THE FAST RED ROAD

a plainsong

THE FAST RED ROAD

STEPHEN GRAHAM JONES

a plainsong

FC2
Normal/Tallahassee

First Edition
First Printing 2000

Published by FC2 with support provided by Florida State University, the Unit for Contemporary Literature of the Department of English at Illinois State University, the Program for Writers of the Department of English at the University of Illinois at Chicago, the Illinois Arts Council, and the Florida Arts Council of the Florida Division of Cultural Affairs.

Address all inquiries to: Fiction Collective Two, Florida State University, c/o English Department, Tallahassee, FL 32306-1580

For more about Stephen Graham Jones and other FC2 authors and books, visit our website at *http://fc2.org*

ISBN: Paper, 1-57366-088-4

Library of Congress Cataloging-in Publications Data

Jones, Stephen Graham, 1972-
The fast red road : a plainsong / by Stephen Graham Jones.--
1st ed.
p. cm.
ISBN 1-57366-088-4 (alk. paper)
1. Indians of North America--Fiction. I. Title.

PS3560.O5395 F37 2000
813'.6--dc21

00-009428

Cover Design: Polly Kanevsky
Book Design: Holly Smith and Tara Reeser

Produced and printed in the United States of America
Printed on recycled paper with soy ink

This program is partially sponsored by a grant from the Illinois Arts Council

Thanks to Ralph Berry, for reading close,
and to Nancy, for not having to.

For
Austin Scott Thomas

CONTENTS

Motionless against the door he listens long. No sound. Knocks. No answer. Watches all night in vain for the least glimmer. Returns at last to his own and avows, No one. She shows herself only to her own. But she has no own. Yes yes she has one. And who has her.

—*Samuel Beckett*

Black Tea: An Old Man Has a Narrative Experience With Prescription Laxatives

Litmus was the sixth one back from the register, which opened onto the buffet. 'The goddamn gate to heaven,' the bearded man behind him called it, and Litmus nodded his head back and forth, waiting. The bearded man was seven feet tall. Litmus drummed William Tell hard into his demo case, until the Indian woman directly ahead of him turned and grabbed his wrist just when his fingers were going their fastest, cadenced like horse hooves. He didn't tell her he wasn't her child, that he was old enough to be her father, but by the time he'd looked hard into her face and she'd turned away in apology, he was holding her hand there, under his own. *Silky Bird* it said on the back of her satin jacket, in thread. He asked her what it meant, and she stumbled through her childhood and her short motherhood and finally said 'nothing, just nothing,' then occupied herself smoothing Litmus' wispy forearm hair back down along his wrist. He was hungry, Litmus was. He'd spent the last two days trapped in a Folsom motel room, hobbled by his big toe, chained to a TV rerunning Jay Silverheel outtakes. He was here to eat and then eat again. He loosened his thin black belt in anticipation, looped his pale hair around his head and over an ear, where it was already falling down.

In front of him and Silky Bird were four cowboys straight from a beer commercial, each more beautiful than the last, their cheekbones chiseled sharp, collective dark hair cropped short against the Clovis sun. The high school girl working the register was defenseless against them, a small nervous giggling thing with braids. When they were finally gone and Silky Bird was digging through her purse for an elusive second party check, the waitress nodded her head down to Litmus' demo case and said she didn't think so.

'This is a buffet, sir.'

'Yes ma'am,' Litmus said back, talking slow and deliberate for her. 'Pitch till you win.'

The waitress ran her pen behind her ear, a violent motion. 'This is a *buffet*,' she said again, harder, pointing to his case now.

The line behind Litmus was quiet except for the breathing giant. Silky Bird was lining pill bottles up on the glass, no checkbook yet. Litmus told the waitress he wasn't going to *sell* a vacuum cleaner to her customers, for Chrissake, in the middle of the day like this, and she just said it again, like it was an answer, that this was a buffet. When she reached for the case Litmus shifted it behind his thick right leg.

'I'm here to *eat*, ma'am.'

'And we're here to serve you, *sir*. But not with that.'

Litmus made a sound to start the whole dialogue over, but saw in the tilt of her face it would run just the same. There were some three tons of people behind him. To his right was Silky Bird, an assortment of glass pipes and needles on the counter now, her on her knees, holding a tintype of her kidnapped son, making oval cooing sounds into the portrait. The giant palmed her head, patting gently, and his fingers came down to her jawline on both sides.

Litmus smiled to the waitress when he got it. 'I'm not going to pack any of your precious food out of here, y'know.'

'I don't much guess you'd tell me if you were.' She said it with her voice flat like the edge of something, and Litmus laughed out his nose, because she was sixteen and there wasn't a thing in the world he could do. He had to eat. He finally just spun the twin combination locks in a grand gesture of defeat, surrendered the case.

It was eighteen seventy-six for him and Silky Bird and the giant. Business expenses, he explained, then collected the receipt and neatly covered the three steps to the end of the buffet, ahead of both of them. He didn't turn around when he heard his case being pried open, either. He was going to eat, by God; as far as he could see were picnic tables with purina-checkered tablecloths, and short Mexican busboys who, tubless yet able, quietly collected the refuse by drawing the four corners of the tablecloths together, throwing the sack over their shoulders, and weaving themselves into the lunchtime crowd. The tablecloths were at least ten deep in places, and the walls in the distance were unadorned, just adobe and chili stains and flies too slow to be all the way alive. The only noise was food: an orange-headed man cracking open a bone and sucking the black marrow out; a woman slurping gravy from a bowl and laughing about something; a child with his lap wet from pee and his mouth attached to a doubled-together straw, the other end going from drink to drink around the deserted table, counterclockwise. He flipped Litmus off and Litmus smiled. He was just getting back to answering the kid in kind when the giant's index finger high in his back told him it was his turn, and then he was taking from each metal bin, heaping it on his plate, going by smell, letting the greases merge together then drip down his hand and off his knuckle, back into the bins.

A kitchen boy came with a new bin and refilled whatever was low. Litmus managed to slip him three dollars of appreciation, and the boy ducked away into the background noise, a background dominated now by a vacuum cleaner being slammed crudely together.

Litmus tried to ignore it.

He scooped more on his plate but it slid off the sides; he wasn't even halfway through the line yet, and already food placement had become an issue: only one more item was going to fit this time around, and even that was going to take a steady hand. Litmus nodded his head as little as possible, chased the saliva down his chin, and finally looked through the plastiglass, for something that wouldn't slide off, something with balance, poise, the proper weight, and as his hand moved through the pork steam, searching, it became hard and harder to follow, indistinct, strobed, moving without him, hardly a part of him at all, and when he concentrated to track it, own it, direct the ladle foodward, the trough-style table in front of him suddenly and with no foreplay lost its horizontal hold and became flattened layers of itself, scrolling up and up, like there were birds on whatever antenna fed the diner, leather-skinned paleolithic things that should never have been able to fly so high. They screamed through the layers, right at Litmus, taunting, inviting, and in a clean snap the vertical went too, a little at first, but finally pushing everything side to side, leaving black at the edges, flecked with nothing. It was the black that made Litmus close his eyes. It made no difference.

He counted twice to what felt like a nervous three, and when he finally peeked out one lid at a time the hair on his forearm was still combed and the ladle was still heavy in his hand, still reaching, the diner and the bins before him were dialed back in, sweating grease, and he had only blinked. Home again home again. The ladle weighed the same, still had mass and even momentum, prior direction, and was still dowsing towards something in the centermost bin, dowsing like no one had blinked and no one would, so Litmus played along, followed its course under the glass, his hand behind but uninvolved, and that was when he saw what had been done, what he had counted into existence: in the bin closest to him was a selection of uncooked man-sized kidneys that had been blue dumplings the moment before last. On the opposite side of the trough an old and out of place Shoshone-looking man had speared a cross section of a tawny forearm and was balancing it across his plate like baby back ribs, his fork making no noise against the anchor tattoo. The blue ink was old, Spanish, *punta* or something, but the *u* had worn away into an *i*, for *pinta*, the disease, the ship. Scattered in the other bins were livers spotted scotch gold, fat sheathed backstraps, stuffed entrails, and more, parts without name, steaming and writhing, like a weak drive-in movie you're supposed to laugh at. But Litmus wasn't laughing. He wasn't even breathing. Five hundred years were slipping away. The giant poked him high in the back again, but this time Litmus didn't move. He couldn't. Everything was coming all at once: the marrow in his own bones, buried somewhere beneath the flesh, untasted; the flies on the wall drifting in and out of this world like small ferrymen; the fevered man in the bathroom, carving fevered words; even the dogs out back, fighting over leftovers as the three busboys huddled under the stoop passed a nervous joint between themselves, left to right. Two of them would be dead before the year was out, the third burying a small caliber handgun over and over, a different place each night, farther and farther out. Litmus watched the never shaved area around the third one's mouth glow red with the joint, then go dim. He was aware again, of everything. For the first time in years, more than he cared to count. It was like waking up. And he didn't want to.

In a last effort to resist, he reached part of himself out, across the horrorshow buffet, locked eyes with the old Shoshone man and pulled him in, forced him too to see what was on his plate, what he had been eating, what they had all been eating. The old man's lower lip trembled. His plate became heavy and fell to the ground. Nobody made to sweep it up. The old man tried to look away, to the sinking sound the anchor tattoo shouldn't have made, but Litmus held him there for a moment longer, because it hurt to know all alone, to have to be seeing through like this. For a moment then they were one, this random old man and Litmus, and instead of the sick buffet spread before them, Litmus tasted instead this old man's vision—Seth's vision—saw his daughter growing into a woman he didn't know, saw the many-hour drive to Clovis for this monthly ritual of food and medicine, but then too, buried deeper than the rest, right below the radio-talking days of WWII, was this scene all over: human flesh in bite-sized portions. Litmus could taste it washing back up his throat, up Seth's throat, and like that the visual tissue they shared tore, and the old man was shuffling away already, his shoulders caved around his chest, suspenders the only thing keeping his pants up.

On his own toilet that night the old man Seth sat reading the tabloid that'd blown up against his leg on the way out of the buffet. 'It's not all crap,' he told his wife, 'come look for yourself,' but she wasn't listening anymore. She had her shows, he had his reading. 'It's not crap,' he yelled hoarsely, and then more came out and he felt emptier than he ever had, hollowed out, pithed by the pharmacist. He raised the half-full milkjug of shitwater to his mouth one more time and let it course through him, doctor's orders: in the morning they would sodomize him again with their oversized garden hose, just looking for something wrong, and then he'd break wind for days, sleeping behind their new trailer, cradling his tender bowels.

The buffet was supposed to have been his last supper before going to the Clovis doctor, a feast of BBQ beef ribs and honeybutter yeast rolls, but he hadn't even eaten his fill, hadn't even had time to smuggle chicken out in each of his pockets, for later, because there at the denuded buffet *later* hadn't began to matter yet. His eyes had been haywired, looking thirty-four years backwards into a survivor's guilt he'd thought outrun by now, a deed he thought buried. Maybe it was something in the food, he told himself. Chemicals, preservatives, radiation, Clovis. Anything, even senility. Call it an episode.

More shitwater. Just get it all out.

What remained of the tabloid had to do with a fledgling porn actor who'd broken his contract and disappeared into the Utah night with a twenty-seven dollar supply check, going feral perhaps, keep an eye out. The silhouette of a watchful Mormon took up the rest of the page. Then too, further in, there was the creeping presence of Saint Augustine Decline among eastern gardens, a Decline backlit by the recent outbreak of Saint Anthony's Fire in the midwest. Geronimo, the California reporter said, Jerome help us. Seth mouthed the words, *Ge-ron-i-mo*, and when the toilet water finally splashed onto his hairless inner thigh again he breathed out and flipped to the center section, the second to the last page. It was the predictions, Big Spring Sally's predictions, made from her padded cell. Seth smiled the side of his face that still smiled. He remembered her, or pieces of her, from way back when. The crazy-ass white girl. The color picture was of her holding both sides of her head, like she was trying to squeeze more out of it, or keep something in.

It didn't matter; she was beautiful.

This year's predictions weren't like last year's, though; they didn't even bother with her hit-miss ratio. It was mostly just the same chest-up picture of her, from different sides of her room, a spider's eye view, fractured angles hard to look from all at once. Except for one, of course, around which the rest revolved; it was centered across the fold, spanning the distance between staples. The back of a legal pad, the cardboard part. Thick magic marker words: *both of him are yet real.* The sideways happy face at the lower corner of the backflap was out of place, with its one lone feather reaching up from the back of its head. The reporter didn't even touch it. She was more interested in who the *him* was, or were, or whatever.

Seth stared at the non-prediction, looked hard to Sally for an explanation, then got nervous and turned the page, where a reader had written in that Sally was not only a pagan throwback, but a public menace; the reader was the health inspector for greater eastern New Mexico. She had included a computer-generated graph showing how Sally's 'woefully inaccurate' eating-of-human-flesh prediction last year had temporarily lowered per capita dining out, not to mention overloading the postal service with health concerns, health concerns she in turn had to allay singly. She noted that she had done this survey on her own time, too, thank you. When Seth got to the end of the health inspector's letter, he dropped the tabloid then kicked it away, off his foot, out the bathroom door. He blew at it, trying to make it go farther. His hands were shaking. He hadn't seen anything, he hadn't seen anything. An episode, it had just been an episode. He tried to make out his wife's shows from pieces of words, but then he was in the diner again, the lights dimming from the vacuum cleaner being plugged in, whining high, inhaling the thin surface off reality, him staring across the buffet table at the pasty-faced man with the stomach, then looking down at his own plate, at what Sally had said would happen.

Get it all out.

He screamed for his wife and still she wouldn't come and hold his head by the temples and make him look away; he sang a song his grandmother used to sing in the fields, but it was no good against this. He was still in the diner, still dropping his plate and watching the pasty-faced man look down into the food bins and shape his mouth around the words once, then twice: *Not again, please, not again.*

Pidgin del Gato

He was the hairy-handed gent in the back of the bus, watching her through a spyhole chewed in a square of styrofoam cup. She was pieces all coming together: slow slope of shoulder, Indian-black hair, Delicious Red fingernail tracing a jaw. Pidgin made up names for her between drinks from his paper bag, finally settling on DK, initials for he Didn't Know what. But it was something beautiful, had to be, look at her, God. Divine Knowledge maybe. When the bus pretty much emptied into the kachina-stained event horizon of the Arizona state line, she was sitting the bench seat beside him for warmth, and he told her the only line he knew: that it wasn't so much the carbon monoxide that killed his dad, but Marty Robbins.

'Marty Robbins,' she said, managing a sluggish fast draw from her right thigh. 'Old time cowboy, man.' Her gun hand was trembling though, her breath hard as kerosene, the rest of her strung out across days.

Pidgin tried to play along, blow the smoke from her gun or maybe breathe it away from her, *for* her, but she just made the barrel into an index finger again, held it over his lips, and told him to wake her at Gallup, lovermine. She nestled into his denim jacket, hiding her face. It felt righter than God: *lovermine*. Pidgin spit out the window and on the fat busdriver sang, a Deep Purple ballad refried slow and Latino. Pidgin moved his lips in the area just after the song, passed his bottle to Rhine, the uneasy rider three rows up, crying for the luggage below: sixty-four and a quarter odd miles back the old man hadn't had the two fifty for his chili burger, and to get out of the cafe in one piece he'd had to stroke his grey beard, lower his head, and promise the dishwasher he'd take care of the ratty Airedale that lived behind the dumpster. Flea the Dog. They'd given him a large pipe and a small piece of time, and when Pidgin had stepped into the lee of the bus for a dip he'd found Rhine's clothes and love letters unfolding with the wind, the old man caught wide eyed and guilty with a weak knee in the sleeping dog's side, trying to close the suitcase over it. The yellowed look in his eyes, cheating death one more time. Pidgin had helped without saying anything and palmed two of the valium tablets stuck to Flea's spit-flecked lips. One of these he gave to DK when she came back to ask what tribe he was. The other he pinched between his lip and gum to make it last. He told her he didn't know.

He didn't wake her at either side of Gallup, and the busdriver sang them deeper into New Mexico. Rhine peed into a mason jar and it rolled around the floor. He told Pidgin he didn't guess he'd ever get to sleep now, not after, and he meant the paisley suitcase he'd packed. Pidgin's eyes were already dilated enough so that before too long following Rhine took all his attention, watching him act out again and again just how it was fending off this mentalcase handicapped truckdriver who'd bitten off the better part of Rhine's still pink-edged ear, offered to spit it back up in trade for cylindrical parcels Rhine didn't yet have access to. But there was the girl, she was asleep. Shhh. Pidgin held his finger to his mouth, please, later. Rhine smiled, said it was later.

'Not that I didn't want that ear back in the end, now, understand.'

He kissed the sleeping girl on the forehead and winked at Pidgin, ran his tongue over his wrinkled purple lips for a drawn-out taste.

'Holy hell, son.'

Pidgin pulled her deeper into his jacket, and between him and the unsedated old man the bottle was dry by the second Vegas, this one at the foot of the Sangre de Cristo mountains, a place sin-black at night. The headlit front of the sign melted by and then the backside, washed tail-light red. Rhine couldn't say anything for a full two minutes. Pidgin passed him the lidless bottle and he peed absently into it, then let it go out the window, his hand steaming in the cool air. He kept saying no to himself, and finally wobbled seat to seat up front to talk to the busdriver about driving around in goddamned circles, there was no time, man.

When the busdriver never quit singing, Rhine finally had to resort to song himself. His Spanish was laced with Germanic from the Mennonites, but his voice was clean and attained heights known only by the ball-less few. Pidgin didn't know either language well enough for song, so to him the operatic war at the front of the bus sounded like horses in love.

He tried to spit out the window, but his body no longer had enough water.

Instead he sucked the chili burger stain out of his shirt when he got hungry, and when it was gone her hair was in his mouth and it was good. In the segmented rearview mirror they couldn't see him. He sat quiet in back and closed his eyes to the passage, and in the miles of creosote and backroads between Las Vegas New Mexico, and Clovis, where his dead dad lay waiting, Pidgin dreamed him and DK onto another bus with amoeba-print couches set up city style along the right hand side. They were traveling still. She was wearing a silk kimono; his horse hair was let down, eyes traced black. He stared at her but she wouldn't look at him, instead cupped herself around something towards her center. Like a mother cat, Pidgin thought, then looked fast out an open window when she raised her head. Outside it was night or early morning, and when the pungent moss smell came cool through the window, Pidgin knew they were in cloudshadow and that the cover was spread out farther in every direction than their diesel supply could take them. Telephone poles cut the night into rectangles and then squares, like a life-science projector at the reel's end or beginning, and there were tar-soaked people stepping from behind the poles to fill the road ahead of them and behind. Their bus was the old kind, though, all cowcatcher and attitude; forward motion would not be sacrificed. It came over the PA like that: *forward motion would not be sacrificed.*

Pidgin tried to catch the girl's attention with a suggestive chin, but she wouldn't acknowledge seeing him. 'Don't,' she said, 'look away,' but she was really hiding whatever it was at her center, keeping it from him. Steam felt up around her ears. Her kimono was pretty much painted on. Pidgin approached her to touch it but timed it all wrong, and then she was the same distance from him again. 'Look away,' she said, 'don't look at me,' which Pidgin took as an invitation, permission. He scrambled over the amoeba-print couches, and she shook her head and said no, and then the bus encountered the first bit of resistance, the first pedestrian, who made cartwheel sounds all along the roof and then was gone. Pidgin felt the thin ceiling where a sound had been, where there had been a hand. He needed to touch someone. But she was watching him. He couldn't let her see. He pretended to look away, faced the windshield and made like he was staring through the tar and the rain, and then when the angry ten-ply tires began getting gummed up with pedestrian matter he approached her in the mirror, during a downshift, and like that he had her, and she had her head in his chest again where it fit, and she was saying remember the diner that was really a gas station—the Petri Dish?—and when Pidgin pretended to, she still had the cup of coffee she'd been nursing then, and Pidgin looked into the cup and reconstructed her over it when it was still hot, and there she was smoking her sixth menthol in a row, the lines in her face highlit by two days of cheap base—both kinds—and as the windows on the bus went lightless altogether he looked into her cup where it had started, and it was no longer coffee. But her mouth was wet from it.

Go on she motioned, their bodies swaying together with the Spanish duelers at the front of the bus. *Go on.*

Pidgin looked into the cup and it swam with shapeless things black and long and single celled, and when he woke there was her hair, her blue-black hair, all but a few strands longwise down his throat, tangled in his insides, binding them together in the backseat, an oily knot. He could hardly breathe and it hardly mattered. There were hours to go. It was Clovis with dawn breaking quietly all around before they finally caught him, Rhine and the busdriver.

'Holy hell, son,' Rhine said. ' I guess you've damn near ate her.'

The busdriver was without song in the harsh light of day.

Rhine cradled Pidgin's head and the busdriver lifted the girl away like a child being born. Her hair came out slow, and it was wet for as long her forearm, the ends sticking together with thinned-out Arizona chili. When they stood Pidgin he fell halfway down, and they drug him up the aisle coughing, getting patted down for some cylindrical parcel he mumbled he didn't have. There on the windshield drops of last night's throat blood going obsidian in the sun, bug guts lending a soft intestinal haze. In the bathroom of the diner Pidgin stared at the indistinct counter between his hands, saying to himself *Clovis, Clovis,* until finally Rhine gestured large and said yes, goddammit, Clovis. He looked Pidgin up and down, winked.

'Tell me about her,' he said.

'Ask her yourself, old man. I've never seen her before.'

'Well what'd she taste like then?'

When Pidgin just kept watching the old man's face, Rhine didn't flinch, asked this time about cannibalism. Pidgin turned to leave but Rhine spun him around by the shoulder, said they had laws about eating people, even in New Mexico, even for Indians, even for half-ass Indians. Pidgin made to leave again, but the busdriver was in the door, carrying the DK girl over the meager threshold. It was a ceremony with him. As he passed going to the stall he said something in Rhine's half ear, then both of them were laughing and Rhine was even crying. He took Pidgin's hand almost as an afterthought and asked again what did she taste like, please. The please part was real.

Pidgin watched Rhine's mouth make the word, and before he could see it in its entirety the mouth was drawing closer, was in his own, a rough foreign tongue probing, blind, touching teeth and gums with the same blunt need. For the second the kiss lasted, Pidgin understood that all Rhine had anymore was this taste of women. He was ball-less, without balls, gelded. But still. Pidgin pushed him away, and they stood in their respective corners. Things were almost tense, but Pidgin was too tired. He just wanted to bury his father and get it over with. He leaned over the stainless-steel sink, holding onto both sides, and listened to the busdriver in the stall with the half-sleeping girl, her clothes giving way to gravity, pearly snaps on porcelain. The words scratched in the door were *love enema*, with a 1-900 number. Pidgin tried to remember horses in love and hoped she wouldn't wake in the middle, to the figure of the busdriver leaning over, laboring. All the same though, he didn't kick down the door. He had been kissed too and not wanted it.

Over a breakfast nobody paid for, Pidgin confessed to Rhine that his dad used to sell pastel bomb shelters here in Clovis, until the end of the world never came. 'The Big One,' he said, and held his hands up in a mushroom cloud. Rhine nodded and ate and said he was color blind, he wouldn't have trusted his dad in the same room with a damn firecracker, pastel or not. Pidgin went on. In a rough gesture of truce over the whole bathroom-mouth thing, he even pulled out the pictogram his uncle had drawn for him, because Birdfinger was evidently still pretending he couldn't write; it said that the Clinic had finally released Pidgin's dad's anomalous body after nine years worth of clinical science, that they'd gotten their five hundred dollars out of him one way or another, there was no cavity unviolated. The seam-ridden heart was back in the wrong side of his chest where it had always been. The Mirror Man. It was time to bury him at last. The rendering of the cadaver was in number two pencil, pockmarked with generations of autopsy, an aged toe tag big as a sail the way Birdfinger drew it.

'Crowbait,' Rhine said, smiling, flashing his hand over the table edge for a nanosecond—one half of a tanned ear neatly palmed, not listening—and Pidgin said no, Stob, *Cline* Stob, then withdrew the pictogram and refolded it carefully. 'Crow, *Crow*bait,' Rhine said again, quietly, about to laugh, and Pidgin had his fork hard against Rhine's throat by the time the busdriver sat down with them and wiped the sweat from his face with a napkin. He was nervous, watching the sloe-eyed hombres at the breakfast bar. Pidgin lowered the fork tine by tine, outnumbered, outweighed. The busdriver almost smiled, and then didn't, instead told Pidgin in fast and rough gringo about an animal he'd seen in a pickle jar once in Mexico City. They'd pulled it from some clearwater cistern high in the mountains, and before it died the scientists learned it could breathe through its skin, it was either the last or the first of its kind, no lungs. Relict was the word. It was three almost four feet long, heavy tail, mottled skin, staring wide eyes that didn't see the sky for what it was. *Atretochoana caecilian*: the busdriver said it over and over like a prayer, and his rolling voice distilled a meter from the Latin and slowly made of the dead tongue something dirgelike and lyrical. Dusty-backed moths filled the room and blanketed the floor finger deep in places. Nobody saw. He was crying soft, the busdriver, maybe for the girl. That was when Rhine pawned the paisley suitcase off on Pidgin, too, when he couldn't say no, when he couldn't say anything, for fear he'd breathe moth and drown. Two hours later, walking south with the suitcase over his shoulder, Pidgin felt for the first time the castrato's spadic hands on him during the busdriver's oral diversion—patting him lightly down for a parcel they must have thought he had—and his boots fell into the even lope of the distraction, the finely-dusted Latin name, and when no one was looking he closed his eyes against the sun and tried to open every pore on his body.

It took every last thing he had.

To even feel like he was doing it, he had to imagine the leopard-skinned woman his dad used to dance with in the technicolored light of the TV, all through *Gunsmoke*; he could see her from behind the safety glass of the El Dorado shelter, where he had been screwdrivered in for most of his twelfth year, safe from the chance of radiation, growing hair all over. The spots of her lycra leggings, *her* spots, opening like scores of hungry little mouths, wide and wider and deep, so real.

Almost.

But no.

Pidgin came to half in the road, on his knees scrabbling for a breath. When the light-green blazer drove back by for a second look, he ducked into the corner store for a bottle of something, anything, and the clerk simply said he had the right reserved to refuse anybody service, and he was invoking that right until he got an FM radio that plugged into the wall. '*That* wall,' he pointed, 'nothing personal.' Pidgin butted the door open with the suitcase but the glass didn't spider away like he wanted it to; the drama was lost, had never been. He walked on. When he reached the tracks he stepped over to the Abergeny side to drink tis-win for a while with a grey-braided man holding down a barrel. Charlie Ward. Indiscriminate blue pills floating seedlike in the wine. When Charlie Ward wasn't lying to him about his hotwiring abilities, how he'd stole damn near every car in town at least once, Pidgin watched him through a small hole chewed in an even smaller piece of paper.

He was home.

He had maybe thirty hours to kill before the interment.

There was an oldstyle iron tractor seat at the foot of the barrel. It was formfit, ventilated. Charlie Ward touched it with his foot and Pidgin sat. In the near distance a group of longhairs were pushing their car over the tracks. It crested and rolled silently down the other side. 'Trying to get away,' Charlie Ward noted, pointing with the index finger of his bottle hand, and Pidgin understood: Clovis was where Birdfinger was, in all his profane glory.

Pidgin had run too, after walking stiff-legged out of sight of the trailer, relations severed. He had been fifteen. He had given one slow-moving over-the-shoulder back-look and then stepped off the front porch for a cool seven years and counting. The last word he had said to Birdfinger had been a hissed *please*. It was about bus fare. Birdfinger had had money then from his song You Look So Pretty When I'm Naked. He had still been red-eyed and deaf from playing the night through. He told Pidgin it was a bad time for a real talk. They were whiling away the afternoon on their respective couches, Birdfinger in his amber-tinted pince-nez, Pidgin with his ruby-eyed monocle, winding and unwinding the long brass chain. Earlier, a beer left for the porch gods had pressured up in the heat and exploded, and, gunfighter-like, neither had flinched.

Pidgin said it: 'Today's the day.'

Birdfinger sat motionless.

Pidgin wound, unwound, wound again. Today was the second year to the hour of his dadless life, the second year after Birdfinger had shown up drunk at the corpseless funeral, singing every hymn he thought he knew, staggering in two days later to usurp in neat order the unsold shelters, the furniture, the trailer, his twin brother's place on the couch, like Cline had never really left. It was a travesty: he had brown eyes like Cline, straw-colored hair like Cline, high-gummed teeth like Cline, a freckled pate like Cline. But he wasn't Cline.

Pidgin wound, unwound, and was planning the next uptake when Birdfinger said it: 'You can either quit that incessance or take it somewhere else, please.' With the ridged back of his long namesake he motioned doorwards. It was an invitation. He had been polite. Pidgin responded in kind, with the proper words: 'You pule, uncle, like none other. We both know this isn't your house, and you hardly my father. There's dried spittle collected there at the corners of your lips. That, uncle, *that's* how I know you're not him. Because it goddamn sure isn't the pallor.'

Birdfinger mocked: 'If only your mother could see you now.'

'Don't tease me with her.'

'Then don't tell me what to do, nephew.'

'Enough with the relations already.'

Birdfinger laughed, said there was more than diluted blood between the two of them; he had also been the one to find his father dead by his own hand. There was that.

Cline wasn't the first one in the family to kill himself, after all, Pidgin not the first to walk in on it. Pidgin said back that there was *only* blood between them, his father the unwilling bridge. 'And he's currently under the knife without sedation,' he added.

Birdfinger leaned forward, looked over the wired topline of the pince-nez. 'I could have been your father, you know.' Pidgin shook his head no. Birdfinger continued: 'I was there, not two feet away. I could smell life beginning, your life. Waylon Jennings was coming across the pasture towards us at seven hundred and eighty-seven miles per hour. You were conceived in splendor.'

'Yet here I am,' Pidgin said, 'concert T intentionally ripped, hair unwashed. Without splendor, without memory of a long-dead mother, with the last image of my father being daily displaced by likeness, forcing me to either accept it or leave. Do you need my bedroom for something, perchance?'

Birdfinger shook his head no, not really, scratched at an armpit, said in a casual voice that since Pidgin was so needful of a father figure, then yes, look on him, he would do his best despite a marked lack of paternal training.

Pidgin said Birdfinger's mask of humbleness was ill fitting even in the lowest light.

Birdfinger argued generosity: 'Are you not my ward?'

'Do you want I should ask for movie money, *uncle*?'

'If that's what it takes.'

Pidgin wound, unwound, his left hand a fist held close to his face. He said Birdfinger could never in any possible world have been his father. 'My mother wouldn't have allowed it,' he said, 'you, I mean.'

Birdfinger didn't laugh. 'You never knew your mother, nephew.'

Pidgin controlled his voice. 'And you know better than to talk of her so freely with me. I feel things falling off metal shelves inside me, and arranging themselves on the floor in strangely familiar patterns.'

'There's murder in yon ruby eye.'

'Fuck you.'

'Tilt it to the floor, spill your blood-red anger there.'

'You pule like none other, uncle, and fail to impress me. Save the wit instead for your alcohol-numbed audience, caught up in their cycle of guilt-driven drinking. They come to you for justice.'

'They come to me for song.'

'Then they leave disappointed.'

'I don't have to take this from you,' Birdfinger said, lip raised, 'from a child so disrespectful his own mother denied him the colostrum every child—'

He didn't finish. They sat in the wake of the half said for minutes, too long for an uncle and a nephew, and then Pidgin's breath caught and his voice broke and he said that Birdfinger did *not* know his mother. 'At least leave me her,' he said, 'since you've already taken him away, replaced him with likeness.' Birdfinger pushed the pince-nez far up the bridge of his nose, hiding his eyes. He started to say something then didn't, instead lowered his head, doled out bus fare when asked, didn't apologize, didn't say come back. He had invited him to leave once already. In the door Pidgin stretched time for a dramatic exit. He silhouetted himself against the heat, pushed his hair out of his right eye, and looked back once, to etch this moment in his memory with acid. It was a mistake. It almost undid him. He carried it with him still, the image of Birdfinger wiping his mouth with the back of his hand, the living room arranging itself around him, embracing him like it too was myopic and didn't know the difference between the two, as if with the spittle gone there was no difference: when Pidgin walked stiff-legged through the shelters he was walking away from the forced image of his dad. He didn't look back again, not for seven years. He ran until the trailer was small, until Clovis New Mexico was small. Until Birdfinger found his address through Dorphin Studios and sent him a monochrome drawing of pornographic intensity and detail. They had now only to bury Cline and get it over with.

Pidgin looked up to Charlie Ward and told him he needed interment clothes.

Charlie Ward said he had some widow weeds back at his place.

It was decided.

With night came a '64 Cadillac left idling outside the liquor store. It was parked backwards, nosing out into the street, a three-quarter view of arrested motion, like the cover of a lowrider glossy. Pidgin and Charlie Ward were through with the tis-win by then, their teeth stained baby blue. They sauntered into the glossy field, and Charlie Ward put Pidgin's paisley suitcase in the trunk as if the car were already his, and in the rearview mirror there was a ski-masked man chasing them, but the getaway car was already getting away. When they could finally slow down, Charlie Ward coasted to the side of the road, stepped out, buried his right hand into the ancient scrotum he had sewn in place of his front pocket and left a red handprint on the flank of the Cadillac, fingerpoints all along the door. He circled one of the headlights, drew a lightning bolt from it across the hood to the windshield. He was breathing fast when he got back into the driver's seat, filmed with sweat, and the car felt different already, ready to run.

They let it. Pidgin had never seen the other side of one-forty before. Charlie Ward clicked the headlights off, and it was a whole nother New Mexico. They rode east, heavy and fast with the railroad tracks, Charlie Ward telling coup stories, Pidgin nodding with sleep, the Cadillac flying low along the asphalt, close to the ground, sparks dragging at each crossroad, houselights in the pastures just dots, just nothing, sparks that only last a second and then are gone. Pidgin said it to Charlie Ward like that and Charlie Ward said yes. They were driving through areas of black that belonged nowhere specific in history. Once there was a campfire. Charlie Ward talked the Cadillac out of another two miles per hour. Pidgin studied him: he had both hands on the wheel, shoulders rounded with age and with speed. Careful grey braids on his chest, tied off with newspaper rubberbands, blue and pink and then blue again.

Pidgin asked him what tribe he was. Charlie Ward rubbed his nose, got his hand back to the wheel, and said Peruna, then changed it to Old Crow, then shook the question off and just told another coup story about a motorcycle he had stolen once when there was nothing else. He pulled the V neck of his shirt down: stamped a quarter inch deep in the loose skin of his chest was the clear imprint of a Mexican wasp at mach 1. A quarter inch deep at the torso. Charlie Ward had had it tattooed in, black body, orange wings veined blue. He said he'd craved unnatural peaches ever since. It was the punchline. Pidgin nodded that he was getting what there was to get, he just couldn't bring himself to laugh: he had come out of Provo Utah heading east and south on a twenty-seven dollar supply check from Dorphin Studios, and now he was overshooting. Texas was approaching fast.

Pidgin told Charlie Ward he'd never been much deeper than the panhandle; when he'd left Clovis at fifteen, the trailer door had opened to the west, and he'd walked a straight and unthinking line from there, with the highway. His first ride was a drunk postdoc anthropologist who picked him up because he was a longhair. Still they went west. The postdoc summoned the filter of manifest destiny, bare breasts and all, said he was writing a paper on the powwow circuit, the migratory habits of the modern-day RV Indian, the Pace Arrow Nation. He had theories about cultural hand-me-downs and the dress-coded identities they begat; he played the epigram for his paper over and over on cassette. It was Johnny Lee, saying how the Indians are dressing up like cowboys, and the cowboys are putting turquoise and leather on. Cherokee Fiddle. The postdoc dressed cowboy to fit in with his subjects. He was counter-intelligence. He wandered into a pay-sweat in California in mid-June and never came out.

That was what Pidgin was afraid of with Texas—never making it out again. He told Charlie Ward he needed to get back to Clovis. Charlie Ward grunted, counted the mile markers with wet fingertrails in the dash dust. Pidgin checked his count mark by mark, turning his head slower and slower from ditch to dash, and then woke sometime later with the side glass saliva-glued to his face. It was still night. They were sitting in a roadless pasture, door-level CRP grass clumped around them. Charlie Ward said it was Palo Duro country, look hard, and listen, you could still hear them screaming their long throats raw, losing their voices.

He said too that the gas tank was dry, then walked off into the scrub, no goodbyes. The night was as black as Utah ever was. It closed around the Cadillac and Pidgin nodded off again, then came to slow and unalone: just to the south was a pale disc of light against the clouds. A spotlight of some sort. It was the only thing. Pidgin stepped from the Cadillac, half-extended his arm towards the light, then withdrew, pushed his hair out of the way, reached again. He told himself it was just a light. But still. It didn't belong. He walked towards it, his jeans tearing against the mesquite, the change in his pocket rattling against lighter casing. The disc drew closer and dimmed. Pidgin walked faster, trying not to spook it, but before he could see it whole it was gone, from the bottom up.

Pidgin stared at the place on the clouds it had been. It didn't return. He pretended to look away then snapped his head around to the same nothing. He stood in the darkness then, defeated by Texas, and finally stumbled downhill towards the dull glint that was the Cadillac, waiting like a vinyl bed. But the Cadillac was no longer alone: standing around it were green eyes, round and unblinking. As Pidgin jangled to a stop, more appeared, turning to see him and his noise. Pidgin held up his hands in apology. He conceded the stolen Cadillac, then squatted in the tall grass and watched the green eyes dance and swirl around it, lowering their heads to the grill time and again, trying to initiate communication maybe. Pidgin moved from a squat to a sit, then slumped lower, promised not to go to sleep, woke a few breaths later to the sound of Charlie Ward coming down the other side of the draw, a five-gallon gas can slung over his shoulder. The green eyes winked out as one, turning to the noise that was Charlie Ward, and then in a rush there were more of them than before, and they were running, thundering past Pidgin, over Pidgin, one of their unshod hooves taking off the heel of his boot. Horses. The smell in the air of clean shit.

Pidgin told Charlie Ward he was glad to see him. Charlie Ward nodded a somber nod. He called Pidgin grandson. He said of the retreating horses that they were a herd of mutes a hundred years old, left alone because normal horses wouldn't work with them. Pidgin said no shit. He limped to the passenger door on his short boot. He asked Charlie Ward where he got the gas and Charlie Ward just filled the tank and drove them back to Clovis, sliding in with the last of the darkness. He parked in the middle of another pasture, in a pair of ruts, walked due north for exactly twenty paces, opened a hatch of some sort, then climbed a solid solid ladder down into the belly of a beast Pidgin refused to visualize at so early an hour. But he followed. And he found a velvety place in the dark, and he kept himself awake by dreading the interment, by saying his mother's name over and over like defense—*Marina Trigo, Marina Trigo*—then woke with a start what had to be hours later, to the real smell of metal, and felt he was inside a bullet, traveling at a hundred and forty miles per hour through the earth. It was an uneasy feeling.

He had slept four times in one night. He said his mother's name again. He wondered if he'd missed the interment, if he had been missed there. His lighter showed hand-sized rivets and body thick pipes and a labyrinth of passages and Charlie Ward sleeping and, along a wall, in block print, a diagram that pronounced he was in a submarine, the USS TommyHawk; in the margin there was even a hand-drawn nuclear torpedo with Slim Pickens riding it hard, one arm in the air. Pidgin backed into the periscope but didn't understand the mechanics of it, couldn't get it to turn away from an unchanging beer bottle in the upper world. He decided it was painted on the lens, maybe a decal. He rubbed and spit and scratched to no avail, climbed the ladder to do the same above ground, stopped halfway up with only his head out, making sure nothing was coming. Nothing was. There was just pasture and heat and the beer bottle hung by woven grass from a yucca spit, deadcenter in front of the periscope, a glassine decoy inviting others of its kind.

Pidgin threw a rock at it and missed, then another, same result, then tracked the rocks to the paisley suitcase out of place under a poisoned-black mesquite. The Cadillac was gone, either backed up in the same ruts or taken from the air. Pidgin sat half on the periscope eye, watching the suitcase for signs of life, knowing it was pointless: the dog would be neither dead nor alive until seen, realized, labeled. Until then it was in quantum limbo. That was the way things were. He'd had it drilled into his head before he was ten, by Sally, with her ergodic theory flashcards and her nicotine lectures on Schrödingerian paradox and Poincaréan recurrence. She said to remember it, it applied to him, he was in a box, too: New Mexico was more or less square. Sally said to Pidgin that he would be two people at once until his personal limbo was over, until he did or didn't become what he had the distinct chance of becoming.

'A cat?' Pidgin's dad had asked, defending Pidgin.

Pidgin meowed inside for his father and ignored her, it, the limbo/cat bullshit, had just about managed to forget the whole education when he was forced to remember in a chemical-driven rush: his second attempt at a life in adult videos came out double-exposed. As if there really were two of him. Meaning no way did he want this suitcase. He couldn't leave it in the sun either, though. He picked it up. Dead or alive, it had the same heft. He resisted shaking it, scanned the horizon for a cool place to abandon it, and then with a sharp intake of breath let it pull him to the ground. He was afraid he'd been seen: not a half mile away was the trailer, the shelters still around it, even more pastel now, the cinderblock shed off to the north. He was here again. After seven years. He pressed his forehead into the paisley print, took late note that the Cutlass hadn't been there, meaning Birdfinger wasn't there. Meaning there was no immediate easy reason *not* to go. Pidgin looked for one anyway, and then, midthought, laughed at whisper level: all those years his father had stood on the porch, leaning over the railing, towards a nuclear presence he claimed to feel in his solar plexus, saying the end of the world was out there. Pidgin himself had slept in the landlocked submarine. The presence was confirmed, but confirmed nine years too late for leadlined shelter promotion.

The end of the world had already come for Cline, visited him in the cinderblock shed. His note had read *let it begin here, with me* and was unsigned, an absence which

Pidgin entertained for a few hours into foul play. But there was none; the windows of the 69 Ford had been rolled up from the inside, door locked, the shin-height vents opened wide, a trick to slow the carbon monoxide enough for the Marty Robbins ditty to play to its sordid completion. That was how the coroner said it. He had no respect for the cowboy ballad. He left the shed blanketed with lovebugs that had been drawn there by the concentrated exhaust. They mated furiously, died just as fast. Pidgin never reconciled it, the bugs, the suicide. Standing in the pasture a half-mile off from the trailer, he collected himself, succumbed to inertia, spun the hatch closed, and left the submarine, looking back once at the painted brown periscope that was part of the landscape already, not even metal anymore.

It was a slow walk, too, his gait uneven from the missing heel, his jeans trailing string like Phil Collen throwaways. Halfway to the trailer he stopped and beat his other heel off with a flintrock, for balance, then threw it as far away as he could. A hawk dove at it and it was gone before it touched the ground. Pidgin said to himself that it meant nothing, that it happened all the time, was always happening somewhere, to someone. Three minutes later he stepped onto the redwood porch for the first time in seven years, the porch his dad had built one week in the heat, shoring things up against the end.

Pidgin's key still worked.

He dragged the suitcase inside, set it under the arm of the couch, then sat on the couch himself, unmoving, wary of disturbing things. On the far wall were successive drafts of the pictogram Birdfinger had drawn for Pidgin, of Cline, of the long awaited interment. He must have wanted it just right, these first nonwords in seven years. Other than that, the place was the same: two couches, two tables, and a pair of stacked TV's, one for picture, the other for sound. The carpet dappled tawny orange and brown, the curtains yellowed with age, the ceiling watermarked. Home again home again. It was like Pidgin had never left. The past welled up around him. There was Birdfinger on successive afternoons, couch ridden, explaining Cline's suicide even when Pidgin was in the bathroom masturbating,

Birdfinger going on about how Cline had never been the same after he took that five-hundred dollars from science, for his body, after he sold himself and became a trespasser. But it was a lie. That wasn't why he killed himself. It wasn't even close.

There was more, that Birdfinger wasn't telling him. A lone Goliard standing squat and misshapen at the edge of the floodlights once, unspeaking the world, pulling Cline from his paranoid salesman life back in time to WWI—Willie and Waylon and the boys—letting him remember how it was before Marina died, when they were postal thieves, the hammer thumbed back every minute of every day, the '69 Ford faster than radio. There was Sally with her insistent voice, keeping time with a metronome—one one one—keeping Cline at bay with a desperate prediction he promised her would never come true: that Pidgin either would or wouldn't finish the macabre work the Goliards had started. New Mexico the box; Pidgin del Gato. There was the graven image of his dad as seen from a shelter, holding the leopard woman's forehead to his limited-series commemorative beltbuckle, both of them framed by the trailer window, backlit by *Gunsmoke*.

And there was more on top of that, untold reams of past Birdfinger probably had stored in fat cells. But even then Pidgin didn't call him on it. He didn't want to be fooled into a trade, into giving up those last few funereal moments before Birdfinger arrived singing, when the leopard woman had stepped into view, face mandrilled red and blue, lycra spots reversed to white in mourning, like she had the pox. Pidgin had both wanted to touch her and been afraid to touch her, and eventually she wandered off, picking through the cars like any one could be hers, settling finally on Cline's crushed Ford, pulled there by police wrecker in a case of mistaken identity and then pulled back to the shed again, padlocked in, windows down and innards filled with kerosene, to preserve.

Kerosene, formaldehyde.

Pidgin spit across the back of the couch and into the air conditioner growing moss in the window. It was oven-hot in the trailer. He didn't know how he'd ever lived here.

He stood, stretched his chest, then slowly removed the heater vent from the floor. He lay down and reached in and birthed a banktube of decomposed pot. One of Birdfinger's countless forgotten stashes, now legal with age. It left Pidgin coughing, and he emptied it into the untumbling air conditioner with his spit, then set the banktube back underground, replaced the vent, decided he would rather be back in Provo, his phone ringing with grip work. Even not ringing.

There were maybe three hours till the interment.

He scrounged a sheet of the foolscap paper littering the floor and left Birdfinger an indirect note, a rough sketch of the pale disc he'd seen the night before, pinioned to the underside of the clouds. He could still see it, was still beckoned. It was both out of place and necessary for that place. Pidgin drew it with care, drew it too well to share with Birdfinger. Again, he couldn't look away. His neck ached and his eyes narrowed and soon enough he had it at armslength, trying to recapture his failed angle of approach, the parched-velvet feel of Texas, but then Birdfinger's Cutlass coasted into the driveway out of some vast nowhere, crunching caliche. One door shut, and then the other, and Pidgin was already running the length of the narrow hall, his footsteps resounding behind him, echoing in the deadspace under the trailer. It was about being caught, about unneutral ground, about Birdfinger assaulting him with the shape of his body, with his features, with how Cline would look plus nine years. Pidgin wasn't ready for it, not now, not yet. He would pick his own time to step from behind the token cypress tree and betray no emotion, no recognition, zero remorse. It would be like that. It would have to be. Later. Now, though, here, he would have no advantage, no dial on the situation, so he leaned forward and ran, and by the time the screen door opened and a woman's floaty voice entered he was already airborne, diving over the old queen bed, out the open window, landing without heels and stumbling the half mile back to the submarine, falling again and again. No suitcase, no note. Just him and what used to be his jeans. He lay down and banged on the hatch with a caliche rock until it unscrewed from the inside and Charlie Ward poked his head out, asking if they were coming.

'Who?'

'The cavalry, shit.'

'No, granddad,' Pidgin said nervously, out of breath, looking over his shoulder for Birdfinger's head sticking out the end of the trailer, or coming for him through the pasture, apologizing furiously. But it was just dry grass and stillness and tin siding. Pidgin dusted himself off, climbed down the ladder and into the widow's weeds, which turned out to be a silk pirate shirt and lowslung leather pants with silver conchos up the side. Pidgin looked down the length of both arms and told Charlie Ward three things: that he was neither a widow, nor a ninja—and he sure wasn't Jim Morrison; he just needed something black for the interment, that was all. Charlie Ward said what they needed now was a fast car for the procession, and then they were off again, to Juanita's for breakfast and a ride. Charlie Ward said there the cars were painless, sometimes he could just lead them away. Pidgin didn't tell him there would be no procession. Instead he held him up by the arm as they went the long way around the trailer, picking tenderly through a prairie dog town taken over by yellow-eyed owls who made them feel like trespassers. Charlie Ward said it reminded him of a story about a man hung like a moose, peeing one day, but then he couldn't remember it all.

Juanita's rippled in the distance for a solid two miles and then in the next step they were there, at a table, Juanita herself making them pay before eating. Charlie Ward laid the money down slap slap slap. They ate breakfast burritos and made them last, waited for the oilmen to roost. Charlie Ward watched for which ones stepped into the bathroom. After the first one had been gone awhile, Pidgin asked, *now*? but Charlie Ward waved a finger close to the table, *no*. Through the plate glass they could see the trucks and cars lined up outside. Over teatwarm goatmilk they kept tabs on who drove what. Finally, Charlie Ward motioned at the one in the laminated straw hat, a single black braid trailing down his spine, silver at the toes and heels of his boots. A turquoise bolo. He even had oldstyle cuffs on, with fringe. Pidgin could tell they had been Wild Bill gloves not long ago. He'd had a pair once; they came with a cap gun.

Together they tried to will the Indian's bowels to move.

After thirty minutes, it worked. He rose suddenly, already untucking his shirt, and stumbled towards the bathroom. In his wake Pidgin and Charlie Ward walked calmly out to his bandit-black Trans-Am. Charlie Ward ran his hand along the hood, over the cowl induction and the firebird beak, and then they were stepping over the doors, standing up through the T-tops, and reclined in the bucket seats. It was theirs. 'Black for the funeral, grandson,' Charlie Ward said, and in the time it took for the dashboard to quit blinding Pidgin it was hotwired and they were gone, easing out in reverse, undetected, smooth.

Once clear of Juanita's, Pidgin said no, please, but Charlie Ward said he just wanted to see what it would do on the highway. It wouldn't take long. They stopped at the liquor store for ice, and Charlie Ward reached into the past and left a yellow handprint on the flank that almost matched the gold pinstriping. It was close enough. He packed the turbo with the ice then, and when it was cooled down and they had a half-gallon of wine, they were the next best thing to airborne, the engine screaming, the wind whipping in and even dragging the headliner loose, so it billowed for a split second then let go, taking the rear window with it in a cascade of glass Pidgin never heard. Charlie Ward had his head out the T-top, being force fed his own war whoops, the tendons in his neck standing out. The speedometer wouldn't do what they were doing, and Pidgin's math was too bad to try and calculate it out. It was wrapped though, the peg broken long ago. When they finally leveled off to a cool one-fifty-something and the gravity acceleration let go of Pidgin, he reached an arm across to Charlie Ward and begged him to stop. But the mile markers merged into an unbroken green line of denial. They were headed west, with the train tracks again, overcorrecting for Texas, missing Clovis altogether.

And there was nothing they couldn't outrun.

Pidgin could feel it for a moment, passing a moving train like it was standing still. In front of them the cars were lining up on the shoulder, to get out of the way. To let them pass. All except the black and white cruiser. Pidgin just made out the trooper's profile for the nanosecond they were alongside him, and his mouth was already held hard to the state radio. And then they were running. And the trooper was running after them, his blue lights in the mirror shifting red, the signs on the road reading Vaughn and then getting sucked up. Pidgin felt Clovis slipping away at a steady hundred and fifty miles per hour. And there was the gearshift just past his left hand, within reach. He pushed the button in and the click went unnoticed. He breathed twice and did it then, pushed the stick up into neutral, the engine winding up to an unhealthy pitch and flattening out there, the aluminum block white hot with anger. Charlie Ward's hand became bodiless and reacted, turned the key back, pulled the machine from the throes. They coasted for a clean and sober two miles, and hung one side of the car in the ditch when there was nothing left.

Charlie Ward looked at Pidgin and Pidgin looked at Charlie Ward. Pidgin said he was sorry and Charlie Ward said back that cars remember people the same as people remember cars. Nothing else. Just the trooper spending hours in his cruiser, preparing, talking himself out of the scattergun maybe. Hopefully. When he finally approached he was all smiles.

'You know that's bad for the turbo,' he said, fatherlike. 'You should let it idle down there, Chief. Go ahead, start it. It's not too late.'

The car came to life between Charlie Ward's thumb and forefinger, loping in place. The trooper slid the stiff leather catch off the back of his gun. It was one of those go-ahead-and-run-boy things. Ten little Indians, fifteen bullets in the clip; the odds were against them. Pidgin had played all their games before; he returned his hand to the leather handle of the parked shifter, to keep it in place, to keep them alive for the interment.

Charlie Ward smiled and said *officer*, and that was all. No cars passed stocked with witnesses. It was only them and a sound, a lone Peano whistle, from across miles, but close, too close. Pidgin felt like they were in the opening credits of a western. The engine climbed to two grand in response to the whistle, and Charlie Ward's eyes went with it. And the sharp corners of his mouth. The three of them watched the tach bounce up and up like a secondhand. Charlie Ward drew his accelerator leg knee to chest, to prove it wasn't him, but still, the trooper already had his gun drawn, hammer thumbed back and not yet clicked in place.

He was laughing, too, in his way. He asked what a couple of blanket Indians like themselves had to do with a *man's* car, like this. Charlie Ward said without emotion that he *was* a man, and then the whistle came again, no train, no anything.

The trooper leveled his gun on Charlie Ward's ear, at an angle where the exit wound would be low down on the other side of the neck, in Pidgin's lap. He told them they were in no position to be pulling schoolboy Indian pranks. It was no joke, though: Pidgin could feel the engine, humming up the metal shifter through the stitched leather handle and into his waiting palm. It was anxious. Over the lakepipes the trooper finally called to Charlie Ward to shut the damn thing off, screw the fucking turbo, but the key would no longer turn, and the trooper wouldn't reach in to see for himself. Not a chance. Instead he just started twitching and talking low, his chin shiny with saliva, his mirrored glasses askew, khaki armpits dark brown and dripping. He was saying to Charlie Ward that he was a *trooper*, not a damn *officer*, and was trying to get Charlie Ward to say it with him when it came without warning—the bullet, the slug, the greased shooter—ripping directly above the T-tops at an easy thirty-two hundred feet per second, whining over their heads and away, the sudden clap from the barrel nudging the three of them out of the ditch and onto a stage where their roles were predefined. Another day at the blood theater. The trooper played his part with precision, with stock movements, looking at his gun as if it was a new thing, watching the smoke rise, and then easing into the initial motions of the solemn shoulder shrug that comes right before finishing a thing already started, out of duty. Everything would come clean in the paperwork. From the corner of his seat Pidgin could read this, and all they had to protect them was the Trans-Am. He breathed out and pulled it deep into first, and for an impossible second the car didn't move, just spun in place, but then it was standing up half in the ditch, traction bars keeping it stuck and in line, fist-sized chunks of asphalt assaulting the trooper's cruiser.

Charlie Ward held onto the steering wheel as best he could, whooping and stomping and shifting into second, the tires scratching at forty-five, the bandit-black car leaping forward into history. Pidgin imagined a sharp-edged 2 carved into the ground behind them, or Jay Silverheels grunting something inarticulate into the trooper's CB, to confuse the cavalry, or Marshall Dillon calling in Chuck Connors, to fan the lever of his rifle and take down everything in sight, telegraph poles and all.

They were running, hard.

Soon a helicopter shadow blotted out the sun. A wide chevron of cruisers fell in behind them too, their blackbird running point. Charlie Ward wiped his eyes with one hand, and looked to Pidgin. The old horse thief was unsure. It was there in his eyes. Pidgin pointed his chin in front of them. There was nothing else to do now. So they did it. And there were no roadblocks, because everyone was behind them and nobody ever thought two longhairs could outrun New Mexico's finest.

But then a thing happened in Vaughn: Charlie Ward eased into the brake and the steering wheel at the same time, trying to make the turn south, towards the fugitive myth of Old Mexico, but the car only swerved back north, and then kept on in a westerly direction. Charlie Ward looked around for a second, then lifted his right knee again. Nothing. They didn't slow at all. He visibly relaxed his hands on the wheel, and it stayed true without him. This went deeper than computer alignment and unbent tie rods. Pidgin put on his seatbelt, and Charlie Ward started laughing, his eyebrows stitched together tight with nerves. Pidgin said his mother's name to himself over and over; half the DPS of New Mexico was behind them, and they couldn't give themselves up if they wanted to. And the gas gauge wasn't falling. And the temperature wasn't rising. Pidgin saw himself a week later wearing a Wild Bill get-up like the original owner at Juanita's. God.

There was still the bottle in the backseat. They fell into it. New Mexico slipped by in a rage of sirens.

When they finally hit a last minute roadblock at dusk on some backroad just outside Albuquerque, the Trans-Am took to the ditch, unplanting fence poles Dukestyle, and then screamed back onto the blacktop. It was unstoppable, a sleek Indian juggernaut. When Pidgin was done with the bottle he held it out the window and it was sucked away. Behind them a cruiser fell. They huddled with their arms in the bucket seats, because night was coming and it was cold in the wind. Above them the helicopter stood on its beam of light, everything in the front seat empty and bright, the dash shining off at crazy angles, Charlie Ward holding onto the wheel because they didn't know when the car would let go.

They were hundreds of miles away from Clovis. Even if Birdfinger had grandstood again, the interment had to be long over, the ground even filled in and tamped down. Pidgin asked Charlie Ward where this car was taking them, and Charlie Ward just shrugged and said it was looking like Navajo land to him, at least what used to be Navajo land. 'But then again,' he said, the end too obvious for him to voice. Pidgin got it, didn't smile, kept to himself, watched Charlie Ward's hands on the wheel to see if there was anything that needed to be said. He couldn't tell, but wanted to say it anyway. He turned the radio on loud to keep from it, but still they had to put their ears to the speakers to hear the news about themselves, how they had become Joaquin Murieta reborn and one of his aged stand-ins, carving up the twentieth century with a single car. They were said to be carrying a payload of feather headdresses, peace pipes and old bones, all museum property, all movie memorabilia, all restolen.

Pidgin said he wanted it to be over.

In another hour, he was answered: they heard about it on the radio before they saw it, but when they saw it they were already there. It was a mile-long line of wooden Indians, pilfered from the cigar-smelling conscience of america. The Hopi had lined them up shoulder to shoulder, strung barbwire through the knees and armpits, and each one was cradling an armful of dynamite the oldtime miners had left behind, beaded now with nitroglycerin like tears. It was Kawliga crying, Tecumseh there beside him for consolation purposes, staid and stoic and grave in the face, frowning hard into the camera. The radio DJ was reading in a monotone, whispering between words *nine-eleven, nine eleven*. A hammer clicked audibly then, and the DJ went on, delivering the message over and over in his coliseum-sized voice: *this far and no farther, this far and no farther.* There was urgent laughing in the background, and fire crackling like static, cleansing the airwaves.

When Pidgin and Charlie Ward approached the fence at one-hundred-plus, dragging interstate cops like tin cans, a gate swung back on skateboard wheels, making an opening maybe six and a half feet wide. The Trans-Am shot through like threading a needle, the passenger-mirror dinging hello, and then the hole closed itself, had never been. The cruisers stood on their noses coming to a stop, but they didn't cross the line, couldn't. And there were no shots, just one warning flare from behind the wooden Indians, at the helicopter, which kissed the blades and made the sky a huge catherine wheel for a brief moment. The smell of radiator water filled the air. There were already vendors set up, for the hungry troopers. From the Hopi side of the line, people were chanting *red rover red rover*. A stray corn chip tossed in fatigue at the wooden Indians could get things started once and for all.

Pidgin rubbed warmth into his face and looked straight ahead. Beside him Charlie Ward said he was sorry. Pidgin shrugged it off. They were on Hopi land, Hopi backroads, and now they were in front of a Hopi prefab that still had a tractor truck hitched to it, stripped, rusting into the ground, the house tilting at a bad angle. The road made an awkward U around the place, banked bermstyle on the far side, but the car didn't take it. It coasted to the other side instead, near a horse trough, and finally rested, the turbo sighing.

The man who came out to greet them was barechested and wearing Jim Morrison pants too, with a brass zipper down the buttcrack. He didn't take his sunglasses off. He just approached the car and ran his hand along the hood, winced at the fence post impressions, inspected the tires and then spit on the sidepipes, making them hiss, stink filling the air; he never looked at Pidgin or at Charlie Ward. Soon enough he was laughing and whooping and doing some cheap stomp dance in the dirt beside his car, knees going high. A group of children joined him reluctantly and together they covered the Trans-Am in a camo tarp. Pidgin and Charlie Ward scrambled out at the last instant, and the children screamed and either scattered or became dogs.

'Hello there,' the man said, then started to say something else but his mouth filled with emotion, and he had to just wave an upturned palm in the direction of the Trans-Am, wait it out. He said it when he could: 'Thank you for bringing her back.'

'She kind of brought us,' Pidgin said, and before he had it all the way out the man was laughing, introducing himself as Grospieler, ushering them inside, handing them each an old chicken bucket of frybread with chili on bottom. As they sat their unevenly-legged chairs and ate, buckets slanted to the side, he told them the sad story of how the car had been stolen from him three days ago, by one of their young men. He said he didn't report it to missing persons because he didn't want the young man to go to jail. But all the same, his baby had been gone, he'd had a hard time even sleeping, and had lost touch with his radio soaps altogether.

Charlie Ward stopped eating midchew, looked hard at this Grospieler, at the eagle bone whistle tied around his neck, made from a juvenile and an adult, so one could slide in the other. 'Tell it like it is,' Charlie Ward said finally. 'Tell us how much you sold it for.'

Grospieler laughed in response, but it came out forced and nervous. He said it wasn't like that. To keep his hands busy he began peddling through a worn deck of Bicycle cards. Charlie Ward shook his head and continued eating. He turned once to Pidgin and said not to play this man's game with him, but Pidgin was already looking around the place, wondering what the man had to lose. He was about to pick up a stray card off the floor when Charlie Ward stood, asked where the shitter was, then walked out the front door with his bucket. In his absence, Pidgin asked Grospieler how far it was back to Clovis. Grospieler shrugged, walked in circles, his hands buried in his pockets, the cards within Pidgin's reach. 'You could get there before morning,' he said, 'if you really wanted.'

'Suppose I really wanted?'

'Suppose you did.'

Twenty minutes later Pidgin was down almost everything he had, which was mostly just borrowed clothes. He blamed the half gallon of wine, his grapeshot vision. The game was two-man Mexican Sweat, a duel. Every couple of minutes Grospieler had to stop, jump up, and run around the room, yelping with excitement, his two legs galloping ahead of each other like a horse, his back hand whipping him faster around and around. He said he didn't get many people up here, anymore. Pidgin said he wondered why. Grospieler smiled a bent-tooth smile, said one last hand between friends.

Pidgin said he would, but he didn't have anything else to bet. Grospieler leaned back and said there was always something else. Pidgin thought about Cline's Ford he still had the single key for, pushed it out of his mind, offered instead whatever small bounty Dorphin Studios had put out on him in a reluctant effort to get their twenty-seven dollar check back. Grospieler said thanks, but no; he didn't have a permit to leave the reservation, much less drive to Utah. And then he left it up to Pidgin, raced the cards back and forth from hand to hand, and within two minutes Pidgin cracked in the silence and had the double-sided Ford key on the table, was selling Grospieler on the 428 Thunderbird engine the truck's motor mounts were practically made for, the 2:11 gears taller than God himself, the powerglide with high and higher, the pony keg in the bed, aluminum-lined for airplane fuel, dual electric pumps.

'It probably won't even start,' Grospieler said, 'shit. After nine years?'

Pidgin said that under the right heel it could still make escape velocity.

Grospieler rubbed his chin. 'It's pretty important to you, yeah?' he asked, and Pidgin nodded. Grospieler nodded that that was enough then, that it mattered to Pidgin. They started in with the last hand, turning the cards up slow, peeking at corners, as if not seeing the whole card somehow increased the chances that it could be something else than it was. But the cards were what they were. When the hand was over and the key duly pocketed, Grospieler said he'd be expecting that pink slip by USPS, within the week. Pidgin left shuffling his feet, wrapped in a two and a half point blanket, still slanting left to stand straight. He passed Charlie Ward on the way in, too, already leaning—Charlie Ward whose face was now caked black with yellow lines bisecting it, his hair tied in a greasy knot on top of his head. 'Dumbshit,' he said right at Pidgin, spitting the word, then closed the door carefully behind him. Liquid discotheque light shot out from the windows and dissipated in the brush. All the female birds in the area laid eggs; Pidgin could hear them falling wetly to the ground, premature, lizards scrambling after the steaming embryos. He sat under the wine-darkened night and waited for it to end.

Two hours later Charlie Ward emerged bathed in sweat, with four things: the key, the widow's weeds, directions to some other prefab, and, below that, a scrawled release of the truck, signed with a thumbprint that had a smiling nutria drawn over it. He kept the release and the key because Pidgin's leather pockets were full with hands. As they walked to the other prefab in the thick Hopi darkness, Charlie Ward said they were even now, but in a sidelong glance Pidgin saw in the old horse thief's wet eyes the glimmer of an old Ford imbued with a Thunderbird's heart—fast, unstolen, maybe the last of its breed.

He told Charlie Ward thanks, and Charlie Ward shrugged. He was bleeding from under the fingernails from gambling so hard. When they got to the next prefab, a bone thin Alaskan bush-pilot with bleached-orange hair answered, smoking a poorly rolled joint.

'You're going south and east tonight, yeah?' Charlie Ward asked.

'I am?'

'You are.'

Eight minutes later they were airborne, the little Piper Cub scudding low, running lights off. Pidgin asked if they were going to Provo or Clovis, but Charlie Ward didn't blink, and Pidgin realized the old man had eyes painted on his eyelids in imitation of a deadcalm poker face, and was already minutes into sleep. Pidgin turned to the small ovaline window then and saw the two of them walking through the cemetery, pushing off from headstone to headstone, Charlie Ward solemn and grave in his medicine paint, Pidgin in his widow's weeds so he could hardly tell where he ended and the night began. They were going to Clovis. They had to be. Pidgin didn't sleep. He didn't say his mother's name. It was going to be over with soon. He was going to stand over the grave and then leave, ride out of Clovis, back to hot handheld lights of Provo, the shadowless sound stage of Dorphin Studios. His name would be there in the credits, both before and after. He asked the slow-witted pilot if he recognized him. The pilot said yeah. 'You're the one in costume dress,' he said like a question, 'at my door.'

Pidgin said no. The pilot nosed them towards a pasture, scattering sheep into a fence and over the fence. He asked Pidgin if that was him in the TV news. Pidgin said no again. He rebreathed the pilot's fourth joint, felt their small engine buzzing, felt them become that buzzing, that circling, that fly over Clovis, and then he was walking down a backroad unevenly on his boots, determined. Behind him was the pilot doing light maintenance and Charlie Ward locating them a necessary ride. The cemetery was only a quarter mile ahead. Pidgin was hours late. All that was left for him was the ceremony of the thing. He had said that to the pilot in parting, when the pilot hadn't asked. He'd offered condolences though, and three packets of ketchup. Pidgin trailed them out his hand, stepped into the parking lot, got divebombed by a bullbat, forced to the ground, to curb level. He talked to the bullbat of deals. He told it about the salty goodness of packaged ketchup. Eventually the bullbat accepted, left him lying there. He stayed for a moment because the asphalt was warm and his shirt was thin.

He told himself to walk forward, but lay still for a few moments longer, surveying, trying to pick out the twin plots Cline had won in a card game forever ago. One for himself, one for Marina. They were still there, marked now by a balloon sagging on its string, evidence of mourning.

Pidgin closed his eyes and opened them again, to make sure everything would remain, and it did, plus one: suddenly there was a form picking through the headstones, in the direction of the balloon. It was a man, a squat, dark, bowlegged shadow of a man with some army-issue helmet over his head and face, incandescent green goggles for eyes, which he kept pointing to the sky and following down, then walking a few steps forward. Like a bug. A carrion-bug. He carried with him a sharpshooter shovel that itself caught the starlight, splintering it across the cemetery. And then, suddenly, hours too soon, he was there, at Cline's fresh grave, digging methodically, and not at the whole thing either, but just part of it, the top part nearest the already old headstone. Pidgin couldn't seem to move, didn't seem to be able to defend his father's corpse. He didn't even think he was breathing. He watched the balloon sway back and forth. It took forty-five minutes for the squat man to undo what the backhoe had done. Pidgin blinked because the water in his eyes was distorting everything: the squat man, done with the skinny hole now, stood the shovel up and unraveled a rope from around his waist. He made a practiced loop at one end just big enough for a wrist and lowered it into the hole, using his supple shoulders to guide it, and started backing away, leaning into it, bringing Cline Stob up by the right arm. He was bloodless white, mouth sewn shut with crude stitches. Father. A pale Y longwise on the torso. Pidgin swallowed, recognized the grave robber in the same instant: it was him, from the edge of the floodlight all those years ago. Birdfinger had called him the Mexican Paiute once, and said it quiet, with reverence. Or fear.

In less than two minutes, then, the Mexican Paiute had all six feet of Cline draped easily across his shoulders, and was loping away, no effort at all. In a nearby tree an owl was punishing itself with names. Pidgin rose up out of the asphalt and stood stonestill at the edge of the cemetery, his chin trembling, and waited to be swept away body and clothes and all.

It didn't happen.

The Piper Cub buzzed the cemetery in military salute and Pidgin didn't look up. He said his mother's name like a ward, five syllables and then nothing. Already the retreating image of his dad had morphed: now he was riding the Mexican Paiute piggy-back, head lolling side to side, mouth sewn into a smile, so he couldn't say anything, or wouldn't. It was a secret. Pidgin knew it was a secret. He had almost heard it once thirteen years ago, lip-read it from forty feet off, through two layers of storm door, floodlight warming the night. But he'd been distracted. The leopard woman had been fussing over him.

'*I* can be your mother,' she offered, and Pidgin at nine-years old recoiled, trained his eyes back out the trailer window; from time spent locked in the bomb shelters his dad kept in front of the trailer, he could watch *Gunsmoke* through the window with no sound, could just read all the characters' lips. It worked in real life too, if he'd been around the person enough to know how their mouth worked. Like his father, out there at the edge of the floodlight, using his hands to recreate what Pidgin lip-read to be a man getting strangled to death with a boa constrictor. Pidgin's dad held the snakeshape in his hands, put a knee against the oblique shape of the man's head no longer in front of him, and leaned back, away from it, his mouth wide open, silent screaming fake rage, finally breaking into laughter, saying it was wonderful, *got-damn* wonderful. The Mexican Paiute nodded slightly, as if assimilating the story into some greater story, then turned to scan the horizon to the northeast and looked right at Pidgin, right into him, touching him in the middle, keeping him there. Pidgin fell back into the leopard woman's hungry arms.

'I had a child once,' she said.

'I could be your mother,' she said.

The Mexican Paiute's face had been dark and deeply wrinkled, flat like a dish and round, cheekbones like wings, nostrils like twin bulletholes, or gun barrels. Pidgin wasn't breathing anymore. The leopard woman saw and after thinking on it, said '*I* can do mother things,' then held him tight to her shoulder and covered him with her breath, stung tears from his eyes with it. Through her hair Pidgin could still see his dad and the Mexican Paiute. But then she took her hair off, replaced it with some that was long and black and dull.

'There,' she said, twirling, 'there. Now I'm her.'

'Look,' she said, and started dancing and clapping whoops from the circle of her mouth, a drink in her off hand. 'Now I'm your mother, doll. Don't you just love me?' She made Pidgin dance with her, lifting him off his feet sometimes, kissing him on the face and neck. 'Let's sit *Indian* style,' she said, and Pidgin shook his head no, turned his back to her, his face to the window. 'Let's braid my *beautiful* hair,' she said, and 'let's not be little spies, now. He's not going anywhere, you know.'

She tried to get a cigarette going then, and positioned herself so Pidgin had to stand behind her and braid, look through her wide reflection to see the small form of his father, who had the rolled-up newspaper out of his back pocket, and was pointing to where he had framed it with band-aids this morning, pointing to the part he said he wrote, that would make everybody cry over Larry.

'Doll,' the leopard woman said, 'be a dear, please.' Her hands were shaking too bad to hold the lighter; she passed it back to Pidgin. He cupped her cigarette with one hand and lit it with the other on the second try, never looking away from his father.

'Let me tell you a story,' she said, 'come here. Here beside me, across from me, like that now.' She positioned him, her long nails in his shoulders. Pidgin drew away, but she both squeezed tighter and said she was sorry with her eyes, raising a row of half moons from his shoulder. 'Let me read you a book,' she said, but soon got bored turning the magazine pages, felt around for the remote. Pidgin pointed out to his dad; there it was, on its camera string, hanging from his wrist.

'What?' Cline barked when the leopard woman called out to him, and then he shooed her away, from forty feet out held her back with an upturned palm, did his head at the Mexican Paiute, who was already starting to fade into the Clovis night air, skittish as smoke.

'Let's not bother your *daddy*,' she said when she came back in, 'heaven forbid,' then changed channels with the flashlight pointed at the lower right corner of the upper set while Pidgin watched his father mime the snake thing all over, this time sweeping his arm to show how many people witnessed it and could never doubt that it had happened, no matter how long they lived. The Mexican Paiute scratched under his ribs and moved his mouth in reply, but Pidgin couldn't follow the words, and then without warning the words stopped and Pidgin was locked in place again by the Mexican Paiute's close-set eyes. His dad shook his head in disgust, placed his broad self between them, spat twice, then walked fast to the front deck, slammed the screen door open, and drew the curtains so tight they overlapped in the middle for longer than Pidgin's arm.

The leopard woman looked up, her eyes sleepy. 'I'm playing mom,' she said, waggling her fingers around, showing all the mother things she was doing, and got slapped awake hard, her one braid slinging around, describing an arc. Cline pulled her face close to his own, held her by the chin. 'I do *not* want my son—' he started then broke off, by sweeping his arm again, this time to the window, to the Mexican Paiute. 'Being influenced,' he finished, his voice almost under control. The leopard woman flinched anyway. He said he didn't want to get into it right now, then shook his head and hugged her, said he was sorry, he was penance in motion, but please, please, and with that he was gone again, back to his snake story. When he left he didn't shut the front door though, just the screen, and it was quiet for too long. 'Let me tell you a story,' the leopard woman said, finally, her voice still half in her throat and not carrying far enough, 'about your mother, doll.'

Pidgin turned to her.

She smiled with the attention. She started telling the story about WWI she always told, talked about it like a war, not a concert, lost it like she always lost it, said she had something even better tonight. She was going to act it out instead, dance like Marina Trigo when she was dancing on top of the kingcab Ford, the nails in her boot heels kicking up sparks from the paint, Waylon Jennings serenading her and four hundred other people, but mostly her. Everything was always for her, Marina. The leopard woman lowered the lights to Canyon Texas level, blew spices into the air to be suspended as dirt in headlights, everything glowing. She said she had been an actress in high school. She pulled on her boots, poured a drink, and began slow, dancing with herself around the living room, her cigarette ash the only thing teasing fire. Soon enough she was crying and asking Pidgin if his father loved her the same as Marina Trigo. Pidgin said he didn't know. He backed away from the vision, eased over to the window to check on his dad, make sure he was still there, and he was: he was going into the snake story for the third time, this time playing the part of Larry, on his knees, getting choked by some masked assailant, tongue lolling out the side of his mouth, face purple. In the scratched glass of the screen door Pidgin could make out of the leopard woman only the end of her cigarette tracing curlicues and swirls, and then in the middle of all the orange lines, the only still image was the Mexican Paiute, smiling clearly at him across forty feet, his teeth even and white, his lips forming the beginning of words shaped like nothing Marshall Dillon had ever said.

The retreating image of Cline's looted body morphed again for Pidgin. This time the Mexican Paiute had looked back over it, his green eyes distended with laughter, with knowledge. Pidgin tried to ignore, tried to slow the development of the image down before he lost it altogether, but the night air was changing around him, billowing through the unreal material of his shirt. He did what he could. He parceled everything coming at him into discrete units. The effort lasted a week; the first day was the rest of the night for him. He walked the six miles back to the submarine, covered in gravedust and gravesmell.

'I filled in that hole,' he told Charlie Ward, and Charlie Ward nodded no, no.

The whole walk back he had been dogged by a tenor saxophone, playing long and gritty like an oldtime detective show. 'So tell me, then,' he had said to it finally, three-sixty, but the syrupy music only backed off for a moment, then came back a little more distant, until it faded out altogether, like it was standing still and Pidgin was the one moving away.

The second day was worse: Charlie Ward disappeared up the manhole, and Pidgin, able to locate neither light nor lighter, stumbled from head-level pipe to head-level pipe. He could no longer find the way out. There were sounds. Charlie Ward didn't return. Once there was a distant tapping, but it was small, hardly real, and then it was gone. 'Dad?' Pidgin asked as quietly as he could, and hours too late. He locked himself in what felt like it had once been a pantry, gorged himself on what tasted like uncooked bread, and slept.

On the third day he was still alone, living underground, and it was like the bomb shelter treatment all over, only now the bomb was in the shelter with him, decaying. He thought the tapping might be his mother burrowed over, so he hid in the centermost place he could find, because Birdfinger had been right—he only knew her by name. And he didn't know how to tell her about his dad.

'I filled in that hole,' was all he knew to say.

On the fourth day he woke with half digested bread in his mouth, and swallowed. Hours later, he licked wetness off relict fiberglass and knew that it was in this manner that people forget how to talk. The saxophone returned, cloying. Pidgin remembered the bus and the girl with the hair, DK: *lovermine*. He remembered the sensation of piping through the air towards the idea of Cline. Around the reed of the saxophone came a gravel-choked voice, mocking, saying the gods were angry, and so was he. Then laughter, then Pidgin angry at the laughter, holding his fist up to the squat figure at the dim edge of his memory who had spirited the body of his dad away.

'I filled in that hole,' he said, jaws corded.

On the fifth day Pidgin woke bent over and unsure, a man's underbelly cold on his lower back, the Custerlike figure leaning over, whispering deep and hard into Pidgin's ear in his best Sheena Easton voice: *now take it slow like yer daddy told ya*. He'd had this dream before, Pidgin, for days on end. This memory. The saxophone was gone, but the anger remained. Pidgin closed his eyes and endured as he knew he had to, but refused to say again *I filled in that hole*, because that would allow Custer those words, and they weren't his, Custer's. They never would be. Pidgin had to keep them. Finally a clammy wet hand slapped him on the shoulder, led him to the manhole, undid the lock that bad luck must have tripped, and with no between stage, no depressurization or anything, Pidgin was standing again in daylight, over some eight-hundred tons of misplaced navy steel. He didn't look back; in front of him was the trailer, and he ran for it for the second time, stood blinking in the midst of the pastel shelters come like worshipers from the pasture. The Cutlass was gone. There were no sounds from the trailer, only a sun-hungry cannabis stalk reaching up through the roof, leaves and trunk monochrome, vibrant. Pidgin pretended not to be seeing it. Over and over.

After a couple of minutes of staring, he turned to the budget blue shelter where a mendicant bass player and his loyal doll were emerging, as if they'd been standing still in the door, waiting for him to look their way. The bass player put forty-five cents in the doll's blown-up hand, made her give it to Pidgin, then led her away. There had been fishing weights glued onto her toes and painted red, a marriage of beauty and function. Pidgin watched them leave, unsure what had happened and what he now held, and when he turned around a pale-haired salesman was approaching, zipping his pleated slacks, shaking his whiskey leg.

'I filled in that hole,' Pidgin told him, nodding that the job was done, and the salesman said I'm sure you did, son, then led Pidgin into the oldest shelter, the once green one, now half buried, crowning. They ducked through the door. It was inky black like the submarine. Pidgin hesitated, but the salesman urged him on. In the center of the shelter there were rocks glowing, heat roiling across the surface entoptic like sunworms. In the meager light they cast, the salesman opened his case, brought out bundles of braided sweetgrass, a pine bough, handfuls of cedar-smelling buds of some sort, more.

'You've got gravedust in your windpipe there, boy,' the salesman diagnosed, touching a thick finger to Pidgin's throat, pointing the gravedust out, and Pidgin began coughing, and then water hissed and the place filled with steam and smell and Pidgin had to hold his face close to the ground just to breathe. The salesman was giving some sort of ceremonial pitch that wilted at the tail-end like one of Cline's door-to-door sermons when he would hold the red-striped straw to his upturned ear and say he had a pipeline to God. Pidgin hid in the darkness, coughed it all out and kept coughing, and when the rocks cooled hours later he was alone again, cleansed, and in place of salesman's case was well-worn banktube, a personal banktube. Cline's, maybe. Meaning Birdfinger's, now. In it he found a sepiatone telephoto that showed the six Goliards, framed up against an adobe wall. Cline and Birdfinger and Sally and the Mexican Paiute and a skunkheaded Indian and there at the edge, playing coy with the camera, maybe the first real picture of Marina Trigo. Appended was a scrawled receipt for the forty-five cents that was gone, that the salesman had taken. Pidgin made himself look away from her, shoved the telephoto into the waist of his pants, and remembered what the saxophone had sounded like: drawn out, moaning, plaintive.

The sixth day was another night for Pidgin, and he found Charlie Ward taking it slow through the streets of Clovis, parking lights on, one hand casual over the wheel of a Chevette, the rest of him duded up in a security guard outfit. The hanger it had been on was still dangling over the backseat.

'You're not the law,' Pidgin said, rubbing his chin, the underlip hair Cline had encoded his direction, and Charlie Ward shot him quick with his finger gun, blew off the extra smoke, then reholstered it. That night Pidgin couldn't go back down the submarine manhole, so they slept at Birdfinger's empty-again trailer. Charlie Ward called it the longhouse, and left his boots at the door. In the kitchen sink Pidgin dyed Charlie Ward's hair Grecian Formula black, and when he went out to rub the color off his hands with caliche dirt the Chevette was already gone. Pidgin turned his face to the sky, looking for the underbelly of the car, listening for the beat of massive wings, the downrush of air.

The seventh day a finger of light reached through the illicit smoke of the theatre Charlie Ward insisted upon, making soft contact with the canvas, and then Mollidell was on-screen, beautiful, lithe, thirty feet tall. Pidgin watched the movie the first time, and the second and third times through he watched Charlie Ward chew his fingertips away—scalp stained black, shortsleeved security shirt tight at the stomach—and he didn't understand: each time Baluk gave it to the moose, Charlie Ward had to swallow tears. Pidgin didn't know if it was for Baluk or the moose even, or Mollidell, not on-screen right. He drifted in and out, Charlie Ward. Their hands were shiny slick in the halflight. Pidgin removed himself to the better lit lobby, restudied the telephoto. It was already worn into quarters bound by frayed-white crease lines. In the lower left were Cline's legs and most of the Mexican Paiute. The Mexican Paiute was built like Yellow Robe from Charlie Ward's movie. In the halflight of the popcorn machine, Pidgin made promises against his person, against the Mexican Paiute. And the Goliards too. He left the theatre in search of an adobe wall circa 1977, a starting place from which he could trace the Mexican Paiute over the years to the cemetery. But there was nowhere, there was Clovis. He did what he could. He walked beside the road until he came to the buffet called the Gorge which rented itself out at night, the building dripping neon, clouded with bugs, the modern brick wall on its south side fingerdeep with bat guano. Tonight it was a moveable bingo game.

Pidgin ran his fingers through his hair, tucked it behind his ears, and stepped through the door with resolve, with purpose, hoping to catch the world off-guard somehow, and was instead bodily halted by the seven-foot frame of Big Truck Rollins, who carried his name inlaid on his plate-sized belt buckle. But Truck didn't make him pay. Pidgin didn't understand: Truck looked at him for a long time and from a great and shaggy height, and then let him pass unmolested. No one else even noticed him. Just another Indian who thinks he's Ted Nugent. The food on the buffet had long been cold, and there were people there with old minnow buckets and styrofoam coolers, collecting the day's overspill in silence, eyes downcast. Pidgin located a soggy chicken wing for each hand, and let the bingo ritual unfold before him in fits and starts. The game was blackout, and there was a fine mist of talcum powder suspended between him and the caller, a long-legged man who smiled at Pidgin and nodded as if Pidgin should know him. Pidgin didn't return the nod. He was surrounded by walkers and wheelchairs and the smell of stale urine, oxygen tanks lined up behind the chairs like house-issued silver bullets. One old man wearing his tank scuba-style, as if he were just visiting, as if this world would kill him if he breathed it in.

A bingo deacon placed a card in front of Pidgin. *N-17* flashed over the slide projector, three feet tall. It was punctuated by sighs, groans, mechanized assistance. Pidgin played his card like battleship and lost. The woman who won rode her three-wheeler sidesaddle up to the stage, and the whole way up the ramp looked into her laprug, careful not to let her eyes stray, like she was ashamed. The man beside Pidgin deliberately sponged away the last game, giving toothless form to archaic cursewords. The caller whispered a prize into the bingo woman's hearing aid, forcing her to turn her head to the side while his fingers danced over the keypad of her silver tank. She held her hand to her mouth when he was done, nodded, then coasted back down. A liver-spotted hand patted her taillight as she passed, and then the offering plates were making the rounds, and Pidgin was behind the curtain that formed a makeshift hall, leading first to the bathroom and then the outer door. One of the plates passed where he could see it and it was spilling over. A voice behind him said that the beautiful part was that it went to research.

Pidgin wheeled around, caught mid-escape, and it was the caller, looming in place, pale and thin-lipped. He had a cold hand on Pidgin's shoulder, on his neck. He introduced himself as Sam, nothing more nothing less, and as he spieled about bingo, Pidgin detected formaldehyde on the air. Sam smiled. 'It's no small accident that you've come here,' he said.

Pidgin shook his head no, it was an accident.

Sam gestured wide and said Cline Stob had made all this possible. He had been worth thirty-eight publications. In his wallet Sam had laminated autopsy photographs; they unfolded to the ground, slapped cold concrete, and then he was gone again, calling numbers with the projector, coordinating the deacons with the subtlest of eyebrow shifts. Pidgin backed into the wall farthest from the bingo game, and through the curtain crack his vision tunneled down to include only the bingo woman, her clear mask held tight to her face, head lowered as if pretending she'd dropped something. The deacons circled like vultures, and when she raised her head, eyes rolled back deadwhite, they closed rank, become one broad back, and Pidgin was breathing fast, holding onto rich blue bathroom tile with both hands to slow himself: he was falling down through lower and lower levels of Clovis awning.

In the bathroom with him was a red-headed college kid accented with demure argyle, leaning into the stall, coloring a white cocktail napkin pencil grey, doing the Vietnam wall thing to the graffiti art. The contour of a face was rising from the napkin, a simple happy-face with a lone feather angling off behind its round head. For the Goliards. Pidgin was unsurprised. At his hesitant touch, the kid wheeled sharply around, backed himself into the corner between the urinal and the stall, and when Pidgin didn't advance, the kid raised his camera slow—as if he might spook Pidgin into flight—and stole three quick pictures.

'Jimmy Olsen,' he mumbled, not extending a hand, and Pidgin said back to him William H Bonney, in the same way he'd heard Jesus H Christ inflected, and then didn't extend his hand either, instead stood open-eyed while the camera probed his retinas, and in the powder-white ceiling he saw the outline of the Mexican Paiute bounding effortlessly across the *Silent Enemy* snowdrifts, dragging a pale blue corpse by the hand, both of them receding in the celluloid, becoming small in the distance, remote. The last thought that Pidgin registered before the concrete floor came rushing up to meet him at thirty-two feet per second per second was *here I am swooning,* and then he was back inside himself, drawn up like a bean, a fœtus, and his father's interment had been over for a week.

A Pagan Groove

Birdfinger was fobless and feeling it at the interment, trying to cover the absence with Vanetta's high-gloved arm. She stood statuesque to the right of him, her red hair in a conservative bun at the back of her head, marmstyle. It was a closed casket, small gathering. Him and her and no kid. The groundsman was a hardnose, too, and wouldn't wait any longer, was already groaning across the cemetery with the tawny backhoe, trainsmoking the cloves he told them kept the stench of death at bay. But, he added, eyebrows winging away, his boyfriends were all narcissists, too, goldenboys obsessed with death, and through him they'd come to truly believe it smelled like cloves. And he sure wasn't going to disabuse them of that notion, he winked. Not him, not their own personal grim-ass reaper. Some of them were even anxious. Birdfinger watched him coming for to carry Cline home. He squeezed Vanetta's hand and she matched him muscle for muscle. His left side was still flaccid from the night before, a nerve writhing in his shoulder like an electric grub. In his palm was a pawnshop pocketwatch, loose but on time, give or take ten minutes.

'He's not coming,' Birdfinger admitted, finally, looking into the watch again, checking it against the sun, and Vanetta said no, it doesn't much look like he is.

'It's not your fault though, Bird,' she added. 'He's a grown boy.'

'Blame the USPS, I suppose.'

'It *was* Billy the Kid day.'

Birdfinger played along, grunted, didn't tell her that the USPS had delivered the pictogram in spite of the holy day. He knew because he had received in reply a business card for somebody named Redfield. It was just his second correspondence with the kid in seven years; the *Redfield* name was crossed out, and the kid had copied something on the back, The Wish to Be a Red Indian, Kafka's long and sarcastic sentence about america. On the frontside, under the crossed-out name, the kid had gotten more personal, offered facts, said that for his first two years with the studios his mentor the recruiter had forced him to read this long sentence at all hours of the day, said it was preparation for a coming part that never came, that it would be for him what thinking about baseball was for white guys. There was no room on the card for anything else, for any apologies tendered or accepted. Birdfinger assumed the card was serving as an RSVP though, that Pidgin was going to be at the funeral. The kid's first correspondence had been just as vague, though. It was from the time when he was making the never-released video that was supposed to catapult him into the national conscience; it was the beginning of that time, when they were shooting and reshooting the Pocahontas scenes from every angle, trying to capture it in its fullness, finding it was deeper than they'd scheduled studio time for. Birdfinger knew because he had had eyes in Provo at the time. Keeping tabs had been an unshirked family duty.

But then the correspondence had come, a back page torn from some desperate magazine, one of the personals circled in pencil: *Wanted. Someone to fill a void.* Because it was so short, Birdfinger thought he should be able to figure it out, but in thinking about it he lost contact with his Provo eyes, let them roll into corners and go dry. There had been no more tabs for years now, only a mail call to come see Cline buried, to come see how he himself was changing, was getting off the hard stuff once and for all, going to. Forty-eight wasn't too late. He didn't want to end up pickled in formaldehyde, naked to the world. Suicide ran in the blood, his father had told him in a note, and every time Birdfinger bled he looked for it, for something.

Forty-eight wasn't too late for reparations, either. Or it wouldn't be if the kid were here to make reparations *to*. Birdfinger looked to Vanetta who was looking away, had no explanations. Excuses were hard to come by in this kind of heat. The sum total of it all was that he'd chased the kid off and done a good job of it, Birdfinger, and now, here, it was all on display for Cline, even the night before rolled in, when Birdfinger had been waiting for Pidgin on the porch Cline had built. He had waited all day for the kid to show himself, too, truly he had, but then night had come wearing stage boots and breathing fire, and he had been alone, and he could no longer deny that down at Clandenstein's they were midway through the Annual Blues Marathon again, when all the slick-bald black men would come together and mainline whatever they could find, playing for hours on end. It was an endurance thing, but it was a baptism too, if you made it through. Last year the winner had been a timeworn lineman called Pops, who'd played for nearly two days straight, all one half-rhymed narrative about a fice dog stealing his trash and leaving it in the ex-wife's yard, night after night; the chorus was the same useless apology to her, then to her new old man, then to the law, and on until the audience was in the song as well, being apologized to one by one, since it seemed they'd all been with his wife at one time or another, had had to clean up the fice dog's trash. It was a house record: forty-six hours. They'd found three of the imported judges dead in the bathroom when it was all said and done. 'They were sad,' the coroner pronounced solemnly, 'shit I would be too.' But he'd got free beer, nobody was complaining, everyone left the next morning wearing plasticlear bracelets that said they were officially dead. Birdfinger still had his, and wore it on nights like this. All the regulars did. It was a badge; it demanded respect.

Striding out of the darkness that the trailer porch had become and into the smoke of Clandenstein's, Birdfinger had only to hold his wrist far above his head and present the bracelet to the all-seeing gaze of Big Truck Rollins, the Bill Walton lookalike who had started WWI, and he was let pass, no cover, another ghost. There at the bar too was Vanetta, darling Net, all six feet of her, metallic red hair down tonight, in everybody's drinks. She tried to ignore him, but he was Birdfinger, leading with his newfound stomach, and the crowd parted before him. The first thing he told her over the din was that he still might be inclined to love her, and the second was that he was afraid to go to the interment tomorrow, without an escort.

'*Interment*, hon?' Vanetta breathed smoke out slow then batted it into curlicues with horsehair eyelashes, her best trick.

'Yeah,' Birdfinger said. 'We had the funeral ten years back or so. I was lead singer.'

'It was a concert?'

'It was my brother, bad gig.'

'I'm sorry, Bird.'

'Yeah, well,' Birdfinger led off, going nowhere, letting his casual invitation worm its way through her red hair while he time-warped to the funeral and back again, a round trip that left him reeling and thirsty. He cast about for Midge, the bandaliered shot girl, and she matched him drink for drink, the camel-colored skin of her throat showing delicate peach fuzz under the blacklight. He said he'd owe her, then got bumped on the elbow and bumped back, with interest, but Clandenstein's was too crowded tonight to let it get personal: out-of-town people milled around in every open space, babbling, dribbling five-dollar drinks which cost two on any normal weeknight. The only thing the same, aside from the waitstaff, was that the stools along the bar were still arranged green brown black, green brown black, a joke about the life of man, the bartender said under his breath to a stranger down the way who didn't get it, but slid from a green to a brown stool anyways, showing his age. The real presence though wasn't the people, but the slide guitar, the blues moan which saturated everything, the focal point no longer the stage but the men's bathroom, where the current contender had dragged the mic, keeping time with his foot on what sounded like a stall door: *one* one two *two* two two.

Birdfinger fell into it neckdeep, feetlast, and when he looked up, Vanetta had wandered off. Now on the black stool next to him was a salesman dressed in a sweated-through three-piece suit, just sidling in place, his loose tie thin and straight as a plumb line. He introduced himself as Litmus Jones, yelled that he was from out of town, just passing through, like a hero in a goddamn western.

'Say what?' Birdfinger yelled back, and when they couldn't hear each other, Litmus hooked his chin towards a napkin and drew a quick pictogram of himself astride a horse, sixguns ablaze, both good and bad guys falling everywhere, their eyes X'd, their women shaped like coke bottles and mannered like doves.

Birdfinger smiled and nodded, then in the way of small talk drew back a pictogram of the view off the trailer's redwood porch, the last five bomb shelters flung out like worshipers, the pre-paid hourly renters crawling out on bended knees: two hungover cowboys and a bowlegged waitress, a truckdriver and another waitress, a junior high kid with a magazine and a month's worth of allowance. It was a living, the pictogram said wordlessly. When the renters were gone, too, the cats would creep bellydown into the shelters to scavenge what was left before the sun baked it inedible. Birdfinger left that part of it unfinished, as potential. Litmus Jones appreciated that potential, responded with like small talk, some offhand banter about lightning rods and vacuum cleaners and sewing machines and hotel soap. Nothing serious, but all the same, he did it with such spare precision and economy of lead that Birdfinger could only respond in kind with his masterpiece, with the machinations and the time that had been involved in getting the tapeworm to come up his throat for the dab of raw meat balanced on the back of his tongue. Pliers and mirrors, bottle flies. Muscle relaxers for the gag reflex. Watching it kick legless in the driveway dirt, the cats unsure for once. His pencil hand shook with effort when it was done. It was a gentlemanly challenge.

Litmus smiled with it, against it, licked his pencil tip, and without even holding the napkin down sketched the most basic outline of a gumshoe, which was a compliment on Birdfinger's detective abilities, his hard-earned gut that had led him to up the ante exactly when the ante needed upping. Birdfinger patted his distended shirtfront and nodded, pulled on his pointy lapels, and while Litmus drew what had to be a monograph or a manifesto at least, judging by the detail involved, he kept an eye on Vanetta, her red hair well above the crowd, close to the stage. A hard act to miss, even on a night like this.

Birdfinger had told her once that her red hair was why he chose her out of all the others in the first place, that it was opposite enough from his long-gone Marina that it didn't remind him of her so much. Vanetta had just looked around and said 'What others, Bird?' then went on, that night, to prove to him that her hair was just dyed red, faux fox. Midafternoon he woke to her watching him. She was smoking a miles-long aftersex camel, her nails witchblack, no make-up. She laughed and said 'You're a hornbrowed, unclever man, Bird,' to which Birdfinger added that he was a little long in the tooth to boot, but who was counting?

'Not me hon, of all people. Surely not me.'

'All the same, though,' he went on, 'I made it a year on the mountain with just a croquet mallet.'

'Mountain?' she had asked then, looking around again, losing the ash off her cigarette into his bed and neither of them caring much about it. They were good together like that, maybe once a month, would leave Clandenstein's early, swinging their hands between them like truant schoolkids. Tonight, though, Birdfinger was trying his best to be a little serious: he hadn't been lying about being afraid of going to the interment by himself, nephewless, unescorted. He had presented himself to her as vulnerable. It was some kind of tacit step or another, God help him.

In a few days everything would be less complicated again. Birdfinger said this to himself three times fast, and when he was just almost believing it, Litmus nudged him, his pictogram complete. But it was more than complete, was more complete than anything in the bar. More real. Birdfinger couldn't look away. The tone of it was confessional, the technique somehow conjuring an act of petty voyeurism, but aside from all that what really grabbed Birdfinger by the jawbone was the stoptime feel it insisted upon, as if the scene the salesman drew had just stutter-stepped, was just waiting for something to rise up, hang for an instant, and kick-start it to life. Litmus blew the real smoke off the end of his pencil, said something about the price of lead, and then the whole of Clandenstein's began slipping away from Birdfinger. He put his fingertips on either side of the napkin, the pencil figures between already swirling, and fell headlong in.

The first thing he felt upon standing was the undeniable urge to pee. It was stimulus-response: he seemed to be in a grey-tiled bathroom, the bus stop facility, none of the tiles bigger than his hand. They were delicately grouted, though, each coarse grain distinct. Litmus had even included the fevered graffiti set once and forever in rhyme. Birdfinger sauntered to the row of urinals and stood by Litmus, who was already there. The liquid click of Birdfinger's zipper going down was loud enough that he looked around, afraid he'd disturbed something unseen. But he hadn't. And God if it didn't feel good to pee. He told himself he wouldn't because this wasn't real, but he closed his eyes anyway, to feel it coming out, the heat splashing on the backs of his hands, his back arching into it, the ceramic embracing his hips.

And now with the warm life he gave it, the bathroom was started, too, in motion with him: Litmus sighing, shaking off, bragging about the ice-cold stainless-steel drain; both of them reaching to flush at the same time; a toilet paper rack squeaking in time with somebody's breath. Somebody small, a child's rapid lungs. No. Birdfinger zeroed in, wary. It was the handicapped stall, God, the big one with stainless handles, big enough for some hapless kid and a game-faced lecher—

Birdfinger slammed the door open, half-expecting the shape of his father's broad back hunched over. The door slapped the wall and slung closed, rattling on its hinges, opening again on its own, slowly, onto a woman lying prone, her black and white clothes opened once in haste and buttoned back up again all wrong, so she looked made from pieces; she didn't even have a face at all: Litmus hadn't drawn anything there, so that she had smooth napkin-colored skin, which brought unaccountable tears to the back of Birdfinger's eyes and made him stumble backwards, into Litmus, who redirected his head back in, forcing appreciation. There squatted by her was the noise, the child, breathing in and out. No child Birdfinger had ever seen, though. He looked like a stony-eyed, prepubescent gargoyle. He had just braided the woman's oily black hair so it came awkwardly out the side of her head, and now, with a pink handled fingernail file, he was sawing the thick braid off to a ragged edge, holding the trailing end in his mouth.

Litmus whispered in Birdfinger's ear that it'd bring ten dollars, twelve if the kid had the patience for an uptown beauty salon. Birdfinger had no idea what to do with this information. The woman was lying there in a half inch of urinal water that Birdfinger knew was rising because Litmus hadn't bothered to draw any plumbing. It was an easy thing to miss. But still. No one deserves that. Birdfinger steeled himself with cusswords and stepped in, ready to lay hold of the kid if necessary, remove him. The expressionless kid just watched him approach, his arm sawing fast and faster, like a thing independent from the rest of his body, a da Vinci study of a pool player's arm. The instant the braid broke free though, he was up the side of the stall and into the mahogany area beyond. He'd moved like a spider, like a lizard, confident of each foot and hand placement, his torso close to the wall. In his absence, Birdfinger sat on the toilet by the woman, watching blood seep into the water from her pants that were on backwards. He couldn't touch her; she was too close. It took Litmus to do it, splashing in, pinching his slacks up over his thighs, squatting where the kid had squatted, breathing heavy like a man, placing two fingers deep into her neck like a man. His face in here was hard and unshaved. He nodded no to Birdfinger, no, nothing.

Everything was focused on Litmus's two fingers now, and then on the index finger alone. Birdfinger could make out each fungal grain of the yellow nail. It was still, unmoving. Litmus said it was too damn bad, he had a friend who managed that grocery store down the way, Squanto's Indian Palace, and he always needed Native cashiers, for authenticity. He laughed and spit into the rising water, tried to tease a response from Birdfinger, an agreement of some kind. Birdfinger neither nodded nor didn't nod. He didn't know what he was doing here. Worse than anything, he wanted Midge, the shot girl, he wanted Vanetta's distracting red hair, he wanted his five-stringed guitar and a Marty Robbins ditty to hide behind, a continental suit to walk out in, incognito. Anything but this, that wooden fingernail, so still.

He watched it, making deals with anybody listening, and was still watching when Litmus could no longer contain his laughter: on the heart side of his twin fingers the skin was rising from the girl's neck, backblood building up. Birdfinger felt his eyebrows V together hard, heard a nurse in some bar whisper *oxygen deprivation* into her drink, and he almost had his arm in motion to begin to save the woman again, but before he got there Litmus made a show of relaxing the now-obvious tendon running down the ridge of his index finger. His fingernail on the girl's neck rose once then, slightly, the clot dissipating, and then again, uneven, falling into a hesitant rhythm over the next two minutes. Slow, but there. Birdfinger looked to Litmus, and Litmus wiped his smile away on the back of his off arm and left it there, nodded no, he wasn't faking it. It was all her. She was too important to die. Birdfinger watched the fingernail rise and fall in spikes, and then looked into where the face should be, waiting for a lidless eye to open, waiting for it to be her, his Marina. That must be why me, here, he said to himself, then just waited, peeking between his fingers, but when the face resolved itself a pencil stroke at a time and there was suddenly a real chance it might be her or close enough, he looked away, made her into just some other Indian girl left behind in a bathroom to try and figure it all out.

'Will she make it?' he asked Litmus as quiet as he could, over the sink, and Litmus shrugged, said sure, for better or for worse. Her kind did. Her especially. He hummed the chorus of the song of women knowing how to carry on, and it cued a long forgotten track in Birdfinger, a Waylon track, let him look away for an instant, and when they left moments later she was propped up on a men-style toilet, knees together, head in her hands, shorn hair straggling through her fingers. 'Maybe you can call that manager-friend of yours about her,' Birdfinger suggested, nearly removed from the situation, already able to hear bar talk again, and Litmus said again sure, but what was it about her? Birdfinger said nothing, probably, and then Litmus patted him on the shoulder, hard, too hard, and suddenly they were arm in arm, made up like gentlemen on a Victorian postcard, and when Birdfinger looked down he saw they were walking on their own water, and that was the grandest thing of all.

Bring Midge the shot girl.

Trade her a cigarette, get her to laugh, love her for a moment.

Tell her about the Sea of Galilee, watch every wonderful line in her face when she smiles, unbelieving, then look beyond, place Vanetta, lose track of this salesman, wad the napkin with one hand, one motion.

Yes.

Birdfinger felt his crotch to see if he'd peed his pants over the last few minutes; he couldn't tell. It had happened before, though. Midge looked away politely, whistled to Truck and aimed him at the stage, where things were developing: one of the judges was emerging from the men's restroom with an unconscious bluesman, the mic wired into some reel-to-reel hardware he had strapped under his flannel shirt. His mouth wasn't moving but the words still came. It hadn't been a chorus, but a loop. The crowd trudged forward to dismantle the imposter. Birdfinger clawed his way out with an empty wingtip shoe and trouser sock, the left ones, and then Truck was sweeping bodies aside effortlessly, maintaining order. There were still hours and days to go. Birdfinger settled into a black formfit stool for the long haul, for the next contender, and just shook his head slow when Litmus ambled up onto stage, not too proud to make use of the house guitar, a duct-taped tool for indigents, pockmarked with generations of cigarette burns.

'Well fuck me,' Birdfinger mumbled, but all the same, it was the life he was born to. He could only accept this salesman's naive presumption like he had all the rest, and half-hope for an unbloody ending: Litmus was the first white guy to ever set foot on the stage during the Blues Marathon. Once there'd been a Plains Indian of some sort, who was dark enough, all right, but nobody'd wanted to hear about high-school basketball on the reservation, and he'd drunk himself unconscious soon enough anyway. Birdfinger had argued it was all part of the act, a dramatic lacunae, but he'd been alone in his thinking. It was him and Vanetta's first fight. He wasn't so sure about this Litmus, though. Nobody was. If he could play like he drew....

Vanetta leaned close to Birdfinger from out of the crowd, some roughneck's hands around her lowslung hips, and whispered in his ear was he maybe covering backup for his new friend?

Birdfinger smiled. 'He doesn't look like he needs my help.'

'He sure as hell needs something, Bird. Some sense, maybe?'

'He's just a salesman,' Birdfinger coughed, buying time. 'You thought any about my proposal, Net? The interment?'

'I haven't had time to think about much of any—' she started, but was manhandled back into the crowd, the end of her answer dopplering away, retreating. Birdfinger imagined it as yes, though, *yes yes yes*. The roughneck she was with cast a possessive eye back to Birdfinger, and Birdfinger looked hard into his drink and listened to Litmus on stage, trying to get the indigent guitar in tune, going one by one through all three sides of the letters, the audience voicing yeas and nays at random. They were all ready to watch this white salesman fall on his face and crack into eggshell. One co-ed table had even broken into song themselves, anglo showtunes, while another gathered around Truck, trying to bribe him to remove Litmus. But Truck had standards, Birdfinger knew; he only took such bribes on a per-pound basis, and when it came down to it, they just couldn't pony up enough for his hedged estimate of Litmus's weight. They were still passing the hat, losing more than they were collecting, when Litmus's whiskers scraped the microphone, filled the holes in the metal screen, and then withdrew.

Birdfinger closed his eyes to let the music come, be what it may. The co-ed table did a slow fade. Litmus touched the strings one at a time, a caress, soft at first, but a full sound. From somewhere to the right there was an audible scoff, an offhand mention of guitarring and feathering, but other than that, just ice in glasses, smoke muffling the rest. Litmus made that first chord last, too; he was feeling out the acoustics of Clandenstein's, the guitar, the crowd. When Birdfinger opened his eyes he caught a head movement from Litmus to Truck, and Truck stepped back, obedient, prepaid maybe, and pulled the side door to. Litmus smiled and picked it up some then, the heel of his wingtip going up and down and never touching the stage, moving his head to the right when he moved it, leading with his chin, almost smiling. When he spoke it wasn't important what name he was stealing for the night, what mattered was that he spoke with a voice pitched like Vern Gosden, Ed Bruce in the morning; it was the voice of God in the old testament movies, where people were smitten down with half-syllables.

Birdfinger felt the long muscle around his femur tremble with anticipation, his hand around the warm glass absently fingering chords. But Litmus, this salesman, this soft seller, he took his time, let it build proper. A half hour into it he finally fished an improvised slide out of his pocket; an hour into it he took his tie off with one hand and hung it off the guitar neck. It was forty-five minutes shy of breakfast before he even put his mouth to the mic again. All the glasses in the place were standing water by then, only one cigar still lit, burning down. And nobody asleep. The song began, once, twice, and then split, going two ways at the same time, twelve bars in each direction. It felt right, though; the lyrics were scrapped together from blacktop words shaped like a foot tent made out of motel blankets and a pair of crossed screwdrivers, never-used flatheads, because they had better fabric grip, and left no rust stain. It was the Gout Blues Litmus Jones was involved with, coaxing from steel and electricity and memory, and already Birdfinger could tell there wasn't going to be any chorus, nothing so tangible; the Gout Blues don't repeat themselves. They don't need to. Once, on a record he'd looted from an abandoned Mississippi trailer, Birdfinger had heard a coathanger version of this same song, but never like this, never with screwdrivers, and never by a white man.

The audience wasn't sure how to respond. Three of the bluesmen near the front were rubbing their smooth heads either with deliberation or with understandable fear. Two of the minors come to dregdrink were holding up zippos, the fat flames swaying. And one towering red head, she was feeling along the outside wall, her hands clenched in balls. Vanetta. Her hair looked lighter, almost faded, and she was crying and trying hard not to. Birdfinger met her at the door, and she said she knew she should fall in his arms, she wanted to even, but goddammit, she had a reputation.

Birdfinger said he understood, and then said that he didn't. 'What is it?' he asked.

'Nothing, nothing,' she said, wiping her face, flinging a hand to the stage. 'It's just, God, Bird, it's just that, my dad, I never used to understand it. Him. The whole pancreas/toe thing. The gout. I had this dog, see, Rahstuff. I know I've told you about him so don't pretend. Not now, please. The best dog ever, too, Bird, *ever*. He ate my first tampon, even. Slept in my bed, guarded my window. And then my dad, and I've hated him for it for so long and I never understood, my dad he just hobbled out onto the porch and gave Rahstuff away one Tuesday night, like he was his to give, to this short family that brought their own scale to weigh him even, right there on the porch, like we wouldn't know, like we couldn't see the tacos and burritos crowding out their pupils. They were standing in their own saliva, Bird. My dad explained it as charity and used the bible for it, but the dinner table it was still turned over sideways from when Rahstuff—'

'Misstepped?'

'It was just the general *area* of his toe, Bird. God, I've hated him for it for better than thirty years, and now,' nodding at Litmus, at his Gout Blues, the pain they were evoking, 'now I don't know anymore, I almost understand why he had to do what he did....'

'And he's...taco meat by now, I guess?'

'My dad?'

Vanetta almost started in crying again with this. Birdfinger nodded no, no, and was about to wipe away a piece of wet napkin from her face when she was turned forcibly around. Her hair hit Birdfinger and the roughneck both. The roughneck was the first to recover, trying to drag Vanetta back into it by the arm. But she angled her boot heels into the ground and leaned away from him. The roughneck shook his head and in a calm voice catalogued the string of drinks he'd bought Vanetta. She slapped him. He kept his chin to the side only for a moment, as if convincing himself this had really happened, and then he was telling her about nerve centers in the upper arm, how he'd seen every martial arts movie there ever was. Every last one. The veins in his arm stood out and Vanetta fell to her knees, floored; he mumbled that he'd be goddamned if he'd wasted thirty-two dollars on her, and when his offhand was moving to return the slap Vanetta'd given him, Birdfinger was there to take it for her, on his unpadded hip. It all happened in an instant, then: the roughneck sizing Birdfinger up and down, Birdfinger not backing down this time but really saving the girl who needed saving, the roughneck's hand on Birdfinger's neck, doing something electric to his left shoulder, something Vulcan, Birdfinger going to his knees too, both his hands on the roughneck's one, like he was penitent, asking for forgiveness, for clemency. But now Vanetta was mad. Her knee was the first thing off the ground, and it lifted the roughneck six inches by the crotch, straight up.

The roughneck collapsed and pulled somebody's plate of eggs and brains down with him. The brains made it look worse than it was. Truck's massive head turned their direction then, and he studied the mess. He nodded his head no to Birdfinger, no, not this night, not this morning, but Vanetta was already dragging Birdfinger out by the collar, pushing him behind the wheel of his Cutlass, getting in beside him.

'I'll go,' she said. 'Bird, just let's get out of here. I'll go with you to that damn thing, okay?'

Birdfinger started the car slow, still no feeling in the left side of his torso, and before Vanetta went to sleep she said to him thanks, hero, and kissed him light on the cheek, like a small girl would. Birdfinger batted his stubby eyelids at the road coming up to meet him and rethought the scene with the roughneck to where what had really happened, or what would happen next time, was that he would tie that salesman's trouser sock around the wingtip and go to school on the roughneck's head and face area. It was just a different version of the poolball-dishrag trick; Birdfinger'd watched his share of movies too. He'd even say that next time. He tried to remember it like he'd said it this time. He had to close his eyes sometimes to get it right, the multiple angles of impact, the molars floating lazy through the air, only landing in the people's drinks who weren't his friends, who hadn't thought he could ever do something like this.

It carried him all the way back to the trailer, and through the night, and now to the interment, where Net was telling him the kid's absence wasn't his fault already, okay, it wasn't a thing of blame. She kicked a clod with her pump. So it wasn't about blame. Birdfinger laughed smilelessly and asked her how could it not be? He *had* run his nephew off, after all, far enough that he couldn't even be here to bury his own father. Vanetta adjusted her glasses, smiled a thinlipped smile, and said they'd talk about it later.

It was their second fight.

Birdfinger cussed to himself, because he was both glad she was here and having to exercise control not to start yelling at her. He had never imagined the grieving process could get undormant so fast, after ten odd years. He was on guard now, not sure what would waken in him next. He wasn't even sure if he was grieving for Cline or the kid. Either way, he told Vanetta he was sorry, and she laughed and said thanks, Bird, but again, this isn't about fault, either, okay? That was the next thing to blame. Birdfinger nodded okay, though he didn't mean it; everything would be worlds easier if he could apologize it away, take it on himself. Then at least the kid would be innocent of missing this, and would probably look better to Cline, like a real son, like maybe Birdfinger hadn't done so bad the two years he raised him.

Which meant that it all came back to him, Birdfinger, an ignoble circle. Start and finish, saving precious face. He was probably even grieving for himself, somehow, hell. He forced his hand into a pocket and started cussing again, actively hating this the first day of his sober life. He shook his head, trying to get rid of everything all at once, and in shaking it, looked up under his combed eyebrows and caught the groundsman who played the grim reaper watching him like he was sizing up another narcissistic would-be date. Birdfinger looked away fast and, trying to worm out of the accusing stare, raised his voice in mourning. His guitar was at home resting, another thing to regret. As it was, then, he had to sing something with no extended instrumental solos. He chose 'Lord You Gave Me A Mountain,' and did it the way Marty Robbins had meant it to be done, and then kept crescendoing up and up, even after the backhoe started in covering Cline. He competed with the diesel engine until his lungs gave out and he was left bent over and coughing tar, Vanetta patting his back. They had brought a red balloon in the place of flowers. It was all the liquor store had had. He gave it to her because he couldn't talk yet, and she tied it to Cline's long-gone-green Veteran plaque. She didn't flinch from the backhoe looming above her, either, packing the dirt, and didn't back away from the rising gravedust. She just closed her lips and her eyes, and kept tying a perfectly symmetrical bowknot. Birdfinger thought he could maybe love her for that and that alone, but then, without meaning to, he thought of Marina, her gravestone right there, and apologized quietly.

'Scuse me?' Vanetta said, and Birdfinger just shook his head no. The balloon had more little balloons painted on it, so it was almost like an arrangement. Birdfinger tried to take Vanetta's hand again, but met it halfway up instead. She was raising it to wave at someone walking their way. It was the leopard woman, and there she was, coming steadily out of the past, black velveteen spots again, the white scabs scraped off maybe, and rebreathed. A survivor. Vanetta took two steps around the grave and hugged her on the neck. Did all tall women know each other? The leopard woman cast an accusing look at Birdfinger, and he nodded his head like Truck, saying no, not here, not on this day. A long moment passed and then she was crying, the leopard woman, snarling at Birdfinger like it hadn't been ten years, being led away finally by Vanetta.

Birdfinger told himself to thank her later, for protecting him. Again. God. But at least he was alone now, with Cline and the grim-ass reaper. It was as close as he was going to get. He reached into his coat pocket, to the plastic bag he had waiting, and his hand came out with the compound he'd traded fealty for in another lifetime. It was fine and blue, chemically designed to simulate ritual cornmeal, with primitive nanotechnology laced into every last grain, circa 1970, that would allow it to rise for days over the grave like smoke, marking it for those with the right battery-powered goggles to see. He sprinkled it because sprinkling was a ritual, connective tissue. He closed his eyes to try and see Cline one last time but somehow called her image up as well, Marina, nervous across the table from him, Cline becoming violent with his three-cheese lasagna, stabbing it over and over.

Birdfinger squeezed his eyes tighter, forcing the blackness, forcing Marina scared like that away, deeper into him where she'd be safe, alive, and in the absence of light found himself in the week after him and Pidgin had watched the eclipse through their *Jaws III* 3-D glasses and were stumbling blind through the trailer, peeing wherever the urge took them, betting each other that the sun hadn't come out from behind the lunar shadow, that that was why it was still dark. Changing their bets everyday, too, feeling the lightbulbs to see if they were warm or not, smelling their fingers. The kid hadn't been thinking of running away then, Birdfinger was sure, or of getting run off, either. Maybe it would have been better that way, he thought, easier. Just being blind. Then they would have been stuck together, interdependent, inseparable. There would have been forgiveness, cheap, reserves of it. He didn't know though. He didn't know if he even wanted to know. He opened his eyes and now the groundsman was leaving. Sitting astride the backhoe, he saluted the grave sharply, then said hidy-ho silver and was crawling away in second gear, yelling behind to Birdfinger a telephone number for love enemas.

Birdfinger tried to forget it.

He was still trying when the two vehicles pulled up. One was a thoroughly antennaed F-350 van, no extra windows; the other was a respectable compact of no particular color. Taupe maybe. The van was the second to park, and it pulled so close to the compact that the driver couldn't get his door open. Two people crawled out the rear of the van, a man and a woman. It took them no time to cross the cemetery. Birdfinger raised his eyes when they got near enough, and said, please, this was the sixth stage of grief here.

'Sixth?' the woman asked.

'He's been dead a long time,' Birdfinger explained. 'Five wasn't enough anymore.' The woman offered her hand and introduced herself as Jane, Finity Jane.

'The *Star* woman?' Birdfinger asked.

A smile, a laugh, a flash of molar fillings, then: 'Yes, I'm with the *Star*. Allow me to introduce our *Star* photographer, as well.' The photographer was Erwin Olsen, call him James.

Birdfinger shrugged him off. He pointed with his namesake to the compact and the torso of the tall man, flopping out the sunroof. 'Who's the sad case?' he asked, and Finity Jane just said 'Him? Don't worry about *him*. Some poor woman's ex-husband, I'm sure.'

Vanetta was watching the three of them from a distance, perhaps having her ear whispered into by the leopard woman, all of Birdfinger's shortcomings suddenly apparent, all the bad things he'd done revealed. Goddamn her. Birdfinger tried to excuse himself, but then Finity Jane was reminiscing about his brother.

'I cut my journalistic teeth on him, y'know. The Mirror Man. Poor Cline. James, dear, you weren't even born then, were you?' She laughed aloud, trilling almost, and Erwin stepped away to take a series of shots of the balloon hanging cheery over the fresh mound of dirt. Finity Jane shook her head and patted Birdfinger soft on the front of the shoulder, almost the chest, the pectoral, indicating his maleness. She said she owed her whole career to Cline, did he know? She was Editor-in-Chief of the *Star* now, in no small part due to the Deviant Gallery Series her Mirror Man debut had spawned. Birdfinger knew her though, already; he never missed any of Big Spring Sally's appearances—manifestations, she would have called them—and most of them were in the *Star*. He even had a styrofoam cooler filled with the issue Cline had come out in, but generations of packrats had homesteaded there by way of the trailer floor, and he was afraid to open the top anymore.

Erwin Olsen wandered off moments after the introduction, mumbling that he really *had* to capture that leopard woman on film, with Vanetta standing like an Amazon behind her: hunter and hunted, sharing a menthol, a moment of repose. Birdfinger told him not to get too close, or he wouldn't be responsible. But he wasn't anyway. He asked Finity Jane why she was here today, really.

She thought about it before she answered. 'Well, to offer my condolences, Birdfinger. That's mostly why. An important part of my life is being buried here, too.' Too. Birdfinger looked at her and waited for the rest, because there's always more. There was. She looked away, started to say something, stopped, drew close to him—her hand on his knee somehow, an earnest gesture—and said if he had a few words to say to the public about his brother...and *things*, then she had a tape recorder? She held it up, small and black, clicking it on and off as if proving that it worked would help her case. Birdfinger shrugged, and then before he could figure out a way to say maybe later and mean never, the tall man from the small car was there, looming and trying not to at the same time. It had taken him a solid four and a half minutes to pick through the cemetery, what with reading all the headstones and trying to dodge the backhoe wandering around, the groundsman asleep it looked like, feet propped on the wheel knob. Birdfinger had been watching out the corner of his eye. Up close now, he recognized the tall man for the menace he was: the lab jacket, glasses, cesium wrist-watch ticking incessantly. The distinct smell of formalde-hyde settled in around them. The tall man apologized and held his hand out to Birdfinger, but Birdfinger could tell it wasn't in greeting: the tall man was staring hungry-eyed at Birdfinger's namesake, hanging a full inch further down his thigh than the others. Birdfinger curled it up into a fist, and then he was punching with his nerve dead side, an awkward thing. The tall man sidestepped it gracefully, like he was used to this kind of response.

'Sam,' Finity Jane said with the flat side of her voice, 'hello.'

The tall man nodded to her as if they were beyond words, him and her, but kept his eye on Birdfinger. Erwin Olsen was capturing all this on film too, the flash strobing some of the compound occasionally, catching the plume of blue cornmeal rising above the grave. And nobody was supposed to see that, nobody. So far nobody had. Birdfinger drew back into himself, so as not to sacrifice that last ritual to something as quicklived as anger. He owed it to Cline. And he didn't want anything else to re-gret, not now, not today. Anyway, he knew where Sam worked: down at the Clinic, cutting people up for ten years at a time, out of scientific curiosity.

The three of them stared at each other, and then it was four: the leopard woman had appeared in the circle too. Birdfinger almost laughed: if they had guns, it'd be a Mexican standoff. He appreciated too that they were stand-ing over his brother's grave in the heat of the day, and he was the only one sweating.

Sam was the first to speak: he asked if Birdfinger would perchance be interested in furthering science to the tune of one thousand dollars, collectable, say, now? It was meant in the way of compliment—twice what Cline had gone for—but still, Birdfinger leaned forward, insulted, wishing to everything holy that that camera boy wasn't here, that he had some control over the left side of his body. That nerve in his shoulder was still burrowing, though. He shook his head no just once, barely, and Sam held his hands up in defense, backing away, saying he understood, it was a bad time, but call him whenever he changed his mind.

The leopard woman was the next to speak: she just pointed a long-nailed finger to Birdfinger, hissed 'Murderer,' and was at his throat then, even Vanetta having trouble pulling her off.

Birdfinger recovered in time to hear Finity Jane ask where *was* the son anyway?

He started screaming then, Birdfinger, not unlike a siren, and Vanetta fell to her knees and held him. It was a maudlin display. The crowd of accusers and unwell wishers departed on cue. From a distance it would have looked like they were leaving out of respect, a travesty of reduction. Vanetta held Birdfinger's head to her chest, and told him it'd be all right, there there, and a host of other mother-type things he needed to hear.

When they stood they were alone again. Vanetta nudged Birdfinger and said 'Say goodbye now,' and Birdfinger did, even waving his hand a little, where he thought she couldn't see. It was a quiet walk to the Cutlass. After Vanetta had seen Birdfinger into the passenger side and was adjusting the driver's seat to her dimensions, Birdfinger looked out at the balloon one last time, red against cypress grey, then felt a cold hand on his shoulder. It was Erwin Olsen, leaning in the window. He had scurried in from who knows what ash-toned bush. He asked Birdfinger where Finity Jane could reach him for the interview, and Birdfinger breathed out and recited the love enema number, finally getting rid of it, and then they were back at the trailer and he was too broken up to go through the front door again, had to stay on the porch and sulk, actively resist his fingernails going blue as they tended to in times of pressure. It hadn't happened for years now, though. The last episode had just been bad luck, too, job-related stress; it had been in the week after GE Allen had played and done the sodomy thing on stage and then eaten his own shit for an encore, the week after the day when it became impossible to negotiate a gig in a suddenly conservative Clovis. Birdfinger had been talking on the phone to the operator about the Crickets, playing nonstop on the radio now, how they were a statement on the pie that had eaten america, and when he tried to trace that out for her over the hills and dales of its meaning into his ameritocracy take and the resultant need for some cleansing tyrannicide, he got lost in agent orange and conspiracies and mirrored sunglasses and his hands went clammy cold and he couldn't play for three days. It had been hell. Blue in the fingernails even. He'd had to hide from the renters out in the cinderblock shed where It had happened, where the truck still sat. Three days. It had felt like Easter all over when he finally emerged and hesitantly strummed what he called a long A flat, a note only reachable by the extension of his long namesake up the rosewood neck. It was a sound like rain coming. He'd played for five days straight then, afraid of losing the feel, plundering his stash of ephedrine, burning holes in his retinas.

But those days were over now.

Listen to the cats fight.

She would have loved it.

But she would have looked away, too, hidden her face in her painted hands, peeked. Maybe. It could have even been her in the salesman's napkin, only Birdfinger'd been too afraid to look.

The rest of the day passed in reverie, idling low through the abridged past, and when night came again it lasted one hundred and twenty-odd hours, and Vanetta, unknowing Net, brought it, handed it to Birdfinger with a warm beer, then retired indoors, leaving Birdfinger at the front edge of five long days living on hardtack and crank, backsliding. What Net had passed through the parted screen door was a note in the kid's unmistakable hand, a third correspondence after all this time, a disc of light pinned to the underbelly of clouds that didn't have to be inferred over Texas, no, but all the same, it was the only inference that made sense of the sketch. What Net had passed through the parted screen door the kid should never have been able to see. He hadn't been born then, yet. Birdfinger watched the blood drain from his extremities, leaving the nerves there raw. He heirloomed the guitar for the time, as it was a bad reminder. He occupied himself instead with pencil and paper. Time passed, a day, days. Finally a sound dragged him back into the world unkicking, unscreaming, unknowing: at the door it was the *Star* woman, Finity Jane. Allfuckingready.

Birdfinger clambered around the living room, straightening the place up as best he could, hiding some of the more damning sketches. The first thing she asked was *was* the fallout from WWI blue like cornmeal? She held the mini-recorder in front of her like a pigsticker from another era, like she could catch him that off-guard, like he would fall over it. Birdfinger stood in the door and scratched himself in irritation, tearing at the scrotum flesh. He fisted his support hand to hide any revealing colors. He turned his back on her and she followed his shamble in, and he thought if he didn't look directly at her for maybe three minutes in a row, she'd just gossamer away, like everything else in the trailer of late. It didn't work: her stripe-toed jogging shoes were undeniable there at baseboard level, a pair of loafers settling in beside them. Erwin Olsen.

'WWI?' Birdfinger asked, wincing from a hangnail.

Finity Jane told him not to bother with the dumbshow. She rolled a vial of the compound across the back of her knuckles, then hid it in her hair. Erwin smiled and handed Birdfinger a photograph that caught him midlunge, Sam arcing his body impossibly away, the blue plume hanging behind them like a cloak about to fall over it all.

'You going to run this?' Birdfinger asked, and Finity shrugged, said it all depended. But it wasn't the usual stock, that was for sure. It was the real thing, *some* real thing. Birdfinger nodded, giving ground, and then Erwin took back the interment glossy and replaced it with five more. Birdfinger held them like cards, drew the second one from the end. It was a bathroom stall done nicely in black and white, to where everything had a knife edge. He studied the sliver of porcelain in the background, winked and claimed to know every can in the region. No facility escaped him. This one was a rest stop on the road that goes to the top of the world. When he pretended he couldn't read the chalk-circled graffiti though, Erwin recited it from memory, shaping the words with his hands:

Lovers who pray thee
From thy door are scattered
Lovers who pay thee—

'—in thy bed are flattered,' Birdfinger finished, disgusted to have heard it said without heart.

'Farewell to the Faithless,' Finity added flatly, the poem title, and Birdfinger nodded again, said he'd never forgotten a lyric yet. Not yet. She claimed the next bathroom had that about WWI and fallout. And there were more, poems and songs and frantic Indian-looking happy faces all over New Mexico: Goliardic spoor. Birdfinger laid the photographs on the table, claimed a couch, left the other for them to share. Erwin chose not to. Instead he paced on stiff legs, then stood straightbacked, regarding the fleur-de-lis sheet Birdfinger had torn from the queen bed and tucked up under the ceiling tiles when he heard the *Star* van circling.

'Something wrong with your posterior there, pard?' Birdfinger asked, smiling, then patted the couch, said have a seat, my man, take a load off. Erwin reddened and said no, nothing was wrong, then hid his face with the 35mm and began bathing the living room with chemical light, the living room which was half the size it usually was, because of the sheet, there to hide the a/c and the damp fairy tale that was going on there. But Birdfinger hadn't had time to hide the rest: taking up the remaining floor space were increasingly detailed extrapolations of the pictogram note Net had passed him. It started as a cone of light, the big end in the sky like a funnel, the point close to the ground, and evolved by stages into a pasture of shinnery and a night with sixty-percent cover, twenty-percent chance of rain. Late Spring in Canyon Texas. Palo Duro country, the soil rich with slaughtered horseflesh. But he hadn't stopped there, or hadn't been able to stop. At one point he'd forgotten whether he was right-handed or left-handed even. Now one of the recentmost drawings was face up on the floor, Finity gauging it with her reporter's eye. Birdfinger held his off hand up like a bug was biting it, then casually spirited the drawing away with his foot, a practiced motion since Vanetta had noticed the new direction he'd taken two days back: the pencil-shaded face was a girl, then an Indian girl, then her, Marina, not Vanetta, not Vanetta at all, *not anybody*, he'd lied when she didn't ask, not really. The portraits of Marina were the main reason Vanetta finally quit nursemaiding him around the clock. She wasn't jealous, she said, just afraid whatever he had was catching.

When she left, too, she'd left in the Cutlass. Birdfinger blamed the kid, the zygote in the sky he had penciled in with delicate crosshatching. Birdfinger hid it too, with his foot, the kid's note, looking at his hand the whole time, then sucking bug poison out the back of it.

Across from him Finity the Tolerant was pushing her lower lip out with her tongue, back and forth, the motion widening to include her head as well; she hadn't bought the bug charade. Birdfinger looked away, half-embarrassed, but just in time to see Erwin get himself involved in an amazing display of body language, asking just what pray tell was behind the sheet he was meanwhile reaching for stealthy as a mime? Birdfinger raised his lip in menace, curled his fingers around a glass ashtray. Finity Jane shot Erwin a look, too, and then Erwin was retreating, backpedaling out the front door, mumbling something about the *Philadelphia Experiment* any damn ways, how it wasn't just a movie, but a mode of military thought. The van's 460 shook the trailer to its rusted wheels, and roostertails of dirt settled on the tire-covered roof, tracing a path from new rubber to old. Finity apologized for him, said he was young and unlearned in the ways of the world.

When the van passed the window, Erwin had the driver's side door open, a metal detector skimming the pasture. Birdfinger shook his head. He said it looked to him like young Erwin Olsen Call-Me-James was being used as a woman by trolls every ninth night or so, which made for a quick-ass education, in some parts of the world. Finity laughed complicitly, then moved closer to him somehow, creating intimacy though they were on separate couches, and said 'Now about this mediæval graffiti artist....'

'He's not mediæval,' Birdfinger corrected, immediately rubbing the bridge of his nose in regret. He sat back and scanned the drawing room like a proper host, and offered that this kilroy shit wouldn't help her sell any magazines, he didn't think.

Finity said maybe not, but it was pretty harmless telling her then, right? Birdfinger thought he knew her game, but still, there he was having to bite down hard on his lip not to stumble into some long-winded confession he didn't really owe her. She whispered that all she needed was what? a name? an address? and Birdfinger whipped his head away fast so she wouldn't see it all in his face somehow. It was that close to the surface, that a rogue cheek muscle could give it away, that a side profile could hide it. He stood to extract himself from Finity's amber logic. He asked her if she wanted a drink, then poured himself two and settled into the couch again, the past welling up all around him. He looked at the queensize sheet and the fairy tale cannabis stalk it was hiding and asked if she knew anybody in the market for, say, a hefty bag full of tea, or perhaps enough brick to build an oldstyle shithouse?

Finity laughed, made her eyes wet. 'You can't throw me off that easy, Birdfinger. And nobody calls it tea anymore.'

Birdfinger drained the tumbler in his right hand and looked at Finity there in her knee-length skirt and kid shoes. 'Why come to me, then?' he asked.

Finity shrugged, said maybe because he had been closest to Cline, the heart of the Goliardic experiment, as she called it. Maybe because Sally, her only other link back to the Goliards, wouldn't talk to her about it, was holding out on her even. Maybe because he was the only other one she could find who still knew. 'There's not that many of you left anymore, you know, Birdfinger.'

'Us.'

'The Goliards.'

'Shit, it's not like there were that many in the first place.'

'Five?'

'Not counting me.'

'It's all public record now, you know, so if you give me this throwback graffiti artist it'll hardly come back to you...?' She trailed off then, because she was in forbidden territory, traipsing around the time when Birdfinger had eaten government cheese simply to get out of eight months' worth of lock-up, to return to the world where she was, Marina. By this time the Goliards were officially disbanded, *federally* disbanded, in spite of what Cline insisted. Their postal crusade was over, and entered in the public record now was the account of Birdfinger's long night in the interrogation room, trading knowledge for nicotine. And Finity knew all this. Birdfinger could see it in the way she sat the couch, as if she'd pulled it in herself, owed him nothing for his hospitality.

'I'm not proud,' Birdfinger said.

'No one is all the time,' Finity said back, urging him on. Again, Birdfinger almost took her lead, too, almost recounted for her how in the early hours of that interrogation night he'd tried to fool the government Pinkertons into thinking it had all been about him, this Goliard-thing, how it was a direct result of having found his father sitting handless and peaceful at his pedal-driven bandsaw one fine summer day in the twelfth year of his life, the sawdust around him clotted with lifeblood, about how his interests narrowed considerably after that defining moment, Birdfinger's, until they included mostly just smoking tea and playing anything with five strings. Once even a roadside loom. He'd held his wrists out in the guilty pose for the Pinkerton men—for Finity Jane, now—but no one was interested in him. It was a wholly unhumored room, an unmisled room, mirrored shades staring back at Birdfinger.

'Your brother,' Finity prodded, the Pinkertons' words exactly. Cline, everyone wanted to know about Cline, to understand him, returning medalless from the DMZ, the brother who of the pair seemed better psychologically equipped to handle their stripmining father's suicide, but had in fact just been saving it all up for the war and the years after, when he would stride bold out of the lunatic fringe, step forward to co-lead the insignificant Familia Goliæ tribe/cult, a group composed of himself, Birdfinger, Big Spring Sally, a Pueblo Indian, Marina, and the other leader, a nameless and numberless half-citizen, likely the one missing from Cline's platoon and presumed dead, his skull counted Asian in the official records. The federal charge Birdfinger was facing that interrogation night was something akin to postal indecency: the thing was the Goliards didn't rob banks, they hit post offices, collecting correspondence, *information*, warehousing it at the Adobe Abode, an old mission out on the flats, white with alkali, registered to one Lanetta Lambright, long since deceased. Never in the public record.

In the telephoto the Pinkertons slid clinically across the table to him, that's where they are, or were, at the Adobe Abode: Cline down on one knee, still in his fatigues, trying to look grim and full of portent, squinching his face like Geronimo, one hand on a vertical shovel, his thigh pocket stuffed with plundered apocrypha; Birdfinger standing to his immediate left, skinny and sideburned like Custer, leaning his midsection out so the camera would see a paunch; Big Spring Sally, a turquoise band binding her orange hair into a skullcap, diluted Cherokee generations deep in her blood, the child inside her already suffocating; Larry the Lapsed and Lapsing Laguna, his arm circling Sally, his oily-black hair done up like a skunk, bleached down the middle—a bullet scar, he always lied; the Mexican Paiute, wearing his handwove sombrero and toeing the ground around his bare foot, his face in perpetual shadow; and then, off to the side a bit, playing coy with the camera, her, Marina, their Indian princess, black hair blowing across her face, hand held delicate across her mouth like a veil, nearer neither Cline nor Birdfinger.

At the time of the telephoto they were three weeks away from the real WWI. At the time of the telephoto

Marina was alive enough for all of them. At the time, they were all so high on purple spot and golden porpoise that they'd willingly stand outside in the New Mexico heat and pose for the forest green unmarked Nova parked in the dry dirt half a mile off, wavering like an oasis.

Birdfinger hadn't told the Pinkertons anything.

He knew that that was all Finity Jane knew, too, or could access: the *facts* of the public record. Not the feel. Which gave him some swagger. 'That graffiti,' he led off, 'it doesn't even have to be about us, you know. It's some drunk college fag probably. One of Erwin's buds on the fairy trail, migrating through to Frisco or someshit. Anybody can draw a damn Indian with a feather in his head, anyway.' He let the silence ride. 'Nobody cares about the Goliards anymore, that's what I'm saying. Surely not enough to...' He motioned down at the time committed to the carved-deep graffiti, and entered that into evidence.

Finity was hardly plussed, though. She crossed the room, took the drink from Birdfinger, said simply *I do*, and in a matter of moments had a blood pressure cuff on his namesake, a penlight stabbed in his eyes. It was a sensual violation. She said sorry, but the skin galvanization patch was in the van, along with the gravy. Birdfinger mumbled what the hell, his skin was galvanized enough already. She drank from the glass and put a piece of ice back, then focused the penlight into Birdfinger's pupils. He mewled. He fumbled for the ice that had been in her mouth and let it melt in his palm, the rest of it scattering behind the couch. 'There there,' she said. He looked down her blouse and kept looking, shook his head twice no when she held up one of the early lightcone drawings and asked *Wicca, UFO*? She straddled him then so she could hold the penlight in her mouth while her hand pumped the blood pressure cuff till the end of his finger went from blue to purple, sad to gladness. Her skirt was hiked up some for this beta-test session. She said she had to establish a baseline, so asked him his name, age, lack of employment, are both of him yet real? all of which he answered or tried to answer in monotone, watching the gooseflesh stretched taut over her sunless breasts. But that last one got him, about the kid, about both of him being real. Birdfinger reached for a laugh, knew he was in deep, kept telling himself—preparing himself—by saying over and over *don't say it, don't say it,* not even sure what *it* would be, trying to retreat far enough into himself that she couldn't find him.

Her penlight was wet with her saliva, though, probing the surface of Birdfinger's eyes, ferreting him out. She told him to tell her the name, just that, tell her who was smearing the past all over bathroom walls, tell her who Big Spring Sally's *him* was, just whisper it in her ear, right there, and Birdfinger whispered Marty Robbins lyrics instead, resisting as best he could. El Paso, Cool Water, Devil Woman. Finity Jane shook her head no and changed her approach, going shotgun style. In quick succession she asked what happened to him at the interment, where *was* the son, why *did* the leopard woman accuse him of fratricide, all of which made his lips contort and mind tilt. The cone of light drilling into his eye was pushing him back inside himself, and he'd been there for five days too long already.

Finally he had to admit to something: he clawed his wet hand into his thigh and recounted for her his big secret, one she hadn't been asking for. It came easy, was right there already. Had been. Marina. It started with him being debooked from the Pinkerton cold storage unit, from his eight months of federal limbo. The debooking took twenty-four hours, so it was night again when he was released, night when he walked into Wyvonne's, dirt still in the weave of his jeans from the grave he had just filled in on the way there. The empty grave. The grave he had *found* empty, yawning to the sky. Meaning she was still out there. She had to be. He told Wyvonne that the postmaster general himself had granted him provisional immunity in trade for nothing. Wyvonne, being Wyvonne, had called him on it, said it wasn't a trade then, dear heart, which made Birdfinger regress into allusion. Though he was the only customer, it was still embarrassing.

He didn't tell it to the *Star* woman like that. For her, he fast forwarded from the bodiless grave to two months later, when he was still in the same booth, drinking coffee and eating two pieces of pie at a time. Lancelot, Orpheus, a chrysalis suspended in a pool of formica. In the interim he had scared off one of the waitresses with his necrotic romance, with all his talk of how Marina had risen, was walking around out there somewhere, her mind wiped blank. He'd point with his hand through the plate glass. Wyvonne bought drapes at an estate sale, but he propped them open with stray silverware, kept watch. Waited. New Mexico was only able to harbor her for another month, and then she returned, was hired by Wyvonne for the nightshift as replacement, was warned within hearing of endearing herself, of taking pity on the sad sack in his usual booth. But the first time she came to his table, God. Everything fell into place, from a great height: the face was different but still Indian, more or less, and the build was starved in the same way, and her hand when she extended it with coffee had the mole there, and then Birdfinger knew.

'Marina?' he said, but the waitress shook her head no, checked her blank nametag for leftovers. No. Birdfinger smiled. 'Felina then?' No. More coffee. He drank until she had to serve it to him in unbreakable plastic cups. He tried for homophonic continuity—Varina Selina Sarina—but she only laughed, looked for another customer who wasn't coming in to save them from each other.

She was Janey, Janey Porivo.

On the second night she brought Birdfinger wet bread, and he ate it on the house and without any names or ownership issues, yet he told her about the kid, left alone, motherless. It had been an appeal to the maternal her. Let the names and the ownership come. Janey Porivo caressed the fingersmoothed cameo she was never without and resisted him and his unsubtle appeal for three weeks, and over three weeks Birdfinger got to know her, her nearly-Canadian accent she tried to cover with book Spanish, her Indian name, unpronounceable outside Montana. It meant something like Bird Woman, but smoother, slicker.

She told Birdfinger not to tell anybody.

Birdfinger nodded; he wasn't in love again, he was still in love.

Soon they were familiar with each other—'Bird, Poor Jane'—joking coffee jokes, sharing breaks, and then one night after an old picture of the kid had done time on the formica, Birdfinger said as she was walking away *Marina*, and she turned around in mock defeat, in play, and then it became a game where she could be somebody else for a shift, let Marina do the waitress work, juggle the orders, but then it went past that: she began asking about the kid, her face solemn. It was the beginning. They'd coast out to the trailer and spy on him through the living room window, Birdfinger the Illiterate reading Pidgin's lips across all that space, repeating his monologues verbatim. They were all about her, his mother he'd never known. It was sad, touching; it worked.

Janey Porivo became quiet.

She wanted both to draw closer to the trailer and to run away. She said she would be no good for him, the kid. Birdfinger said no, no, but was afraid she would concede. The first line he had used on her had been the one about her being the kind of woman that makes a man remember he's married. She had fallen into it, wasn't from Clovis; she'd told him too bad, then, and Birdfinger had drawn the line tight, told her he wasn't really all that married. The second line he used on her was when they were in the Cutlass, driving back from a night in the scrub past the trailer. It was the night before she gave him her Wyvonne earnings—twenty-five hundred dollars—to take care of the kid while she was away, keep him out of the whole Primate of Order/Big Spring Sally bullshit. They still smelled of dry grass, both of them, the Cutlass too. Janey Porivo had looked straight ahead and said it like she'd been practicing it, that this was all going too fast. Birdfinger had agreed over two-tenths of a mile, nodding into it, the second line he gave her: he told her she was right, it was all going too fast. Someday he was going to have wanted it to have lasted forever.

Finity Jane, still straddling Birdfinger's lap, each knee on a different cushion of the couch, said she didn't think Birdfinger would have had that in him.

'You'd be surprised,' he said.

'So she left, then?'

Birdfinger nodded.

'And you spent the money how?'

'Looking for her. A seance in the foothills of Marfa, with the lightshow. Spelling Relief with too many letters, too many baggies. Same old.'

'And this...Primate of Order?'

'The Ape of God.'

'...'

'Spoken one night while Sally was faking sleep.'

'*By* Sally?'

Tics were kicking themselves awake all over Birdfinger's face.

'And now,' Finity continued, rushing him through to the end, 'now you would try to redeem yourself in this other Marina's absent eyes by paying your estranged nephew the money that by rights should have been his, money that perhaps would have kept him out of Sally's spoken world.'

Birdfinger nodded yes and no.

'I *would* say this happens all the time,' Finity led off, unable to finish.

Birdfinger buried his face in his hands. Finity relaxed the cuff, clicked the penlight off. She tapped her lips with it then, looking off into nothing, eventually pacing couch to door, couch to door. She muttered logic problems between pen taps, how this second Marina never could have had a cameo of the kid, Pidgin, as she was clinically dead for the duration of his abbreviated gestation. As in no brain activity the monitors could pick up, even when Cline hotwired them into the lightsocket while the doctors weren't looking. 'I still remember her story,' she said to Birdfinger. 'Two sides of it. We had facing pages to orient the reader. The pro faction of the staff opted to run Maculate Conception in gospel-like letters; we, on the other hand, chose Nine Moons Wasted? in a skeptical font, kept ourselves to one question mark.'

'Who won?' Birdfinger asked.

'Not her.'

Birdfinger shaped his mouth like he was going to speak, pronounce, but he was just killing time, stalling while Finity Jane poked and prodded his experience for possible *Star* inclusion. At the least, she had been sufficiently distracted. But it was becoming a column for her too, and then, with a pen dismissal, it wasn't. She said the pictures they had on file to fit this type thing didn't jive with Birdfinger's age group: her readership preferred senior citizens for love and/or ghost stories. Birdfinger said it wasn't a ghost story. She was real, had been. He said if only Janey's cameo hadn't been water-damaged in a fire, they'd have had proof. He reached for his glass but it was empty. He drank anyway, and drank again. He started to offer a counter story about this light triggered temporal lobe problem he thought he was having lately, that made him compulsively dishonest, but then Finity was drilling him for details on and wording of Sally's so-called Primate of Order prediction.

She was implacable, omnivorous.

Birdfinger closed his eyes against all this prediction shit and just gave her what she'd originally come for: 'Larry, okay? Larry the Lapsed and Lapsing Laguna. Larry Lambright. Thinks he's an artist. Born August twelfth, nineteen fifty six. No social. A thing about bathroom stalls. Shit. Shit shit shit.'

Finity looked down, maybe hiding surprise, then pinned him to the couch with a look: 'Larry Lambright died thirteen years ago.'

'Choked with a feather boa down on main street, yeah.'

'Meaning he's dead.'

'Just the name, that's all. We just killed the name.'

Finity smiled a real smile, for the first time, and waited.

'Atticus Wean,' Birdfinger mumbled when he still saw no way out except the name. 'He's Atticus Wean now, okay? Face done up like Hank Jr, mirrors and beards.'

'Atticus Wean of Wean Construction?'

'He thought the boa was a poetic touch.'

'I never knew him.'

'He was like that.'

Finity leaned down in gratitude then, allowing Birdfinger one last look he wasn't up for anymore, kissed him soft on the upper lip, then scribbled something on one of the portraits and tore it off. She handed it to Birdfinger, said quid pro quo: it was a poorly-drawn picture of a new bagboy up at Squanto's who was said to be speculating in pot futures this month. His distinguishing characteristic was the patch that could be on either eye, a trick Finity Jane had accomplished with arrows going back and forth. Birdfinger asked was this a legitimate contact, and Finity nodded yes with her eyes, blew him another kiss, didn't look behind the bedsheets, and in a flurry of foolscap paper was gone, the van rumbling to life from nowhere, as if on cue. In her absence, the room was suddenly swirling with failure and missed opportunities and guilt. Birdfinger was sure his voice was already being replayed and copied and dubbed and distributed and transcribed down into yet another public record: Larry Lambright, goddamn him and his skunk-headed self. But he was the only one literate enough and still around, with access to men's bathrooms. He'd done it to himself, though, Larry, or was still doing it to himself, if the spoor was as fresh as Finity Jane suspected. Birdfinger said it in a convincing fashion, but still, it was his voice on the tape recorder, not Larry's, and as far as physical-type evidence went, he was now twice a traitor.

Farewell to the Faithless, yes.

He shuffled around the room until his legs hurt, and pulled the bedsheets down in anger, slinging them across the room like a fishing net. Ceiling dust paled everything. Everything but the cannabis plant. It had grown some even in the past hour, beanstalking its way from the a/c roofward, already mature, green as life. Birdfinger cut a bud off, using Cline's old tin snips. He cured it a bit in the microwave, impatient, and after he'd handled it, rolling one Cheech-size wad and then another, something large and thick placed itself between the sun and the trailer window, and Birdfinger saw that his fingers were tinged green with microwaved tea—lambent, pulsing—and he thought of his father in the dark, wringing his uranium-working hands against each other, his genes stained with radiation, on fire, aglow, his foremanlike laughter filling the house until there was nowhere left to hide. Birdfinger wrapped his hands in his shirt and lit one of the joints on the gas stove, holding it in his mouth with his lips, inhaling hard to keep it going, the threat of his own laughter making him tremble and close his eyes, balance feet and butt on the thin paisley suitcase and draw his knees up to his chest.

The old man was home for the night.

There was no music playing anywhere, no cars passing.

Birdfinger didn't know how much less he could take.

At the end of the second joint a pagan cat crept onto the porch, left an offering, a rat or a mole. It was still a little bit alive, scratching into the redwood. Birdfinger stepped outside, stepped on the small creature's head out of mercy. The crunch woke one of the renters. The renter sat up coughing, stabbed himself in the face with a lit cigarette. Failed to find the vent hole right above his head. They never could. He coughed into the night, giving up, and Birdfinger let him, just stood there and breathed deep, until he got it together enough to feel his way over to the outer rail of the porch, the uncloying Clovis night opening up just beyond it. There was always that, after everything. It had made the difference before. Birdfinger placed himself at the edge of it, watched the renter's cigarette share its flame with a candle, and from there it graduated to a rotten board scrounged from under the trailer probably. Birdfinger could care less: the light was playing soft against the inner walls of the shelter, becoming for Birdfinger a Marfa lightshow from his past.

In its remembered glow was Larry and a bottle of ether and the ancient Mexican woman chanting unMexican words from the depths of her shawls, Birdfinger trying to hear in them the only name he needed to hear: Marina. To her left Larry was recalling tonelessly the day at the top of his life when he had stolen a kid's husquevarna from in front of a sieged post office, torn back and forth from flagpole to flagpole, emptying the trooper's guns. Birdfinger listened for Marina's name just once, even Janey, but the old woman wasn't saying it. Instead Larry inhaled deep and fell face first into the small fire and didn't get burned. Instead the old woman struggled with the american words and said *look, there,* and where she was pointing, like clockwork, the lights appeared pale blue and white and did what they did in a huge and delicate silence. Let them be ghosts looking for the mothership or mothers looking for their dead kids. Let Larry's Indian beard burn away from his unblistering skin, his mind frozen into a tight, guilty fist. Let the old woman point until her finger rigor mortises and she has to bandage it in the daytime and pretend it got caught between the rocks, grinding corn into meal.

Birdfinger looked into the chrome top of the starter-fluid canister only a moment before he inhaled and became fireproof as well, ethereal, but in that moment he saw her like he had that last night, Janey, Marina, different but the same, at the asphalt edge of the parking lot of Wyvonne's, winter coming on fast but the sweat on her anyway, and the way she had shied away from his hand on her waist, then offered the money she'd rat-holed, her getaway money, for the kid, all of it, a gesture not located in time, a mother's fist held in the hollow of her throat as she backs away—*please, promise*—and then one hundred and eighty days without her, the money heavy, a burden. Birdfinger had watched the kid himself, for her, but was just going through the motions, physically sick with nostalgia. Once the Mexican Paiute had appeared on bare feet beside him, watched the kid for a while too, in silence, and he hadn't returned for months then, Birdfinger.

Now he was just here, back in Texas, the ether and the lights dancing like candleflame for an old Mexican woman who was no way all Mexican, who was looking at Birdfinger and smiling like she too could see Marina turning slowly away and becoming a crude girl-shaped obituary cut out of the *Phoenix Sun* and kept safe between bible pages. Who was looking at Birdfinger and still pointing in such a way that Birdfinger, starter fluid wiping his mind clean, came to understand that the crook in her index finger wasn't just dried up tendons, but a likeness of the earth's slow curve, which meant she was pointing past the foothills, past the mountains, past all of New Mexico even, all of america.

When morning came cloudless and red, Birdfinger paid her everything he had, then deliberately packed

Larry's mouth and nose with ceremonial ash, because Larry had to have heard him say her name. And Cline wouldn't forgive that kind of coveting. But Larry was immortal: he showed up back in Clovis six days later, hair like a skunk, teeth stained grey, thumb sore from hitchhiking, Birdfinger hugging him hard, too hard, until he pushed him away, knowing better than to talk of the old woman Birdfinger had paid half of Janey's money to try and forget.

The next week Birdfinger invested in coyotes, mules.

They'd let him down too.

On the porch now, in the prepaid glow of his renters' slow moving nicotine ritual, Birdfinger cradled his belly and held the potsmoke in, sighting along the old woman's finger with hesitation, following it on stiff legs to the cinderblock shed. God. He hadn't felt guilty enough to sleep here for years. He was haunted the night through by thirst, cottonmouth, and then before he was ready for it to be, it was morning and the sun was coming through the roof slats like an alien inspection, scanning first the back wall and then in due time Cline's Ford with the chalk foot traced on the cement just under the driver's side door. Each layer of eight-minute light tynsdaled a little different from the last, the dust swirling paisley in it like damascene steel wrought into evenly spaced bars. Birdfinger, trapped in his corner—barred in by shadows—watched the chalk foot inch into view. It was the only part of Cline the law had marked off. Size 11 mule-eared boots with real silver conchos. Birdfinger still had them in the closet. In leaner days, Sam had sold them to him out the back door of the Clinic for fifteen dollars and a half pack of smokes. In the silence of the shed, Birdfinger told Cline he was sorry, about the boots, for not paying what they were worth at least, but then took it back.

He wouldn't get into that again, couldn't. It took too long.

He stood instead, trying to wipe away the possibility of Cline, and was left with the petroleum smell of grease and an associated awareness—the just-surfacing aftersound of creeper wheels and ratchets, the heat of an old kerosene lamp that was still flickering, a lamp Birdfinger had never learned to use.

Which meant he wasn't alone: there was a visitor with him in the shed, had been, too. Birdfinger's muscles locked into place, and it took him five long minutes to relax them, because now there was breathing other than his own to deal with. When he was calm enough, the affront washed over, that he was being trespassed on. He dropped to the floor silently to scan for the denim shins television said should be there, found none, then crawled under bench and over cardboard, green-beret style, on fingertips and toes, gut scraping. Still though, nothing, and then in a harsh instant more nothing—the light winding down under an unseen thumb, becoming wicksmell and kerosene smoke, leaving Birdfinger spreadeagle in the darkness, assaulted by smells. He didn't feel military anymore. The affront was gone. He tried to force himself into a grasshopper flashback, for guidance, but found himself unbald instead, in the past with the unpredictable specter of his father. And the old man hadn't taught him anything. Except to hide. Birdfinger did. He retreated to his corner and made himself small, watched the door the truck the window all at once and close, but still, the trespassing mechanic managed to evaporate into the new morning under the cover of a phillips-head screwdriver left slowly spinning, and in the following four hours on the sunside of dawn, Birdfinger came to know that it had been Cline after all, come back to do preventative maintenance on the only love his brother had left him.

Birdfinger watched the size 11 chalkprint, waiting for the naked foot to appear that would be the first part of him, Cline, toe-tagged, raw soled, ill humored. He apologized again, but took it back again, replaced it with the two most important things he'd said to him in life that last week, over six different payphones: that I knew her better, and that it isn't the end of the world. On his fifth retracted apology, he listened to himself at forty-eight years old, talking with what would have to be a truck, a reminder of absence, and listened at first with pity, but then looked at himself feeling sorry for himself and grew sick of it all, to where he could taste it in the back of his throat. He rose in disgust, in contempt, blood rushing back to his fingertips, the rest of him walking forward through the layers of guilt-colored light. With the floorjack handle he caved in the windshield of the truck and did it so it looked like a fist impact, over and over, hammering ten years back into the dash. There. Standing amid the shelters minutes later, breathless, the shed locked again, he rubbed warmth back into his hands, and before he could stop himself said he was sorry, and one of the disembodied renter voices sleeptalked *no, no,* then fell into a coughing fit.

No: apology unaccepted.

Birdfinger closed his eyes against the sun, against the voice, felt himself losing ground already. 'Twenty-five hundred dollars,' he offered then, weakly, above the sound of hacking tar, realizing for a moment what the *Star* woman had meant—that that was what redemption would cost: for Marina to return, he had to keep his promise about the kid. And she had to return.

But Cline. There was Cline. Birdfinger looked back to the shed once, listening for the windshield healing itself, and when he couldn't hear it, when he couldn't allow that he would be able to hear it, he turned away fast, sank an axe deep enough into cannabis flesh that it sang out of the living room and beyond, steel on stalk, scattering cats and birds the same. When it fell it left the trailer gutted on the backside, a/c ripped out, hot days ahead. Birdfinger climbed onto the roof with a half roll of tarpaper, used bricks for nails and fixed it good enough. The stalk wasn't so easy, though; it weighed better than three-hundred pounds. And he still didn't have the Cutlass back.

He called Clandenstein's, and after a bit Vanetta got on. She said she'd come if he'd tell her what it was all about.

'Why?' Birdfinger asked, staring into the receiver.

'Because my mother didn't teach me any better, Bird.'

When she got there Birdfinger got mealy in the mouth, asked if she knew what a weregild was.

'Lycanthrope, you mean?' she asked, leaning forward. 'Is that what's kept you holed up here all week, werewolf problems?'

Birdfinger shook his head no, said it was more like money problems, now. Vanetta rubbed her eyes, asked what else?

'Cline,' Birdfinger said without lip movement. 'Cline's back.'

Vanetta laughed in her nose, wet her lips with nerves. 'No, Bird,' she said, 'Cline is *not* back. We buried him, remember? You sang. And there aren't werewolves in Clovis anymore. And if you need gas money...'

Birdfinger shook his head, held it between his hands, and then in a series of instinctual motions he was lying in Vanetta's lap, not looking at her, confessing about that last week talking on the phone with Cline.

'How'd he get the payphone number?' Vanetta asked.

'I was the one calling him,' Birdfinger said. 'I used to call once or twice a month from wherever I was, to ask if she'd ever come back.'

'Marina? You asked *him* that?'

'No. Shit, Net. But I'd ask if there were any new Indian waitresses in town or anything. My voice was disguised.'

'But she was dead, Bird. Even I know that. It was in the newspapers, all the *Stars*.'

'You don't understand. She'd come back once already. For me, I mean.'

Vanetta rubbed Birdfinger's hair into his scalp; he could feel her fingers shaking, dislodging flakes of unwanted skin. She said he must have finally guessed then, Cline? Birdfinger nodded yes, head going back and forth in her lap, eyes looking over the edge of her knees with every forward motion, then drawing back into the velvet safety of her thighs.

'He said it was the end of the world. He said it wasn't fair to take away a swath of years from somebody and make them see them different. I told him he'd hadn't been seeing them right because he hadn't wanted to. I told him all kinds of shit. That I was sorry, too.'

'It's a long time ago.'

'He was right.' Birdfinger closed his eyes. 'He told me I wasn't his brother anymore.'

'Ten years, Bird? Jesus H.'

'It still matters.'

Vanetta shook her head, no, it doesn't, it can't, it shouldn't, and then Birdfinger went on, told her in no great detail about the weregild money he owed the kid, the money the stalk had to be worth, how it was all going to work out, how she was going to come back again, Marina. For him. The only illustration he had for his story was the stick-face picture the *Star* woman had drawn him, with the pirate bagboy and his roving eyepatch.

Vanetta batted tears into her mascara, her worst trick. 'Bonito Bonita,' she said quietly. 'Shit, Bird, he'll skin you alive. Especially you. Especially now, when you're all simpled out.'

'He's just a bagboy.'

'No. Nobody's just one thing. This is Clovis, after all.'

'He's got to give me something, at least.'

'You might not want it.'

'He can't be more than fifteen, Net.'

'I've heard about him though, Bird.'

'He works for minimum wage.'

'It's not about money with him.'

'Come with me, then, keep guard.'

Vanetta stared into the porch boards then shook her head no; if he was going to see Bonito Bonita, he had to do it alone. That was how it worked. Birdfinger wanted to ask *what*, that was how *what* worked, but before he could, the Cutlass keys were warm in his hand and Vanetta, skylined, muscles jumping under her skin like horseflesh, had the stalk easy over her shoulder, free of the a/c. They doubled it over and tied it across the trunk like a green deer, a fresh kill. She said she shouldn't ride with him, and Birdfinger said he shouldn't even ride with him. But they couldn't stay at the trailer all day either. On the short ride to town he could feel it between them, too, his words, how everything for him led to Marina returning. But Vanetta didn't voice it, and Birdfinger didn't know how to unvoice it, didn't even know if he would. He remembered how she'd closed her eyes against Cline's gravedust though, enduring, her metallic red hair the opposite of anything he wanted but beautiful all the same.

He left her at the convenience store down from Clandenstein's, bought her a popcorn lunch from the clerk who was trying to hide his Wonder Woman wrist armor. It shone through his thin flannel though, and when Birdfinger fastdrew into his pocket for change, the clerk had the armor out just as fast, arms held forward, wrists crossed at forehead level, mouth open banshee style.

Birdfinger smiled, shot him in the ribs with his finger gun, then blew the smoke away and reholstered, leaving him with sixty-seven cents and a twitching lip.

In the parking lot he hugged Vanetta and said he didn't see what she was so worked up about, he probably outweighed this bagboy by a solid seventy pounds anyways. He patted his gut to show her, but she only held his head to her chest and said it was nothing, she was just afraid for him, afraid his life was catching up with him too fast, afraid he wouldn't be able to outrun it this time. 'If you need me…' she led off, and then Birdfinger was backing out slow, preparing an involved shrubbery lie for if the law flashed him down. But they didn't. They couldn't. He made it to Squanto's parking lot with no hold-ups, narrowly avoided a luckless pedestrian, then coasted into a lowspot pregnant with carts and sat there in prime bag-boy territory, because he wanted control of the dealings from the start, wanted this Bonito Bonita to see what was tied over the trunk and have to solicit *him*, Birdfinger, enter the carsmell he'd cultivated over the years, sit in the seat he'd adjusted, listen to the music he'd dialed in; he wanted Bonito Bonita to feel like he used to feel in Cline's presence. There was no way he'd be able to skin him then, no way in hell.

But the solicitation was long in coming, and Birdfinger grew sleepy, rested his head on the wheel, smoked one to let time dilate around him and woke in the dark, unalone, Bonito Bonita sitting patch-eyed in the re-adjusted passenger seat, the radio dialed in Spanish, piña colada thick in the air. He was already losing, Birdfinger was. Bonito Bonita even had his apron with the generic geometry folded over the rearview, which meant Birdfinger couldn't see the area above the trunk without turning his head and thus showing how little control he had of things in the real world. Bonito Bonita sat there inhumanly calm in his seat, inspecting the lukewarm car lighter, tonguing it even, smiling over the chrome at Birdfinger.

'It's my break, ese,' he said, 'fifteen minutes. And you've slept through nine of them already.'

Birdfinger said he'd sort of had a rough week, but Bonito Bonita waved it away, asked why'd he come here to see him like this, even, in public, where he could endanger his livelihood? He had mothers and grandmothers to support, man. Birdfinger shrugged, squinted, then said he didn't know where he lived, Bonito Bonita, nobody did.

'I would have found you, ese. I would have smelled it on the wind. I always do. Now though'—he motioned past the side glass, at Clovis in the general sense—'the market, it's bad, weak, watered down.'

Birdfinger looked around and nodded agreement, then caught himself midnod, turned to the bagboy to tell him the market was always good in Clovis, but then hardly recognized him with his patch suddenly and with no warning on the other eye.

'Breathe,' the bagboy said, and Birdfinger did, in shallow breaths.

'Drive,' the bagboy said, and Birdfinger did. They only pulled behind Squanto's though, where there were no more houses or stores or people, just blowing trash. 'Now,' Bonito Bonita said, 'look,' and out past his lifted hand, small in the distance, was a figure so thin it looked tall, like at the end of a movie, a figure walking with deliberate steps, placing each foot, so that Birdfinger was forced to remember the Old Old Indians he'd heard whispered about in a bar once, from a lush anthropologist—a horseless people who moved across the plains on lodgepole length stilts, each step two car-lengths apart.

Bonito Bonita looked at him though and just said *no, ese. That's me*. He tapped himself on the chest, did his nose in a proud way that showed his teeth. Birdfinger swallowed, forced a laugh, and said there was no way in hell, muchacho. He shook his head to prove it. Bonito Bonita just pointed with his chin though, and then Birdfinger watched as the figure stopped, looked around, then squatted and reverently buried something, tamping the earth back over it, shaping it. Bonito Bonita smiled like it was hurting him, the burying. 'He'll be back.'

'He?'

'Me. I will.'

'. . .'

'For the gun, you know.'

'Bullshit.'

'You can't leave it in one place too long. Someone might find it, and then it'd be evidence.'

'I'm not falling for this.'

'Watch.'

Birdfinger did, again, not wanting to, but before he could focus, the dock lights behind the car flipped off and the figure all but disappeared. There was only after-image. Birdfinger reached for the ignition to run the figure down, have it done with, but Bonito Bonita stayed him with his left hand, his right holding ruby-lensed mini-binoculars to his face.

'So you don't believe it, ese,' Bonito Bonita whispered. 'You don't believe this about a person or a thing being in two places at the same time?'

'Listen to yourself.'

'I can't hear that far.'

'Logic won't allow it, sabe?'

'But the data, ese. Me, him.'

'Logic doesn't change to make room for bullshit.'

'It's changing right now.'

'Then it's not logic.'

'I can see it disturbs you, ese, this possibility, this *data*. Maybe I'm that one's Don Genaro though, his doppleganger, his shadow self. Maybe pronouns only exist in grammar school. Maybe sometimes the recoil of a small caliber handgun can split a person right down the middle, when it's too much, when nobody's really paying attention to what you're doing anyways, because you don't matter in the first place.' With his right hand he made like there was a zipper down his front which would bisect him further even, into quarters maybe, and Birdfinger looked a fraction of a second too long, against his will. Bonito Bonita pulled the mini-binoculars from his face then with a distinct suction clap, the patch falling into place. Birdfinger had already forgotten where it started even, the patch, the dealing, this whole ride. Was it Bonita Bonito or Bonito Bonita?

Bonito Bonita held the mini-binoculars over the glove compartment that split the bench seat. 'You don't believe me,' he said. 'Tell me to wave, then.'

Birdfinger stared at the binoculars. 'Wave,' he said, but then Bonito Bonita winked, said nobody waves for free, ese. Nobody nobody. He tapped the headliner with the back of his index finger, waited. Birdfinger looked at the receding presence of a figure, walking north into the dark past Clovis. He blew out his nose twice, to show his dissatisfaction, but he did it, he tugged on the corner of the headliner that let what he'd pruned off the stalk fall into the bagboy's lap. Maybe half a pound in four flat plastic bags. 'Goddamn you' he said as he snatched the mini-binoculars, 'now wave.'

Out in the red distance, image doubled, he did.

Birdfinger didn't say anything. He looked hard through the binoculars instead, hanging out the side window, sitting on the door. 'I can't make out the face,' he said. 'It could be anybody. You could have this all worked out.'

'With our Spanish ESP.'

'With mirrors or pigeons or synchronized watches.'

'You were only asleep for two hours, ese.'

'Shit.'

'And I was working anyways.'

'You waited till dark on purpose.'

Birdfinger turned on his headlights to try and freeze the walking figure, but they wouldn't reach far enough. Bonito Bonita laughed. Birdfinger turned on him, not sure what he was going to do, but wound up not doing anything: held to the bagboy's face now were 10 x 50 night binoculars with saucer-sized lenses, a nine-volt humming, collecting light.

'Like looking in a mirror,' Bonito Bonita said from under the binoculars, then angled his chin up, like at a half mile out he was searching for the hair that wasn't there yet. Birdfinger lunged for the binoculars, missed.

The bagboy ran his finger in circles over the glove compartment.

Birdfinger slammed his fist into the dash, throwing dust and skin cells and cigarette ash everywhere. But he opened the glove compartment just the same, let Bonito Bonita remove the grocery bag he had a quarter of the way filled with tea, took the front-heavy binoculars and slammed them to his face so hard it hurt.

In the artificially green distance now the figure had his back to him, hands in pockets, shoulders cocked up.

'It's cold out there, ese. The wind.'

'Fuck that. Turn around.'

Through the wandering binoculars and for just an instant, when their rates of vibration harmonized, he did, he saw him, the walking figure, and it was Bonito Bonita's face. Birdfinger dropped the binoculars into his crotch, crossed his thighs at the last second. 'Twins,' he said, not looking into the passenger seat anymore. 'You're goddamn twins. Like me.'

'You?' Bonito Bonita made eyes about Birdfinger's stomach.

'And my brother, asshole.'

'See I don't have a brother, though, Paunch.'

'Tell me about it.'

'If I did though, it'd be the same.'

'That zipper bullshit?'

'It can happen in the womb.'

'It can't happen anywhere.'

'It disturbs you, doesn't it? Me being out there, in here. You being like me.'

'I'm undisturbed. Look at my hand.'

'A real sideshow, ese. Now look at mine.'

When Birdfinger did though, Bonito Bonita said no, out there, and Birdfinger drew the binoculars up, tried to make out the hand. But the image was shaking, a blur standing in place, and he couldn't get it together again.

He rested the binoculars on the steering wheel, but then the windshield got in the way. 'I can't hold them steady,' he said, with full reluctance, and just reached under the dash for the last bag when he saw the tripodded spotting scope Bonito Bonita had out.

'It's got zoom,' Bonito Bonita said as they traded, 'an important feature,' and Birdfinger didn't answer. But he used it, zoomed in tight to the Bonito Bonita figure's hand that was flipping him off from half a mile out. The other hand too.

'I invented that, goddammit,' Birdfinger said, fed up with the games. But he was alone in the car again. Only the smell of piña colada and the total absence of anything to smoke. He turned the cha cha off the radio, gunned the Cutlass, and headed out across the dry grass, driving by way of the spotting scope.

And he did it, too, he ran down the figure at a rough seventy miles per hour, pulled slow alongside. The figure got in. It was him, Bonita Bonito. 'I told you, ese,' he said, 'but break's over.' He made the cut-off motion with his hand. On the slow ride back Birdfinger tried to remember which eye the patch should be on, but everything inside him was failing, and he didn't trust his voice not to crack.

He dropped him at the front door, curbside service, just to be rid of him.

When he was gone, the bagboy, his apron a geometric bundle now, Birdfinger coasted back down to the low spot, looked in the rearview for the first time and saw some longnecked birds stowing away on his trunk. Two sandhill cranes, eyes bleeding. He got out, waved his shirt at them, and they lifted themselves into the mellow night air, let the wind do the rest. Birdfinger put his shirt back on unbuttoned and then with loving hands inspected the stalk nub; what the birds hadn't got, his seventy mile per hour defeat had. He tried to imagine a hotline for this particular situation but couldn't do it, couldn't think of a seven-letter word that would capture what he was feeling. There was nothing else to do. He reached instinctively to his headliner, but it was still plundered. He was stashless. He thought about calling Vanetta, but couldn't take it, the way she'd just accept him and keep accepting him, skinned or no. He laid his forehead on the horn instead, in public deliberation, and the sound attracted a different bagboy, this one with a fake braid and wraparound hearing aid.

Birdfinger traded him optical gear for information.

The bagboy told him three things: that the new cashier girl had some gordo juice, he thought; that if he really needed money that bad, he could do that Deaf Smith gig in Aztec that nobody wanted; and that Bonito Bonita was never there.

'Deaf Smith?' Birdfinger said quietly, and the bagboy crammed his pinky into his ear, adjusting, and said it was a cowboy dance, did Birdfinger know any cowboy songs?

Birdfinger nodded yes, he knew them all. For the price of a spotting scope then he was hooked up with the promoter's phone number. Before the bagboy ran off after an errant cart, Birdfinger asked how'd he known he was a music man, and the bagboy, trotting away, turned around and ran a line over his stomach in imitation of Birdfinger's slanting guitar callous. Of course. Birdfinger felt back and forth over the yellow ridge as he approached Squanto's, all done up in adobe, mission style. He was supposed to look for Stiya number 6. He buttoned his shirt in anticipation, concealing his musical bent. Once inside, it was the same grocery store as ever: harsh lights, registers done up like a Mayan temple, vegetables corkscrewed around mini tepees trailing paper smoke, Rita Hayworth's vinyl heartbeat steady and soft over the PA like a drum, all the cashier girls wearing the exact same nametag as near as Birdfinger could tell from the descending slope of letters, Stiyas all. He absently counted down the registers to 6, heedless of appearances, of revealing his narcotic intentions.

As he passed register 4 the security camera zeroed audibly in on him and he didn't care. He smelled his shirt, to see if the decomposing luggage in his living room had tainted it, but couldn't tell. He hoped it had, though, because it would make him an undesirable presence, someone you throw gordo juice at just to make them go away. Midstride then, he timewarped back to how he used to get Sally's food the same way—because she had a delicate nose, was an easy gag, because it made Marina laugh behind her hand at him, in spite of Cline—and when he returned he was there, register 6, and Stiya 6 had her back to him, was windexing her station, wearing hair that was a wig fishnetted on but that was beautiful all the same, long and braided and shiny wet. Birdfinger reached for it before he could stop himself, like he'd never seen its like, and when Stiya 6 snapped her head around at the camera buzz he'd brought with him, slinging her braid out of reach, it was her, from the salesman's napkin trip, lips and nails startling red, and Birdfinger swallowed hard, shied away from the sound of things slamming together in a perfect, violent fit. He'd heard it before, once.

She was pretending she didn't know him, didn't remember him. Embarrassed, maybe. But interested.

And not pretending, Birdfinger made himself remember: not pretending. He told himself over and over *not too fast, not too fast, she doesn't know yet*. A case of Unwrought Simplicity. He recited lyrics to himself so he wouldn't aneurism. Her lips and nails though. They were the exact same shade of red as always, the same as the first time him and Cline saw her, right arm snaked down into the blue maw of a federal drop box. In the salesman's grey bathroom, colors done with crosshatching, Birdfinger hadn't been able to tell. But now, God. And the hair, and the skin. It was her again, Marina. But not too fast. Birdfinger straightened his voice out as best he could and said he'd heard she was holding.

'Holding?' she said, loud and unMarinalike. 'Nobody *holds* anymore, mister.' She stepped closer then, her eyes dancing, and said from whom did he hear this lie?

Birdfinger moved his mouth noiselessly. Stiyas 1-5, 7, 8 and 9 were looking their way, the security camera drowning out Birdfinger's unformed words. He was the only one there without his finger on a panic button. He had to get her alone, tell her, reeducate her, make her remember.

'I've got money,' he lied.

She stared him down then, challenging an ear to twitch twice or a rogue eyebrow to give him away. But

Birdfinger stilled his body, and finally she smiled, Stiya 6, slow around the eyes, at the mention of money. She drew close to Birdfinger, her cheek almost on his, his skin never so sensitive, never so unshaved, and said two thirty-five, her break time. 'In the Apache room, lovermine.' She winked then, reached to her thigh like she was maybe going to shoot him bye but got interrupted by a man with sardines in one hand and silver in the other.

At her unstated request, Birdfinger attempted to fade into Squanto's, go native, let the other Stiyas get back to what they were doing. But he couldn't lose her either, not now, not after twenty years without her. He positioned himself at the endcap of one of the aisles, sat in a pharmacy seat with a *Star* held over his stomach, watched her small and distant in the Aztec meat department's stainless-steel mirror.

She was everything beautiful; the years had protected her, fallen for her too. God. It was happening again: *lovermine*.

Pidgin Boanerges

Pidgin came to slow, to the sound of his own voice. His unwashed hair was dried to his teeth. He wasn't talking. No way was this the bingo-parlor bathroom. He gagged and spit and dragged the back of his forearm across his lips, burrowed a spyhole in the pastel finery billowing around him. He was in a canopied queen bed that was in the corner of a bedroom with one window. On the backside of the only noncloset door was a black-edged poster, dog-eared so that one corner slumped forward. The picture on the poster was a dummied up photo of a UFO, a familiar disc of light hazed against the clouds. Behind the door was Pidgin's voice in surround sound. He tried to filter towards it, stumbled instead over words leftover from a woman who smelled like the room smelled, words from when she had been standing just to the right of the bed: 'So this is Billy the Kid?' Hours before that there was more interference, a slightly male voice this time, the argyle berdache with the strobelight camera, talking movie Spanish—'He knows too much, señora Finidad'—then laughing nervous at his own joke, his hand touching the bed there, there, the heat from his flash bringing sweat to Pidgin's upper lip all over again. He let his spyhole collapse, cocooned himself in the sheets, and lied that his surround sound voice in the other room with the spastic drums and the scripted one-liners wasn't *The Scræling*, his second double-exposed production effort, a skin flick ranging from 1492 until 1953, Discovery to Termination.

It simulated time shifts with camera angles and light tricks. Pidgin was the second main character, the loinclothed Scræling, scrambling across decades and centuries, a side-haired Custer figure inexorable behind him, unrelenting, engorged. The director was one-sixteenth Choctaw on the job, slightly Dominican on the phone, and Sephardic on Saturdays.

In the sit-down before the movie, he had told Pidgin that *The Scræling* was going to revolutionize the porn industry, take Amsterdam by the balls and make it beg for the return of its pubescent soul, because *The Scræling* was going to be the first adult video that made of skin an honest medium; the message between every frame would be that the Indian always gets it up the ass. Pidgin had looked past the director's spiel, though, at the Custer lookalike in the glass antechamber of Dorphin Studios. Redfield, the veteran porndog, couldn't even get hard for a flesh and blood woman anymore without pharmaceuticals and an encyclopedic spectrum of visual and aural stimuli. But he was doing *The Scræling* pro bono. It was unheard of. Pidgin asked the director if the unseen script called for him ever getting caught by this Custer. The director smiled and rallied his Choctaw blood to the surface, so that skin-deep he was Indian. He said that the Scræling would get away unviolated, into an alternate future, as yet unwritten. But it was a tactical lie: the penultimate scene was in the soundproof room, dolled up to look like a BIA director's office. It was authentic. It tore Pidgin in two and forced him to remember Sally, consider limbo.

He convalesced for weeks afterwards, holed up in his trailer.

One morning the director's assistant called with the bad luck news about double exposure, blamed it on magnets in the camera man's headset. She delivered an uncut copy to Pidgin, no slipcover, COD, and when the master tape was filed away it fathered generations of copies from its dark interoffice cove, bootlegs of bootlegs, disseminating itself over all of america, hounding Pidgin into isolation, into a bedsheet cocoon. Here he was. And there he was out there too, past the door, running, the berdache saying his lines rote before they came through the speakers, so Pidgin had to hear it twice. It had found him again, run him down again. The berdache was even ad-libbing lines in the empty spaces, during the camera and light posturing. And not only ad-libbing: during one extended time-shift sequence in which one hundred and seventeen years were traipsed over like nothing, Pidgin heard the berdache whispering in Cowboy and Indian terms to the woman, organizing a raid of some sort. An old-time attack. And by their names, they were the Indians here. Meaning Pidgin was the cowboy this time. He stood from the sheets then phoenix-style, on impulse, answering the drama crackling on video tape, and looked down on the starched-slick wranglers he was wearing like a second skin, the boots without heels he still had on. On the bedpost was a 4X hat, sloped crown, rolled brim, frontheavy feather band brittle to the touch. But it was a hat. Pidgin set it on his head, pulled it down over his eyes.

In the other room the two Indians were announcing themselves as Rabbit Head and Yellow Snow.

Pidgin was Billy the Kid.

He said through the door that God was on *his* side now.

Yellow Snow asked back did God have-um any guns?

Pidgin looked at his waist, scanned the room for the piece that had to be. But it wasn't. There was just bedroom trash: mirrors, dirty clothes, a wedding album tilted in the corner, the bingo caller smiling out of it, past an endless row of pointy lapels. Nothing remotely Old West. There would be no glory blazes this afternoon. Pidgin sat on the foot of the bed and tried to wait them out instead. In response they adopted federal siege tactics, watched the movie on loud loud. Pidgin paced back and forth, back and forth, assaulted by his own interoffice screams, refused to give up. The movie played to completion and was started over. The voice of the woman came and went, as if she were walking from room to room. Only Yellow Snow remained. Pidgin asked him where he got a name like a joke, and Yellow Snow responded with slumber-party tactics to get the door open: he poured water back and forth, deep pitcher to deep pitcher; he sighed hard and flushed the toilet in the other room; he told the story of Tycho Brahe with the piss-golden nose and the toxic levels of urine in his own bloodstream. A zipper went up and down on stereo somehow. A beer was opened and its drinking narrated. Toilet bowls swirled invitingly to the left.

Yellow Snow said to Pidgin *you're in trouble now,* and Pidgin could taste it in the back of his throat. But still. He refused to surrender.

Five minutes later he unzipped, palmed the only piece he had. He said to the Indians that this was their last chance, he was dead-fucking serious. Rabbit Head came alive, spoke of stain resistance and three-year warranties and empty threats, what she could do to him in next month's editorial. Her words accelerated time inside Pidgin. He clenched every muscle that would clench, finger muscles too, then stumbled around the room, unbalanced, shoulder heavy, looking for the bathroom door that wasn't there, threatening every object, establishing hierarchies of the possible and the electrical, then finally let go in a rush, leaning back where he used to have heels, using both hands to hold on, and at first, when the jamb split and the door crashed open and Yellow Snow and Rabbit Head appeared in full regalia, Yellow Snow yelling *shit shit shit, this was supposed to be therapy for Chrissake* and simultaneously letting fly his nerf arrow part of the attack, at first, Pidgin's neck muscles were the only major group to respond, turning his head to the door, but then, as the arrows made contact and bounced away, oblique torso muscles kicked in and he turned his piece on them as well, on the one with the neon bow, and Billy the Kid was in action, white hot, and Yellow Snow was catdancing like he was born to it.

When it was over he stood there, Pidgin did, drained, not shaking off, bladder contracting. He'd done it. Rabbit Head looked him in the eye and said with zero inflection that she thought he could put that smoking piece away now, it appeared to be spent. Pidgin zipped up with both hands, then took what initiative he could salvage and asked where she got her an Indian name, being so blonde and white and fortyish.

'Prom night at Chippewa Falls,' she said flatly, like a challenge. 'I'll tell you about it someday when you grow up.'

Pidgin said he was grown up, was something of a professional lambskinner, even.

Rabbit Head stepped out of her soiled regalia and said it: 'Lambskinner?'

'Skinhawk.'

'The trade?'

'The craft.'

'The life, of course.' She smiled, and in the digestive lull that followed Pidgin took note of her salmon-colored panties and her legs, one forward, one to the side. She chamoised the urine off with her breechclout, like it was just water, nothing of consequence, and when Pidgin looked from her to Yellow Snow and gauged the space between them, he saw that the bows and the arrows were just something she allowed for his sake, toys she granted. But she could just as easily take them away. This was her home. She was in control, the mother here. She looked at Pidgin and said that technically a grip wasn't a performer, even an indentured grip. And she also knew how much he was worth in the bounty world these days: forty-five dollars.

'It used to be different.'

'Before *The Scræling* mistake, yes.'

Pidgin looked away fast, asked with all due humbleness why was he here.

Rabbit Head shrugged, said she imagined it had to do with his father, Cline Stob, the Mirror Man, puppet leader of the Goliards, son of Hardwick the government stripminer, grandson of Glasscock the land tamer, himself a twin too. 'It skips generations,' she said, 'you know that?'

Pidgin nodded, did his best to betray no emotion about the two new progenitor names in his blood. He sat the couch through her thirty-minute shower with the scrapbook of *Star* columns she'd given him, updates on Cline under the knife, month by month. Yellow Snow stood in the door and introduced himself again, this time as

Erwin Olsen, call him James. Pidgin grinned for the other side of the room, then in his best Clark Kent asked Erwin for a beer, didn't get one, just got stared at while his skin crawled and his throat audibly parched.

When Rabbit Head returned in terrycloth, she introduced herself professionally as Finity Jane, and Pidgin already knew the name from the clippings, from the Deviant Gallery.

'The *Star* woman,' he said, and she did her smile, shooed Erwin into the darkroom, and said she'd missed him at the interment. Pidgin said he was more or less detained. But he'd gotten there. Rabbit Head aka Finity Jane aka *Star* woman rose then, careless of her robe, and brought Pidgin his beer, took the first drink deep and gave it to him like a kiss.

They were seated in intimate surroundings.

'A Goliard,' she said, defining as Pidgin drank, 'a Goliard of mediæval times was a wandering student of song and revelry, not unlike yourself, who would eventually go mad with the knowledge life gave him.'

'Or didn't give him.'

'Yes, of course. You can ask me.'

'Ask you what?'

'Tell me what you were doing in the bingo bathroom.'

'I was looking for somebody.'

'Ask me who.'

'Who?'

She smiled, then pulled from somewhere in her hair the yellowed telephoto the salesman had given Pidgin after the sweat. 'We have a common interest,' she said, 'yours personal, mine journalistic, nostalgic.' Pidgin stared at the Mexican Paiute, framed with wipe-off highlighter. He wiped it off. He asked Finity Jane why she wanted to find the Mexican Paiute. She did her eyebrows and said she wasn't interested in yesterday's praetors, and in the pause she left afterwards Pidgin realized he'd been played. This was her house, her couches; she was in control. She talked over it like nothing had happened, though, said the Mexican Paiute had been AWOL since Vietnam, underground, only seen once. She tapped the photo to show Pidgin when, but he was already looking at his mother, saying her name inside. He could hardly make her out anymore, except for the black hair and hipshot way she stood into the wind.

'She was something else, alright,' Finity Jane said like a concession, and when Pidgin pulled his head up she was watching him like a cat, and then before he was sure what was going on she had washed his hair and shaved him, leaving a nascent line of hair under his lower lip, and was sitting cozy in his lap in the back of a Ford van Erwin was trying to drive, going to the Big Springs State Hospital to grill Sally for answers Finity Jane said she owed the both of them. Pidgin said he hadn't seen Sally since he was impressionable. On the passenger side of the van, the video unit was rolling *The Dark Crystal*, the only one of Erwin's role-playing games that Finity Jane said did anything remotely therapeutic for her: she was the Aughra character, and Pidgin was a lowly member of the vulture set. Finity Jane said she'd made the domino masks herself, delicate eyepieces held on sticks, a stylized armadillo and a vulture done up in rhinestone. Pidgin held the mask in one hand, Finity Jane in the other, and during the low spots in the road, when gravity lost its grip just a little, felt he was in some cocktail party gone awry years back, that was being subducted en masse to a yet lower plane of existence; he tried to remember where Big Springs was, even, but couldn't begin to place it.

'Texas,' Finity-as-Aughra hummed deeply through her mask, letting it build, 'West Texas. You'll do just fine, lover, just fine.' When she was through talking Pidgin found her mouth was on his, and he drew back, unsure, but then the gravy was a familiar prick in his arm, the needle nose probing around the scar tissue for something non-muscle. It found it; the syringe bloomed. They spent the rest of the drive trying to join themselves together again at the waist, Pidgin's glass eyes touching hers singly, painlessly, with small sound, Erwin with his left hand unsteady on the wheel, making words over the coupling, anticipating aloud the *Dark Crystal* dialogue, hurtling on into Texas breakneck style.

When they pulled into Big Springs a handful of hours later, piece-mealed again, distinct and uncomfortable with it, Pidgin watched the buildings slip past empty and dry and said he'd been through here once, riding the skinny dog east for some reason or another. Maybe a desert shoot or a scheduled pick-up and delivery snowjob. Finity Jane, hairdrying the masks and packing them back in their velveteen cases, looked up. 'Everybody comes through here at one time or another, lover. Big Springs. The interstate. And by the way, nobody says skinny dog anymore.'

Pidgin shrugged, stepped down into the state hospital parking lot, tasted lithium and phenobarb in the air, instinctively thought of Birdfinger and instinctively tried to will the image of him away. Walking to the main entrance, he looked back to see Erwin fingerwriting WET SPOT over the rear window of the van and had to smile. He apologized to Finity Jane for peeing on her carpet. She brushed it off with her left hand again, like nothing of consequence to an Editor-in-Chief, and then they were there, one door sliding out of their way, the other jamming, Pidgin walking nosefirst into the glass, Finity Jane leading him through correctly like he was a new patient not yet wholly familiar with three unyielding dimensions. In the antechamber to Sally's cell, Finity Jane debriefed him for the second time in as many hours, said the thing with her and Sally was that the *Star* had negotiated a contract with Sally allowing Finity Jane first publication rights to any and all of Sally's predictions.

Pidgin said he understood, asked what was the hip-pocket clairvoyant's end?

Finity Jane smiled, drew close, said the only thing the same about Sally from when Pidgin knew her, aside from hair color, was that she still claimed to have no sense of taste, yet insisted that during her prescient moments her sense of smell became painfully acute. 'But I don't think that'll become an issue today,' she said, 'her performance this year has been dismal to say the least.'

'So you're here to milk her?'

'I'm here to get what's legally mine.'

Pidgin pocketed his hands, asked where did he fit in, got no answer. Finity Jane stared at him instead, tapping her pen against her upper lip, then as Erwin loaded his camera said that the only thing that might become any kind of issue was that Sally thought she was a wendigo these days.

Pidgin only had time for one last question before Finity Jane ushered him into the room: 'Wendigo?'

'Anishinaabe cannibal,' Finity Jane said with distraction. 'Sally miscarried after WWI, and her body partially reabsorbed the fetus before expelling the leftovers. It's a guilt delusion, a legend, probably fits in with the no-taste claim somehow. Don't worry, you'll do fine.'

With no more words then, they were buzzed into the padded room with Big Spring Sally, Erwin holding his light-meter aloft geiger-style, Finity Jane arranging the chairs around the round-edged safety table and absently humming the *Lone Ranger* theme. Sally looked the same as ever. She took the chair opposite Pidgin but didn't speak. She inspected him instead, did her mouth in a slow O which her tongue described in minute detail, the slowest inner lip licking episode Pidgin had ever witnessed. Erwin caught it on film, too, using the strobe flash adjustment, and Sally didn't flinch under the hot and fast light. Had been born to it maybe. Or for it. Finity Jane presented Pidgin to her in grand fashion, the specimen.

'I'm the dog here, I think,' Pidgin said to Sally, 'maybe the pony.'

'Yee-haw,' Sally said back.

It was started. Pidgin said to Sally he'd heard she got committed. Sally said she was sorry about Cline. Pidgin said that was nine years ago already, he was over it. Sally smiled. Finity Jane interrupted with half a word about business, but Sally stayed her with a raised finger.

'What is it?' she asked Pidgin, the years between them erased.

Pidgin looked around. There were cameras in the corners, mirrors in between. He didn't even know the Mexican Paiute's name, if he had a name. And the image of Cline being shouldered away like a feedbag wouldn't stay still long enough to put into words. And they weren't alone. Finity Jane spoke for him: 'I gather he's looking for your Mexican-Indian friend.'

Pidgin nodded bullseye.

Sally never broke her smile. 'The grave,' she said.

Pidgin nodded again.

'Ask me something different, Pidge, anything, square roots, presidents, lottery numbers.'

'But that's the only thing,' Pidgin said, 'I saw him.'

'And he doesn't get seen. That says something.'

'I just need to find him, talk to him.'

'You will.'

'If you tell me where to look.'

'The morning after,' Sally said after some deliberation.

Pidgin let his forehead touch the tabletop, kept it there.

Sally smiled. 'Eighteen-ninety mean anything to you?'

Pidgin asked if she could be a little more specific.

Sally said she wished she could. Pidgin looked up and said she *could*, but she was shaking her head no, saying he'd be back soon enough, Pidgin—both of them—and then it might be the right time, or at least less wrong. Not now.

'But I'm never coming back here, Sal,' Pidgin said, eyeing the padded walls, trick mirrors, 'not to Texas, shit. I hate it here.'

'For me you will.'

Pidgin shook his head no like an apology, pressed the side of his fist into his forehead for long seconds then slammed the other side hard into the table, driving a cup and two pens into flight.

'You've developed a temper,' Sally said.

'Over the last nine days, yes.'

'Your father too. He was like that.'

Pidgin closed his eyes, felt teased with information. She was still Sally. If she had access to scissors anymore, there would have been flashcards in the game already. Pidgin sat back and looked at her, told her if she was withholding because foreknowledge might disturb the whole Schrödinger's cat graft, then she should know it was a lost cause. 'I figured my way out,' he said, holding Finity Jane at bay too, 'the trick is, *I'm* the one in the box, see? *I* know whether I'm A or B, alive or dead. I'm both the observer *and* the subject. The realization doesn't hang on the damn thing opening from above. It's with me.'

Sally talked over Finity Jane: 'You're saying it yourself, Pidge.'

Pidgin held his temples in one hand and relistened. He was saying it: *and*. As in A *and* B. Given away by a conjunction. Goddamn her. And she was even committed. Pidgin polished his thumbnail and felt transparent on closed-circuit Texas television. He only had one card left to play. He desleeved it, told Sally that this *Star* woman was here to gather predictions, her predictions, and he knew one, anyway, an old one, and not just a corollary. Sally broke her smile, stared hard, said she was sorry it had to be this way between them, she really was, and then Finity Jane was in edgewise, talking monotone to Sally, reciting that both of *Pidgin* was yet real, yes? Sally was stone. Pidgin nodded for her to Finity Jane, said yes, then added that it went further, the gist of Sally's prediction. It was that he would finish whatever it was the Goliards had promised to finish. Or not.

'Pretty sophisticated stuff there,' Pidgin added: 'Either or. Hard to be wrong, right Sally?'

Finity Jane said thank you to Pidgin before Sally could answer in kind, then turned to her, mentioned specific wordings, contexts, printable matter. Sally said yes, there were those. A dramatic recreation wouldn't be too far out of reach either. If she wasn't mistaken, there was even a telephoto of it around somewhere. She even had the scent environment categorized, parsed into animal, mineral, and other: 'There was mint julep,' she said, 'fresh. One of the officers staking us out, resisting sleep in his little Nova. He was drinking it with his thermos of tea. A real southern man.'

'Well.'

'They were half a mile off, upwind.'

'Okay. Validity attained.'

'His partner's deodorant was breaking down too.'

'I get the picture,' Finity Jane said. 'But your prediction? The Primate of Order?'

Sally narrowed her eyes about the Primate of Order, no longer had anything like an upper hand.

'From his uncle,' Finity Jane explained, indicating Pidgin. Sally looked to him and then away. 'Not while he's here,' she said.

Finity Jane turned to Pidgin, a polite demand. Pidgin shook his head no. 'Why can't I hear?' he asked Sally, calm-voiced again, and she just said that it was a matter of timing still, with him. Pidgin laughed because there was nothing in the world he could do here. You couldn't argue with her, not face to face.

Sally shrugged apology when Pidgin didn't look away, and in that shoulder motion Pidgin realized that the way she saw it, she was martyring herself—their relationship—for the greater good of the Goliards. He told her they were dead, the Goliards. She corrected him—*dying*—said if he wanted a clue, that was it.

It lodged in Pidgin's mind, meant nothing.

Finity Jane started her recorder then and said to Pidgin *please*, turned her face to the door languidly enough that there was room in there for her to indicate the corner-mounted camera.

Pidgin stood slow into understanding, into the deception it seemed Finity Jane was offering. He didn't want to play her game, but he had to know. He told Sally goodbye and said thanks for everything.

Sally nodded once, waved her fingers on the table like dominos falling.

Pidgin walked to the padded door and got buzzed out on cue, held it open long enough to hear Finity Jane say to Sally that there was a delicate legal matter pending between the two of them—an *obligation*— long enough to hear Sally agree, click the recorder off, and say to Finity Jane *you first, though, Miss McCrae*. And then he was alone in the hall. He hooked his hair behind his ears, tucked his shirt in, did his best to look sane, then followed the red dots on the floor that led from Sally's cell out, through the cafeteria where predigested food hung in stalactites, through the maze of leaning halls decorated with mounted fully-caped bullheads around every corner, undiscovered pellets for sawdust, and finally got to the tight room Finity Jane had meant, the room with the two morphine drips punching each other in the arm, fighting over chair privileges in front of the closed circuit TV, pot-smoke thick in the air, vents taped over. They drew back from Pidgin when he entered, hid behind their white jackets and touched him first with a pencil tip, then a hand, then Pidgin stopped the inspection.

'You have sound here?' he asked, and they fidgeted and toed the tile floor and said if by sound he meant noise, then yes, there was significant interference, the signal was either garbling in route or was garbled intentionally from the source, in an effort to use reverse psychology on theory, which *had* to be impervious to such assaults, yes? Pidgin closed the door, locking himself into the chamber with them. They didn't seem to notice, continued wrestling over the chair. Finally Pidgin touched them with the toe of his boot, insisting he was there, and they wheeled as one, feigning pre-teen adoration, saying in concert *look*, it's the Indian Ken doll. Their eyes were going four ways at once, like iguanas. Pidgin stood still and made like a lizard himself, blending into the wall, and when the chair wars were over and the victor seated, he watched closed-circuit television with them on eight tiny monitors, colors tinny, no sound.

Centerstage was Finity Jane on four screens, flanked on either side by running loops of Pidgin striding out the door in timeless fashion. Above the eight monitors was a black and white printout of him with fangs and horns and a patch eye. He asked the drips if there were microphones in the cell, and they said that they weren't gestapo, man, more like lifeguards with magical binoculars. Pidgin massaged the bridge of his nose, trying to leech out the anger: so Finity Jane had played him again, right out of the room. And, though he knew her mouth intimately, he wasn't the lip-reader he used to be. And he was no closer to finding the adobe wall from the telephoto and seeing through it back to 1977. And the only person he knew who might have any answers was Birdfinger, and he'd already run from him once. To come to him with questions now would be to lose the advantage with him, to *need* him, to admit that he was necessary. Pidgin said aloud that it might come to that, humbling himself on the porch. He waited for the drips to reply in cute unison, but found that they were in a frenzy, were suddenly without *Frankenhooker* dialogue to supply their mute subjects with: centerstage, moving in quadruple, Finity Jane-as-Jane McCrae was slowly unbuttoning her shirt, Sally sitting across from her, no table between.

Pidgin looked into the monitor's concave reflection then without forethought, looking only for help, explanation or institutional evaluation, and accidentally caught the morphine drips midmolt, their face muscles slithering under their skin, locking into scholarly expressions, like something within them was waking up. Pidgin backed away, toe to heel.

'Terms of the contract,' the chair war victor said in a deep and clinical voice Pidgin didn't think he had.

'Yes,' the other replied, leaning back from the hips where he stood, holding his head up by the chin, arm in crook, 'a time honored tradition.'

'She feeds the fear—'

'—She sates the cannibal.'

'She gets her scoop.'

'The primal, journalistic instinct.'

'The need to know.'

'But the price.'

'Perhaps it's become ritual.'

'Perhaps she's addicted.'

'Bloodletting is hardly new.'

'Not in this facility.'

They shared a well-patted belly laugh then, and coolly observed Finity Jane stepping out of everything but her control-top hose.

'A forty year old woman,' the victor noted, pointing with his eyebrows.

'In fine shape.'

'Let's not rule out exhibitionism.'

'On a limited scale.'

'Notice her own need.'

'The dynamics of any contract.'

'Legal innuendo.'

'Mutual self-delusion.'

'Ritual mutilation.'

'Yes, indeed. Very interesting.'

Pidgin, flat against the wall, lock-kneed and blue in the lips from it, zeroed in on how Finity Jane in her control top hose looked half-Indian, from the waist down, like she'd waded through it to get to Sally. Waded through him. But then things went cinematic: Sally approached Finity Jane, her lips writhing, overpronouncing—*her first*—and Finity Jane silently told her to wait, wait while she removed from her hair a shiny black scalpel and inserted the edge of it delicately into the aureolic base of her nipple, shallowly circumscribing it counterclockwise.

'Right-handed.'

'It goes without saying.'

'Notice the blade.'

'Obsidian, yes.'

'Divides at the cellular level.'

'No scar tissue.'

'Appearances, after all.'

'This is the Western culture.'

'Masochistic tendencies.'

'Madonna imagery.'

'Unavoidable.'

'And her neckline.'

'Prominent adam's apple, yes.'

'Head thrown back.'

'Symptomatic.'

'Superfluous.'

'Orgasmic.'

'Evidently she enjoys it.'

'This.'

'The scoop.'

'The knowledge, yes,' the victor said, making a fist, 'the power.'

When it was over, when the talking heads were scribbling furiously into their notebooks against the time when they would regress to morphine drip state and toke up in celebration of the obvious, Pidgin slipped out the in door, invisible as ever, the image of Sally still before him in quadruple, blood at the sharp corners of her mouth, eyes closed, about to mouth specific wordings to the *Star* woman, about to recreate on demand.

In the parking lot Pidgin lay in the bed of a custodial truck that eventually carried him to an abandoned USAF base, and he walked from it through the empty hangars and barracks and to the interstate. He crossed over to the westbound lane, back to Clovis again, back to the trailer to humble himself before Birdfinger and get it all over with.

He walked and sang to avoid sleep, but still his blinks lasted, and once he was caught in the headlights of a long heavy Buick which whipped past like a train, spinning him back into the ditch, making him live. He hugged his ribs against the cold and kept walking, avoiding anything vanlike and westbound, and the forty-third car to whoosh by was primer black and rocket-made, brakelights flaring, nose diving. It coasted alongside, the window humming down, the driver half-drunk and hollow-eyed.

'You sure?' Pidgin asked, but the stranger was already pulling away hard. Pidgin closed the door twice, took the beer offered him, then jerked his knee up as something vaguely reptilian scurried across the thin toe of his boot. The stranger smiled, toasted, said drink up, it's a long ride and a longer walk, and then for two-hundred odd miles angling northwest on skinny roads chosen at the last possible instant he told Pidgin all about Texas radio and the big beat, and Pidgin sat his chair and listened, obedient, anxious to know more, the 4X image of Sally still locked in his head but being overrun by frogs locked in the fractal background. When he woke, not even sure he'd slept, they were in the road, the frogs, wetbacked from some rain, puzzled together collarbone to collarbone, and Sally was gone. There had been a division. The stranger told him this as he calmly picked through amphibian matter at twenty-two miles per hour. There had been a division. He also said he could heal him if he wanted him to, Pidgin. He had that ability.

Pidgin regarded him, miles away in the driver seat, his arm spanning the distance somehow, sleeve vomiting of all things a plastic-red watergun, pointing it at Pidgin, who shied blindly away from the barrel, narrowly avoiding the warm stream of water that passed in front of his face, on its way to the fat-tailed gecko suddenly sleeping on the side glass.

'Lizard,' the stranger said, explaining, and then laid the gun in Pidgin's lap. 'Came with the damn car.' Pidgin raised the gun and his finger convulsed on the trigger, filling his road-dried mouth and wetting his shirt. The stranger laughed a deep bass laugh then, and didn't stop, and in his laughter Pidgin heard a whispering of what was coming, saw an image of himself, dead in a motel room, peanuts spilled in a crescent around his feet, the lizard on his face, drawing the last of his moisture up through the capillaries, the stranger in the next room clicking through the channels faster and faster.

He looked over at Pidgin from his bed or from his seat, Pidgin could no longer tell which, and said *I can't stop, man, I just can't stop*, and then Pidgin had the door of the rocket car open and he was stepping out at twenty-two miles per hour, rolling in the dry grass like a rag doll. He lay there for hours. A convoy of dairy rigs thundered by, and the silence it left was glass placid. In it, the frogs prayed deep in their throats for order, for guidance, for surcease. When Pidgin arose, his knee didn't work right, so he split the wranglers around it and stumbled from mile marker to mile marker to home, to Clovis, to Birdfinger.

He walked into the trailer at daybreak, opened the door, and presented himself to no one.

He sat on the couch he said he wasn't going to sit on too long. He woke with his arm dangling off the side, and when it came back to him it had retrieved some under-the-couch matter: one of Birdfinger's sketches. A woman in number-two pencil. His mother. Marina Trigo. He recognized her outline from the telephoto. Pidgin held the picture until it tore, and then hid it in the cushions, and then questioned his absent uncle who drew beautiful pictures like this and hid them. There was no reason, there should be no reason: Birdfinger wasn't Cline. No matter what he thought, no matter how he looked. He didn't know her. He had no right to draw her.

On the way off the porch Pidgin emptied the spittoon of change, for lunch money, maybe the movies, where

Charlie Ward might still be. He wasn't though. There was no one. Only *The Silent Enemy*, Baluk and Neewa, rolling over and over, living and dying. Pidgin sat in Charlie Ward's seat, smelled kerosene, pushed the sensation away, and on the third time through, his mind numb with animal fat, he felt someone behind him, and then a plastic-handled nerf knife was at his throat, scraping away skin cells, and the whisper was in his ear, telling him that Rabbit Head didn't like to begrudge people anything, especially those so easily taken as Pidgin. Erwin's breath was like a baby's. Yellow Snow. He was laughing in his nervous way.

Pidgin imagined the nerf knife penetrating his transparent skin.

Erwin said to count the people in the telephoto out loud, name them. Pidgin did: Cline Stob, one; Birdfinger, two; his mother, three; Sally, four; the Mexican Paiute, five. Erwin held Pidgin's head in place by the hair. 'Now how many people are up against the wall?' he asked.

Pidgin saw it, admitted it: 'Six.'

The sixth one was the extra Indian to the right of Sally, with the white stripe in his hair. Pidgin said he couldn't name him. Erwin said his name was the easy part: Atticus Wean. He made Pidgin repeat after him, then added that Atticus was the owner of a horse called Weanie, and Weanie was putting on a Sunday show in Aztec. 'Ride or don't,' he said, 'whatever your *in*clination.'

Erwin laughed some more then, about the sodomy gibe Pidgin distinctly felt, and under the cover of his laughter Pidgin steadily withdrew the water pistol from his shirt, pointed it where the flat under Erwin's chin would rest when he drew close again, when he pulled his feathered head down out of the finger of light pointing out Baluk and the moose, the scene which had Pidgin nervous like Charlie Ward, unblinking, clutching the armrests, afraid to miss a single step, afraid he'd miss everything if he did.

Two hours later he was still there, whiteknuckled, the gun leaked empty, his skull fake scalped, the rest of him danced over in victory, couped to exhaustion.

He hadn't been able to pull the trigger.

He rubbed the scratchy line of underlip hair the *Star* woman had left him. He was a study of indecision. He had a pocket full of change. From a booth outside Juanita's he placed three calls. The first was to Birdfinger. A languid-voiced woman answered. She asked was he taking a poll? Of course Bird was there. Pidgin swallowed and recradled the receiver before anything could be said. The next two calls were collect to Dorphin Studios to beg for busfare to Provo. The first was a misdial. The manvoice on the other end accepted and listened to Pidgin's tale of woe and asked how he felt now in the aftermath. Pidgin said he felt cashed, and was afraid the aftermath wasn't come yet. The second call to Dorphin Studios the operator apologized for. It rang and rang. Pidgin explained Dorphin Studio quality control to the operator when she didn't ask; he said the secretary wasn't at her post because they probably needed a redhead for a group scene, to complete the visual palette, lend via diversity a realistic sheen to the whole shebang. The operator took offense to *shebang*. Pidgin said the wigs involved pretty much quashed the sought after realism anyway. The operator said it sounded like a fetish game to her. She accused Pidgin of knowing a little too much about Dorphin Studios. In a continuing moment of weakness, Pidgin confessed: he was Dorphin Studio's friendly neighborhood Spiderman. The operator dial-toned him.

Pidgin left the phone hanging, walked into Juanita's and chose a back booth, ordered coffee and more coffee, watched a platinum-blonde underaged barrel-racer origami her stack of green paper into a chain while waiting out a chalupa, got hard watching, recalled with fondness the Spiderman stint. It was his first double-exposed failure. It had paid room and board and naked women. Pidgin didn't even have any lines; the three-fingered sex prop man hadn't had time to design a face mask that would allow words to pass unmolested. Pidgin had been lightheaded all week from lack of oxygen. He was sixteen then, had just followed his mother's surname to a dead-end at Browning Montana when Dorphin Studios found him. They manufactured a tribal ID that said he was four years older. It was a Salishan ID. Pidgin practiced saying Kutenai.

Three days before the ID, too, he had been Mohawk, because the recruiter from Dorphin Studios was casting someone sure of foot and steely of nerve. But Pidgin wasn't the only one antsy to trade Browning in on the next thing, whatever it was: suddenly every male standing outside the IGA was claiming Mohawk blood.

The recruiter rubbed his chin in deliberation and said he only needed one. He held his finger up, talking sign language for all the Mohawks. They squinted and looked at each other and played the game—piling onto the flatbed, riding west towards Glacier, holding their breath while the junked-up blonde stepped out of the passenger side of the Ford, looked them head to toe, straightened her halfshirt with twin, kidney level pulls, and then, using the recruiter's leather belt and her spike heels, shinnied up the nearest telephone pole and reclined on top like a Vargas girl, one knee drawn to her chest, one hand trailing a red bandanna like second nature.

One of the Mohawks said something in Blackfeet that made the rest tear their eyes away and notice the truck, but the recruiter just held his finger up again, turning them back around; it both stood for the number and pointed to the girl. He said he needed a *spider* man, gentlemen, if you please—or, *she* needed one. There were seven of them there, besides Pidgin, and they all made it to the pole before him. He was still looking at the truck, trying to figure out what had passed between everyone. By the time he got to the pole two of the Mohawks were already halfway up, hungry-eyed, crotches bulging, but they were pulled down by the remaining five. Then a lone climber made it nearly to the top until the next in line telescoped his wrist an extra twenty-four inches and pulled him down by the heelskin. It happened over and over, until it became a cycle; the pole swayed back and forth. Pidgin didn't know where to get in, how to get on, whether he wanted to even. He watched the blonde and saw she was watching him too, from her crows nest, disinterested in who would eventually win her, or whether they all would. Maybe sure they wouldn't. The bandanna fluttered.

'Go away,' she mouthed twice, her lipstick framing her words, and Pidgin ignored her invitation, turned sharp and soft-shoed his way to the passenger side of the flatbed. He crept in, hoping the keys were there, finally understanding the theft the Mohawk had been suggesting in Blackfeet. The recruiter was sitting guard in the driver's seat though, reading Mickey Spillane and smoking an everyday pipe. He said he was fluent in most of the north american language groups, and could get the gist of the rest. And he was nowhere near naive enough to get marooned, truckless in the middle of nowhere. He closed the book and asked Pidgin what was up, little big man?

'She's got to come back here,' Pidgin said, 'that's what.'

The recruiter tapped his temple in minor key applause, looked in the rearview and started the truck, eyebrows suggesting flight. 'On any other day, I might agree,' he said, pushing his foot ankle-deep into the floorboard, spilling tobacco between them and letting it smolder into the seatcover.

Two hours closer to Utah, he bought Pidgin a burger and shake deal and fashioned a makeshift belt out of head and chest shots folded together like a dollar-bill hatband. Neat interlocking triangles of skin and hair. Pidgin tried not to look impressed. When asked, he said that he was in Browning because Browning wasn't Clovis New Mexico, and the recruiter agreed, then added that neither was Provo. Pidgin nodded and ate, and when they put the contract before him he traded Browning for two renewable years of employment, and when they gave him his homemade webshooters he wore them and didn't complain that they were chrome flasks JB-welded onto turquoise bracelets. He said Kutenai inside his hermetic mask and stared at his ID. The picture wasn't even him, but some other crossblood, someone not dangling from a webline outside a stage window, someone not play-acting the perfect voyeur, the ideal narrative vehicle. Pidgin's only job was to masturbate for the camera at a pretend forty feet and not say anything the mics could pick up.

He did, convulsively, defensively, in the back booth of Juanita's, under cover of the table, his mouth muttering, eyes zeroed in on the barrel racer's idle origami, seeing past it to the seven nonMohawks and the one fake blonde, the orgy that was always a handsbreadth away, held in front carrot style, just to lead him on, tease him. It was an abreaction of the nerves. *100 Strokes a Night*. That had been the title of that first video that never made it through postproduction. *100 Strokes a Night*.

The third-shift waitress poured him another cup of coffee on the house and nodded her head no way in hell, not in here, not on her watch. 'Take it outside,' she said, but Pidgin looked away and put both hands on the table instead. In the waitress' absence one of the crippled Indian truckdrivers began laughing into his chili cheeseburger. The barrel racer was cutting her chalupa up into fourths and then eighths and then Pidgin had to look away even more, had to stare out into the parking lot where the fleet of dairy tankers were parked nose to tail, chromoly blue, pasteurized. A sea of milk. Twenty-eight of them, still pointing west. For the nth time in nine hours, Pidgin mulled over the nonclue the *Star* woman had forced on him, baited him with; Aztec was more or less west. And tomorrow was Sunday. The Goliard's name was Atticus Wean.

Pidgin kept both hands in view and drank his coffee slow. He outlasted the barrel racer and collected her paper ouroboros before the busboy could loot the table. He broke the circle it made, unfolded one of the isosceles links, and like it had to be—like Sally had preordained it all before he was born, giving everybody else time to memorize their cues and exits—the green paper was an official flyer for the SHY KIDNEYS SHOW AND RODEO in Aztec New Mexico. It was shaped like a belt buckle, all the information in unfurled banners: horses, riders, and entry fees. Pidgin told himself he'd found this without the *Star* woman's charity. He tried to fold it back along the same lines, too, but couldn't do it, and finally just flattened it with a plate, leaned onto it with both hands, elbows locked, shoulders at ear level. When the plate cracked, Juanita's went silent and Pidgin was on stage.

The crippled truckdriver began laughing again, chili-cheese settling on his part of the counter in an alluvial fan.

Pidgin stared at him hard then left, took it outside, waited for Charlie Ward to appear out of nowhere and drive him fast out of Clovis one more time, one last time. But Charlie Ward wasn't on patrol. Pidgin stepped out of the floodlight, feeling along the clapboard wall for the bathroom that used to be there when Juanita's was Wyvonne's. It was still there, door ajar, abandoned. But the sixty-watt worked. In the feeble light Pidgin leaned over the sink, waiting to fill his own shadow with vomit, give it substance, waiting for the truckers to charge their meal so he could steal a ride west and then north, and while he was waiting, his spidey sense echo-located something carved into the stall door, a series of names with all but the last four entries scratched out; they were *Lucayos, Wovokans, Tupamaros* and *Goliards*. It could mean anything.

Pidgin scratched them out with a screw nub, denying them importance, then dropped the screw nub into the drain, backed off to admire his handiwork, and found if he looked at it just right, the stall door, the letters came together as cross-hatching, and a happy face six feet tall was smiling out at him, one long feather angled off the back of its head. Pidgin stumbled backwards into what used to be the paper towel rack, then shook his head no, stepped purposely out into the sea of milk. He picked an idling cabover by license plate—TALLBOY—and squatted down behind the fairing, tried to camouflage himself in the boomers and brake lines but couldn't manage it, finally just gave up and webbed himself to the belly of the tanker with stray bungy cords. Just past his feet were the trademark dummy udders, each rubber teat as thick as his forearm.

He didn't feel worth forty-five dollars.

In *100 Strokes a Night* they hadn't even used him for the waist level close-ups. They said his foreskin was too dark, that Peter Parker was anglo if he was anything, and in all likelihood circumcised. Pidgin didn't argue. He clung to the belly of the great metal cow and waited for her to lumber off. He watched in silence as the drivers filed out of Juanita's, every last one on twin polio crutches, blinking to unblear their eyes, moving forward in jerks, none of them bumping into each other. It was like watching puppets move, but it was so choreographed. Three feet to his left, two of them exchanged pill bottles and patted each other on the back. Headlights came on, a horn bellowed towards the rear of the line. It was a convoy, a stampede. Pidgin saw himself stepping out from under his chosen tanker at seventy-plus miles per hour, set up like a bowling pin for the grill of the one directly behind, the driver reaching for the air brakes with his crutch and not finding them. Pidgin closed his eyes to pass the time, to not think, but was pulled out of the oblivion by heavy breathing, by someone laboring above.

He stiffened, expecting the bite of the sharpshooter shovel already, the noosed rope reaching for him, but he was still under the tanker. Down by the udders there was just an old Indian driver, squatting, bronchial tubes thick with tar, camo-pantsed, wearing a once-blue Alcatraz '69 shirt, faded at the sternum and armpits. He coughed to clear his throat and held onto a teat while he did it, so he wouldn't tip over. He was old in the same way a turtle is: skin etched and leathery, every move deliberate, knees knocked. Tallboy. He pointed with one of his short silver crutches to the cabover. 'Got some coffee up there,' he said. 'Pretty good windshield too, if you're into that kind of stuff.'

Pidgin was. In the cab, in answer to the unasked question, he said *Aztec*. 'Y'know, the town.'

Tallboy shook his head no, pointed straight west with his chin, gesturing over two states: Bakersfield. He nosed out onto the highway, not twelve feet behind the truck in front of him, gathered speed and then breath, and apropos nothing said 'I am a cowboy,' directing it straight at Pidgin and enunciating with his whole face, like it meant more than the words.

Pidgin sat there unsure, rubbed time from his underlip.

Tallboy smiled, teeth sharp and even, and said it again, slow for the meaning-impaired: 'I am a *cow*boy.'

'So I hear.'

Tallboy was going to say it again too, Pidgin knew, say it until he got it across or until Pidgin buried his head between his knees in defeat, withdrawn. Pidgin studied it, restudied it, and when Tallboy downshifted for a rise, checking his ten mirrors in a glance, it came to Pidgin all at once: they were riding herd, eighteen-wheeled horses, et cetera. He said it to Tallboy like that, but Tallboy shook his head no. He looked Pidgin over, asked who *he* was, then. 'I am an *In*dian,' Pidgin said, weary of the game already. But Tallboy had led him to the response he wanted. He patted Pidgin on the thigh, smiled wide, then motioned his head in a way that meant the rest of the dairy tankers, the remainder of the polio drivers. 'We're *all* cowboys, here,' he said, clicking on the domelight to fish out another cigarette. Pidgin drew back, realizing that he was being nudged down yet another blind alley, handfed breadcrumbs, just enough not to starve, but then he saw it laid out on the dash—all the yellowed demonstration clippings, the CUSTER DIDN'T DIE ENOUGH bumper stickers, the I SHOT AGENT COLER paraphernalia, the narrow 2 Samuel 12 broadsides, the End of the Trail silhouettes crossed over with a thick red slash like a No Parking sign: Tallboy was an AIM veteran, a media warrior, a real life TV star. He kept a cigarette between his fingers at all times.

The light clicked off. He asked Pidgin what tribe he was, and Pidgin said Piegan, pronouncing it like pagan. Tallboy said he thought so, there was a Blackfeet back at Alcatraz those first few days, looked like him. Something about the hands. Pidgin lied yeah, then asked Tallboy what he was.

'Narcoleptic,' he yawned, weaving off the road. Pidgin didn't fall for it; he'd heard it once before from a yearlong RV ride. 'Navajo,' Tallboy finally said, the sloshing milk still rocking them. 'Jemez.'

Pidgin was half nauseous from the motion, intolerant.

Tallboy thumbed a cassette in and it was drums, chanting, footstomping. In a cinderblock community center it sounded like, or the basement of a church. Pidgin listened as long as he could but finally begged for mercy with a sidelong look Tallboy got. He quit tapping his foot, muttered something like a cussword, then smudged the cigarette out in his palm, filling the cab with flesh smoke. But he turned the drums off. They rode in silence then, pastures washed in the light of twenty-eight trucks. Pidgin counted telephone poles and regretted getting into the truck. Thousands upon thousands of pounds would have to roll to a stop just to let him out. He could feel it all behind him, pushing him forward, and it was like he was a movie hostage, a damsel tied to the front of a train, the train collision-bound, the orchestra nervous. Tallboy slammed the electric locks closed, cleared his throat, spat out the window, and in a low voice told Pidgin that that Alcatraz Blackfeet had stolen away with all their peaches one night, and ran back to Montana. 'Like a goddamn packrat,' he said, 'he wasn't a real cowboy,' and Pidgin couldn't tell if it was good to be Blackfeet or not anymore. He decided it wasn't. He told Tallboy he wasn't really Piegan, and Tallboy told him he wasn't really from Jemez, nobody was.

Pidgin pulled his seatbelt on, all five points.

Tallboy smiled the passenger side of his face. He offered the coffee like it meant something too. Pidgin looked into it, smelled it, declined.

'I don't like peaches,' he said. 'It wasn't me.'

'Good,' Tallboy said back. 'But that's not peaches there, either.'

Pidgin turned away, watched his elbow in the side mirror, tried to breathe around the smoke. An hour passed. They were on the interstate now, Tallboy on the CB, talking low and double guttural into it, some tongue Pidgin knew wasn't Navajo. He'd heard Navajo. The sentences weren't near that long, and there was more repeating. He made himself not listen, thought about the telephoto of his mother instead, about Birdfinger's cocksure posture in relation to her. He couldn't decide if it was honorable or not. There was no way it could be, though, not with him, not with Birdfinger.

He should have never come back to Clovis. Even for Cline.

When Tallboy finally recradled the CB handle, he told Pidgin to pay attention, it was ballot-casting time. Pidgin looked straight ahead, just waiting, preparing himself for whatever miscarriage was next, but still, he wasn't ready when the twenty-eight trucks turned their headlights off as one. At eleven-odd feet in the air, he clamped onto anything solid, could feel the earth turning under their drive wheels, pushed back by them, rotated by diesel power. Tallboy's voice came out of the darkness: 'The Pochtechan Chapter is unanimous yet again. Looks like you're officially in, *cow*boy.'

Pidgin was uncomforted by the news. He studied the relit tail of the truck in front of them, noted the straight-up fists embossed on the mudflaps. He weighed his words as best he could: he told Tallboy thanks, but he didn't want to be in, no offense.

'None taken.'

'But I'm not a cowboy.'

'It's an Indian thing.'

'And I'm not Navajo.'

'Neither am I.'

'And I don't want to drink that.'

'Well,' Tallboy said, holding a cigarette up for the screen of smoke it offered, 'we'll have to talk about that one.'

'It's not coffee.'

'No sir it's not.' Tallboy breathed the steam off of it, a deep and congested sound. 'It's more of a...mitochondrial type brew,' he said, 'special blend, y'know. Tidepool stuff.'

Pidgin sat up against his seat belt, but was restrained for the duration. Tallboy shrugged an apology.

'Why me?' Pidgin asked, and Tallboy said they needed some new blood, it wasn't 1970 anymore. They were getting arthritis and prostate cancer and having colón problems he couldn't even talk about in mixed company.

'Sorry I asked.'

'Don't be. It's endemic to these americas.'

'These?'

'As if there's another, yes. You're catching on already.' Tallboy's smile was audible.

Pidgin cringed. 'But I don't have...crutches, either.'

'They come with the kit.'

'With the drums on tape.'

'With the drums on tape.'

Pidgin closed his eyes, pushed the back of his head into the seat, and breathed, in and out, in and out. When he had it going regular, no more throat catches, Tallboy cleared his phlegm, spat it, and outlined the Pochtechan Chapter, overdetailing the Shipment-of-Laced-Vaccine / Victim-of-Government-Scientists / Indians-as-Guinea-Pigs part of it, skimming over the WWII part—where some of them met over radio waves, taking heavy fire from their CO's who were no longer in the communication loop—and then getting bogged down tarboy style in the archaic part, sticking one fist into the coffee that wasn't coffee at all, but genetic extract distilled from a seriously old Cowboy Gulch Indian the government scientists had found, only to have it seized back in bone court, then sticking his other fist into the double-guttural language the Pochtechan Chapter spoke on the odd channels between two and twenty, how it was like all the other languages mixed, like before the Indian Tower of Babel.

'The Indians aren't in the damn bible,' Pidgin said, trying to slow things down.

'No shit,' Tallboy said back. 'I'm talking pre-pre-Columbian here, and then some.'

'It comes with the kit too, I guess.'

'It's in the inoculation, yeah. The coffee. You'll trade your femur integrity and not regret it.'

'That's all I have left, I think.'

'Then it'll mean that much more.'

Pidgin swallowed, leaned forward, said wouldn't it be easier to just talk Navajo and forget the whole crutch game?

Tallboy smiled, said back to Pidgin that he'd get more than language with the vaccine, *Ponce*, but then got longwinded again, explaining how Navajo hadn't been safe since WWII, since the military assimilated it, then rambling on further, about how the dairy line they ran was really a highly-evolved communications network, udders as mailbags, manholes as dropboxes. He paused and said they were like the goddamn Indian Pony Express.

'Except on cows.'

'It's not 1880.'

'No shit.'

They stared at each other. 'I'm not drinking that,' Pidgin said finally, but then the truck was weaving and the thermos was to his mouth and it was down his shirtfront like throw-up, warm and recombinant on his lips. Tallboy spun the top back on.

'We've got more,' he said, 'and it's a long-ass way to Bakersfield California, I promise you that.'

Pidgin was too paranoid about osmosis to reply. They rode. Tallboy eased left to pass a rocket car in the slow lane. Pidgin watched it go by his window, saw Birdfinger with both hands on the wheel, fingers aglow with dashboard light, the rest of him duded up. They stared at each other, forgetting. It was a dull moment that lasted.

'Goliard,' Pidgin said, classifying by genus, saying that instead of uncle, relation. Tallboy looked him over, Pidgin, asked if he'd said what he thought he'd said? Pidgin said it again—*Goliard*—then took a stab, read something off the bathroom stall of Juanita's: 'They used to be the Lucayos, back when.'

Tallboy shook his head no, but didn't mean it, and from his side of the truck reevaluated Pidgin. 'Goliards,' he said just once, then spit into the floorboard, as if even the aftertaste of the name was that bad.

Pidgin considered spitting with him, but was too self-conscious, too stared-at.

'You don't like them,' Pidgin said.

Tallboy swept his chin up and down the line of dairy tankers. 'They took something important from us a few years ago,' he said, then loosened his hand as if he were going to pat Pidgin down. 'What's your name anyway, cowboy? How do you know about these Goliards?'

'I don't have whatever you're looking for.'

Tallboy smiled the passenger side of his face, maybe the other side too, Pidgin couldn't tell. 'I'll be the judge of that,' he said, and was almost through bungee-cording the steering wheel in place so he could cross the cab to Pidgin when a double-quick guttural voice came over channel eleven, excited, going three ways at once. Tallboy listened reluctantly and looked past Pidgin out the side window, into the distance. He hummed the glass down from his side. There was nothing, though. Just cold air, flatness. Pidgin watched Tallboy watch it, felt the line of tankers collectively sag with attention. Tallboy stalled out when he didn't downshift. Pidgin told him that was bad for the turbo, no joke, but he no longer existed as far as the Pochtechan Chapter was concerned. When Tallboy opened his door, Pidgin felt his five-point harness relax. He tried not to show it. Tallboy stepped out, hardly breathing, intent on the distance. He crutchwalked to the front of the truck, did something repetitive and mechanical by the bumper, metal on metal, the claymore signature. Pidgin released himself and looked over. Tallboy was sitting butt-down. In the rearview mirror, their next in line was doing the same. In a matter of seconds then he stood, Tallboy, and his head was suddenly level with Pidgin's, and Pidgin choked on the closeness. But Tallboy wasn't seeing Pidgin anymore. His old wrinkled face was blank, expressionless. Of another time almost, seeing some other world. He turned back to the distance and stepped gracefully towards it, without his crutches, on the aftermarket carpenter stilts he must have had stowed up under the bumper. This was his natural state—his calves artificially extended—had to be. The reason the muscles of his upper thigh were so malformed.

It wasn't polio. Something worse.

All up and down the line he was joined by the other drivers, uncrippled now too. It was like homage, somehow, fear and respect in one skin; Pidgin could feel it: they wouldn't go more than a few of their long steps out. But they couldn't look away. Enrapt was the word. Pidgin followed Tallboy's head, his line of sight, and over the course of six minutes it moved the smallest bit along an arrow-straight route from Clovis to Aztec, from Texas to Utah, a diagonal across the face of the earth, the dry tide of Ptolemaic epicycles maybe. But no: for an instant—from the cab of the truck where he was almost as tall as the truckers—Pidgin thought he saw it, the form of a man miles out in the scrub, his torso compressed, his legs impossibly long and slender, black birds ushering him along. He moved like fluid, too, and so fast, so effortlessly, eating the miles up.

Tallboy turned to Pidgin, saw that Pidgin had seen it, was seeing it. Smiled. 'Old way,' he mouthed, nodding out there, then, as he was turning back to the distance, something else, something that looked like *new way*. Some of the truckers were moving their legs in unconscious imitation of the form, some of them were crying, and none of it was right. In the quiet moments before the night swallowed them all, Pidgin stepped down from Tallboy's side, didn't close the door.

It was four in the morning again.

He skulked ditchward, followed it west, hid from any Cutlass-like headlights and finally got picked up by a kingcab dually, non-GM. The passenger door swung open. Behind the wheel was a grease-painted apparition, nostrils bleeding cocaine. Bandywine the rodeo clown. He wasn't funny. Pidgin didn't try to make the Pochtechan Chapter into words. By breakfast they were in Aztec, eating at different tables.

Pidgin caught his breath finally.

The waitress asked was he okay, then made him pay in advance. He ate three pieces of spearmint gum, washed down with house coffee. He bummed a dip off a bullrider with Popeye forearms and a Bill Laimbeer plexiglass facemask. The bullrider said his zygomatic arches were that delicate. Pidgin understood. He turned away, saw himself haggard and spent in a small oval mirror, and then turned further away, towards the real Navajo man in the corner, unweaving his western omelette into a story for those within hearing distance. Pidgin was. He pretended to drink coffee, to stare out the window at the powwow crowd waking up from the night before, and listened to the old Navajo man recount a long list of the legendary bucking horses, his voice going up and down with them like a mnemonic device, like he knew their individual rhythms. There was A Horse Called Sleepwalker. There was House Afire, Hemlock. There was Brick Shithouse, Leperkisser, Holy Roller and Rockets Red Glare. Iron

Mountain, War Paint, Tipperary, Odelay, Danzig, Old Red, Hard Eight, Dusty Lane, and he just kept on and on, the old Navajo man, forgetting to swallow until his words became thick with saliva and another old Navajo man slammed his fist into the table. He was on the other side of the room.

When the silverware settled there was silence between them, and then a word from the second: *Gunjumper*. It was a challenge to the sanctity of the first man's list. The first man was uncowed; he replied in a hallowed voice with a horse called Weanie, then was hit hard with *Grand Mal*, with *A Horse Called America*, and after that the situation spun to another level, and they were circling each other, recounting other lists, naming off the longtime riders, the first opening with Cathode Ray Bill and Billy McLaine, the all-around cowboys Joe Mack and Billy Jack, the second slamming the door closed on that list too, with *Tom Black*, the unpale horseman who had made the national news five years back when he rode some mechanical bull to death in a Colorado bar and started an electrical blackout that rippled out two states in every direction, leaving him wasted-drunk at the middle of what the newspapers had called a black hole, a singularity, a one-Indian revolt. And then they began comparing horse and rider lists against each other. The first Navajo man palmed a butterknife and swore that Weanie would remain unridden, the ten-thousand dollar prize unclaimed. The second surrounded himself with tables and said that in the five years since his unretirement, Tom Black had ridden a horse a month to death, like revenge. And it was the end of the month.

Shy Kidneys Show and Rodeo.

The green flyer had had Weanie in one banner, Killer Tom Black in another. The coming showdown had trickled into the diner, even. And Pidgin wanted no part of it. He ducked out behind the waitstaff, leaving the two Navajo men locked together in their flaccid anger, shoulder to shoulder, fighting as old men fight. Pidgin's waitress made eyes behind her order pad and said they were brothers, that this was usual Sunday morning fare for them.

The long order cook was rubbing some defib paddles together to restart their hearts once the match was over; the short order cook was taking bets. The register girl was filing her fingernails. She looked at Pidgin and said she wasn't above fisticuffs herself. Pidgin didn't look back. Coffee cup in hand, he faded into the milling crowd, into the arms of a short Mexican man at the exhibit building door who hissed into his ear that for the price of a tamale he would kill him dead. Pidgin gave him his coffee and hoped it wasn't enough. He was let pass. Inside were nearly two acres of pens and little light. A pig screamed by and then a crewcut Navajo kid, chasing it with his showstick, crying. Pidgin flattened himself against the corrugated tin wall, involuntarily listened to the booth barker on the flipside, hawking his beef-fed-beef, which was double the flavor. Pidgin saw cannibal cattle, a solipsistic food chain, self similar at every link, artificial. He remembered the castrato on the bus calling him a cannibal. He remembered the pigs in the bible. He remembered four stylized heyoka piñadas he'd seen at another stock show, hung by the neck, legs beaten into hard candy, eyes X'd over with electrical tape.

He pushed hard away from that wall, paced himself, made the rounds like he was looking at livestock and not for some fresh hay to lie down in and hide. Near the back corner he found it, occupied by a white-faced Hereford. He stepped in, talking nonsense but keeping his voice even, and squatted down by the sweet feed, picked out the molasses chunks, ate until he was tasting rum then kept on till his muscles were sluggish with it. The Hereford rose, nosed Pidgin out of the way, and Pidgin circled around to the steer's shitwarm place, sat back against the wall again, tried to cover himself with hay that kept sloughing off. Refused to lie down all the way. He had slept enough. He told himself that, threaded it into a song, lullabied himself senseless, four stomachs ruminating above. In their ungulate shadow Custer loomed, scowlfaced, quirt in hand.

Pidgin sat up hard. The steer was either gone or had become industrial-strength hairspray smell. And the noise pollution he had evidently been tuning out for a couple of hours was a bullhorn voice, getting strident. It was waking people in the pens all around, and they were rising to a reserved stance, like prairie dogs tracking a wounded owl slouching their way. The man beside Pidgin was wearing a bottle adhered to the nape of his neck; his ear was spiderwebbed over, thick white. Pidgin rubbed his eyes, focused through the haydust. On the distant wall was the crisp black outline of a man standing in front of a jerky eight-millimeter movie. On her knees in front was the one-woman audience, tightlipped in a beaded-buckskin dress and satin jacket. She was staring at the man's chest, and at first Pidgin thought it was just the movie in miniature that she was watching there, but when the man stepped suavely out of the projector light, Pidgin understood: the man had a banktube like Birdfinger's slung around his neck, stuffed with cash. Ten thousand dollars cash: it had to be. He had a white stripe down the deadcenter of his head, too. Yellow Snow and the Navajo brothers and the telephoto all held hands in mute testimony, pointing him out, and it was so easy for once. Pidgin thanked the *Star* woman from afar, but then cussed her and thanked the salesman instead.

The man with the webbed-over ear burrowed back into his hay.

Something ran over the roof and its footsteps made all the livestock angle their necks heavenward. It ran with four feet, padded like a coyote. The skunkheaded man looked up for a moment too, away from the movie he was offering to the woman who wasn't there for the movie. Still though, it played, plodding through the opening credits about Wean Construction of Clovis New Mexico sweeping down godlike to the glue factory in the mortal form of Atticus Wean—white hairstripe and all—buying the unridden and unridable horse by the pound. It cost him the equivalent of nine bags of dogfood. He paid with a company check. Atticus Wean. The sixth Goliard. He leaned down to the woman, kissed her on the top of the head and couldn't see her lips snarl.

Behind them the movie flickered on, clips spliced together about the horse now renamed Weanie. Atticus Wean pulled himself away from her and did the penside lore in a booming voice, tracing the saddlebronc from its Nordic roots to the Lippezaner training facility to its first stint with fame, fancydancing in neat, equine circles for dukes and duchesses. But it didn't last, couldn't have. Next were the grainy still shots which the woman didn't flinch at when Atticus turned too early to comfort her: Weanie was tearing through a Rotary Club meeting, spinning and kicking, leaving six white men dead or dying. He wasn't destroyed for it. Instead he was imbued with whatever he took from those dead Rotarians; he went tearing across the countryside, leaving dog corpses scattered in his wake, knocking the sides out of livestock trailers, mocking the docile string of contract horses. There was a shot of him by one of them, and he was six hands taller, hooved like a primeval Clydesdale, bleach-white nosetip to tail, nostrils wide. The woman squinted her eyes he was so bright, stood to leave, but Atticus sat her back down, begged her to stay, pointed screenward. There was Weanie surfacing as White Lightning Two at the Calgary rodeo, where he paralyzed his first cowboy; there he was surfacing at Vegas, as Cuts Both Ways, where they barred him after the first go-round, when he got into the stands somehow; there he was in Billings, as Moby Dick, where he was ridden for 6.7 seconds before dragging a Crow's leg off at the knee. In the background of the moving picture, offset from the half-leg dangling from the stirrup, was Tom Black, watching with his devil eyes, fully absorbed.

'He'll never ride him,' Atticus said to the woman in his own voice.

'He'll bend its horse ass over,' the woman said, 'and then kill it dead.'

'It's my damn money.'

'For maybe eight seconds,' she said, then drew close to him, placed her palms on his chest, leaned in, got him off balance, and in a whirl of beads and fringe had the banktube tucked under her arm football style and was running, stiff-arming livestock, Atticus sledding behind on his knees, drawn by the neck, hands made into fists around the leather holding strap. From forty feet out, Pidgin could tell it was a seduction gone awry: she hadn't played doe-eyed squaw to his moneyed Indian, had only been impressed by his technical mastery of the projector, the bullhorn he had somehow kept concealed in his rhinestone jacket. But not by him. When Atticus finally tripped her, they fell together and their struggling shadows were huge and delicate on the wall like a Chinese play. Pidgin watched and forgot the shadows had originals, thought that because they didn't sweat and lie they were of the first order. By the time he retrofigured back to Atticus, Atticus was alone on the ground, buckskin dress in hand, neck raw, banktube still in place. He yelled cusswords after the woman, but they were ineffective. He deliquesced in the projector light, the spent reel slapping the back of the plastic case in derisive applause. 'Fuck you,' Atticus said, and then in a pen nine down from Pidgin, a dark squat man rose on greased joints and clapped ponderously in imitation, his hands driving the air into sound, his thin mouth curled into a thin smile.

The Mexican Paiute.

Pidgin didn't know whether to duck or call him out. He could do neither. He had never seen him this close, this real. But his face was the same as thirteen years ago, and he was still looking at Pidgin, smiling for a brief moment, then turning and fading into nothing all over again. A brief noise at the side door and he was gone. Against the far wall Atticus inhaled some vital piece of his bullhorn and screamed in a battery-assisted croak *not yet, you bastard, not yet,* and then he was scrambling for the door as well. Pidgin vaulted out of the pen, intent, moving loose like the scarecrow he was dressed as, and then he was running after them, not even sure if they were running after each other.

It wasn't so easy anymore.

He ran pinball style for what felt like five minutes, and four nonpaper heyokas fell in behind him, mocking him, his indecision writ large on their faces. One of them snagged a broomstick somewhere and wore it across his shoulders like a cross, like support, and the other three fell into their crow patterns, diving and swooping and finally not being scared. Pidgin hated them. He tried to lose them behind the beef-fed-beef stand, but they were glue, and in shape, or maybe not even breathing people-air. Pidgin was tasting his lungs. He slid to a stop, spun a likely man forcibly around, and was gone before the man could stop him. It hadn't been Atticus. Nobody else mattered. His second time through the vendor row part of Shy Kidneys Show and Rodeo, he stopped and leaned over a hitching post, coughing, the heyokas fake coughing around him, rolling in the dirt with comical pain, pulling the straw from Pidgin's shirt and wearing it in their armpits. A crowd gathered, eddied, then dissipated in swirls of inattention, back to their ubiquitous beer smell. The heyokas went with them. Pidgin didn't mourn. His head was still in motion. He pulled himself a couple of feet above mob-level, balancing on the fifteen-inch tire of a vendor, and tried to see Atticus' rhinestone jacket. But there was nothing, only straw hats, a pregnant woman in a serape, the heyokas filing away in their levis and horizontal stripes, two braided teens standing on top of a camper, slamming beer through an ear trumpet, their breath distorting the air before them. Pidgin envied them their seared insides, their inviobility; he hadn't been expecting the Mexican Paiute until the end of the shitslide. Not now, not yet. He wasn't ready.

'One Goliard at a time,' he said, 'please,' and then the fifteen-inch vendor tire rolled under his weight and he was chin down in the dirt, pulling the last few minutes into him before they became indistinct. The first most pressing image he shied away from. The second most pressing image was Atticus Wean in the absence of the undemure woman, holding his raw neck in such a way that Pidgin had no choice but to reconstruct his father behind and above, knee in the back of Atticus' head, every last bit of his fake weight pulling on both ends of a snake, head and tail. Larry had been the name in the obituary, Larry, not Atticus, not Atticus Wean. Even his dad had said it, wrote it. From the ground Pidgin kicked the aluminum side of the vendor trailer, and the aluminum gave. He didn't bother to run, just waited for reprisal, anticipated it even, but was approached instead by wingtips worn through on the sides, swirled ice cream dripping on their toes. He followed them up, and as the suitlegs widened into massive thighs he found himself again in the presence of the fishbelly-white salesman. The salesman tipped his coke bottle at Pidgin and introduced himself as Litmus, Litmus Jones.

'I know you,' Pidgin said, standing.

'The sweat.'

'The picture.'

'The shelter.'

'Tenderfoot.'

Litmus smiled, helped Pidgin stand, spirited the coke away when Pidgin made a grab for it. He held Pidgin under his arm and steered him away. He pointed to the beef-fed-beef stand, the fifteen year olds hovering around it, said they ate the meat not for the flavor, but for the hallucinogenic side effects of the anti-spongiforms. Litmus told Pidgin not to eat of that. He spoke like a bassoon. Pidgin nodded, but it smelled good, normal, legal. The next stop was the Torus Donuts booth, a dozen glazed. Litmus didn't offer to share; Pidgin didn't ask. He told Litmus he probably had to be going, he was chasing somebody.

'Right this instant?'

'I was taking a break.'

'Is that them up there?'

Litmus pointed at a woman, child in tow. Pidgin said it was a *him*, and no, but still, found it hard to look away. Litmus claimed to know a thing or two about pursuit. Pidgin turned away from the mother and child, looked this salesman up and down, then said he really had to be going, thanks for the no donuts and zero coke.

'And the picture?'

'And the picture, yeah.'

'It's a good one, enit?'

'Not good enough.'

'Oh, but you're in hot pursuit.' Litmus swivelled his head secret-agent style, which required him to get down in the stance. Pidgin gathered his spit and strung it from his mouth, broke if off with his middle finger.

'You're not that funny,' he said.

Litmus shrugged.

'I'm in a serious chase.'

'Yeah, I saw you and your four friends. Some serious business there.'

'Fuck you.'

'You really want to catch this...'

'Larry. Atticus.'

'...this Larry Atticus?'

Pidgin nodded yes, but wouldn't say why when asked, because he'd played too many games already, with too many people. Litmus kept him under his arm, steered a different direction, said again that he knew a thing or two about pursuit, and one of those things was that you needed a good nose dog, first and foremost.

'A dog?'

Litmus nodded, stepped behind the exhibition building, checked to see if they'd been followed. They hadn't been. In the shade of the building were some dilapidated pens, roofed over. There was a door. Litmus presented it to Pidgin. Pidgin knocked and an eye-level slit slid back, asking what already?

Pidgin looked to Litmus. Litmus nodded go ahead. Pidgin said he was a cowboy. The eyes on the other side laughed, said it was a goddamn rodeo, looks like he's at the right place. Then they drew close to the slit, whispered that that was *his* line, capice? Pidgin held his hands up, palm out, apologized, waited for the words to come through the slit: 'I am a *cow*boy.' Pidgin answered that he was an *In*dian. The voice said good, this was a powwow. He was in the right place. The door creaked open, shut behind them, and inside it smelled like sweat and dollar bills. And dogs. Overbred German Shepherds with lead weights tied to their tails and dyed-black water to drink, to make them wolflike. But they were the right size: feet like saucers, ribs gaunt, wary in the eye. Pidgin said he didn't want a dog, he'd find Larry with his own nose. He didn't have any money anyways.

Litmus said you don't always need money. He pulled one of the handlers over, asked what were the odds?

'On the next one?'

'On the next one.'

'Even money.'

Litmus asked Pidgin if they were in, if Pidgin really wanted to catch this Larry Atticus?

Pidgin looked around, told Litmus it was either Larry or Atticus, not both. 'And I'm not much of a gambler, either,' he said. 'I'll pick the loser.'

'Sounds like a bet.'

'It's not.'

'You're on.'

In the first fight Pidgin chose the dog that started on the right. The two dogs circled each other like choreography, like a spirograph, and had their legs all coiled to spring when the left one began dry hacking. It threw up fourteen fluorescent pills, half digested. Its handler couldn't take the resulting limelight they cast him in: in two long steps and a vault he was gone, his backside splattered with chili and sugar flecked tomatoes. Everyone kept their frybread. The two dogs lapped up the vomit side by side, litterkin. After some heated discussion on what would have happened had the fight gone on, complete with idle pictures drawn in the sand of the two dogs' respective sideboards of moves and tactics and records, the left dog was declared the winner by default.

'See?' Pidgin said, and didn't know for sure whether he was into Litmus or Litmus was into him. Either way, and before he could stop himself, he'd said it: double or nothing. Litmus accepted, and then an old man and a young man came forward, sticks in hand, and traced out the record of the next fight, and the one after that, complete with orated stats and vials of colored sand that everyone seemed to have on their person. There was no longer any need for the physical presence of the wolf dogs. They huddled together in back, growling and weaving. Pidgin was consumed. He bet on the dirt dogs with his eyes closed, trying to pick the loser in order to win, uncertain even whether Litmus was playing by the same regression anymore. But it didn't matter so much: there was a stick-game song being adapted and adapted well, and he could almost remember it, in whatever tongue.

For two hours they played. Pidgin kept telling Litmus he had a chase to get back to. But he couldn't leave: he was down to his boots and underwear and nothing else; he'd been betting straight bets on the side, in hopes of counterbalancing his winning losses to Litmus. He told Litmus it happened every last time he put his money down. Litmus smiled, said *what money?* then left his red handprint on Pidgin's bare shoulder and pushed his way to the middle of the crowd, stepping onto the fighting area like he owned the colored sand there. The old man handed Litmus his stick with reverence, as if returning it; the young man bristled.

Pidgin smiled with nerves.

All around him money was changing hands, the handlers betting their dogs' registration papers, Pidgin's new and slightly torn wranglers making the rounds. It was almost dark. A floodlight came on and the group stilled, one man saying this barn had never been electrified before that he knew of. But it was now. The moths gathered, cast shadows on the dirt where the figure of an old old buffalo bull twice dead already was appearing under Litmus' stick. The bristly young man across from Litmus drew a midwinter pack of wolfdogs in response, the last mooncalf two weeks ago already. At some point all betting stopped and the stories and sounds began, the old bull bellowing fear, looking side to side at the coulee it'd backed into, the wolf dogs fanning out through the downwind trees. Pidgin, because the last round was always all or nothing and this had to be the last round, talked the handler to his left into taking a late bet on the bull. The odds were seven to one, because there were seven wolves. The handler called Pidgin a long shooter, a fifty-caliber man; he settled the sights of his fake Sharps on the old bull, pulled the trigger, ba bam.

Pidgin moved to a different part of the crowd, away from the handler and his fake gun, and the fight began, slow at first—the stories of the bull and wolfdogs dovetailing at uncomfortable angles—but then quicker, one dog clamping nimbly onto the bull's ratty tail, the next two lighting on his back, the bull trying in vain to reach them.

He fell to his knees—Litmus too. Pidgin looked to the motionless representation of the bull in the dirt and realized the outcome had been there all the time in the initialmost lines, in the drawing sticks themselves. All that was left now was the drama, all that was ever left was the drama. He should have seen it. He should have always seen it. He wasn't a real gambler; he began looking for the door, but suspected many eyes were keeping tabs on his boots. He turned back to the fight, to the old bull breathing pink froth, trying to stand. It wasn't good to watch. It hurt, even: seven to one. Pidgin didn't know what he would owe the handler when judgment came, and he didn't want to know.

He breathed in and yelled for the falling bull until his teeth hurt, until the rest of the men were yelling against him, until everything was undifferentiated noise, and then without warning the stories were swept away: the young man, lips pulled back from his teeth, dove into Litmus, and Litmus bellowed and rolled with the attack, shifted his weight and threw the man into the wall. It rattled. A bridle fell to a lower nail like a huge spider moving slow. The man came again then, growling, dove into Litmus and emerged spitting ear pieces, wiping them on the back of his forearm. Litmus pinched his slacks up over his thighs, blew, then leaned forward and charged, all business. The man took a shoulder under the ribcage that lifted him into the hayloft, where he limped back and forth, exchanging ends quick like a flipturn, like a wolf. Litmus scratched his left scapula on the wall, and was trying to disentangle his suit jacket from a nail when one of the handlers kicked his boots off and attacked in sock feet. Litmus was helpless, pinned, and his weakened state drew five others to him.

Pidgin watched it happen, and it occurred to him that he hadn't called out a warning, that he wasn't helping, that they had come here for him in the first place. It occurred to him the frame of mind Litmus might be in if he made it out, and that he still probably owed Litmus things he didn't have. Among other people. He decided to leave. He kept close to the wall, the alpha male above watching him from his hidden place. Three of the seven men-as-dogs-as-wolves staggered out of the fray bleeding; two of them wandered back in. The old man was in the corner taking his insulin. He offered the thin needle to Pidgin, but Pidgin didn't have time: he was unburdening an unconscious man of his ribbon shirt, then taking his oversized levis as well.

Clothes underarm, he opened the door. Litmus bellowed a congested bellow and Pidgin didn't look back, couldn't, because he knew he'd see black horns wet with blood and would have to carry that with him too. He dressed fast, leaning on the pens, and was approached stealthily by the dog that had thrown up pharmaceuticals. He instinctively put his back to the wall and told the dog he was sorry. He tried walking away holding his pants up by the front, but the dog paced him, dragging its rope.

'I've already got one like you,' Pidgin said over his shoulder. 'I keep him in my suitcase, okay? You weren't my idea, anyways.'

The dog threw up some more in response. Pidgin looked away. The salesman's harsh breathing was muted now, a long ways off. He was quarenciaed. Pidgin listened for the sound of his heavy body falling, but heard only struggling feet and then, closer, the door beside him getting nosed open, spilling small light. The rest of the dogs filed out, belly to ground, ears flattened, noses wet with this new world. They carried themselves without sound to the exhibition building, where the prescient among the sheep were already screaming. Pidgin smiled, told the pharmaceutical dog a thing or two about pursuit: he explained Larry aka Atticus Wean—rhinestones, bullhorn, skunkhair, Indian beard—and said he'd have the scent of money about him, behind him. Ten thousand dollars. He did his fingers like a trail along the ground. The dog didn't follow. Pidgin shook his head, reached for the dog with a vague pity-pet, but got snapped at, forced into respect. He backed away slow, bantering nonsense, tying the torn beltloops of the levis together for support, telling the dog about Larry and Larry's scent, then completing the joke the salesman had started by reaching into his pocket for cash he didn't have, for the dog to sample. To continue the chase. But the joke wasn't over: his hand came up out of the loose pocket with two-hundred dollars in fives, and three sets of registration papers. Pidgin looked at the money in wonder, instinctively threw ten dollars at the dog, and when it went loping off, the dog, money in stomach, Pidgin found himself lagging behind, picking through the regurgitated pills with a twig.

He shook his head no twice and made himself walk away.

He had two hundred dollars now. A hundred and ninety. He could pay for it. And he would. Screw the salesman's dog. He would find Larry himself, later, at the last go-round, the showdown, the exhibition match. Right now there was the matter of forbidden cowmeat to attend to. Pidgin counted to ten and stepped back into the people flitting from stand to stand as if trying to hold on, trying not to be swept away. After a few hesitant crowd-testing steps, he found himself in an alleyway walled by bodies, a deadspace left by the dog moving silently through the unconscious, between legs and strollers. It was the path of least resistance. He followed, passed the turkey remains, the chili dogs, the three different breeds of frybread, the sundance booth where a white woman would either massage your chest with novocaine then pierce you with twin diaper-size safety pins or go the economy route, brand you with a hotshot and give you a Dick Harris cap, name inverted like a phonebook listing. Around the booth Indian men were comparing chicken-pox scars and telling stories about deep scratching, craters and keratin. Pidgin remembered how it'd felt, then didn't, was still following the dog running in whisper mode, going unnoticed but felt, going somewhere. Maybe towards Larry and his moneysmell. Maybe even the Mexican Paiute. Pidgin stutterstepped with the Mexican Paiute unwanted in his head, fell back to an even more discrete distance, and then the dog alerted, hit hyperspace, and disappeared. The crowd swelled shut and began breathing up all of Pidgin's air. The one landmark he could make out directly ahead was the beef-fed-beef stand wavering like salvation, like the dog had known and led him to it. His momentum carried him forward.

At the booth tension was high. The vendor was nervous, making no sudden moves: the dog was standing hip-level behind the counter, taking over the place with non-verbal threats. There was a moneybox involved. Pidgin pretended not to know the dog. It wasn't hard. He bought three pounds at ten dollars per, left the vendor to be ransomed by someone else, and ate mechanically under the stands of the arena, listening to the pounding hooves of the barrel racers. The meat was salty, denser than beef, and it numbed his gums, made his eyes water. For the second time that day though, he was full, and for the first time he was under the influence of anti-spongiform hallucinogenics.

He knew very little.

He was thirsty, that was the first thing.

There was a bar on wheels. He'd seen it. He transported himself there, shook the beefstand paper bag off his hand at the bar, kept slinging his arm until the goateed bouncer guided his hand down for him and hooked his thumb through the levi beltloop. He smiled like the devil. Pidgin nodded thanks, then laughed at the edges of some joke the bartender was telling that began with *these four skins* and ended suddenly trap-door style with *an antibacterial handjob!* It had nothing in the middle that Pidgin could make out, no connective tissue, no steps to follow. The beginning and the end just slammed together. The bartender asked him what-the-hell-was-so-funny-chief?, and Pidgin moved down a few stools, standard procedure. He laid his money on the bar and bought two rounds of whiskey with water back. The difference between the two was trivial. Every time someone touched him, he coughed.

He sat, watched. The vendor had translated beef-fed-beef for him into Indian, called it double-slow elk. Pidgin's anger came minutes after the fact, passed. There was still almost a hundred and fifty dollars in his pocket. He transported himself to the bathroom and there were no urinals, no toilets, no sinks, just a grating-as-floor, set up on cinderblocks. Steam rose around him; he breathed it once and then held his breath, let it out back at the bar, where there was a woman with either hepatitis or jaundice: yellow eyes, sallow skin, bony hips. She was wearing a HEAVY PETTING t-shirt tight across her breasts; under the bar she was doing the handjive in some cowboy's pants. It took little attention. She made conversation with Pidgin.

'Kutenai,' he said when asked, then Clovis, lambskinner, twenty-two. Yes no maybe. He felt milked when it was over. She said she was mostly from Isleta, and that she was on break from the warpaint stand. Pidgin could see through her shirt the tribal tattoo under her collarbone. It was intricate, Mesoamerican, three days' worth at least. She said don't ask. He didn't. She told him she had many names, but they all boiled down to her personality: Unshy.

Pidgin said he was Spiderman.

She tried and failed to contain herself when he showed her the memory of his webshooters, his middle and ring fingers moving in slow motion to his upturned palm, sapping every last bit of his attention. Her laughter straightened the backs of those around her. Pidgin saw it happen a muscle at a time. He asked her if she was the middle part of the joke, and she said she was just laughing from pity, but she had what he needed. He gave her fifty of his dollars, one five at a time. She tucked it in her jeans vegas-style with a stray coathanger, then whispered something to the cowboy she was nonchalantly pulling off. The cowboy closed his eyes and shot all up under the bar. She walked away with his wallet, nodded for Pidgin to tag along. He did. She ran her wet hand along the shirtbacks of everyone bellied up to the bar and they just grunted, didn't turn around. Pidgin expected them to break into song at any moment. He expected many things. As they left the bar-trailer he told her he was chasing someone named Larry. She said she didn't know him herself, but she did know a thing or two about pursuit.

Pidgin stopped with those words, watching her recede, *letting* her recede, wishing her on. He didn't need any more help, any more prodding. He knew all he wanted to about pursuit. She was ten inches tall already. A six-foot man stepped between Pidgin and her. He had sterilized safety pins through his chest and the pins were beaded and he was showing off how many grams of fishing weight and goose feathers he'd tied on. Pidgin shoved him hard for the disturbance he needed, then made a sly getaway into a series of booths that yawed and creaked and ultimately dead-ended at hers. The warpaint stand. She was there waiting. She guided him into one of the two empty barber chairs. His face rose closer to the canvas ceiling, one pump at a time. To his immediate left were her shirtcolored breasts, prehensile nipples; to his right was her palette. He closed his eyes and tried to start over, tried to eat the beef-fed-beef slower, long enough that a lemonade cart came by and he then had no need of the bar, of her. It didn't work; he couldn't let go of the joke he'd nearly got and was nearly getting.

Shuffling feet entered the booth from another door, then there was a man-shape under wraps in the second chair like an overgrown homunculus. Pidgin was morgue-sheeted himself. There was a hand in his pants, hers. It was casual. His pores filled with paint and his face lost all expression. She said she was glad to get out of taco hatland for a few minutes. Pidgin nodded that he was too. She said the first thing about pursuit was that you needed a good disguise. Pidgin said he thought the first thing you needed was a dog. She said dogs don't disguise well. While part of Pidgin's face was drying she picked straw out of his hair, flicked it away like lice. She painted with smaller and smaller brushes, down to a single horsehair. She took her hand out of Pidgin's pants and straddled him, dry-humping slow, her hand now holding his cheekskin tight for the brush.

'What are you making me into?' Pidgin asked.

She said she was getting him ready, painting his outside white so it would match his insides. She said it tonelessly, and Pidgin was half unsure what she was calling him. He said he wasn't really Spiderman. He fumbled with his pants to prove it with dusky foreskin, but was weak, uncoordinated, sluggish. She said Spiderman was red on the outside too. 'If you were real Flathead or whatever,' she said, 'then

I wouldn't have this many clothes on still, okay? That's how you'd know.' She dry-humped him with emphasis through the plastic sheet. She was treating him like the cowboy in the bar. The white cowboy in the bar.

Pidgin said he had a chase to get back to.

She asked if he was going to read sign like a real Indian.

'Fuck you already,' Pidgin said.

She laughed and Pidgin's back straightened, and he imagined driving himself up into her, using the plastic sheet as prophylactic, proving his Indianness. He was so hard it hurt. She smiled. Pidgin could hear the lines in her face. She said if he raped her, that would make him even more white.

Pidgin disagreed.

She said his bone structure wasn't shaped by commodity food.

Pidgin argued potted meat and contraband Dr Pepper.

She said he probably didn't have diabetes.

Pidgin made a face like his pancreas hurt.

She doubted whether he even knew his enrollment number.

Pidgin gave her line one, Dorphin Studios front office.

She said it had too many numbers and not enough letters.

She said he was generic, a movie Indian.

She said he probably couldn't even play basketball.

Pidgin tried not to hear her, but she refused to stop, was talking now about the new skin test. Pidgin said he'd pass a color chart any day of the week. She laughed again, shook her head no, said it was a question that was more of an easy-to-follow instruction, really: draw a composite sketch of what you used to think you might look like if you'd been born white.

The dry-hump friction was hurting now.

Pidgin didn't have any answers. 'My mom was Indian,' he said.

'Then it probably stopped there, cowboy.'

She tapped him then on the forehead with the butt end of her paintbrush, said she was finished, no hard feelings. Pidgin pushed against her through the plastic sheet and said he still had some hard feelings to get over.

She smiled, dismounted, said do something about it then.

Pidgin tried. He rolled out of the chair in a lysergic stupor, stumbled after her. The rush of circulation rekindled the beef-fed-beef inside him. The booth was a haze. He had been manipulated into small pieces and broadcast like seedcorn. She finally let herself be caught, waited against the wall for him, feigning helplessness, corneredness. When he shoved his hand down the front of her pants, she whispered in his ear that *that* was more like it, and he nearly came, which would have been some more of him scattered around the booth.

He closed his eyes and turned away.

She was already gone.

He felt in his pocket and his money was too. He wanted to yell after her that that proved he was Indian, that he'd fed ten dollars to a dog and had nothing to show for the other one-ninety. All in under thirty minutes, too. He slid down the wall and tried to collect himself, piece himself back together. It wasn't so easy. His face wasn't skin anymore, but paint. In the mirror he was halogen white, colorless, a mime. And it wouldn't come off, not in the sink, not with a towel, not under his fingernails. He found her palette by touch, dug out a small brush, a tube of black ink. He applied it first to his lips and then made a star around his right eye and colored it in, eyelid and all. A Paul Stanley disguise. It wasn't the first time. He wished she were still here, the unshy woman, to see what he'd done. He told her out loud to go to hell, and then began squeezing her paint out into crayon-looking turds on the floor. He used both hands; his mouth was full of caps. He spit them out one by one, and then a voice from behind asked if petty vandalism made him feel any less the disillusioned caucasian. Pidgin didn't say yes or no. He recognized the voice, though: in the mirror the overgrown homunculus was standing, folding his sheet with military precision, snapping the edges. His face was painted in a cruel smile, eyes pulled down in the middle, overblown tearducts. Bandywine the rodeo clown.

Pidgin didn't say hello.

Bandywine said two things, holding his gloved fingers up for clarification—stay away from his wife's supplies, and Paul Stanley is no Indian—and then in a shuffle of his huge feet he was gone, running. Everybody always running. Pidgin closed his eyes for just a moment, gathering resolve, and then continued the chase, tracking Bandywine by the clap of his rag-stuffed shoes against the packed dirt. They ran back past all the booths, past the charnel house of an exhibition building, past the pens. At the arena gate another clown was waving them on. Bandywine raced through and went into a tumble routine; Pidgin ducked left at the last second, pulling himself up into the stands. The audience made a pocket for him, around him. He sat, cradling his tender-blue balls, wondering what an inch-square negative of himself sitting in the stands might look like right now, lights and darks reversed through the magic of make-up. Maybe that's what the unshy woman had been getting at. But maybe he was already too old for it to count. Maybe it was too late. Pidgin hated her.

Beside him was an abandoned bag of beef-fed-beef. All around Pidgin was abandoned food and drinks, as if left for the dead. But this was general seating. Pidgin ate the beef, drank the warm beer, watched the round dance going on below and at first thought he'd sat in those people's places, was eating their food, but then saw Bandywine and his helper clown goosestepping on the in-side of the dancers and understood: the audience thought he was one of them, that he was involved in the mocking. It was the face paint and the oversized levis. He didn't try to explain. From the opposite side of the stands a group of fifteen year old longhairs were headbanging, hands and fingers in the air, elbows locked. It was for Pidgin, for Paul Stanley.

The beef-fed-beef was dense, but he was getting used to it.

The round dance went on and on, spiraling in tighter and tighter on Bandywine and the other clown, playing Cavalry and Indians, Greasy Grass. It was a massacre. The drum measured it. In the halflight of dusk fourteen bullbats dove at the traditional dancers' plumes and roaches, and it rained porcupine quills. When it was full night the riderless horse came out dragging the harrows, erasing the round dance, and the dancers filed away. In their absence the arena went black for three long minutes and then two crossbeams spotlit the announcer on his scaffolding, a Tony Clifton lookalike with band-aids for eyebrows. Sitting beside him, jacket aglitter, was Larry aka Atticus Wean, banktube in place for the big showdown.

Shy Kidneys Show and Rodeo.

It had all come down to this go-round: man versus horse. It began slow, with Tony Clifton whispering names and rankings, Larry intent upon the section of bleachers Pidgin was at the wrong angle to see. Pidgin tried to follow Larry's gaze, but suddenly people were standing in anger, in laughter, because Tony Clifton was whining about Indian rodeos, about the wild west in general. He said he was an Auslander, then stood there shining in the heat of the twin spotlights, trying to read names from his list and reading them wrong, unable to distinguish the riders from the horses. He could get as far as knowing that Dago Red and Dutch Oven were in the chute, but couldn't tell who was riding who. It was the same with Bushy Head and Braided Tail, Hump and Old Man, Runs Back and Fool Bird, No Vitals and One Ear, Crow Hopper and New Jim. Pidgin thought it was all part of the Tony Clifton act, but then the mic-power was cut midsentence, and the riders who knew who they were rode the horses who knew they were horses, rode them in spite of the words that said otherwise, in spite of the unresponsive audience. The silence they rode through was the silence left when the collective ire directed at Tony Clifton had resettled into apathy. The chutes swung open with no intake of breath, the eight-second horn blared without a cathartic sigh, the fancy dismounts went unapplauded. The people were saving themselves for the showdown, dispassionately enduring the ungentle foreplay that led to it. None of the riders were Tom Black, and none of the horses were Weanie. And their ride would be all that mattered.

Power was restored to Tony Clifton's mic for it.

The previous rider was being stretchered away face-down, his left spur lodged in rectal tissue. Tony Clifton grimaced over the PA, then said the Indian always gets it up the ass, no? It was an apology; his band-aided eyebrows drew together in supplication. A woman below Pidgin yelled back what would he know about that, white eyes? Tony Clifton replied in a somber tone that he was Wayne Newton's second cousin by marriage. Pidgin wasn't sure whether it was small slander against Wayne Newton or a claim to comfortably distant Indian blood. Either way it was accepted; people laughed around their beer because they didn't get it, and Tony Clifton read from a hastily-prepared index card, paying reluctant homage to the sponsors and paying most of it to A-1 Auto Salvage of Albuquerque New Mexico. He asked for a round of applause for their representative here tonight—the beautiful Salvage Queen—and Larry was the first to bring his hands together for the woman rising from the area he had been watching. Pidgin could barely make her out: old and nondescript, thick and grey, wrapped in enough shawls that she couldn't have a corporeal middle. Her face was dark and deeply lined, had years of sunlight folded into it. Pidgin clapped with Larry, who was clapping with desperate speed and force, like he was afraid, like he could clap the vision of her away.

When the applause was over, a late family who didn't know any better sat in the deadspace around Pidgin. The children stared. Pidgin stared back. One of them feinted with his head like a cat and Pidgin flinched into the new old man beside him. Beer was spilled between them. The old man creaked his neck around to Pidgin and said today was the day the Indian would ride the white man back into the ground once and for all. It would begin here. Pidgin followed his crooked finger, and it pointed to Weanie being paraded around the arena, dazzling white, highstepping, mane and tail uncut. One of his forelocks was already caked with blood and dirt. Tony Clifton said he'd maimed an Indian pony back in the pens. The crowd rose, booing, throwing whatever was at hand: plastic cups, broken watches, pacifiers.

Larry smiled, pulled his rhinestone jacket together at the neck, and Pidgin knew then that it was bulletproof. When Tom Black appeared, straddling the pipe railing, never taking his hat off, the PA simulated wooden mallets upon sheet metal. From fifty yards out Tom Black pointed a steady finger at Larry's banktube, and Larry tucked it into his jacket. The crowd writhed with anticipation; Pidgin lobbed his empty sack into the arena and it was one of many. Tony Clifton fell all over himself with words, and his mic was cut again. He had been out of character, involved in the wild west, calling for espontaneos and laughing when there were none, only his own caustic voice, resisting, saying this is bullshit, there aren't any legends like this, this isn't how they're made.

But it was; Pidgin was part of it. He stood with the crowd, held his breath when Tom Black lost his footing over the chute, breathed out with Weanie when they pulled the cinch tight and tighter, until Tom Black nodded enough, enow. It was time. The two replacement clowns setting up styrofoam crosses-as-grave markers scuttled over the fence and then the bottlerockets trailed sparks across the sky and finally the chute swung open, spilling horse and rider into the dirt hooves first, already in motion. For a full eight seconds, Pidgin forgot he was painted. He stood on his seat and yelled as Weanie spun right then left, changing direction midjump. Tom Black angled his body and followed, his spurs flaying Weanie's shoulder skin away in inch thick strips. It was art. Women were crying, babies were screaming with anger, men were bleeding internally from pesticides and cigarettes and feeling no pain from it. The rush circulated faster and faster through the bleachers. Weanie spun, kicked, nosed dirt up into the air, and Tom Black held on, one arm raised, the other light on the hackamore, constantly adjusting. Weanie slammed hard into the railing and one of Tom Black's boots cocked out at a wrong angle, ceased raking. But he didn't let go. The next jump, Weanie came up breathing something black, slinging it from his nostrils. It looped through the air for hours. People got lost in its motion, moved their shoulders with it, and then it hit the dirt and rolled itself into a tube snake. Suddenly there were only two seconds left. In them Weanie reared Silver-style, bucked into the air off his hindlegs, all four feet clear of the ground, and then twisted, starting the motion with his head, screaming, floating, hanging aboveground long enough for people to write songs about it, this.

And then it ended: Weanie came down hard on his back, came down with all his horse weight on Tom Black. Fifteen hundred pounds and then some. Pidgin felt his eyes heat up and didn't understand. The eight-second horn blared. The audience quieted, and in the lack of noise Weanie rolled, tried to stand once, then did, and Tom Black was still there, his arm driven down past the saddle, deeper, his gloved hand tight around Weanie's spine, the rest of him lifeless and lolling and crushed. But the forearm muscles were locked, a deathgrip. Weanie bucked like a spasm, walked a few feet, stood in the face of equine science and bled from the nose. No pictures were taken. No music played over the PA. Shit ran down Weanie's hindquarters, and then the back half of his body followed, pulling the rest of him down. He fell with Tom Black amid the styrofoam crosses. It was a boothill postcard, a half mile past the end of the trail. The old man beside Pidgin said *now*, and when he said it Pidgin expected the ground to open up and swallow rider and horse the same. But it didn't. The old man refused to look away, though. The spotlights remained on Tom Black and Weanie. Across the arena, the longhairs had their lighters going.

It was over. Eight seconds.

All that was left was for Larry to get caught trying to sneak down the scaffolding. Under duress, he threw the banktube in the direction of the two bodies. It rubberbanded back to his waiting hand. The elastic was cut and he threw it again. This time it opened and the cash went every direction, and the crowd became individual people fighting their way over the rail, their fingers blind with desire. The dirt they stomped up settled on Tom Black and Weanie, coating them, covering them with a brown veneer which made of them one body. The centauric image aged in fits and starts. The old man beside Pidgin smiled, contented.

'Now,' he said. He looked at Pidgin, shook his head in acceptance of the day, and left with his grandchildren.

A twenty-dollar bill blew Pidgin's way, and Pidgin collected it.

Shy Kidneys Show and Rodeo. It was time for an exit. There was nothing else. Pidgin ducked out the way he'd come in, chasing no one, sure he could find Larry aka Atticus Wean in the yellow pages if he needed to, if he decided to, if he ever made it back to Clovis again. But he would. He knew. He stopped to gather some spilled ice and was rubbing his face with it when he looked through his fingers and saw that the night wasn't over yet: there was the Salvage Queen being helped down the next ramp. She was on the elbow of the Mexican Paiute, and his posture showed a deference Pidgin couldn't reconcile with the image of him stealing away, a corpse slung easy across his shoulders. They locked eyes as they had to, and the Mexican Paiute bared his filed teeth to be seen in such a vulnerable state. But he couldn't run this time. Not without letting the Salvage Queen fall. He continued to walk, slow and away, shawl tips whipping in his wake. Pidgin stood, watched, trying to understand, and when they were past followed them for a few hesitant steps then lost his nerve and turned away. Not yet.

Maybe if the Salvage Queen hadn't been there. Maybe if the Mexican Paiute's upper legs didn't look so familiar.

Pidgin walked in circles, rubbing his face with ice and getting nowhere with it.

No one talked to him. No one said anything. One woman walked by with a square of white horseflesh, spurcut, rowel-edged. A wolf dog was following her. Pidgin left the rodeo grounds, kicked a timeless hole in the dirt and tried to shit out all the anti-spongiforms he had in him but couldn't even begin. In the dark with the bushes his eyes played psychotropic tricks. He used his ears instead, followed the seven year old sound of You Look So Pretty When I'm Naked. It led to a circle of campers and pickups and canvas tepees grouped around a makeshift stage, planks and barrels. The song was dovetailing with the 49s starting up two camp circles over. Pidgin approached, was met by a blind man with pink socks who was already haunting him. He was let pass. He was joined even. The blind man held onto his elbow, nodded towards the sound of the stage where Birdfinger, wearing Pidgin's dad's Mexican-heeled boots, was sitting on a three-legged stool with his five-stringed guitar.

'Let's do it,' the blind man croaked, leaning into it like he'd ever been young, and Pidgin the Glutton walked in, following the outside of the oval dance floor, the inside of the campers. He was seeing Birdfinger from all sides; he wasn't just wearing the boots. He also had on the many holed belt with SUBSTANCE ABUSER tooled into the nameplate. The belt and the boots were a set; the buckle was hidden by new belly fat. Birdfinger's t-shirt read 2003 MINUS 25. It was as old as Pidgin almost. He told himself to breathe. Misstepped when the song changed from You Look So Pretty When I'm Naked to Feeling Bonny. From his left a woman's scratchy voice said *thank you*, and the old man's grip loosened as he accepted the thanks and the dollar bill that came with it. Pidgin followed the appreciation and the retracting arm, and it was the leopard woman at her own card table, unaged, a pile of cigarette ash piled before her, each side a delicate thirty-two degrees and holding.

'Hello,' she said. 'Long time, hun.'

Pidgin nodded, sat when the chair beside her was offered. Here he was. They watched Birdfinger in silence. He was Deaf Smith tonight, on a stool on top of the world. He played Polled by Death and said it was in loving memory of his long-lost brother. His voice cracked. The leopard woman laughed a derisive laugh.

'Ask me to tell you a story,' she said.

'Tell me a story,' Pidgin said.

She did.

'Your mother,' she said, 'your mother she was beautiful in her own Indian way. I'll give her that. Your father loved her, at least. Do you even know what she looked like? Good. You've got something like her around the nose, I don't know. And of course the hair and the skin, good God. Even with that awful paintjob.' The leopard woman paused, crushed out her cigarette, allowed Pidgin to light the next one, as if testing that they still knew each other that well. 'Ask me why,' she said.

'Why what?'

'Why she died.'

Pidgin unfolded the empty cigarette carton mechanically and began rubbing a hole in one of the corners, a hole to see through. He didn't ask Why, was afraid she'd say because she had you.

There was Birdfinger, huge, singing, eyes wet with stage life, fingers sure.

The leopard woman regarded Pidgin, answered anyway. 'She died because the human frame can't support the weight of a truck. Ask me about the truck.'

Pidgin rubbed the carton between the nails of his thumb and index finger, trying to make a hole, something to crawl out of. 'Was it his truck?' he asked dutifully, nodding once towards Birdfinger.

The leopard woman looked stageward and said no. It was Cline's truck, the Thunderbird Ford. 'He put it back together,' she said, 'while you were gestating in the *Star*. It's that same one. And then he died in it too.'

'I know how.'

'Yes.'

'I don't want to know why.'

'But you do.'

They watched Birdfinger together, and he was in his element, the pagan groove, unaware of New Mexico vast and penetrable all around him. 'Ask me,' the leopard woman said.

'Why are you doing this?'

'Because now he's with her and not with me, Pidge. There's a noticeable lack of justice in our immediate area.'

Pidgin watched a line of ash cascade down her pile without sound.

'Ask me,' she said.

Pidgin held the carton to his right eye like a second mask. There was paper fuzz around the spyhole frame. He licked it down. He didn't ask, and then he did, his voice involuntary, betraying him. The leopard woman flicked her cigarette Birdfinger's direction. 'Marty fucking Robbins is why,' she said. 'It was fratricide. I promise you that.'

Through the spyhole Birdfinger was manageable, in focus.

The leopard woman held the bridge of her nose and recited. Because Pidgin was empty, her story filled him. She said it was a record of the last two weeks, of Cline's last two weeks. Pidgin nodded with the rosewood neck of Birdfinger's guitar. Birdfinger was introducing his next old song, Filibuster, a cheap take on The Cowboy in the Continental Suit, redone from the horse's point of view. The horse was self-named in Birdfinger's version, delusional, and longwinded as thoroughbreds are. It was a Marty Robbins ditty. The leopard woman held fast to her nosebridge, holding the song at bay, and said that Pidgin's father wasn't perfect, she wouldn't have had him if he was. She was no spring chicken and all, not even then. But Pidgin's father had been imperfect in a different way altogether.

It wasn't Vietnam, and it wasn't Marina, not really— or, not *first*. It was more the genetic imprint of his own father, Hardwick the stripmining foreman. That was where Cline got his insides turned around, if Pidgin wanted to know, where he got intimate with Revelations: Hardwick used to read it aloud through hollow-cored closet doors and say he saw things like that in the mineshafts, that it was all underground, building—that he was uncovering it bit by bit, the end of the world. He held it in his hands and knew its number, its atomic weight. Cline listened because he was firstborn, had to bear the brunt of duty, the weight of generations, then forgot it all on purpose, out of fear, then listened again, watching the closet door swell and recede in anticipation. He weighed each word against reality.

That was why all the post offices: in the years after the war Cline had become sure there was some pipeline of apocalyptic apocrypha circulating underground, through New Mexico and all over the world, coded messages about the end, the time and the manner. Everything else was just happenstance.

'Not my mother,' Pidgin said, aware of who he was saying it to. The leopard woman's pupils narrowed to slits. The card table was suddenly between them.

'Your mother,' she said for the second time already, 'your mother was trying to steal foil-wrapped car payments from a drop box when your father met her. He wouldn't have noticed her otherwise. Not if she hadn't been bent over.'

'This isn't a story,' Pidgin said back to her, all the while conceiving grand designs against her ashpile. In them he was a receding figure, she a Pompeii husk soon to collapse into the foreground. He rose to leave and find an appropriate bellows and a pint of glue, but before he could manage an escape, the leopard woman had pulled him back down, said she wasn't finished with him, not yet. Her hand on his leg had been almost maternal. He'd called her *mother* once years ago, to appease her. He told himself that: to appease her. Not because he'd needed to. He redirected his attention. Birdfinger was into My Heroes Have Always Killed Cowboys now, the verses spooling out. The dancing lovers were becoming mere two steppers under his spell, and dropping into chairs from exhaustion. One couple was leaning into each other, asleep on their feet. The leopard woman let Pidgin light her another cigarette and asked did he want to know the cause and effect part, then?

Pidgin shrugged himself smaller. He'd dropped the carton already. He half knew anyways: the last two weeks, implied fratricide, the sketch he'd found under the couch at the trailer. The leopard woman said she was going to dummy it down for him: the situation was that Cline's upbringing made him particularly susceptible to tales about the end of the world. He was hardly discriminating either. She said that was just character setting though, psychological landscape. She formed her words from smoke. 'The cause,' she said, 'the *cause* of your father doing what he did to himself in his truck was that your miscarriage of an uncle took something Cline couldn't replace—yes, you know already? Your mother, Marina. His three years with her, wiped clean, rewritten. He made her into a stranger. I'm sorry to tell you like this, Pidge, sincerely I am.'

She paused, looking past Pidgin, and when she began again, saying she was there just after so she knew the truth of it, Pidgin saw it happening. He knew what his dad looked like back then: yellow-haired, asymmetrically freckled, everything not Indian. Birdfinger the same, mister spitting image. His mother he had to extract from the telephoto, walk her into motion until she could do it alone, then let her sit on the couch in the trailer one night when his father was miles away, poring over letters by flashlight. Her hair was still half over her face, though there was no wind. She was staring at the wall, uncrying. As happens, then, her irregular breathing drew lurkers, *a* lurker: there was Birdfinger on the porch, collecting himself, throwing an off-brand beer bottle end over end into the scrub brush. Before it fell he was in the door. WWI was still a year away or more. The leopard woman was still working the school cafeteria in Jal, doling out child-size servings of goulash.

Through the window the cutout she'd made of Birdfinger took a hesitant seat, the lamp on the opposite side of the room casting his shadowshape against the amber curtain. He had his hat in his hand, in deference to beauty. They were on the same couch. It held both of them somehow, and they talked until four in the morning, Birdfinger making her laugh, her confessing to him maybe about how she was conceived at the Land Trust House and had never been able to get too far from Texas since, maybe about the book she'd been reading since she was fourteen and a half and was afraid to finish. That first night there was only useless words, nothing biblical. But it went on for months—Birdfinger escaping letter duty via feigned illiteracy, Pidgin's mother husbandless at night because of that letter duty, because had to pore over each one. He did touch her once, finally, Birdfinger did, removing something from her face with his long namesake, as if it was shaped by nature solely for such an intimate and profane gesture, and Pidgin looked away from the skin on skin of it, pushed the leopard woman faster, past WWI, past his own birth, up to the last two weeks she'd promised.

It was about phonecalls, about voices from the dead giving heavy-handed hints about the end of the world.

The voice from the dead was Marty Robbins, part and parcel; Birdfinger thought he was being sly. He traded the hints to Cline for information about any new Indian waitresses or cashier girls or dancers in Clovis, who might look like Marina had looked. He said he needed to know because the presence of some certain one would be a sign by which he could tell other things. But his slyness broke down; his voice was recognized when the operator refused to put through a call from the afterlife, when the operator demanded a new fake name out of respect for the dead. On the line, Birdfinger stumbled, said Jimmy Martinez like a question, then began apologizing and had to create lies on the spot for Cline, to explain the apologies from nowhere. He hung up. He called again at the appointed time, with a handful of change rattling against the receiver, and when that some certain Indian girl wasn't yet in town as far as Pidgin's father knew, the voice of Marty Robbins explained her in more and more detail, and two days later Cline was dead.

'Cause and effect,' the leopard woman said, shrugging the relationship into existence.

Pidgin said no. The leopard woman said back yes. She said she understood it was hard to assimilate all at once. She said there were chemicals especially designed to make the process softer. She happened to have some in the false lining of her jungle-print purse, red pills that looked like ladybugs and tasted like ladybugs. Pidgin was spitting out the hard candy shells when Birdfinger waved his guitar over his head in grand goodbye and stepped clumsy off the stage.

Pidgin said it: 'Yonder dickhead this way roams.'

Birdfinger grew steadily larger with approach, until he was lifesize, seven years thicker than the last time, but still the same, Cline plus nine. The leopard woman was ready, had a cigarette in each hand. She passed one to Birdfinger. He coughed over it, too drunk to inhale. She presented Pidgin in grand fashion.

'Allow me to introduce your long-lost nephew in whiteface, a trifle late and in the wrong town.'

'Long time no see, Pill,' Birdfinger said in the way of hello, then, about Pidgin: 'A gift, you say?'

'An accident.'

Birdfinger cocked his head, studying Pidgin with one eye. Pidgin didn't look away. He was Paul Stanley.

'In whiteface?' Birdfinger finally said. 'Here in Aztec New Mexico? After missing his own father getting buried?' Before Pidgin could draw away then, Birdfinger was holding him by the chin, crucifying phrenology, saying that Pidgin wasn't Pidgin, was different around the eyes and temples. He did the fingers of his right hand around his own face, to show, let Pidgin's chin slide and burn.

The leopard woman shrugged failure too soon, too easily.

Pidgin held his thumb in his fist. First the *Star* woman had brought him to show and tell, now the leopard woman. But the leopard woman was doing it different. She was in the front row, all smiles. Pidgin sat, his lawn chair incognito and sacrificed as little movement as possible. He was a spy in close quarters. The leopard woman got Birdfinger talking easily enough, about his razor line singing, about Marina at WWI. She looked a flat look at Pidgin. There was a matchbook in his hand with one match left. He was half-afraid it would flare and give him away. It didn't. He contained his heat, contrived it into words to dry gulch Birdfinger with: 'Your swan song there, Deaf Smith, it did bring me to mine knees, though only to disgorge.'

Birdfinger stilled, rotated his eyes to Pidgin. The unattended guitar fell over in a din of misplaced chords. Neither registered it. 'Paul Stanley,' Birdfinger said, 'your manner of speaking. Were I a lesser man I'd be unnerved.'

'Then unnerved you are.'

'You're not my nephew.'

'If only saying it were enough.'

'You're just another Indian,' he said, 'coached by my brother's commonlaw widow, and coached well.'

'Take the credit yourself. Perhaps your fatherlike appearance has elicited some sonlike reaction in me.'

'Your words are not your own, Paul Stanley.'

'Agreed. I have one that belongs to you. Adultery.'

The leopard woman chimed in with *fratricide.*

Birdfinger smiled at her, asked her what she wanted from this slap and tickle?

'Apology,' she said, 'that's all.'

'So you can twist it into a guilt admission?'

'You're wearing the guilt,' Pidgin continued, 'my father's old cowboy suit. Handpicked by my mother.'

'A story you no doubt have second or thirdhand. And careful with that word.'

'Marina Trigo?'

Birdfinger reevaluated Pidgin. 'As I was saying,' he said, 'you've been coached to near perfection.'

'I've been suckled on lies.'

'And I don't have time for this.'

When he rose Pidgin rose with him, accused him of standing in his brother's stead before his brother was even dead. Birdfinger said to Pidgin-as-Paul Stanley that he didn't know anything about how it really went down. Pidgin said he was not Paul Stanley. Birdfinger said he didn't have to explain himself to every Indian that came along with the right lines memorized. Pidgin threw the matchbook gauntlet-style into the edge of the grey ash. The cover was rolled back like a sleeve, the lone match extended above the knuckles of the others, the white match-head like the back of an unwholesome fingernail. It was Birdfinger's call sign, his signature piece of old. It validated Pidgin. Birdfinger fell off his stool on top of the world. His lip quivered. The leopard woman clapped like a seal. Pidgin was stone; Birdfinger wavered in place.

'So,' Pidgin said.

'Say it,' the leopard woman said, a cool observer.

Birdfinger apologized.

Pidgin said it didn't undo anything.

Birdfinger looked away, blinking, then fumbled with the hidden buckle of the SUBSTANCE ABUSER belt. Pidgin said making an exhibition of himself wouldn't help. He turned on his missing heel to leave, looked over his shoulder to make sure he wasn't being shadowed, and Birdfinger said he probably had some of the answers Pidgin was looking for, he knew what Sally wanted him to finish. Pidgin lied that he no longer had any questions.

He turned to leave a second time then, looked over his shoulder again, and this time saw recognition in Birdfinger's eyes—not of a person, but of a movement.

Said Birdfinger: 'You're walking away.'

Said Pidgin: 'You're not my father.'

Said Birdfinger: 'Wait.'

Pidgin did. Not because he wanted to, but because he was held fast by the vision taking shape over his shoulder: it was Birdfinger, balanced against the card table, taking off the mule-eared boots, the tooled-leather belt, the cowboy suit. Pidgin shook his head no, it wasn't enough. Birdfinger emptied his pockets of spare bills and a sweated-through Deaf Smith envelope. Still Pidgin said it wasn't enough. Birdfinger never looked away. He undressed in the bonfire light, stood naked, unbold, arms apelike and dangling. The leopard woman was giddy with herself. People were gathering, hiding their mouths, ashamed. Birdfinger's body was pale and uncut, had never known the scalpel. It was dusted with curly yellow hair, matted down by years of unattended sweat. This was the man who had foretold the end of the world for twenty-five cents a minute. And his mouth was still moving in supplication, but there weren't words anymore. Pidgin's breath caught with the sight and the soundlessness, of Cline plus nine, and he walked away until he was free of the light, and then he ran. There were bushes to crash through, depressions to roll into and out of, blanketed lovers to bound over. He ran, not chasing but chased, and when his legs gave he lay on his back, the ladybug pills entering whole into his bloodstream, talking to each other over the dendritic space with telegraphic precision.

They were apologizing furiously, Birdfinger-style.

Pidgin accepted, then didn't. He reduced it to the simplest terms, said that since Birdfinger had been the first one to sacrifice neck movement, he had lost, and it was fitting that he have to play the fool, walk naked to his Cutlass.

But still.

The clouds overhead were pregnant with rain. In the occasional headlight they were lead-colored, heavy-bellied. In the near distance, tribal memory recalled all this, prefigured it. The stars absent from the sky journeyed earthward, coalesced, took the shape of a man's torso and approached, leaned over Pidgin, said it would be alright, man, really. It was the mortal form of Wean Construction of Clovis New Mexico, wearing pilfered batwing chaps with silver dollars hammered into extravagant conchos. The form lifted Pidgin as a child and Pidgin didn't resist. They moved back towards civilization, batwings flapping. The exhibition building smeared past. They made the corner to the pens, made the door without need of a password. Pidgin was laid on the ground. The form peeled a cigarette and offered it high and low, side to side, then backed away, out the same door. Pidgin's neck muscles were rigid. In his field of view was the old diabetic man from the dogfights. He was sifting colored sand into the uplifted corner of an antless antfarm; the sand was separating itself into backgammon stripes. There were vials all around him, like crack leavings in a city stairwell, midwinter, two AM. Pidgin smiled, tried to laugh, then the old man was blotted out by shaggy legs which became a twice-dead buffalo. The old bull approached slow, limping. He leaned over, breathed Pidgin in then blew. His mouth was a handsbreadth from Pidgin's face, his coarse beard on Pidgin's straining neck, and then there was a Gene Simmons tongue licking away the white paint, licking the skin raw, and the old bull was whispering to Pidgin with a man-voice, and Pidgin could feel his face changing under the rough tongue.

He became aware of the mule-eared boots in one hand, the many-holed belt in the other.

The rain came in glass sheets and shattered over New Mexico.

A los Muertos

Birdfinger was a surly migrator: in the afternoon heat of Clandenstein's, he was kept in motion by the nameless sweeping boy. He grunted disapproval, covered his beer glass with a cupped hand, avoided eye contact. Moved, moved again. Traced fingerwide lines in the windows soaped over to defray overhead. On the jukebox was a bootlegged Bodhisattva and a drunken Donald Fagan. In the ashtray was a flesh-colored hearing aid. It was caucasian. Birdfinger prodded it with a toothpick. It screamed in the upper range of audible frequencies. It keened. It got chased across the tabletop and duly pocketed.

Back to the hard stuff.

In not so many words, Birdfinger told the sweeping boy to go to hell. The sweeping boy declined. Birdfinger's beer grew cloudy with floordust. He filtered it through a napkin back into the bottle. He occupied himself with an unfinished game of pinochle from his childhood. Cline stared at him over the cards. Birdfinger looked away. Through the fingerwide window-lines was the parking lot, and in the parking lot was a chrome three wheeler and the flyblown carcass of a deer. The deer was straddling the bike, reclining; the bike was abandoned. The bartender said Indians were darkeyed creatures, uneasily spooked; there was a Salishan old timer in the corner, waiting out the bugs and the worms and the joke, his tab erased nightly by mites in the ledger. Birdfinger nodded to him. There were three exits from the bar, one of them an emergency. Vanetta occupied all of them, her red hair sinuous, alive. She triangulated in on Birdfinger, sat.

'I knew you were bottlefed,' she said, taking his beer from him, and Birdfinger smiled a little, confessed that it was the nipples, those sanitary rubber nipples, then moved again as the broom approached. Vanetta followed in half as many steps, resettled.

'Never a dull moment,' Birdfinger said.

'Always something happening.'

'A veritable hotbed of activity.'

'Around the clock.'

'Shit.'

They sat. The floor was clean under them. Birdfinger drank and tried to gauge where he was in relation to her, Vanetta. There was more than the table between them of late. Or less. He talked to her only in passing now, on the way to pick up Stiya 6 from Squanto's. She still insisted she was worried about him. He told her he was doing fine, wonderful, *extra*-ordinary. The Deaf Smith gig burned in effigy in his near past, though. He blamed it on Pill, smug in her leopard print. He no longer had his guitar or his good jeans. But things could be worse: he was well into reeducating Stiya 6, Marina. Vanetta said that was why she was here.

'Don't you like the beer?'

'I love the beer, Bird.'

'Then do we have to?'

Vanetta nodded, stayed the nameless sweeper with a steady stare. Birdfinger tried one last time to avoid her; he said he had what felt like a dog in a paisley suitcase out in the trunk of the Cutlass. Vanetta shrugged, didn't look away. She was here to talk. Birdfinger called for another pair of beers. They came. Time drag-assed past them and out the door, shaded its eyes, slumped into the heat left by the rain. Birdfinger felt himself become disheveled in stages. He slumped in his chair, rested on his gut.

'So if I understand correctly,' Vanetta said, choosing her words, 'it's her again, right?'

Birdfinger nodded, squinted.

'I'm not jealous, Bird, you know that, right? But I'm not blind, either. And try as I might, I can't look at you and not think about where you'll be tomorrow, or the day after that. *How* you'll be, I mean.'

'You're worried about my well-being.'

'I care about you for all the wrong reasons, yes. Like the song. Maybe it's just pity too, I don't know.' She stopped, drank, drank again. Birdfinger followed suit. She started to speak then took it back, as if she was waiting for something on Birdfinger's part. He cracked under the hint of pressure. He told her he was pretty sure he'd seen the kid in the northwest corner of the state.

'Aztec?'

'The damn rodeo, yeah. I gave him some old clothes and shit. Money too. Four hundred and change.'

'Why?'

Birdfinger laughed in his nose, told her it was because he owed him that and more. Vanetta wanted to know about the *more* part. Birdfinger said it came to two thousand-odd dollars or so.

'You mean he prorated it all somehow?'

'I don't even think he took it.'

'Then he doesn't want it.'

'Yeah, that's what I thought.'

'Past tense?'

'...'

'He corrected you, you had divine inspiration, what?'

'I almost fell in love with you once, Net, y'know. I was maybe six, seven feet away.'

'Bird.'

'At the interment. You had your hand in the dirt, the shovel of a backhoe looming.'

'Bird.'

Birdfinger peeled his beer. 'I'm going to get the rest of the money together now, yes. Obligated and all.'

'Duty stricken. Odd notion for you.'

'He's family. It's a debt. His mother gave it to me, for him. Marina. Way back when. When she was Janey.'

'And you spent it on the Cutlass?' Vanetta asked, eyebrows V'ed. Birdfinger shook his head no, said there wasn't much to show for it outside a spinal tap. He switched beers with her, drank the rest of hers. It was hot by the window, even with the soap.

He moved them again.

The sweeping boy was brushing the pool table now. Birdfinger overplayed a coughing fit, didn't get any free beer out of it. Vanetta paid for the next round, left Birdfinger even deeper in obligation. She said she wasn't so sure about this cashier girl.

'Stiya. Six.'

'Like I said.'

'Well I'm sure.'

'How is she taking all this?' Vanetta swept her hand around at Clandenstein's, a compact motion emblematic of Clovis, the whole Marina-thing. Birdfinger said she still thinks she came here by accident, got on the wrong bus. But she's listening. 'It'll take time,' he said, 'but hell, y'know. Shit doesn't happen in a day. Reality's constipated.'

Vanetta wasn't smiling with him; she granted that reality was becoming an issue here. Birdfinger, backed into a corner, offered his best defense: that Stiya 6 was showing maternal instincts by urging that he follow through with his original plan and get together the rest of the money somehow. He was proud of the insight, but Vanetta refused it. She just shook her head and said she would probably say the same thing were she dislocated, in the wrong town against her will.

Birdfinger shook his head no.

Vanetta held his hand that was around a beer. She told him that Stiya 6 was already on cash-drawer probation at Squanto's. Birdfinger said the whole night shift was, simply on principle, and did she have surveillance equipment in that grocery store, or what?

'Was I wrong about the bagboy?' Vanetta asked.

Birdfinger told the technical truth: that he still had the stalk.

Vanetta said she couldn't watch this happen anymore. She wouldn't.

Birdfinger warned her not to get involved with his lovelife, but she suggested that she already was in a way, then let that hang awkward and unfinished between them.

'I'm not your charity case, anymore,' Birdfinger said.

'It's not about charity, Bird.'

Vanetta plead with him with her eyes, her hand on his, and at the first derelict thought about Stiya 6, at the first sign that Vanetta was getting to him, Birdfinger put his foot down and made himself say it: that if being motherhenned by her meant ending up like Rahstuff or her tenderfooted father, he didn't want any part it. He was better off without her on watch. It was his holecard, his panic button, a fabrication, false correlation; he chased the sour taste away with a beer, kept drinking. Vanetta removed her hand from his a finger at a time. The muscles in her face were slack now, her hair pale again, not quite red but more strawberry roan, a girl's hair. She was reduced by words, had been. Birdfinger couldn't look her in the eye. She said she was sorry, really she was, about Marina, about him having to say what he'd said, about everything, and then her footsteps trailed out the door. Birdfinger recognized the sound: she was leaving Clovis. He closed his eyes and tried to force the backhoe and the dirt into her mind again. He meant it as an apology, something good to take with her. He hadn't wanted the talk, *to* talk.

Birdfinger felt like his father for some reason.

He didn't pursue the sensation.

There were still almost two hours until Stiya 6's shift was over, until he could reeducate her about WWI, that pivotalmost night in their history. Birdfinger made a conscious decision to fill both of those hours with alcohol. The first hour was ninety-proof, six-percent grade. The second was slower. He approached the Salishan man in his leather and fringe and nodded to the beer he held in each hand, by the neck.

'Bottlefed, yeah?' Birdfinger said.

The Salishan man studied his two bottles, said he was visited nightly by memories of synthetic milk and inhuman nipples, that they reminded him of his android infancy on the reservation. Birdfinger thought it through a word at a time. He tried to match the Salishan man. He told him about the backhoe and the dirt and him six maybe seven feet away from falling in love with the moodhaired opposite of his intended. The Salishan man admitted that Birdfinger was no small poet. Birdfinger walked away content, nodding, was drawn to the soaped window and found himself again in the sweeping boy's path. He stayed just one step ahead of the hostile broom, became nomadic, abandoned many color-coded stools, broke off many stilted conversations. He finally found an inaccessible patch of clean floor between the jukebox and the payphone. He staked it out. He wanted another beer but couldn't get anyone's attention from the cubbyhole. In the back of his throat was the aftertaste of his harsh words to Vanetta. But they had had to be said. She'd done it to herself. It was her own doing.

He finally broke cover when a nonregular silhouetted himself in the doorway for a long moment, announcing his lanky presence with formaldehyde and presumption. Sam, the dissector of brothers, profaner of burials, lord of the pantywaists. Birdfinger opted for stealth and approached at a casual pace, checking his step, freeing up his right hand and making it look like swagger. He was almost within striking distance when Truck's long arm extended from the woodwork. There was no way around its reach or its girth. From the hairy backside of it, Sam said he was the maker of deals, was Birdfinger interested?

They met at the bar.

Birdfinger said he was a hard bargain driver. Sam said he was in the mood to deal. Birdfinger said he was unmisnomed, then showcased his anomalies, starting slow, letting things build auction-style: he opened with what Sam already knew, his aberrant namesake. Measurements were taken, the finger was framed on a cocktail napkin with a bottlecap for scale. A spy camera clicked twice. They moved on; Birdfinger turned his hand over. He had no fortune lines, no life no heart no children. Smooth like the liver-spotted pate of an old man, he said lyrically. Sam was giddy with it. He said the amount of collagen necessary to both deny identifiable palm wrinkles *and* allow a modicum of dexterity was more or less unprecedented in the human hand, maybe indicative of a whole new cell structure. Birdfinger asked if Sam was calling him fat. Sam curled at the shoulders, suggested Birdfinger take note that his fatty deposits might yet be weighed by the ounce, mined for radioactive isotopes. Birdfinger patted him on the back. Plaster casts were taken, beers were put away at a steady rate. Birdfinger drew close to Sam, said, too, he suspected his heart was in the wrong place, at least that was the word from the womenfolk—from a certain woman noticeably absent here. But Birdfinger refused to be stethoscoped in public. He held out; it was a bargaining tactic. The crotch of Sam's no-color slacks was engorged. Birdfinger asked what would happen on that autopsy table? Sam said his interest was purely scientific. Birdfinger unbuttoned his shirt, exposed the yellow skin piled in place by the guitar, lied that it was congenital like all the rest, though he didn't know the evolutionary advantage of it, not yet. Sam touched it with a latexed fingertip, said he would pay one thousand dollars cash today for exclusive rights.

Birdfinger feigned insult. He said this wasn't 1979. He needed at least twice that much. He said he hadn't even shown Sam everything yet. He led him to the men's room, dimmed the lights, unzipped, told a tale about regenerating foreskin. Sam said the conditions of the contract would be that Birdfinger stay within the county at all times, as extradition procedures from neighboring morgues were tricky at best.

'So I can't steal myself?'

'Not legally, no. Though ownership doesn't actually transfer until death.'

'And I would get the three thousand immediately upon signing?'

'Three thousand?'

They talked more at the bar. Birdfinger enlisted the bartender's help; the bartender said there were oddities about Birdfinger that defied rational explanation. Like the night he drank strychnine on a bet that his liver could egest it before last call. Birdfinger lost the bet, but lived to pay it out in weekly installments. There were vague allusions to a vestigial mole tuned in to the magnetic poles, its lone hair a directional needle. Sam said he was only budgeted for fifteen hundred dollars per case study. Birdfinger said to count him as two then, he was worth any pair of corpses from around the Clovis burg. Sam said the paperwork, Birdfinger didn't understand. Birdfinger corrected him: it wasn't that he didn't understand, it was that he didn't care. He was the one with the merchandise—he *was* the merchandise.

'You don't just dabble in the flesh trade,' he said, 'it's all or nothing, herr razor boy.'

Sam's chin trembled. He said he would go into his own savings, maybe, if it came to that.

Birdfinger said if he was going to go into his savings, then he'd also make him a deal on a conversation piece, a dog that might or might not be alive. He said it was a grab-bag thing, like at the carnival. But he'd heard a muffled bark at six in the morning three days ago, and the bag weighed in at about a labrador, maybe a retriever, and the cats around the place kept their distance from it, even though the wheels were rusted in place. In the parking lot Sam donned his X-ray specs. Birdfinger asked did he get them out of the back of a comic book? Sam asked for quiet, please. He leaned over the trunk, counted to ten on his fingers, said he could possibly take the dog as part of the package, at the aforementioned price.

Birdfinger shrugged. Sam offered him the paper to sign. Birdfinger said he was born forty-eight years ago, not hours; he needed cash money, and soon. He had debts to pay, rats to kill. Today's price wouldn't be good tomorrow. They leaned against the Cutlass together and watched dusk embrace Clandenstein's. Sam extracted from his pocket a roll of twenties that added up to a thousand. Birdfinger noted that they were alone in the parking lot, yet he was without an adequate stick-up line. That was always the hardest part of the crime. Sam said consider the thousand a down-payment. Birdfinger said any salivating on his part was strictly obligatory. The money smelled, had heft. Legal tender. Birdfinger wiped his mouth and said Cline had been a goddamn bargain, then demanded the rest of the money Sam had on him: fifty-two cents and a pocket full of pesos. And the X-ray specs. Birdfinger sketched the upper-left quarter of his signature pictogram on the lower-right of the contract, waited for twenty-five percent of him to slough off. He'd weigh what he did twenty years ago.

Sam filed the contract in his slacks, said not to leave the county.

He held onto the suitcase as collateral.

Birdfinger stole out of the parking lot in the Cutlass, felt suddenly constrained by Curry County at night. He rolled down both windows to further dry the stalk remains in the backseat. It would still be smokeable and/or salable if mulched down to long grain. And, as luck would have it, at her register Stiya 6 had heard the rumor of a well-outfitted gardener man on third, who bought lawn bags by the gross, on a weekly basis, suggesting he had the necessary mulching equipment. That wasn't all, though. She also claimed to know people in Gallup who dealt more in quantity than quality, if Birdfinger knew what she meant. She didn't even want a cut, she said, just a ride; the first thing she'd asked that night in the Apache breakroom was whether or not he had reliable transportation. Birdfinger had only had fifteen minutes with her, after two decades. He said yes, then recounted the first time he'd seen her, pilfering money from corporate america, within shouting distance of the main post office.

'I did all that?' she said.

Birdfinger nodded.

She told him she didn't remember ever being a hippie in eastern New Mexico.

Birdfinger said give it time, give it time.

He feathered the brake pedal, and Stiya 6 maneuvered into the passenger seat with an armful of day-old groceries. They made a picnic behind the store, on the dashboard. She said none of their bagboys had eyepatches. It was an Indian-themed store, not pirate. Birdfinger said it was just a question. She told him he still had a cheesy-varnish from driving naked all night in highway exhaust. Birdfinger said he'd already bathed twice. He smelled his shirt to give himself time for a comeback, then realized it was an argument they were having. Low key, but still, evidence of conflict. He felt them drawing together in it, through it. Back together. Marina. She was here. Eating long pickles and turkey. Talking about the assistant manager and his display fetish. Pushing her hair out of the way with the side of her hand, hooking it behind an ear, finally just taking it off. Underneath, her real hair was schoolboy short. Birdfinger tried to sustain the conflict, draw them closer together; he asked if the wig was Indian hair or non-? Stiya 6 directed him to the house on Third Street, didn't answer, didn't say anything. Just pointed left, right, right.

When they were parked in front of the blue-shuttered family house, car killed, she depocketed some camo paint from the hunting aisle, 12b. Birdfinger let her apply it to him, then applied it back, lingered with his finger to her face. They were hidden in plain view. They moved against the family house like thieves, the stalk slung between them. Birdfinger kicked a ball midstride and it rolled noiselessly through the manicured lawn. Breaking and entering: Stiya 6 climbed the gate and opened it from the inside. The cool air wicked the sweat from Birdfinger's unlined palms. One foot after the other. The lights were off. Stiya 6 fell back, drew as close as the stalk would allow, whispered that the automatic sprinklers had just gone off. She said half of it with her hands. They balanced the stalk across the armrests of a lawnchair. Birdfinger held Stiya 6 by the waist so he wouldn't lose her in the quarter-acre backyard, in the hulking shapes tarped over, arranged for display. The centerpiece was the shape of a riding lawnmower. Spoked out from it were the smaller shapes of its accessories—weights, canopy, snowplow, fertilizer rig, two-wheeled utility trailer, three-row disc, different grass catchers for different seasons. They were each on a dias of sorts: pretreated 2 x 12s hammered into mini-decks, with sled-style rails and slender strips of galvanized steel under those rails, so as to minimize grass damage. Each had a tongue so the lawnmower could pull it, and each a hitch so they could be trained together if necessary. Birdfinger tried to imagine a scenario in which they all would be. He held Stiya 6 closer. He had never been this deep into suburbia; there were shapes he couldn't even identify, implements of yard management mediæval in design. Stiya 6 was immobile with fear. Birdfinger told her not to worry, coaxed her into motion because he couldn't move himself.

Towards the alley was what they were looking for: the industrial-strength mulcher, with a dial range from CHOP to LIQUEFY. It had a neck like a sauropod, two black rubber tires. And under the tarp, a pullcord. Meaning two-stroke engine. Birdfinger felt his throat lump and tried to swallow around it; he had been expecting a flipswitch, like a blender. He had told Stiya 6 they could get in and out unnoticed. He had told her they used to do shit like this all the time. Him and her, letterbags over their shoulders, tiptoeing with their whole bodies. Residential was supposed to be a joke compared to the federal outposts they'd hit in their youths, together. But now here he was. He folded the tarp to delay starting the machine. Stiya 6 was on the back porch, had the top of her head at windowsill level, keeping guard. She was beautiful, lithe. She turned to Birdfinger and whispered across the grass *now, now*. Birdfinger saw it frame by frame, followed her finger when it pointed down: *now*. He couldn't refuse her—he couldn't have lied to her, not already, not this soon. They could do this. They had to be able to do this.

He pulled on the cord as little as he could. It spun, kicked back. He closed his eyes and pulled again, a fraction harder, leaning away from it. The mulcher woke. It stood on its hind legs and roared over the neighborhood. Birdfinger fell in the wet grass, crabcrawled backwards until he had a tarp behind him. Through it he could feel tiller blades filed razor sharp. He realized they hadn't even brought any lawn bags—*he* hadn't brought any lawn bags. He saw the head of his shadow just past the tiller-shaped shadow. The back porch light was on. The storm door opened, shut. He pulled the head of his shadow down, wanted to be out of the county.

A barefoot man walked by in just jeans. The gardener man. His cuticles were impeccable. He choked the mulcher tenderly. It went quiet. He turned to maybe inspect the rest of his equipment and at the last instant Birdfinger closed his eyes, to hide the whites, to merge with the tiller-shaped shadow. The wet footsteps drew in, circled, slowed, then went back to the porch. The tarp was still folded, lying there. The storm door didn't open and close. Dogs up and down the alley talked to each other about the mulcher. Under them were voices, questions, a hum of conversation. From the other side of the tiller, from Stiya 6's former post. An interrogation maybe; she must have got caught in the light. Birdfinger ran through plans for getting her out of there, but all of them involved a fleetness of foot he didn't think he could manage. And the stalk, God. He fingered rapid chords against his thighs. The conversation continued, just out of reach, just under the dog news. Birdfinger took out his new cash. Maybe he could buy their way out. They hadn't disturbed anything aside from sleep. He had made the decision to stand and do something and was counting to three for the fourth time when he found something knotty in the thousand dollars: the hearing aid. He spit it clean and inserted it in his good ear, the right, adjusted it with his pinky and some elbow motion, promised to do something good in return for this if it worked. It did. The conversation funneled to him:

—It was just a no-name bus.

—No name bus or not…

—I'm already forgetting it, okay? I'm even trying not to remember any of this.

—You could always stay here, of course.

—I'm not looking at you on purpose, y'know. No offense.

—I understand. I watch them in repose too.

—Them?

—The garden tractor and his familiars. Its, I mean. It doesn't have a gender, or so I'm told. But personality, yes. Like your mulcher there. A precision instrument with a blunt purpose.

—Reporting live from the Valley of the Green Giant.

—Some men have religion. I have a lawn and a therapist to guide me through the moral intricacies of herbicide. He could schedule you into group.

—I don't have any issues.

—You woke to a busdriver brutalizing you in another language…

—Maybe an identity concern or two.

—You were essentially scalped for bounty…

—I'm repressing all this as it comes.

—Of course, of course. You don't have to look at me. Note how the grass past the porch unfolds from my footsteps. The trick is to step from the outside in, just lay the blades over, walk with them, not on them.

—Is that cookies I smell?

—My wife and her snack compulsion. You're a guest.

—*My* mulcher, you say?

—At your disposal.

—We don't even know how to walk properly in your backyard.

The gardener man laughed. A leg pat came through the hearing aid. He was touching her leg with his hand. Birdfinger could even hear the attentive posture he relaxed back into, index finger running up the side of his face, chin on thumb, legs crossed at the thigh. Birdfinger stood, blood rushing. His shadow could go anywhere. To hell with it. Stiya 6 seemed to have already been watching the space he rose into. The gardener man tipped his lemonade glass to Birdfinger, waved him in. He said he was glad Birdfinger was here, two in the AM or not. His voice was huge, deep, an inner-ear assault. Birdfinger reeled back, blinked, approached. The gardener man said he had been talking to Birdfinger's lovely but understandably nameless associate. Birdfinger adjusted the hearing aid with the tip of his pinky, but still, everything was loud, in stereo: a handmixer in the kitchen, an only child smoothly aping sleep on the couch. Birdfinger said his associate wasn't nameless to him. The gardener man said she was trying to forget this whole scene, so the less memorable the talk, the better for her. But blackface was a considerate precaution. Birdfinger offered two hundred dollars to him, nodded to the stalk, their unfinished business. The gardener man looked from Birdfinger to Stiya 6, for final permission to do this thing. Stiya 6 nodded yes.

'Anything I can do to help,' he said, 'moonlighting included,' then offered Birdfinger his seat. Birdfinger took it on his own terms, folded a twenty under the lemonade pitcher. When the gardener man had the stalk shouldered and was stepping carefully out to the mulcher, walking with the grass, Birdfinger slipped in two more twenties. He said he didn't want to begrudge the man anything. Stiya 6 said at least he wasn't calling the law.

'So, you, here?' Birdfinger asked, meaning was she going to stay?

Stiya 6 didn't answer. Birdfinger realized he was whispering. He asked again, louder. She shrugged, rearranged her lips. The gardener man pulled a lawn bag from a dispenser up under the mulcher. He spun a catalytic converter extension onto the exhaust. It was a silencer. He could do no wrong. Birdfinger tried to pick up where the gardener man had left off: he said he understood Stiya's aversion to mass transit, to public facilities. She looked from the gardener man to Birdfinger.

'I still have the Cutlass,' he offered. It was his most remarkable feature to her right now, he figured.

Her head motion continued past him, though. She was looking at the porch, the swept cement, the bricks all in a line, the windows properly caulked. Birdfinger tried to cover as much of it with his body as he could. He swished lemonade in his mouth and spit it into the corner. Half a backyard away, still too close, the gardener man was feeding the stalk slowly to the blades. The mulcher exhaled backseat dust, the uric acid of sandhill cranes; the gardener man tore off a layer of his motocross goggles in response, pressed on, undaunted. The mulcher was set to CHOP, and he had enough lawn bags lined up to go through all the dial settings. Birdfinger figured that gave him some fifteen minutes to convince Stiya 6 that this wasn't her life, that she had another. He pulled his chair closer to her.

'WWI,' he said, his voice on reverb in his right ear, 'Willie and Waylon, Canyon Texas, God. I was already calling you Felina by then.'

'And I was liking it.'

'Not so much around Cline. But yes.'

'Felina.'

'Marina.'

'All these names.'

'You were wearing a mail-order skirt with spangles, an animal-skin mantle I found in a cooler with dry ice.'

'An intercepted wardrobe.'

'There was cold smoke still in the pockets.'

'And your brother already had that letter thing he'd been looking for?'

'I told you that?'

Birdfinger drained the gardener man's lemonade just to have a glass to his mouth, a handle to hold onto. Maybe she'd remembered it, maybe she *was* remembering it. He hadn't meant to tell her about it, at least, the letter, the parcel. He was going to build her better this time, program a Marina that wouldn't die or run away. He refilled. He started over.

'Canyon Texas,' he said, 'nineteen seventy-seven. We were drinking coffee by a plate-glass window and through it were watching the Mexican Paiute smoke his handrolled cigarettes at the edge of the parking lot. And he was watching something too. There was something coming. Cline said the police wouldn't already be out, not this soon. Larry was pacing the floor, saying how wearing other people's clothes was suicide, how those people could be getting an urge for diner food at any fucking moment, and then what? It's not like a spangled skirt was *quiet* or anything, *didn't* draw undue attention to itself, especially with that much leg showing. Cline said to Larry that Larry didn't have the necessary mettle, then from across the table, from over her stomach, Sally defended her delicate Laguna man, said necessary for what? Cline didn't answer. It always went this way. He withdrew to you, Larry withdrew to Sally, I spilt myself all over the table. You laughed. Nobody was expecting a concert. There was no concert planned.'

'What was coming?'

'A dark bus, a man built like a flagpole.'

'Same old story.'

'You looked right in that animal skin.'

'It accessorized the Indian blood?'

'I couldn't tell you then, I mean.'

Birdfinger slid a hand across the table. Stiya 6 didn't cooperate. He played through, pulled the lemonade to his mouth and drank, said no scurvy tonight, trying to get a laugh. She was watching the gardener man, though. Birdfinger said the gardener man was paid labor, doing their grunt work. Stiya 6 said Birdfinger couldn't have planned this.

Birdfinger started again.

'We were in Canyon because Cline thought we could catch the mail before it went underground, before it tunneled under New Mexico. He was right, too. They weren't using trucks yet, so it was easy pickings. We had to leave caches buried all over the Llano Estacado, for later reading. Lazbuddie, Nazareth, Vigo Park. We picked what we kept by a show of hands. Your outfit. Some magazines for the road. Vitamins for Sally that it was too late for. Birthday cards were always good for cash money and balloons. The Mexican Paiute kept guard for us, too. Have I said that before? It wasn't like he didn't agree with Cline's missions or anything, it was just like he needed to smoke his cigarettes worse than he needed to get his hands dirty with meter ink. I don't know. He was the first one to see it coming though. WWI. The bus, the thin man with a valve-core remover held in his teeth like the dagger of God.'

'And then the Pinkertons.'

'Two in a Nova.'

'And me.'

'Dancing on a truck.'

'In a truck.'

'Felina.'

'Marina.'

She laughed, Stiya 6, over the wire-topped table, into her lemonade glass, her shoulders convulsing together. It wasn't a good laugh. Birdfinger felt it in his spine. He was losing this, losing her. To the gardener man and the stable image of life he could offer, the pruned backyard and weatherproofed house. Birdfinger had accepted the idea of a duel for Stiya 6 as a matter of course, but WWI wasn't turning out to be the weapon of choice. He palmed another one, a more abrasive one: 'You're not really what I'd call houseguest material,' he said, but before he could honestly start spieling, about quaaludes and cartoon shows and social sedimentation and american pie, the door opened behind him in a flood of augmented noise and there was the gardener man's wife standing in it, the cookie woman, all smiles, leftover facial cream around the jaw and hairline. Maybe frosting, the face a cheesecloth mask. The cookie platter was still warm. She clicked off an intercom built into the brick and apologized that she'd found the recipe on-line, which meant they were her guinea pigs. Birdfinger snorted once, compulsed by inner demons. Stiya 6 made eyes to him that reminded him that they were the guests here. Birdfinger made eyes back that meant no, they were the criminals. Another fight. The cookie woman pretended not to hear or see. Instead, she touched Birdfinger with the underside of her fingertips and said Stiya 6 most definitely *was* houseguest material. And Birdfinger had potential too. Birdfinger shook his head no, he didn't.

'You were talking about the concert?' the cookie woman asked then in what had to be tea-spot falsetto, and Birdfinger caught the afterimage of bridge cards on the table, tupperware balanced on every flat surface, napkins blowing into the fence and not being able to escape, ever. She was a conversationalist. 'The concert in Texas?' she asked again when the minimal amount of time had passed for clarification. Birdfinger nodded because there was nothing else to do.

The cookie woman picked the story up.

'WWI,' she said to Stiya 6, then turned midsentence to Birdfinger for support, validation. 'You do mean the first one?' Birdfinger nodded again, all the same nod, really. She nodded with him. 'The first one,' she said to Stiya 6, 'was something of an accident as I understand it. Evidently, or the way it was related to me, the conditions in Canyon Texas at that point in time were such that they nudged the concert up from just being possible to being absolutely probable, and then, of course, it simply became inevitable. This is the way things happen. Why inevitable?

Perhaps because your associate here's friend saw it coming—perhaps his native awareness that such a thing was actually probable added that last little bit necessary to make it unavoidable. Either way, though, it was Texas, dear. Things happen. I'm sure you know. It's too big a place for things not to happen.' She stopped, tore off a dainty bite of cookie, ate it, and closed her eyes in response, in a show of pleasure. Birdfinger felt the rest of the story being offered back to him while she chewed, but it was no longer his weapon. He had been disarmed. He looked at her and waited. She flowered under the attention, continued as if pressed into service. 'But I digress. Forgive me. When I got there, and on whose arm and why is irrelevant—it was another time, another mindset—the first thing that got me, aside from the *raucous* smell of beer, was all the headlights, how Monday morning the battery business would be booming, if you'll allow me a bit of alliteration. And it was in the middle of a field, of course. Isn't everything, though, on some scale? I don't know what kind of field. Dirt. There were rows of some sort, all piled up or dug out, though they could have been from the previous year or last century altogether. I've never lived outside town. A cultural ignorance, but one I own, and hard-earned, I might add. My husband would know, of course. Damon. That's more his world.'

Past the back of her hand the gardener man was two clicks away from LIQUEFY.

Birdfinger ate three more cookies. 'Where was your group parked?' she asked him, dragging him in, making him necessary. Birdfinger dug his heels in, shrugged like he couldn't recall. Ate another cookie. Chewed Fletcher-style.

'To the left?' Stiya 6 said. The cookie woman clapped and said you *do* remember, but Birdfinger ignored her social antics. Stiya 6 hadn't remembered; she'd said it like a blind stab. She was either filling in the hole in the conversation the cookie woman had set like a trap or she was taking the heat meant for him, Birdfinger. Birdfinger opted for the latter, because if it was the former, he'd need to save her, and there was no way. He was outgunned. He tipped his empty glass to Stiya 6 in acknowledgment, but she missed it. Maybe they were still fighting, still drawing closer and closer together. The cookie woman sopped up the silence Birdfinger wanted to extend.

She was talking about the left side of the audience now. She had been on the left too, parked in the ditch. 'The stage was barrels and planks, wasn't it? I believe so. My escort said it looked to him as if there'd once been a pond there, of all things, and what we were seeing was the marooned party barge. He was perceptive like that. A student of the petroleum arts. He later compared it to a Dali print...but, again. It's so hard to stay on course. I should have known you were on the left side, too. Didn't mean to put you on the spot. I apologize. That's where most of the trucks were, all clogged up from coming off the road. There was obviously little attention paid to proper parking. Like I said though, or, like you said, it was an unplanned affair, to say the least. Which is why we both remember it fondly. And you'll have to tell me about the tall, thin man who started it all. I'm simply awash with curiosity.' She drank what lemonade she could between sentences, dabbed her lip corners with a napkin that appeared at will.

'And the right side of course is where there was that awful disturbance. A disgrace. Not that the music stopped, heaven's sakes no, not mister Waylon Jennings, but, and I'm not sure what was going on—and believe me there was none of this at the second WWI, the one that got the album and all that—but it looked to my escort like someone had installed a police flasher-light on their dash and was playing freeze tag or Marco Polo behind the wheel. He talked colorful like that, my escort. It ended quick enough though, of course, the little flare up of activity, *par typi-cale,* with cars chasing each other across the field, limping like football players at the end of the season, but, did I tell you this? No. Shame on me. I got my name in the national papers for *being* at that first WWI. For having a camera. My claim to fame, yes. I'll get it.'

She scurried inside, disappeared down a hall. Birdfinger watched through the glass, tried mentally to construct a buglike exoskeleton that could bear the weight of all this, the backyard they'd traipsed into like it could be just another backyard. The oven buzzer went off. The child rose instantly from the couch, slithered across the livingroom, killed the noise, returned to his spot on the couch. Or its.

Stiya 6 said to Birdfinger *maybe*.

Maybe she would stay.

Birdfinger told her it wasn't like the cookie woman was telling it, WWI. It wasn't her story to tell. It was his, theirs, the Goliards. Housewives don't know the true meanings of things. He ate another cookie, paid for it with twenty dollars, got the back of his hand slapped by the cookie woman herself, moving silent on moccasin slippers. She had a rolled-up poster in her hand. As she chased the rubber band off the end of it, she asked what was that smell, were they smelling it? Incense? Birdfinger put his nose to the air. There was stalk kindling on the mulcher exhaust. And it was sweet. Airborne THC. The gardener man was moving in slow motion through it, watching his hands, his individual fingers. His world was becoming reenchanted. Birdfinger smiled with the corners of his eyes: it was the first good thing all night. Maybe the only. He looked at the unrolled poster. It was a dummied-up UFO shot. It was the same thing the kid had drawn. The zygote in the sky. Birdfinger leaned back on two chair legs, unable to bear it, tried to jack the hearing aid up to mute the cookie woman and instead tuned into the last conversation he had had with Cline: it began in 1977 and ended ten years later, over hundreds of miles of phone line. Their voices were distorted by distance and signal decay and by intention. There was a lot left unsaid.

In 1977 Birdfinger was in a diner in Canyon Texas like he'd told Stiya 6, his hands symmetrical with each other on the burnt-orange formica, as if holding himself in place while Cline and Larry argued. It almost worked; two years later he was still there, over and over, the revisitor, compressing the hours, milking them, distilling what was distillable and stowing it away in unlikely fat cells: WWI. It began in the diner, with Cline positioned near the window so the leadlined bulge in the left side of his BDU jacket would be less noticeable, so his right arm could contain Marina. There was Larry pacing, going through the cigarette motions without the luxury of a cigarette. Sally gestating the dead on nothing but willpower and apple pie. The Mexican Paiute a three-inch figure at the edge of the parking lot, smoking his homerolled, cupping his hand around the glow and keeping his eyes up the road. It was a military stance. He was full of purpose. Birdfinger looked at him from his vantage point of two years after the fact, and he wanted to run from the diner and pull him away by the arm, deal with the consequences later. But he never would have been able to touch him, not him. And he didn't know to try. He was caught up in the moment, in high spirits. 1977.

Texas had been good to him, to them, the Family Goliæ. He called the waitress Brandy because she was a fine girl. Sally said he should court her. Cline said his brother wasn't the courting type. Birdfinger said he'd been known to woo a girl or two in his day. He pointed at Marina by not looking at her. He whistled to scatter attention. He fancied the idea of being a bonafide bodice-ripper. He adjusted himself; in his underwear were birthday balloons filled with pills and powder. The walking talking stash. Cline said he didn't all the way trust him with it. Birdfinger said he didn't all the way trust himself. Bladder problems and all. It was a long-running joke about heredity and Hardwick in his last days before the bandsaw came calling. He laughed alone, ate the premeal fries singly and in pairs, waited for Marina to thank him for the Manual Lisa he hadn't pawned, listened to Larry stew about how they should have left that USPS driver tied up for the night, that just because the guy showed them where the good stuff was stowed didn't mean he wasn't still a federal employee with guns to stick to.

Cline said it was a field decision, not open to indoor analysis.

Marina was in her same boots. They ended midcalf. She asked Sally how was the pie, miss america? It was another joke. Larry climbed aboard, got bodily removed just as fast, moped back and forth. Birdfinger contained himself. He played El Paso on the jukebox and hummed along with the key passages, watching Marina in the plate glass, her chin in her hand, her shoulders outlined by Cline's arm. He surrounded everything that was her. Almost. Birdfinger looked deeper into the glass. There was the Mexican Paiute, intent upon the distance. When the waitress carried his plate out she left it by him in a blonde huff, collected the change already there. Birdfinger counted it in her hand: thirty-seven cents. He didn't apologize. He tried to use the Mexican Paiute as a relay station instead, to see what was coming. Because something was. Even in the booth, half-blind with Marina scent, Birdfinger could feel it, could see it in the Mexican Paiute's posture. Maybe Larry was right. Maybe it was the law again, which meant lying under the surplus tarp in the bed of the Ford and trusting his life to the Thunderbird engine and to the wheel bearings and to the tires and to the u-joints and to the rear end. And to Cline, God. But it wasn't the law. Birdfinger watched in slackjawed silence. At first it was a southbound bus, dark and shiny, black nosetip to tail. It pulled up to the first row of pumps, every last window slit trailing smoke. The Mexican Paiute flicked the end of his cigarette into the section of asphalt it had driven through, as if marking it down in history: this time, this moment. Next, only moments behind, was an impossibly tall two-dimensional man running barefoot in jeans and a high-school basketball jersey. He had no sharp angles, moved like a fluid through the night. He was young, white, cleanfaced, an easy seven feet. The back of his jersey read ROLLINS in an arc over the number, 41. A post player, running behind a bus, something clenched in his teeth, a silvery purpose, a mouthful of determination.

This is how things happen.

Birdfinger held his breath, didn't adjust himself, knew he could never render again what was taking place beyond the plate glass, because he was already holding it too close to the bone: number 41 folded himself under the rear end of the bus and became a spidery arm reaching around the tires, gutting the valve stems, releasing geysers of wet air from other states. It commingled with Texas.

The bus lowered by inches. An across-the-road light became just visible over its roofline. Sally dug her fingernails into Birdfinger's forearm. It was her maternal hormones: if the post player hadn't been as thin as he was, the lowering bus would have pinned him to the concrete. But it didn't, it couldn't. It was Canyon, it was 1977. The bus was outside a diner. The post player rose when it was done, lips drawn back in victory, and loped off into the Texas night not like a person but like a thing that had had to be, that could have been no other. The Mexican Paiute lifted the burger from his plate and ate it with one hand, fortification. Cline said goddamn twice, low in the back of his throat. Larry was unpacing, forehead to the window. The waitress crossed herself. Birdfinger mouthed a tasteless fry. It was a concert bus, roadweary and tinted against the daytime. Longhaired gentleman outlaws and their leather-slick ladies stumbled out the door, the first step shorter than usual, their knees locking against the rushing concrete. Their faces in the light of the pumps were pasty white. One of them kicked a flattened tire and studied his boot. Waylon Jennings. He smiled through his beard, rubbed his nose with the back of his hand. Four hours later the concert began.

In those four hours, the Birdfinger who knew how the Thunderbird Ford would fall slow and quiet on Marina when no one was supposed to be looking took her by the hand and led her over the state line and back to the trailer outside Clovis New Mexico where it was still sixty minutes earlier and listened to her talk everything all over again and carved each word in his memory, to repeat back for her when she returned. And there was so much. A catalogue of lives. To make room, he forgot large pieces of himself. He promised to keep her alive in him, above all else, for the times she couldn't do it herself. It was a chivalrous gesture. She looked into her lap in maidenlike response. She said she couldn't stay any longer. Birdfinger opened the door for her, followed her back to Canyon Texas, to the buffalo wallow where there was already something like a stage risen from the grass. She was in the cab of Cline's truck with him, Birdfinger. Cline was on self-imposed reconnaissance detail. The Mexican Paiute was just out of sight. Larry was leaned over the truck beside them, drinking a slow beer, and Sally was on the tailgate, trading information about the postplayer for birthing tips she'd never need.

Five minutes before, Cline had been in the cab too, with. It still smelled of his intense sweat, his knowing demeanor. The three of them had plundered Birdfinger's underwear together. Birdfinger had looked away and said he usually got paid for this sort of thing. Cline said he thought it was the other way around, then left before Birdfinger could respond in kind. It was their game. It was winding down over the years too, all they had left, really. Besides Marina, Felina. Their long-lasting conversation wouldn't begin for another two hours, give or take. But it would be the same. In the brief absence of Cline, now, Birdfinger had his right hand on the seatcover a finger's width from Marina's uncovered leg. It was as close as he'd ever been. Time dilated around them. A soundcheck for a waltz: one one two one one two. The rumor of Willie Nelson waking in the back of the bus. The truck pointing away from the stage, a kingcab Ford pulled alongside. Birdfinger adjusted the rearview mirror to track Cline's silent approach whenever it might come. He talked to Marina of small things and tried to load them with hidden meanings so he could unpack later, at his leisure. He told her the perfect sentence that applied to him: that he was an overfed, longhaired, leaping gnome. Marina considered it, rolled her skirt between her fingers, and said the perfect one for her was still out there on the FM band, awaiting the proper ear. Birdfinger opened his mouth and more lyrics spilled out, because at twenty-six he still didn't know anything real to say; what he came out with was that the devil made him do it the first time, the second time he done it on his own, with the proper pause between lines so she could think he had just been singing, not talking, if it came to that. She took it as conversation, though. She popped her neck unlike a lady and asked what *it* was.

'Coming to the trailer that first night,' Birdfinger said on impulse, then remembered that he'd meant to say it was providence that led him there, the world trying to make up for the myopic mistake of pairing her with his brother. But here she was beside him.

'You know I didn't really hear that,' she said, and Birdfinger nodded, cracked the driverside window because his heavy breathing was steaming up the glass. Cline still wasn't approaching from any mirror angle. Marina drew geometric shapes in the dust on the dash and said the way she could always tell Birdfinger from Cline was that Cline had the potential for a significant gut. Something about pelvis carriage and the wear of his cowboy belt. It was halfway intangible, she said, but there, for her, in the sway of the back, maybe. She patted Birdfinger on the stomach. 'You, though, you're a skinny boy,' she said, 'a wastrel in cowboy clothes.'

Birdfinger looked at himself and said again that he was overfed.

Marina laughed, said maybe, maybe not. Either way he was still lanky, his body indecisive about what and where it wanted to be. She didn't say *unlike Cline*, but Birdfinger heard it. He felt awkward and adolescent in the cab of his brother's truck, with his sister-in-commonlaw.

'In the dark I bet you wouldn't know,' he said, 'between me and him.'

'In the dark,' she said, absorbing the word, 'you'd glow in the dark, Bird, I'm sorry.'

Birdfinger smiled in pain and told her some about Hardwick and the closet days. He told her about looking in the rearview mirror and seeing the cowcatcher of a moving train. He told her about the lightless sky over an abandoned Mississippi trailer park him and Larry found once, the backs of floating carrion birds hot with the sun and crowblack, coloring the land with their collective shade. Marina said he didn't even want to hear her stories like that. 'It gets darker on the reservation than anywhere in america,' she said, 'until we start burning things, I mean. And places.' She did her eyebrows, laid her head on his shoulder like a schoolgirl playing at fear, at love. She'd said it before, too, about the reservation; it was her standard line for killing all talk, an Indian Great Wall. Birdfinger said he was sorry, his stock line. Marina said don't be, then amended, said the only apology she would accept came in a brown bottle.

A knock on the rear window and the beer appeared, blessed by Sally. While Marina wrestled with the lid, refusing help, Birdfinger gathered the stray page of a magazine off the floor, tried to glean a pattern from all the circled letters and pieces of letters. It was Cline's handiwork, his theory on how to decode the enveloped message they'd intercepted earlier in the week that he now kept folded inside an X-ray apron, next to his person. The closest he'd come so far was the ingredients label off of an outdated can of condensed milk; it had a similar cadence and line count. He thought it was maybe Indian, the message, like from the second world war, when they talked, but Marina claimed she was Plains of some sort or another and Larry the Hedger didn't think it much sounded like anything he'd ever heard, and the Mexican Paiute only lowered his head and walked away when asked. His broad back only strengthened Cline's case, though: he said the letter—because it was evidence of encryption which was itself evidence of guilty knowledge and because it was on acid-free bible paper and because it had a vague federal stamp—justified their existence, their mission, made it past reproach, a noble enterprise among noble enterprises. Birdfinger didn't feel ennobled, though. And the world wasn't almost over, as near as he could tell. It was just beginning. But all the same, he let Cline pore over it day in and day out. He even left odd labels in his path. Time-consuming labels. They all did.

Birdfinger never saw him coming, either, Cline, below mirror level. He knocked on the window at the exact moment when Birdfinger was about to give Marina a limerick shaped like a handful of posies, when he had just been watching the individual hairs on her nearside thigh reaching for his finger, attracted by the static coursing over his skin. Love, he called it to himself, then flinched from the sound of Cline's hand, forgot to protect Marina, cursed himself for it. It was bad instincts. He wasn't military. Cline was. He opened the door, beer in hand, offered them the twice-circulated rumor of Willie Nelson waking in the rear of the bus and suspected nothing untoward between them. It wasn't trust. Birdfinger listened, half relieved he wasn't a threat in his brother's eyes, half belittled. But it was the life he was born to. He rolled with it.

There she was outside the truck now, with Cline's hands under her ubermink, under her shirt, her own hands plaiting her hair in the meanwhile, getting it out of the way. There she was dancing on the cab of the truck next to them, in answer to a bet. In eighty or a hundred minutes the concert was going, after a few false starts, now that there was no more honking, no more glasspacks throttling low into the mics and seeping from the speakers like thunder come too close. There was only dirt coating everything, baked on by halogen light. Tailgates lowering, urine splashing, bugs collecting. An unmarked Nova pulling off the road because the road was littered with lawn chairs and people and was unpassable. In less than two hours Birdfinger would be in the Nova's backseat, surrendered. The Pinkertons asking no questions, respecting his silence, his rights, the unspeakable. The Family Goliæ scattered, one less in number: Marina. There was nothing he could do to stop it. But neither could he leave, neither could he look away. For the hundredth time he watched her lead Cline to the cab of his truck, pull the door closed, wet the windows with their labored breathing. Birdfinger retreated, followed kegsmell through the crowd. On stage, Willie and Waylon stumbled through half sets and talked to each other and shared smoke and held the attention of some three hundred people and maybe a quarter as many trucks, drawn in by CB like radio moths.

Birdfinger the Rubbernecker could see it all at once, WWI fisheye-style, from bird height. Strange animals raced by agrin. He concentrated them away, slowed down what he could of the night, localized it, let the winch truck approach *him*, let Larry pull him into line behind it like nobody would see. The winch truck was the beerstand, the endline of the kegsmell; the lift arm was rigged with a canvas tent, edges flayed back so it looked like a field-dressed tepee. Larry said it like that. Birdfinger shrugged. There were body shapes moving behind wet glass in his mind. One of them his, or almost. Practically. A matter of names, of order, of subtleties of build.

The beer was a quarter a cup, depending on who you were or weren't, and the line winding and involved with itself. In it, Birdfinger heard of Palo Duro and the horses massacred there, now deathless and unbreakable, disregarding all fence lines. He hummed Ghostriders in the Sky until the story quieted; he was only here for the beer. Larry talked beside him like a television show but he was easy to tune out. Soon enough he was talking to a passing woman instead, getting her to touch his skunkhair, jumping forward in his small-boned way when she had her arm raised, her beer scared down the front of her white tube top. Her pair of boyfriends remained after she'd left, keeping thankless track of Larry and Birdfinger's place in line. They were either patient or slow to anger. Birdfinger pretended it didn't concern him. He was trying to gain weight at a breakneck pace. He was reliving his time in the cab with Marina word by word. Larry pulled him out of it with a rib elbow: approaching down the windless side of the line was the recentmost customer, two beer cups in each hand, the rollbumper still impressed on his thighs where he'd leaned against the winch truck.

His face when Birdfinger got up to it rushed at him like one of the two was falling towards the other, and Birdfinger distinctly heard the door of the Adobe Abode creaking open on the Family Goliæ: it was the USPS driver, his left ear purple from Cline pressing the side of his head into the federal property steering wheel, whispering paranoid, unreal demands for information no mortal could have. There was recognition in the driver's eyes too. And fear. He was still the lesser number. Birdfinger tried to make himself smaller. Larry was two steps ahead, already making necessary friends with the driver, reliving the hijacking as if it were a bad part of a worse movie, the low point of the day, an accident, bad circumstances. He piled the words on until they became apologies without admissions of guilt. He made eyes to Birdfinger to play along.

Birdfinger did. He drank the driver's beer and nodded that there wasn't much money involved with knocking over mailtrucks. But then again, that's what they were—small time, making the small hauls. Birthday cards and the like. Gentleman bandits for a tamed West.

Birdfinger nodded with Larry's story, kept nodding, and in the moment before the driver began nodding with him and said he had been going to rob his own truck any damn ways—fuck the postmaster general—Birdfinger saw a thin grey film roll into place over the man's pupils: he was talking his way out of it too. They were all play acting. Nothing was real. Just that they were in line. When they weren't even that anymore, Birdfinger didn't mention the pupil-thing to Larry the Bullet Sweater. He couldn't: he had the rim of a beer cup clenched between his teeth, three in each hand, and four spilling against his chest. Eight dollars worth they'd bought and shared with the driver. Happy birthday, Larry said to all, someone's money put to good use, and when he took the lead, Birdfinger hung back, took a shadow route. Left Larry the Lapsed and Lapsing Laguna to his fate with the two boyfriends and their hard hands.

He followed the driver instead, lost him twice, found him again with the CB handle held hard to his mouth, his remaining beer lined up on the dash of a foreign truck like in a shooting gallery, bam bam bam. Birdfinger swallowed. He couldn't run with all the beer he was holding close, so he walked long sloshing steps, but they weren't long enough. As he approached, he saw *Nova* register in Sally's openwide eyes, heard it behind him, on his neck, and then the beer was falling and he was light on his feet, diving into the steamed-up cab of Cline's Ford, telling him go go go. Cline never needed to be told anything twice. He was always almost already in action. He pulled out of Marina and the Thunderbird engine came to life, competing for a moment with the oversized speakers of WWI. Marina didn't bother to cover herself. There wasn't time. But she still had the fur wrap around her shoulders, a fetish in-the-making. All three mirrors flooded the cab with strobing blue lights. The truck lifted maybe two inches when Sally rolled off the tailgate, and then the right tire was spinning in place, the passenger side pulling chrome trim from the kingcab beside it, fishtailing into the motionless congestion of trucks. It was always like this. A bottle spiderwebbed the windshield and Cline had the presence of mind to click on the wipers. His military training. Marina wasn't screaming. She was a calm nude, fingers dug into the saddle blanket seatcover. They ran. They grazed a one-ton Chevy and tore the rear bumper off Cline's Ford, a parting gift. Beer bottles rained their way. The Nova was practically chained to them. They pulled it from the audience in first gear, no longer able to even see the stage for all the dirt they'd thrown and were throwing. When they got to the first fence a quarter mile out, Cline didn't hesitate. They drove through the five strings and the wire was new and tight and it almost made a chord sound when it broke, and it was a concert they were leaving.

Birdfinger held onto the dash and could no longer slow things down. He planted his feet and rode it out, because the part of him that was looking back knew where they were going, and how, and what he would have to do. Ahead was the Mexican Paiute, always near but never quite close. He was standing on top of a leaned-over horseproof fence with new metal poles that hadn't been planted deep enough. Cline's truck limped across the pasture, backlit by the Nova. He drove over the fence screaming, one arm out the window, and behind him the Mexican Paiute stepped off the fence, and it stood again, before the Pinkertons. They slid into it, stretched it, and even bent three of the poles, but the Nova was a light car against a good fence, and its city tires couldn't get the purchase to push through. It backed away, breathing radiator smell, exhaust growling, then followed the fence north for the chance of a gate, one Pinkerton sitting on the window with binoculars, tie streaming. They would be twenty minutes getting through. Birdfinger stood for a moment with the Mexican Paiute, trying to decipher his role in all this. It was useless. He was native stone. Together they watched the Ford taillights draw together in a kiss goodbye. This was the last part of the night where it still might look like the good guys were getting away again. But the vision was shortlived. And the Mexican Paiute seemed to be in on it; he looked hard and knowing at Birdfinger the Revisitor like he always did, like maybe he was looking through him, taking one last look at the concert, and then he lowered his head, retrieved a long bundle from the base of the fence, and walked south, away, to wherever he went at these in-between times.

Birdfinger followed the truck. It never let up—Cline never let up. He still had a hard-on, was still yelling, the windshield wipers still keeping time. There were demons in pursuit. There always were. He led them through the dry grass, traded the hard dirt part of the pasture for the shinnery part, where there was sand for ground. It grabbed the front wheels and locked them sideways. The Ford pushed a mound in front of the remaining headlight and then tried to turn out of it, rolled slow instead, first onto its side, then all the way over, bodyparts groaning.

Cline killed the engine.

Birdfinger remembered it against his will, what came next, what had to come next: their bodies reslapping together, Cline and Marina's, Birdfinger playing unconscious, face pressed into the headliner, neck cocked at an unhealthy angle, Waylon Jennings coming at them across the pasture. It lasted for hours it seemed. Cline whispered that heaven and earth couldn't stop them tonight, and Marina just made animal noises into his neck. Once her hand touched Birdfinger's sleeve. He thought he heard his name breathed. It was too much, sensory overload, depraved indifference. He could smell it when they were done. Cline rolled out of the truck for a damage report. Birdfinger felt himself pulled through the window, because the doors were jammed. He played along—groggy, unaware—but then something broke inside of him, and he quit stumbling and rubbing his eyes, just told Cline the truth for once: He'd been listening. It was the opening statement of their twelve-year conversation.

They shared a broken cigarette, listened to Marina dress in the cab. Moved slow and ponderous like the giants they had become. Bragged about Ford body strength, how the truck was unharmed in the soft sand, how the four barrel had even worked upside down, in the face of gravity. Maybe a mile off a gun popped one two three: the Pinkertons, running the padlock through with lead. There wasn't much time left. Cline said something about snipe hunters. Birdfinger nodded, smiled, smoked.

'So you say you were listening,' Cline said.

Birdfinger nodded, said he'd seen it before.

Cline smothered the cigarette. 'But not with her, not in real life, at least.'

Birdfinger looked at him and stared, like that would make him unguilty, shrive him clean on the spot. But then he realized he didn't so much want to be clean anymore. Cline stood into his pants and asked Birdfinger if she'd sounded the same as he'd thought she would. They were maybe three sentences away from violence, in any direction, and Birdfinger had no combat training. He chose his words carefully. He said he'd never stepped over any bounds.

'I know,' Cline said, making eyes, 'not you. Shit.'

Birdfinger swallowed, scratched his chin on his left shoulder, stood. They were the same height, same everything. It was funny. He didn't care anymore about combat training. He was tired of their game. He couldn't will himself to water the tension down with a fitting comeback. He talked low and even and didn't look away when he said it: 'Not that I couldn't have now, Cline.' He didn't have to say it twice. Cline swung openfisted into the side of Birdfinger's head, and Birdfinger fell to his right and smiled to be breaking capillaries for her, Marina. It was sweet. It tasted of iron and rust. He milked it for years. He said it again—*anytime*—and Cline kicked him, and he rolled with it out of time, and when he returned they were fighting on the ground like brothers, knees and elbows and teeth. Hardwick's twin sons in the dirt. Birdfinger yelled to be yelling, sang El Paso through his bloodied teeth, stanza by stanza. It was beautiful, a high point. Cline held Birdfinger's head down by the hair and told him to fucking eat it, the song, the singing, the claim, but Birdfinger refused, turned his head towards the truck and sang to her, for her, a serenade. Cline locked his elbow and pressed the side of Birdfinger's head harder into the ground, and it was because of that that he saw it and couldn't look away, had to witness the cab of the truck crumple slow under its own bodyweight. It just happened, gravity calling in its marker. Birdfinger saw it in its three seconds of fullness and felt it in his spine forever. And he made Cline see it and feel it with him: they hadn't escaped, weren't escaping.

When they got to her she was still warm, she was dressed, she was dying, trying to make words. In them, Birdfinger heard his name again, one avian syllable, and then he was pushed away, flying along the fence for help, towards WWI.

A half mile back he met the Pinkertons in their wounded Nova and surrendered, traded himself for a radio call, traded the Goliards eight months later for a cemetery visit, traded his waking hours for coffee at Wyvonne's.

Two years passed while Birdfinger stood in place in the Canyon diner, afraid to move, then ten more.

He said into the receiver to Cline that there were probably birds on the line, great speckled extinct things sent to censor communication between the dead and the living. He was talking like Marty Robbins, even though Cline had heard through it two calls ago and said so. But it was the only voice he had. They forewent any formal greetings. They were brothers. The preliminaries were all gainsaid. Cline spoke first. He said Marina wasn't just going to show up in a damn waitress apron in Clovis New Mexico, unmartyred, serving coffee to the living. Birdfinger said she already had once, for him. Cline said he wasn't your everyday fool-sufferer. Birdfinger pressed his face hard into the holey side of the phone booth, breaking capillaries for love again, chemical flares bursting behind his eyes, where he was looking.

He lied to Cline that he was out in the West Texas town of El Paso. It was in character with the voice. He was still serenading; it had never ended: he was Orpheus; he had brought her back once. Cline laughed through his nose, funneled it through the line somehow, then told Birdfinger enough, it stops here: Birdfinger had never crossed any boundaries except in the tea-stained twists of his tea-stained mind. Birdfinger recalled what 1977 had tasted like—sharp, bitter, necessary—and then purged, gave voice to what he'd kept bottled up for ten years: 'She said my name, Cline, right at the end, when it counted most.'

'She didn't say your name, Bird.'

'She thought you were me.'

'Fuck that.'

'Even before, in the truck.'

'Is this what you tell yourself?'

'This is what's true. You never knew her.'

'I knew her in every way.'

'And I knew her in more.'

There was silence on the line for too long, then Cline breathed through the small speaker that even if she had ever come back, if such bullshit were possible, it wouldn't be for him, Birdfinger. He wasn't her husband, the father of her child, the one in disguise in the waiting room of the coma ward, apologizing. He wasn't anything to her.

Birdfinger swallowed, closed his eyes to whatever town he was in.

He said he knew her secret name: Felina. He said she had her grandmother's mole on the back of her hand, climbing with every generation. He said he knew where she was when she was four years old: Heart Butte, peeking over a junked car at the northern lights, waiting for them to part like a curtain. He said even her commonlaw husband didn't know these things, didn't know the real her like he did, Birdfinger. 'You never really had her at all,' he said to Cline, 'not in any lasting way.'

There was unmeasured silence on the Clovis end of the line, and then Cline said to tell him more. There were three distinct breaths in the sentence. They satisfied the part of Birdfinger that needed satisfying. He said again that he hadn't really been knocked out: he heard her say his name in the throes. It might as well have been him under her. There was no real difference. They were the same body, him and Cline.

Cline said no.

Birdfinger said when she came back she didn't even want to see her former husband.

Cline said no again, but his mouth wasn't to the phone, and Birdfinger could hear that on that end everything was gone in life, nothing was left. He was still singing inside. He couldn't help it. He had bitten through his lip for love and was bleeding from the mouth and into the receiver. He didn't apologize. He promised himself never to. He had said what needed to be said. And now there was no more. Only a drive in the Cutlass back to Clovis to get the news, attend the funeral. But that was hours and days away. He had time to go through it one more time still. He crumpled in the phone booth, kicked the door closed, and started the conversation from the top, staring at his hands twinned on the formica, controlling his voice and telling Cline he could court any woman he pleased, any.

After two times through, Birdfinger finally had to acknowledge that the formica under his hands was wire-mesh tabletop, lawn furniture, and WWI had been unvoiced in the real sense, reduced to a poster, to a stray episode in a comfortable woman's life. And it was more. Birdfinger leaned forward, back into suburbia, four chairfeet on the ground again, then stood, plowed through the cropped-short grass to the gardener man. He looked back once at Stiya 6 and she already seemed a part of the back porch scene; the cookie woman was explaining about her close encounter, the light in the sky, how her escort had noticed it first, pointed with his lightly-furred arm. There were royalties involved, check stubs to be seen, tall tales to be told. Stiya 6 was nodding: *maybe.*

Inside, cookies were burning.

Outside, the man of the house was stoney-eyed, grinning.

He told Birdfinger the stalk conformed to no known taxonomy.

Birdfinger said he understood. They bagged the last load together. When it was done, Birdfinger squatted up against the fence, extracted paper from his wallet, rolled a thin joint, lit it slow and painful off the exhaust. The gardener man sat by him. Stiya 6 and the cookie woman were Siamese-twinned over the wire-topped lawn table, forehead to forehead, the cookie woman's mouth racing over the held-down poster, Stiya 6's eyes darting now and again to Birdfinger like she was unsure, like she could feel the trap closing around her. But she'd wanted the trap too.

Birdfinger asked the gardener man if he was serious about his offer to the girl, about staying. The gardener man asked in return if his eyes were bleeding. Birdfinger said no, it was only crying. He said he didn't know him well enough to say why. But give him time, give him time. He clapped the gardener man on the knee, handed him one of the cookies he'd pocketed for later. The gardener man showed sincere gratitude. Birdfinger said there was nearly three hundred dollars under the lemonade pitcher. He said he was sorry. He said Stiya 6's name was Marina, Felina.

'Like the song?'

'Exactly like the song.'

The gardener man smiled, simpático. Birdfinger told him to hold his joint while he fertilized a bit. He didn't give him a chance to say no. He passed it to him, walked to a corner, but didn't pee, just held himself and spied: the gardener man balanced the joint under his nose, squinched his eyes, looked to see who on the back porch might be watching. Only Stiya 6—Marina to him, Felina. She instantly scanned the fenceline. Birdfinger closed his eyes to hide. When he opened them she was in motion, Stiya 6, stiff-legged, walking on the grass to the gardener man, backhanding the joint into the alley, sparks fizzling in the sprinkler dew. The gardener man said he could get up himself, thank you. He said this was his own damn backyard, this was america, he paid his taxes. Birdfinger eased back into the floodlight, appraised Stiya 6.

'You're doing this on purpose,' she said in a serious voice, 'just so I'll go with you in trade for leaving him be.'

'Its just that I'm not houseguest material. Bad habits and all.'

'These are people, though, a family.'

'We're people.'

'They don't deserve this, us.'

'There's only three bags. I can go it alone if I need to.'

They stared at each other. The gardener man navigated the area between them, pushing the grass to the side and then applying one-sixth pressure on each foot, his legs bowing out, trying to displace body weight. The back porch was silent, expectant. Grass blades folded and didn't unfold. Birdfinger turned to the muffled noise he could still pick up: the cookie woman was patting her face rapidfire with her napkin, maybe trying to dab away the sight of her strain-faced Damon, plundering the cookie platter now, fisting them into his mouth two at a time. The gardener man looked at his hands and then at his failed footprints and then to his wife for help, but she could only dab and dab some more, mutter about her petroleum-arts student and the wrought iron sculpture he had in front of his red-roofed house, halfway across town. The gardener man's shoulders spoke of defeat. But then he straightened them, forced them straight. He removed the tarp ceremoniously from the lawn mower. He eyed the implements radiating out from him, looked from hitch to trailer tongue to hitch. Birdfinger could just make out a caravan in the gardener man's pupils, an escape route in fourth gear, no PTO, utility trailer stocked with munchies, the rest strung out according to size and function. On to greener lawns, other yards in different climes. If the gate was wide enough. He started the lawn mower, and under the engine sound the smoke alarm in the house was screaming about the cookies. Stiya 6 lowered her head and said *Okay already, okay*. Enough. It was. They each shouldered a bag, dragged the third between. Birdfinger only looked back once, when he was closing the gate, forcing uncounted money between the boards in apology: the kid was standing behind the double french doors, unasleep, inhaling smoke, watching, androgynous face framed by hands on glass.

First Vanetta, now a whole family.

The dogs talked about it through the fences.

Birdfinger pulled away, headlights off, feeling his way out of residential. Stiya 6 was silent. Birdfinger put in her

Buffy St James cassette but there was only one good song on the tape and it was already over. A fire truck ran them off the road, into another family's lawn. Birdfinger fish-tailed across the wet grass, caught an art deco mailbox with the passenger side, and didn't say anything either. They were fighting. There was conflict. Things were going by fast for town. There was one hundred and fifty-odd pounds of mulched pot in the trunk. It conformed to no known taxonomy. Birdfinger broke down and said it tasted like shit, like real true shit, like no sane person would ever buy it, not even in Gallup New Mexico. No response. The streets played themselves out. He knew where he had to go. He told Stiya 6 he had a stop to make, a thing to do, a rat to kill. In the parking lot of the Clinic he counted the money he had left: three hundred and eighty dollars. He checked his pocket for burn holes, found none. He counted again, then killed the Cutlass, told Stiya 6 to keep the windows up, radio down. She said he just didn't want her to get away. She was right. Birdfinger had no response, had to back away slow.

In the windless space by the Clinic's glass door, he smoked the rest of another thin joint and tried to spit out the taste as it came. He knocked on the door with one of the cement ashtrays lined around the entry, rehurt his hurt shoulder. He threw the ashtray into the glass and it rebounded, fell to pieces on the ground. He kicked them back into the glass, saw himself in action. This was where he'd bought Cline's boots. He'd thrown the ashtray before, too. And three beers out of a six-pack, two of which he came back for later that same night. The other he regretted. The kid had never come here with him, though, not even on the bad nights. Pretending it didn't exist, pretending he didn't care, that none of it mattered. Birdfinger counted the money again. He was six hundred and twenty dollars short of having a cool thousand to bluff Sam with. The new bargaining tactic was to pretend he wanted out, wanted to buy twenty-five percent of himself back: two bidders would drive the price up. It was the law of the auction block. Birdfinger inhaled, held it in and wished Vanetta could have seen the decision Stiya 6 had made, to protect the family, to sacrifice herself. It was evidence of her maternal nature, her true self coming through, her old self. But too, she'd been protecting the family from him. Birdfinger rubbed his face on the knee of his pants, became white and yellow again.

He said to Vanetta that Stiya 6 was real.

He yelled to Sam the Bastard and tried to melt the plastiglass between them with the end of his joint. It worked, made a pinhole he could yell names through, trying to keep his lips small and pointed to focus the sound down the long hall. Finally a labcoated figure rounded the corner, wheeled oxygen canister in tow. Sam. He walked in zigzags, wall to wall, as if reorienting himself. He ditched the canister with a host of others. He put his ear to the pinhole. Birdfinger whispered through. He said he wanted Sam to take a down-payment on buying himself back.

Sam said through the hole that all deals were final. He pointed to a sign on the door: NO DICKERING.

Birdfinger said he didn't come here to dicker. He came here to get out.

Sam's pupils were uncapped wells. When he talked through the hole he looked like an armadillo, kissing. Birdfinger mentioned it. Sam didn't see the humor. He said it was late, he was no longer in the mood to deal. Birdfinger said he would pay more, Sam could turn over two-hundred dollars inside of six months. He flashed the wad of money, made it look large. Sam was uninterested. He said the only profit that concerned him was the scientific kind. And that was called progress. Birdfinger said please, said he would get on his knees but the pinhole would be too high to talk through then.

Sam shook his oblong head no.

Birdfinger walked out of the doorway, walked back in, all part of the show. He said he wasn't like Cline. Sam agreed: Birdfinger was no Mirror Man. Birdfinger said that's not what he meant. What he meant was he wasn't too proud to say he didn't know what he was getting into, he wasn't too proud to get on a payment plan. He humbled himself in front of the glass. Sam laughed without his mouth. He placed his lips to the hole, drew back, coughed, returned. 'I've got to get back into the lab,' he said, 'my senior citizens aren't going to dissect themselves.'

'A king without clemency?'

'A man with a contract.'

Birdfinger said it then, his second sleeve-ace of the day, a threat: 'I'll leave Curry County, die under a false name. And then what?'

Sam admitted that he still owed Birdfinger some money.

Birdfinger lied that he could pay his debts without science.

Sam hemmed and hawed, made a show of going though his pockets, lipsynched the standard alimony dirge, verse and chapter, detailing his son's extravagant therapeutical needs and the costume fees involved. Birdfinger sagged into the rough wall. Things weren't going as planned. There was no dickering going on, no bidding. There was no hard bargain being driven. Not by him at least. It was the damn sign. It was on the inside of the glass too, so he couldn't scratch it off, pretend he'd never seen it. Birdfinger said to the Vanetta in his head that he was a loss cutter, that he knew when to go out, when to stay in, when to hold and when to fold. He made her smile, beam, nod approval.

When he returned to the Cutlass minutes later, it was overheated. Stiya 6 asked how much, already? and Birdfinger pretended not to hear. In the final stage of bargaining he'd been stethoscoped through the unlocked mail slot. He had a hundred and twenty dollars more in his pocket now, rubber-banded tight, insulated with a stray wrapper. Which made five hundred. Which was what Cline brought twenty years ago. Stiya 6 asked again and then didn't ask anymore. There by the headlit dumpster was the paisley suitcase. It belonged in the trunk: nothing free for Sam. After collecting it the Cutlass followed the road back to the trailer, radiator steam streaming along the hood in a tight column and then snaking up the windshield, green smell coming through the vents. Birdfinger tricked long-grain stalk from under his fingernail, let it slide out the side window. The silence was complete. In it, Birdfinger could hardly recognize Marina.

Soon enough, the trailer rose in front of them. No lights, just a long low shape with seventy-one thousand miles on it. Birdfinger coasted in, parked midyard, sat, watched Stiya 6 jimmy the doorknob open, close it behind her. She was beautiful. Her wig was still tucked behind the visor.

Birdfinger carried it with him, woke the renter in the nearest shelter and explained about him and Stiya 6, about drawing closer through conflict, through long and mutual silences. The renter introduced himself as PFC. Just the letters. Ex-Navy, surly-nerved, unshaven. Here in Clovis looking for the hatch he crawled out of thirty-four years back, a born again lover of dry land and analog clocks. His story involved signed waivers and retroengineered alien bean technology and a conspiracy to deny him retirement benefits. Birdfinger ran his fingers through the wig and endured. At least PFC didn't want anything besides a shelter for the night. He was straight up with his intentions: to locate and salvage his old submarine for scrap iron. Fuck 'em, fuck 'em all. Birdfinger touched him on the back when he started coughing, wasn't sure where to put his hand. PFC touched him in return, on the bicep, lowered his voice and said that after a while, the silence between a man and a woman can become a gulf. He said he got that out of a vending machine in a bar in the Southern Pacific, pick a port. Birdfinger traded him the X-ray specs for it. PFC slid them on carefully with both hands and said tomorrow he would find the damn submarine, be a rich man, and then it all would have been worth it, what they had to do to survive. But tonight he had some sleep to be getting back to, if Birdfinger was through with him.

Birdfinger was. He helped him into the shelter, shooed the cats away, stood guard for a bit, adjusted the hearing aid and then homed in on a flapping on the backside of the trailer. It was the tarpaper over the stalk hole. His house wasn't weatherproof. It was moveable. He gathered stones to weigh the tarpaper down at the bottom, but when he drew close he could hear Stiya 6 breathing irregularly on the couch, her feet rubbing together in the corner, changing places. He wanted to wake her and tell her it was the right, they were parked to the *right* side of the stage, *they* were the disturbance that defined the concert, but she was sleeping. He let her sleep. He had promised to do something good. He said it to himself like that. He said it to Vanetta. Tomorrow he would tell her about their truck, Cline's Ford, limping off into the pasture. Or the next day. For the moment, he weighted the tarpaper down, made it secure, and then returned to his post over the Navy man's shelter, throwing stray beer bottles away from the trailer just to keep his hands busy, to keep from waking her.

Pidgin Agonistes

It was a graceless ride back to Clovis. Larry said there was no need for language. Pidgin told him to go to hell. His face was raw, sensitive to the heat, the rest of him ill-tempered. Larry suggested a stage name: Rothchilde. As in anger. Pidgin said he didn't need his help, thanks. He tried hiding behind his visor, but on the vinyl flipside were stillshots lifted from *The Scræling,* dummied into oldstyle postcards. The words on the back of the postcards were love lines to Sally, unsent. Larry said he'd send them but he was still in Indian Witness Protection. He said the government called it Relocation. Pidgin didn't laugh. On the back of Larry's visor were postcards addressed to *Atticus Wean,* from Sally. The pictures on front were daguerreotypes of mutilated white settlers, riddled with arrows. Sally had drawn in more arrows with a thin eraser. There were no pledges of love in the blank spaces. Larry said it was understood. Pidgin looked away. They were passing in daylight now what he'd passed twice already in the night. It was the same. It was inevitable. Larry claimed diarrhea and stopped at every bathroom, shuffled in with a dull jackknife and his leatherbound *Carmina Burana*. The diarrhea he said was from the Weanie feast he'd attended in the predawn; the *Carmina Burana* was in Latin.

Pidgin opened the door on him at a rest stop, caught him transposing translations onto the side of a stall. Larry had three lines of verse half-framed with the *L* of his thumb and index finger, the book pressed open just to the upper left, held with an elbow. They stared, held the moment, parted. In the truck again Larry didn't explain. His hands were blurred though, nostrils flared and shiny. He rubbed Rogaine into his thin beard, a defense mechanism. Pidgin read his love lines aloud, littered the ditch with the postcards one by one. Larry responded with a story Pidgin didn't want to hear. It was about the Mexican Paiute. It was a warning. It was the verbal record of Cline Stob in soiled fatigues, dislocated from his unit, moving from broadleaf to broadleaf across a delta Larry refused to call by name. Indian Country, Year of the Monkey. It was Cline's first tour and his last. He was following the path of least noise. It led him to a birdless place maybe forty feet wide, with gravemounds spaced regularly, within arm's reach of each other. The centerpiece was the Mexican Paiute. He was motionless but unsleeping, ptomained in war. He had created a sacred place in a foreign land. Cline recognized it from his own internal landscape, recognized the calm determination necessary to collect bodies, the compulsion. He breathed the oily air with difficulty, but didn't cough. Manners pressed: he approached the Mexican Paiute, and the Mexican Paiute let him. He asked who all was buried here. The Mexican Paiute shrugged with one shoulder, his left, then looked around. Cline told him about Clovis New Mexico, used apocalyptic terms to do it, gestured wide, brought it all back into himself in a tight, sternum-level fury. He traced a line in the humus that led from Vietnam to the trailer and rested his fingertip on the trailer like it was the center of the world. Larry leveled his voice across the bench seat and said to Pidgin this is how things happen. He laughed. Rogaine beaded on the many tips of his beard and dripped into bulletproof rhinestone.

Pidgin said the Goliards were bullshit.

Larry said again there was no need for language. Pidgin said go to hell. It started over. Larry suggested a stage name for Pidgin: Archilde. As in *our*. Pidgin asked him if he had a mouse in his pocket. He fingered the penultimate postcard Larry was tracking and pretending not to. He dwelt on Birdfinger and Marina Trigo and causality, on the Salvage Queen even the Mexican Paiute had deferred to. The image of Cline's verbal record settled twenty-five years after the fact. Pidgin told Larry he didn't get the warning. He held the last unsent postcard hostage, demanded the particulars of Sally's related prediction. Larry overkilled: there was Sally sleeping, talking in her sleep, unrandom collisions with her sensory mucosa presaging the end of the upstart Goliards and the rebeginning. Nestled in her stomach was their child, Larry's and Sally's, the rebeginner. The prediction was originally for it, for him, a tailormade quatrain, validation for the pact the six of them had already made. But then. Larry said Pidgin was just a stand-in for the real replacement. Pidgin said replacement for what? Larry opened his palm for the promised postcard. Pidgin surrendered it. Larry let it go out his own window, drew from his jacket of many interior pockets an electric screwdriver. It whirred the three screws from the triangular base of his love-lined visor. He held it out the window, let go, put his sunglasses on close to the face, told the pending story of how he planned to recoup the ten thousand lost at Shy Kidneys: he was going to start a new religion, one even more eucharistian. The sacrament was stick gum laced with prechewed peyote. He had six starter cases behind the seat, a jerked thumb indicating them. Pidgin didn't look, wouldn't be diverted.

'Replacement for what?' he said.

'Telling you screws it all up, y'know,' Larry said without lips. 'Sally drilled it.' He pressed a fingertip into his forehead, tuned in some obscure Van Morrison from a station with too many call letters. He said it was cover. He talked under it. He said he loved Sally, don't get him wrong, but he had personal reasons for *wanting* to screw it all up: he wasn't ready to die. He told Pidgin that the child he almost fathered was supposed to have been the next Golias incarnation, come from within the group, as had to be. The Primate of Order, yes. He spoke carefully of the unborn dead. Pidgin understood: no names. Only

Golias, Cline Stob, Marina Trigo, Big Spring Sally, Birdfinger. Larry. Now there were six. He asked it: 'The Mexican Paiute then, he's her Golias?'

Larry nodded. 'For now,' he said.

Pidgin said to consider him warned.

'What does he do, though?' Pidgin asked.

'Thought you knew.'

'He steals dead people, as far as I know.'

Larry nodded, said he didn't sleep anymore.

The image of the Mexican Paiute and tightlipped Cline morphed again: they were in colorless fatigues now, flowing through the dank underbrush, outrunning history. Pidgin could feel the corpse-weight on his shoulder. He resisted, replaced the image with Utah, but in Utah he was in Provo, and in Provo he was bartering a second-party supply check for busfare to Clovis. And then here he was again. The ligature dents on Larry's neck swelled red in the unvisored sun. Van Morrison carried them bodily to the next gas station, Finder's Keep. They sat the offside of the pumps in silence, unable to look away from the dairy tanker not fifty feet ahead of them, the bandy-legged Pochteca on the payphone, the udders positioned over a drain, an arm extended from that drain, milking steady, kneading information to the end of the teat. Larry said he'd been seeing too much of that lately; Pidgin said he wasn't seeing it in the first place.

They left the truck gassing up—Pidgin to the store, Larry to the bathroom. The clerk called himself Atanacio Morena, said *¿quien es usted?* Pidgin didn't give his name up so easy though, anymore. He said to Atanacio Morena just the burrito, please, but Atanacio Morena didn't so much deal in money; he had the store to himself.

'Where you going,' he asked Pidgin, '¿á donde va?'

Pidgin got Atanacio Morena to repeat the question slower, syllable by syllable, and during the *o* of *going* looked down Atanacio Morena's throat for the see-through webbing he suspected. There was none. He discounted his eyes: he'd *seen* none. He confessed: 'Clovis.'

'Who with though?'

'Atticus Wean.'

This was a funny thing to Atanacio Morena. He watched himself laugh in the convex mirror, his mouth huge, teeth individual. He gave the burrito to Pidgin out of pity. Pidgin ate in silence until Larry swaggered in, folding the knife against his thigh. He nodded to Atanacio Morena. Atanacio Morena asked how was business, kimosabe? Larry-as-Atticus Wean said the rodeo hadn't been so good to him this time around, mi amigo. Atanacio Morena let his smile ride, asked if Larry had anything special for today's display case. Pidgin caught Larry looking at him. Larry shook his head no once, and then again, quick and discrete. Pidgin felt uninitiated. Under the glass were miniature coyotes made with real hair patches. The claim on the label was that they were mounted life size. Above the case was the token jackalope, the tortoise with the snake head and matching rattles for tail. Larry approached the counter with a handful of plastic lemons, traded three sticks of gum for them. Atanacio Morena smelled the gum, looked from Larry to Pidgin, then smiled ear to ear and told Pidgin to hold on.

Pidgin swallowed the last of his pity burrito and pushed both glass doors open, left before things could escalate, Larry in tow.

His stage name now either was or wasn't Golias.

He told himself it wasn't. He pointed to the dairy tanker and told Larry there was the underground channel of information the Goliards had wasted their youth looking for in post offices. Larry pulled away, squelched Van Morrison, then said they had wasted nothing—two days before WWI they *had* found what they were looking for, Cline's resistance piece. *That's* what the tanker drivers were still trying to reclaim, the parcel they had lost in shipping and been looking for ever since.

'I never saw it,' Pidgin said, 'not for twelve years, anyways.'

'It was in the truck with your mother. There were full body searches.'

'I never heard of it, either.'

'Because he never decoded it.'

'Then it was nothing, more bullshit.'

Larry shook his head no. Pidgin said their secret was safe with him. Larry slowed, said he knew it wasn't bullshit because the tanker drivers were willing to pay big money for it, after all this time he knew it wasn't bullshit because he still *had* the damn thing, because the government never caught him that night—they couldn't recognize him, face swollen blue; he knew it wasn't bullshit because they had left the truck where it rolled until the following Monday, giving him time and darkness to recover the letter Cline had stashed on instinct in the last possible moments. Larry had then wrapped it in Marina Trigo's hair-on mantle and buried it deep deep, to hide it.

'And now you've got yourself a spy ring?'

'I figured it out.'

'And?'

'And it's about the end of the world, just like your dad thought. But more poetic, more stochastic.'

'And.'

'It's a suicide note, okay? Some panflash Fermat of a skin. He starved himself to death writing the note, over and over. Trying to figure it. There's some kind of lesson there.'

'They're not that hard to write.'

'I guess you'd know. Sorry. His was, anyway. All numbers, a fingerlength optimization algorithm.' Larry paused for dramatic effect, and Pidgin's *and* was implied this time. Larry continued: 'In simulations it allowed certain DNA strands to replicate aggressively in a liquid suspension that more or less matches american drinking water standards. Makes of genetic lability a liability. *Is* beautiful.'

'*Is* bullshit.'

'That's what you're supposed to think. You're supposed to think Indians couldn't come up with a resistance this sophisticated. That's why it'd be so easy to pull off.'

'It's never even been tested I bet.'

'It was never even delivered, mi amigo, thanks to us—to your dad. And the DNA strands?' Larry laughed, said this was the poetic part, the part that made it all worth it, almost, was why the tanker drivers were willing to pawn everything to buy it back: 'The only variable ever ran through it, the only algorithm that *worked*, was, you guessed it, indigenous, was that Fermat skin's own DNA—

'Meaning he was a throwback.'

'Meaning that that coded letter your father interdamncepted, coupled with some of that throwback blood, some likely drop points, and about five parallel years underground, is something like plans for contaminating the american watershed, retaking the northern half of the continent from the marrow on out. Heritage reclaimed and all that BS. Poetry, my friend. The stuff of songs.'

Pidgin turned away, faced the ditch: america on polio crutches, on stilts, moving forward in choreographed jerks. But moving.

He told Larry to go to hell.

Larry said he wasn't going to die.

It didn't start over. Soon the grain elevators of Clovis approached, and Larry took to the backroads, feeling along fencelines, telling Pidgin about his geodesic dome home by Portales, the wealth he had amassed there—the conquistador breastplates as bedpans, the exsanguinated horses, gelded clean, mounted on their sides in a perfect ring of burnt astroturf, the extensive foil collection dating back to privateer times. Pidgin said Larry wasn't a pirate; New Mexico was landlocked. Larry said he was the best fencer ever to escape the Acoma reservation, and not a bad taxidermist either, on the side. Pidgin cut him short, asked how long till they got there? Larry laughed with the outside corners of his eyes, said in deep falsetto that the home of the brave wasn't for them or their kind anymore. It was off limits, uninfested. He hadn't been there himself in nine days now.

'I'm in quarantine,' he said, 'you too.'

'I don't feel like I'm in quarantine.'

'It just started.'

'Infested with what?'

Larry didn't answer. Pidgin could hear him sweating, though. He asked where *were* they going then? Larry said he had traplines to check. Pidgin said this wasn't beaver otter or weasel territory. Larry said he was more a coyote man. Pidgin said he believed it. They were out of lines to trade back and forth. They felt down the rutroads in silence, moving in the direction of dead and dying animals. The first trap was on the backside of a wash, with the wind blowing downhill towards it. Larry was breathing hard as they stepped out of the cab. He said they had to prepare: from somewhere in the inner folds of his jacket he extracted two matched rapier handguards, threw one on the seat by Pidgin and polished his on his sleeve, careful of the jagged rhinestone cuffs. Pidgin inspected his handguard; it had a threaded female mount. The male turned out to be one of the twin mirror-mounted stubby CB antennae. Larry unscrewed his with care, then coupled handguard to blade, aligned his thumb, and swished it once, twice, until the rubber antenna sheath slung off and he could trace sword motions back and forth, a smooth left-handed Indian duelist, blade awhistle. Pidgin couldn't help but acknowledge the shapes he cut through the air. He didn't even assemble his own four-sided rapier; it was enough to watch Larry slash his way into dusk, pink and hazy, fist on hip, off elbow jutting, a rudder. For a moment he envied the Goliards their ignorant bravado, their sense of mission, but in the next he denied them.

Larry stopped long enough to assemble Pidgin's weapon for him. 'For the birds,' he said, flinging the sheath off neatly, and again, Pidgin agreed. But when they got to the trap there really were birds, great hulking buzzards walking in clockwise circles around the barely breathing coyote. They walked like old men, careful of each foot placement. Pidgin asked did they get tired of flying or what? Larry never missed a step: he approached the buzzards cutting the blue air into ribbons, and they lifted themselves reluctantly away, tangled in it. Pidgin took two fast practice swings, felt the blade flex when he changed its direction, then relend its weight, the tip completing his swing. It was nice. He held his lips in a thin Spanish line like Zorro, shadow-fenced a poisoned mesquite, then looked around in time to see Larry run the coyote through the neck, pinning it to the ground, the blade cleaning itself on the hair-lined wound. 'Point,' he said. They carried the coyote between them back to the truck, hefted it into the bed, and then covered it with the fur wrap Larry said had special significance for Pidgin: it was a lady's accessory, once soft, still stained with the dirt it had lain in for years. The lady was Marina Trigo.

'Why?' Pidgin asked, and Larry said again wait.

He held his finger up.

At the next trap there was only a porcupine leg. Larry recocked the trap, left the leg for bait. The third trap was in a tangle of deadfalls. Their rapiers were useless in the close confines, and the trap was gone anyway, dragged off by something with plate-sized pawprints, unretractable claws. The fourth trap had another coyote, almost separated from its leg. Larry dared Pidgin to run it through. Pidgin did, felt metal on bone, told Larry again to go to hell. The coyote watched Pidgin even though it was dead. They carried it back to the truck, laid it on the other side of the bed. Larry said they had enough for tonight, it was almost dark. They followed the truck's lights back along their tracks to a fence, and then crept along the fence to a low spot where there was a dim structure from the remote past. Pidgin half recognized it, and then, when Larry finally pointed the truck towards it, washing it in halogen light, he did: it was the adobe wall from 1977, from the telephoto, one side of a still-standing old mission supplyhouse or halfway station or one-man monastery. It didn't matter. Here it was, the hideout. Pidgin looked deep into the weathered adobe and tried to trace the Mexican Paiute across his own twenty-two years, to the night of his father's interment. The adobe was unyielding though, uniform, no matter how hard he stared. It was just a wall. Larry said it: a wall, not a window. Pidgin shook his head no, but Larry said just because it started here in Pidgin's head didn't necessarily mean that's the way it went. 'If the world were only so kind,' he said. Pidgin turned on him with the rapier. Their blades kissed once.

'Where is he, then?' he asked, and Larry backpedalled to the truck in step with Pidgin's advance.

'Look,' he said, and with the tip of his rapier lifted the mantle fourteen inches. Pidgin did: underneath were two sluggish, miniature coyotes—not pups, just smaller than the original dead one, and mucus-wet. Larry said they equaled the original body weight down to the gram, matter had been conserved, nobody was getting damned to physics hell for this. He lowered the mantle before the two coyotes could get away. He asked Pidgin if he understood yet, and Pidgin shook his head no, realized he was being distracted but couldn't get back to the matter of the Mexican Paiute's location, not just yet.

'How?' he asked.

Larry shrugged, said he found out about it by accident, trying to hide a coyote from an unbribed game warden. He said it only worked on dead ones, and that he would kill these two again in the morning, to make of them four, and then on and on, smaller and smaller, on to absurdity, to fame, to a miniature petting zoo touring the southwest, cleaning up. He called the mantle the Shroud of Marina Trigo, because she'd pretty much died in it, because now it could raise the dead into diminutive sets of two.

'Animalkind, at least,' Pidgin said, pointing it at the tail end like a question, and Larry confessed that the thought had occurred to him too, but he'd seen too many movies. Pidgin looked at the mantle, at Larry, asked it: 'There's more?'

'My home away from home,' Larry said, looking towards the adobe, 'you guessed. It's infested.'

Pidgin approached the box of a house, leading with his rapier, and when Larry clicked the headlights back on, Pidgin saw them inside, coating everything, fingerlong full-grown coyotes, weaving, leaping, snarling small snarls. In a matter of moments they covered the window, drawn to the heat the headlights had to offer. Larry said there were even smaller ones than they could see; there seemed to be no reduction limit.

'This is wrong,' Pidgin said.

'So said the young Indian.'

'I'm serious.'

'So am I.'

'I'm not sleeping in there.'

'Maybe you're not invited.'

'I'm not in quarantine, either.'

'You've been in contact with me, I've been in contact with them. Connect the dots. They have.'

'Which way's Clovis?'

'Miles and miles, mi amigo.' Larry swept his rapier to the vague southeast. But Pidgin could see the lights.

'Just tell me where he is,' Pidgin said, 'and I'm gone.'

Larry shook his head no. 'I don't want to die, remember?'

'I won't tell him you told me.'

'You'll become him. And then you'll just know.'

'I won't.'

'Or you will.'

'Fuck Sally, okay?'

Larry said for the last time, there was no need for language.

Pidgin said nothing this time, instead came across the front of Larry's rhinestone jacket with his rapier. It trailed blue sparks. Their fight was begun, Pidgin all roundhouse slashes, Larry all smiling finesse, light on his feet, secure in kevlar, stinging Pidgin in navel and armpit with the tip of his rapier, then moving on to the many-holed belt, counting as he went, telling Pidgin it was his swordplay and dash that got the Goliards out of many a postal scrape. He had been their advantage. There were ninety-six holes in the belt, two rows of forty eight. Larry claimed boredom at eighty, went to his right hand, asked Pidgin was his fury spent yet? Pidgin redoubled, held the rapier like a baseball bat. Larry looked away and riposted neatly, said he was using the shadows for reference, giving Pidgin the time-lag advantage, however long it took light to move from them to the wall. Maybe a blink, an eternity. It was enough. In the end he flipped Pidgin's rapier out into the scrub, and Pidgin had to look for it in the dark if he wanted the fight to continue. He thought he did. His hands were shaking, forearms veined, shirt wet with sweat. When he finally found the rapier and returned, the headlights were off and Larry had retreated into his home away from home, the hideout.

Pidgin watched him through the lone window, resisting sleep on his cot, wrapped in mosquito net, the toy coyotes massing over him, drawn to his heat, biting him awake, jaws too reduced to even tear through the initial layer of skin. He was already dying. Sally had said it. Pidgin breathed out, checked the perimeter, found it empty, sought the softness of the truck. His fury was spent, and then some. In the blue-black sky the last of the sun glowed in a rocket contrail hundreds of miles away. White Sands. It looked like waves crashing.

He dismantled his rapier then, remounted the blade as CB antenna, didn't tune it in for company: there were double-guttural voices on the air, talking a tongue too old for radio. Instead he watched the Shroud of Marina Trigo in the bed writhe with coyote flesh, finally parted the rear window—grabbing mottled hair with stray pliers—and pulled the Shroud slow off the two half-sized adults. They stretched, moved as one to inspect their still-dead brethren, then wove back and forth in the bed, unsure what was past it anymore. Pidgin slid the window back in place and laid down to the tinny howls coming from the one-man monastery. There was spirit gum to chew but he pocketed it instead, because his beltline was bruise-colored and tender, meaning Larry owed him. Like tomorrow he would owe him a ride, and unvague answers. Pidgin locked the door and in half sleep saw himself walking into Clovis in the daytime, his knee jarring because he wasn't watching where he was stepping, because he was seeing a Custerblonde woman on the other side of the road and feeling the same wind that was blowing her skirt up, revealing man parts.

He came to sharp, pushing back with his locked knee, and caught the shape of a single full-size coyote loping off, back slick with mucus and starlight. He counted to a hundred twice, then tracked it braille-style through the crusted dirt back to the truck, to three feet shy of the bed; there was one set of tracks, not two, like there should have been. The tracks were deepest coming down from the bed: two had become again one. He watched Larry's adobe fort for signs of life death or limbo and crawled back into the cab, waited the night out, closed his eyes against the wind whistling through the dried weatherstripping around the vent window, said his mother's name to drown out the other—Golias. The rabbit population exploded around him. He warmed his hands in the glove-box light and pared the last two days down to a sentence: Cline Stob had forestalled the end of the world, and then Birdfinger had quickened it for him.

Pidgin felt it run through his fingers, and he caught it again and again.

Dawn came like a blessing. He sat on the hood wrapped in his mother's shroud, because he was still two people. He said it to Larry like that when Larry emerged, whisking his jacket clean with a handbroom, and Larry stretched and yawned and said there were stranger things in the world, not the least of which would be a well-balanced breakfast. He didn't notice the missing brace of coyote, didn't cover the still dead one, and then the truck only turned over when Pidgin closed the glove compartment, giving it back the light-bulb juice. And still, it was close. They had two antennae again, like an insect, feeling their way towards Clovis in the daylight hours.

'What about quarantine?' Pidgin asked.

'I don't care about Clovis,' Larry explained. 'I just don't want them in my house, y'know?'

They didn't eat at Juanita's. Instead Larry rented a double hotel room just for the continental breakfast. He left the key on the desk where the clerk slid it, and then they gorged on bagels and donuts and cream cheese. Larry said this is New Mexico. Pidgin had his mouth too full of cartoon cereal to respond. On the way out he grabbed one each of all the leftover newspapers and magazines, and then Larry-as-Atticus Wean began his morning surveillance of the jobsite, cruising slow, blocks away from the yellow color of construction, so there were just brief flashes of hardhats and backhoes seen down occasional throughways, sightlines passing like snapshots, moving pictures. He finally found a high spot with the sun to his back and binoculared in on the workers stealing his money by the hour, explained to Pidgin that they'd been digging a forty-foot hole for twenty-two days now. It was supposed to be simple: basement and foundation. He said Cline Stob would have billed it as a bomb shelter; Pidgin said it looked like Clovis was digging its own grave. The cereal milk was curdling in his stomach already, like always. He chewed Larry's chalk-tasting pills and scanned the newspapers, hesitating a moment on the front-page shot of last night's iridescent contrail, hesitating next on the births and deaths, ordered in three columns: Protestant, Catholic, and Other. Under Protestant was a long list of senior citizens, presumed fallen into death-still waters; under Catholic was a like-sized list of the missing aged, considered ship jumpers, bailers, damned; under Other was a Ms. Sarah Lunn, a pagan death. Pidgin didn't ask Larry what Sally's last name was. He held his breath and dug deeper, to yesterday's *Star*, was afraid, went through it slow.

The crossword was already done, with unused boxes colored in and diagonal slashes drawn through others, to allow two letters. Larry looked over and said bang-up job there, then became Atticus Wean again, owner operator of Wean Construction. Pidgin turned a fingerful of pages, to the Deviant Gallery flashback that was a photographic epilogue to the Mirror Man saga: a single sharp-edged black and white shot of the interment, with the interesting twin brother lunging through a blue plume of dust at Sam the chironic bingo caller, Sam's body shaping itself around Birdfinger's fist, a recoil two seconds in advance. The leopard woman was in the background with an Amazon. And the *Star* woman, of course, overdrawn, everpresent in mock veil and black hose. The only one missing was Erwin, because he was behind the camera with the audience, with Pidgin. It was uncomfortable, crowded. The caption said it had been a closed-casket service.

Pidgin swallowed the chalk down a grain at a time, then turned the page to RELATED NEWS, which was all small print, the extended obituary of the *Star*'s very own Big Spring Sally, who had ingested runny-warm candle wax some three hours before press, and then suffocated when it cooled. There were Finity Jane-ish intimations that she had predicted her own suicide, and below that a last-minute retraction by the managing editor, stating in boldface that predicting one's own imminent actions was more veiled threat than evidence of premonitory cognition, meaning it didn't quite meet those quality standards without which the *Star* would devolve to the level of the rest of the weeklies, and be taken hostage by its subject matter.

Pidgin ignored the managing editor and the *Star* woman both: Sally was dead. She had killed herself. Hours after he left. Because of his visit. Because he had been there, visited. He visited her again in recall. He said her words to Larry: 'The Goliards are dying.' Larry breathed hard to hear it, shook his head no. Pidgin passed him the *Star* and he read it three times without emotion then turned back to the jobsite, forcing the binoculars hard against his face, cupping his eyes with rubber. Pidgin didn't say anything. Halfway to Big Springs they stopped and swordfought again, Pidgin saying no about wrapping Sally in the shroud, Larry arguing special circumstances. Pidgin tried reminding him of the movies, but Larry explained it that if *she* died, then it was all coming true—meaning he wouldn't be far behind. Pidgin had no response, because he was implicated in it all, because from inside the nonsense cycle, Larry was making sense. But he couldn't be. They hung from gravel-heavy rest-stop roofs and fought one-armed. They kicked trashcans at each other, and the trash hung at shoulder-height. They fought through it. Larry switched back and forth from hand to hand so often that his blade dismounted on the backswing, planted itself in the side of a passing truck, traveled on. Pidgin dropped his rapier, stepped in front of it. The fight was a long draw: Pidgin finally traded Larry the truck keys for the shroud, and they left it on a fencepost under a transformer leaking voices down the shadowside of a telephone pole, where the creosote lunged for Pidgin's already withdrawing hand. They apologized to each other at the Howard County line. They didn't stop until they got to the hospital, rested the front wheels against a parking curb. Big Springs settled around them, already a residue.

Larry eyed his speedometer bottomed-out behind glass, his hands useless on the wheel but still holding tight, and said this is what mourning is. Pidgin sat in the parking lot of the state hospital and summed his insides into a like response: 'This is the face I make right before I start laughing.' Larry touched him on the leg, perspired resignation, said maybe it was too late for him—for both of them—things had been rolling for twenty-two years already: Sally's prediction was a threat *too*, the editor couldn't retract it all in one column. Pidgin said no, it didn't have to be like she said just because she'd said it, talked them all into agreeing with it. That was a bullshit way of making sense of the world. But still, here they were. Because he couldn't admit it to himself, he admitted to Larry that Sally had said he'd be back. Larry said he didn't doubt it. He didn't doubt anything. He stared at his hands. Time passed. The glass doors of the hospital parted for them automatically, and when Larry asked the nurse for the martyr Sally, he offered his real name in return, and Atticus Wean had died in the doorway, unnoticed. Pidgin failed to comment. In the unclean hall there was a bald man telling a story about Bob and some ducks. Pidgin didn't know if it was a joke or not. For five dollars palmed away from the corner-mounted cameras, the nurse led them to Sally's old cell, her living quarters, the air-conditioner vents lined blue with ritual cornmeal. She wasn't there. The nurse said she was in the freezer, of course, and pointed her words up at the tail end like a question.

Larry didn't rifle through Sally's belongings.

They sat and looked at the finger impression in the candle stub.

Pidgin tried laughing but almost cried instead. He left Larry and wandered the halls ten feet in either direction, then eight, then a bodylength, then settled in front of the door made up for him like a gravity well. Quarantine was over. The hospital was technically infested. Soon enough a rhinoplastic candystriper approached, consoling Pidgin in the lower vocal ranges. The name on her badge was Anodiana. She explained that it was a pet name—she was only licensed to distribute aspirin and third-level platitudes. She ushered Pidgin back into the room, gave him and Larry four tablets each and said Sally was in a far, far better place now. 'Utah?' Pidgin asked, weak-voiced, and Anodiana had no response in any of her pockets. She smoothed her skirt, played at shame, said she was only level three and said it this time like an apology, like she was ashamed of it. Around her neck was a mass-produced medicine bundle, never-opened. A single tissue made the rounds. Anodiana made it clear by her reserved body language that she was in a position of knowledge. Pidgin finally said it: 'What already?' The attention transformed her into a coquette. Her new straightbacked posture wakened Larry to her presence. His jacket got wide at the shoulders.

'You're the second set of people here today already,' she said.

'We're not a set,' Pidgin said.

'The other was that journalist woman and her ensign.'

'Erwin Olsen.'

'James,' she added, playing innocent eye games with the floor now, 'yes. Will there be more?'

Pidgin shrugged, looked to Larry. Larry nodded yes without any head motion. Pidgin relayed it to Anodiana, held his finger up for One, one more, yes. Anodiana said everybody comes when you're dead, no? and then took it back, said she was overstepping. She rubbed the Roman line her nose made, touching lightly, as if it had yet to harden. She said when Einstein died, the bedside nurse didn't speak German, meaning she didn't listen to it for what it was, either.

Larry licked his lips, looked to Pidgin for forward motion. 'Sally only spoke american,' he said with hesitation.

Anodiana nodded, said herself too. 'I was there. Here, I mean. On the volunteer clock and all. Under the electronic eye.'

Pidgin and Larry didn't disturb the lull she'd made. When it had passed and they were in a different mode of discourse, Anodiana confessed that she hadn't shared her bedside experience with the journalist woman, that she'd hid in the supply closet for the duration of her visit. That was why she smelled of ammonia. She'd even resisted the cash reward that came over the PA.

'I've got money,' Larry said, 'if—'

Anodiana shook her head no. 'Some of the less articulate patients thought it was the voice of God, with new tactics and all. But no, thank you. It's not about money with me.'

'Mrs Morena?' Pidgin asked, before he could stop himself.

Anodiana flashed him a worried eyebrow dip and said no. Larry said it didn't matter. He asked what did she say, Sally, what were her last american words? Anodiana held up her fingers peace-style, rabbit ears, said there were only two, then stalled, hedged, kept them there tempted with information, told them about the wendigo she knew from the hospital library, how it was a spirit that visited the occasional person and then left for another, always one step ahead. She looked at Pidgin when she said it, and the surety and the lope in her voice was all Sally's.

She illustrated the wendigo by way of the underbed reading material, the Comico Grendel, another entity that manifested itself trans-historically, hopped from person to person like a virus, outrunning time and the delight destroyer. Pidgin chewed the inside of his cheek, thumbed the proffered *Grendel*, stopped at the ad-girl from the 50's with the leadlined bra, seen through X-ray specs. He smiled, angled it to Larry who cocked an appreciative eyebrow, but Anodiana in her Sally role was over-sensitive to disinterested airs, flared her symmetrical nostrils in response and drew the two of them back to her, her bovine eyes and placating mouth, saying now *Golias*, then, okay?—the original one, he was of the same pulp stock, had started out hiding dead noblemen from an arbitrary thirteenth-century God he thought would appreciate the humor, the mockery, the decomposing court he arranged out on the heath, but after the night's drunken work there had been no deep laughter from the heavens, not even a nod, nothing like an explanation for why his life after that long and quiet moment was to become suddenly open-ended for him, overextended; he was being denied that which he had violated in jest, Anodiana pronounced, spittle gathering, and in time he threw his ringed head back and his eyes bulged with his stomach, and he laughed at this judgment visited upon him, lapped the irony and asked for more, and like that he slipped the mortal coil and fell willfully into wine, debauchery, poetry, railed in meter against everyone not at the tavern with him—meaning God, the Undelighted—railed until he began to fade into the whisp of legend, into the series of undocumented hosts necessary for there to be no *physical* laws being broken here, the hosts necessary for his so-called punishment to continue to be meted out, the hosts necessary if he was to *live*, teach God humor, ape him, hold his figged hand skyward and taunt.

Anodiana breathed deep and said the macabre and still-practicing Golias was evidence both of the divine Id and of the infallibility of God, if you took it that far, but Pidgin declined, commented on her over-aqualine nose in hopes of stopping the force feed. It worked. Anodiana turned away and gave up those last two wax-shaped words: *Henry Ford*. Pidgin looked to Larry and Larry looked back over the erect collar of his rhinestone chest and said she didn't even like cars, did she? He was already some two feet closer to Anodiana, drawn there by the answering tone of her voice, by how she was reenacting Sally's last two words from her new supine position, tracing with her hand the immaterial wendigo flitting from host to host, carrying hunger with it, deeper than need. She nibbled Larry's fingertip when he offered it, said he tasted canine, gamey, good.

Pidgin watched it happen, didn't warn Larry, was busy trying to make sense of Sally's still operant strategy, how she'd programmed this candystriper to exhibit a pattern of metempsychosis that would in turn program him, Pidgin, to accept that such things could and did happen—that if Sally was alive in this candystriper, so could something be wakening in him, Pidgin. Sally had sacrificed herself to nudge Pidgin into the role she'd prepared for him, prepared him for. Grendel, Golias. Pidgin said aloud *no*. He wouldn't let this comic book happen. Couldn't. Anodiana laughed at him, her teeth mercurochrome in Larry's shadow, a game of light. Pidgin told her her little stalking horse gambit wasn't working here, he wasn't sold, he was seeing through. Anodiana said Sally was smiling on him from her far far better place right about now. Pidgin flipped off wherever that was, and during the three-hundred and sixty-degree display, Anodiana closed her mouth on Larry's, and Larry was dying in stages. Pidgin left him to meet it alone. He told himself it meant nothing, was an accident of timing. His hand was full of something, though: another banktube. Sally's banktube. Standard issue for the Goliards, evidently. In hers there was a picture too, not old like the telephoto but cut from a tourist brochure. The picture was of all these dead Indians in the snow, their fingers frozen at wrong angles, their lips drawn back from teeth gone cold. Nagasaki kind of stuff. The caption was 'The Morning After,' just like Sally'd said the last time Pidgin was here. This is where he was going? Pidgin crumpled it, left it in the hall behind him, followed no lines or dots or clown footprints. Not anymore. Not anyfuckingmore. He located the parking lot, sat the crossbed toolbox of Larry's truck, waited again for night, another round.

It came maybe a carlength ahead of the figure of the Mexican Paiute. Or the Mexican Paiute brought it with him.

He was the same: squat, dark, without sound.

He was wearing the green-eyed goggle helmet too, scanning back and forth across the hospital roofline. Pidgin remained motionless this time by choice. The Mexican Paiute crossed the parking lot against the white lines, rolling like a monkey from vehicle to vehicle, never parting his lips for breath. Golias. Pidgin didn't see himself in the primal gait, now or ever. The Mexican Paiute didn't acknowledge him either, but Pidgin nodded anyway, because he wasn't that naive: he was the audience here, the intended student. This was all for him. Big Springs had been built for the hospital, the hospital for Sally, and Sally had lived and died for him, Pidgin, her son born of another woman, the one who could loop the old days to the new for her, a filial duty, a parting gift of immortality. To think of it any other way was to fall behind, fall prey to her story. Pidgin understood. He hadn't asked Anodiana why she'd saved those last words for him and Larry, didn't sell them to the *Star* woman. He didn't need to.

He watched the Mexican Paiute skim the grounds, gain access to the building through an air-conditioner vent, emerge minutes later with the body of Sally slung easy and cold across his shoulders. No alarms announced the body snatching, no one pointed long and shrieked. Sally was wrapped in an aquamarine sheet, her red hair a contrast even in death. She trailed dry ice smoke. It was miles and miles back to Clovis. The Mexican Paiute showed no daunt. Pidgin stood in the bed of the truck and yelled to him that he knew who he was. It had dual application, and he meant it that way. The Mexican Paiute didn't look back at Pidgin, acknowledge his ambiguity, and Pidgin in turn didn't dignify the Mexican Paiute's exit by waiting for it. He turned away, denied it all with a head motion, with a physical act.

He waited for Larry, dead or alive. Larry stumbled out in between the two male nurses trying to blindside him, overbalance him into their white wheelbarrows. He dove into the truck, said he was deep in the third stage of grief, yes, but still, that wasn't Sally in there. Pidgin said no, it wasn't. Larry let him drive because his blood was still thin from all the aspirin and he was unsure about things in general. He asked Pidgin if he was dying and Pidgin shook his head no, avoided eye contact. It was another graceless ride. Pidgin decided it had to be the destination, not the truck, the company. Larry's utility-pocketed jacket visibly weighed him down, almost to sleep. He rummaged under the seat, emerged with a cassette about sales strategies, double-baiting and switchbacks, how to think standing up, what footwear best promoted entry, what best facilitated escape. He told Pidgin about his petting zoo, described it in such microscopic detail that it became invisible to the naked eye. He groped for it then fell back again on the larger than life letter, Cline's resistance piece, patted his jacket, said the code could only have been broken by an Indian on Bastille Day.

Pidgin cringed behind the wheel, said he wasn't up for the decryption process, not now, not ever.

Larry smiled. 'Your dad, he almost had it, though. The dairy angle.'

'He wasn't Indian,' Pidgin said. 'French either.'

'He didn't have to be,' Larry said.

Pidgin grinned displeasure, ejected the sales tape, drove faster. There was religion on the radio and maybe two hours until Clovis. In them Larry detailed the unamerican prison cheese of the Bastille, how the aged taste made it beyond reproach, let it pass inviolate through doors and doors to the real heart of matters, let it smuggle large things in a small piece at a time, to be assembled later. Larry closed his eyes, salivated out the driverside corner of his mouth, talked then of the commodity cheese of his youth, chipped into frybread dough, how, years later—weeks ago—with gunpowder still in the air from Independence Day, he'd gone looking for the process by which to make it again, the cheese, and stumbled across a short list of ingredients in a scuttled file cabinet, mentally laid it over the remembered letter of Cline's. Days later he found that the decryption only worked if he read the letter aloud, liasoned the word endings together, kept contrapuntal time with both feet. But it did work. There was the algorithm, the tagged-on coefficients, the layered exponentials, the lone catalyst, the plan for the end of the world.

'Of america, you mean,' Pidgin said.

'Right here, I mean,' Larry said back, patting his chest again, his jacket.

'I don't want to see it,' Pidgin said, 'you can quit hitting yourself already.'

'It was your dad's, though.'

'That doesn't mean it's mine.'

Larry held his hand out then drew it back to his face. At the first rest stop he spent a half hour in the bathroom with the *Carmina Burana*, carving. When he came back he said Sally was really dead, wasn't she? Pidgin said she was riding piggy back into the afterlife right about now. He asked Larry why the Mexican Paiute did what he did, buried white people. Larry said Indians too: Marina Trigo, yes. He explained that some people collect stamps—a shoe can be a fetish, or holding a cigarette English style, heat close to the palm and dangerous. 'Sal,' he said, 'when she used to smoke.' Pidgin eased back into the lack of traffic and said in a nasal voice that now they were in a far far worse place than her: New Mexico. It didn't allay the sluggish regret circulating through the cab. Larry ran his finger over the blank visor, and Pidgin didn't know if he would throw the postcards out again, given the chance, given foreknowledge. The preacher on the radio preached damnation and preached it hard. They passed a redbrick Ford house with the side entrance labeled Parts, and Pidgin understood Sally's Einstein words: he was a replacement. The machine he would fit in was history, her history, her machination. He laughed at the simpleness of it, milked it in silence until Clovis, and then let it go at the elevation sign, simply because there was the chance he was meant to milk it, the chance that he was playing into it all. And chances were certainties.

Larry directed him to the floodlit construction site.

Pidgin second-guessed himself into a proleptic wordlessness. He let Larry make their decisions, followed him to the edge of the Clovis grave, helped him sink the plumbline down thirty-eight feet, reel it back hand over disappointed hand. They wore hardhats because the workers were shooting bullbats with nailguns. One man even had his fly-fishing gear out, his tool belt heavy with the down of flatnosed hawk. His Indiglo line whipped slow, back and forth, described languid S shapes and then reversed them with ease: *2-S, 2-S*. Larry asked the closest worker if this is what he paid them for? The man pointed to the lone jackhammer and then to his ears in mock deafness. The foreman approached with private words for Larry. Pidgin squatted within earshot at the edge of the pit. The hole was down to stone, bedrock maybe, but that should have been long ago. This was a second bedrock. The foreman spat a teal stream of tobacco and said it was fucking Precambrian he'd guess, but that wasn't all bad, either. Contractual deadlines could be extended—they could throw up plywood walls around the lot for privacy and then build it up another two feet above sea level if necessary. But that was all later. What mattered now was the worth of fossils in yen. He had called some people. Larry said it was his dig. The foreman said that's why he had called *his* people. Back pats were exchanged, became knowing punches, unvoiced apologies, credit due.

'Well let me see it already,' Larry finally said.

'*Them*,' the foreman corrected.

Larry reminded him then of pecking orders; the crane lifted him down deus ex machina style, a grand entrance, one leg dangling. Pidgin and the foreman took the switchback stairway, no handrail, every third step blazed yellow with BIOLOGICAL HAZARD. It was a fire escape from a condemned hospital. They descended. The foreman carried his hardhat underarm and leaned back to counterbalance his gut. Pidgin smelled his moist scalp, tried to hold his breath the rest of the way down, greyed in and out. The visual effect was akin to time travel in *The Scræling*. Pidgin resisted the association, placed one foot after the other. At the Precambrian level the air was richer, unbreathed, restoring. From the perigeed crane hook, Larry announced Sally's name through a second bullhorn, and it didn't mean anything to the workers in the pit, and it didn't echo. Larry's eyes flared. He breathed in to eulogize, but the foreman lowered the bullhorn with tact, with the hard side of his hand, said there were more pressing items to deal with than names. More rewarding.

This was a funny thing to Larry. 'Business,' he said, and then rubbed his nose, admitted he was grateful for all this last minute distraction, for his life intruding on his death. Because it was coming. He lined crank down the ball joint of his thumb and inhaled, licked it clean. The foreman quickened a flare on his rough jawline and showed them the night's find, the take: there were three Volkswagon-sized rocks chiseled out of the earth, the lone jackhammer working on what might be the fourth. The foreman handed the flare to Larry and hosed down the biggest of the three with twenty-five hundred pounds of pressure. The magnesium light was trapped in the water rolling down the rock, filling the regular indentations with life, and in the lambent-wet skin Pidgin found himself holding Larry hard by the wrist: it was a snail shell. Pidgin made his cusswords into a string of white noise, a hiss of involuntary awe. Larry motioned for tarps, cameras, sketch artists, historical biographers, dancing girls. None of them appeared. Instead there were sudden dumptruck headlights peering into the hole, rumbling loose shale down the side. A blue van entered the scene to their left, taking control. Pidgin touched the wet snail, left his hand there—the water running up his forearm, joining them—and imagined a herd of massive snail flesh, moving slow and inexorable across the plains or the swamps or the boreal forests or the tundra or whatever New Mexico was before it was New Mexico. Miles behind them were the whipthin hunters, touching the damp trail, tasting it, advancing. Always advancing.

But it was an eon later.

The modern-day hunters silenced their blue van. Its door swung open over the pit, and the passenger thought better of it, crawled back between the captain seats. The magnetic sign on the hanging open door read Damon's Mowing for a moment, in rich green, and then the door was pulled shut from the inside, and in its place were the khaki people, representing the benign interest of foreign investors. The middleman here was Atanacio Morena. He had been the one in the passenger seat, aware of that first step. He was all swagger and pomp. He single-filed down the staircase with the khaki people, wired into each other with headsets. Larry did three quick lines to Pidgin's nervous one. He said that as owner-operator of Wean Construction he was forced to take part in these international dealings from time to time. He said as a potential witness Pidgin was entitled to 0.25 percent of the net, in yen; changing it to dollars was up to him. Or he could just silkroad it east, make a home in the Orient. Pidgin accepted the idea of the payoff, rezipped his lips in trade. Atanacio Morena approached, smiling the same smile as last time. The khaki people were already crawling over the snails like ants. They were to scale. They were wearing Spiro Agnew masks so as to protect their university affiliations, their collective tenure.

Atanacio Morena said they were hoax dogs, here to sniff things out. Necessary evils in this day and age.

'Like I could carve those ever,' Larry said.

'Cement and a plastic swimming pool, my vainglorious friend.'

'There are better words.'

'Not for you.'

Larry took it as a compliment. He reclaimed the crane hook, eyes veined red, voice large through the bullhorn but still shaking. It was a last stand. He rejected the preliminary price Atanacio Morena offered without the hoax dogs' report. Atanacio Morena said in Pidgin's ear that Atticus Wean was a shrewd capitalist, streamlined by evolution for black-market trade. Larry the Paranoid heard somehow, said back with amplified voice that Atanacio Morena was a callow man among callow men, and that wasn't all bad. They nodded respect. Pidgin said to Atanacio Morena that the Atticus Wean he knew had died in a doorway in Big Springs Texas. Pidgin had almost caught it in his peripheral vision. Atanacio Morena didn't respond, was pressing his earpiece in deeper with his thumb, following a conversation. He smiled, looked again at the snails. 'No shit?' he said. 'Fucking south-ass america?' Spiro Agnew nodded a collective no shit. Atanacio Morena squatted on his heels, threw rock shards at other rock shards.

'What?' Pidgin asked.

Atanacio Morena looked up at him through his oily bangs, collected in points. 'Do you watch your toilet water?' he asked.

'Who doesn't.'

'Then you know already.'

Atanacio Morena had to reclimb the stairway to negotiate price with Larry, who was swinging back and forth, chain in one hand, bullhorn in the other. He had been listing his coups over the office of the postmaster general, arranging them by zipcode, trying to get it all in. He said it was his death song. Sally was in there, waiting between every line. He turned the bullhorn off when negotiations loomed, and still his voice carried. He came down to

Atanacio Morena's price too quick it seemed, sold the three snails for fifteen thousand apiece, but then charged six-thousand dollars loading fee—six thousand per shell. He said they could go by weight if Atanacio Morena wanted to face the scales, if he had that kind of time, if night would cover him and his deeds that long. Atanacio Morena surveyed the lot as if there was anything he could do. There wasn't. He nodded defeat and Larry accepted it, dictated corollary terms in small print. Inside five minutes the biggest snail was chained, Larry straddling it, captaining it. He gave the thumbs up and rose, rode up and up to a dumptruck, unhooked when there was enough slack. His hands were sure; the night wasn't: he was rocking back and forth, settling the second snail into the second dumptruck, when there came a thumping across the sky.

It was helicopter blades.

From his perch Larry narrated a spotlight approaching, clamped his teeth together in the face of adversity, let his hair whip around his shoulders. His carriage was twenty-five years younger than he was, and he truly was something to behold. They had the third snail chained up by the time he returned on his oversized hook, and then the rushed crane operator swung him and the load wide, tilting the crane base off the ground even, testing God. Pidgin expected Larry to die then, when he was up there in the thick of things, thinking it was the old days again and he was invincible, but he didn't. Instead the crane settled and Larry fell soft the ten feet to the pit lip, played hognose in the millions of candlepower the helicopter directed around him. The voice from above announced that they had the law on their side, this time. It was a museum booster, an airborne covey of them. The foreman said this had happened before. He was double-fisted. Pidgin hid under the stairway as the khaki people raced up three steps at a time, their hard-plastic Spiro Agnew faces betraying zero emotion.

The dumptrucks gunned to life moments later, found reverse, rained gravel down into the pit, sped off for the far east on 84 west. The Damon's Mowing van didn't lead them. Instead it lagged behind, the frontseat crowded with presidential motion, would-be getaway drivers. From their midst Atanacio Morena emerged, coalesced with both hands on the wheel, ten and two. He smiled across the pit at Pidgin or at destiny and took hold of the column shifter and in the same instant was crushed from behind, pressed into the glass, and as he let himself be arranged against the windshield with the other bodies, the van nosed forward with their weight, over the lip of the pit, its headlights melting down the opposite wall, then feeling along the raped Precambrian bedrock until the halogen line was perpendicular to the ground, collected in a hot puddle. The van fell slow into it, brake lights tracing descent, and caved in on itself in a splash of glass, stood there, already a headstone. Pidgin was up and running by then, out of the Clovis grave, dragging Larry by the collar and away. It had been stimulus-response. They hid bellydown under one of the orange doghouses tucked between dumpsters. The helicopter dopplered away, attached to the dumptrucks by law. A Spiro Agnew peered over the lip of the pit, face caught in a plastic snarl, and crawled away.

Pidgin said he'd heard of worse things happening.

'I had the scrapies once,' Larry said, making the face.

They chewed a grim piece of spirit gum each.

Larry's workers emerged from under I-beams, from under deerhide blankets that matched the ground. They moved to purge the jobsite of fossil evidence. It was instinct. The foreman used no words, just aimed fingers here, there, across the street. He made promises of overtime that Larry said he was going to let slide, considering. Pidgin kept a hand on Larry's ankle just in case. Jackhammers jackhammered. Minutes later the fourth snail breached groundlevel for the first time in millennia, an unlicensed crane operator in control now, beer in hand, glass cab filled with cigar smoke. The snail floated over the jobsite, across the street, settled on the asphalt behind a derelict car with its flank handprinted. A Cutlass. Birdfinger's. Pidgin snarled. On their way to the bar to construct workable alibis, one of the men lagged behind, smiling, and looped the fourth snail's chain around the axle-housing of the

Cutlass. He left whistling, kicking a can ahead of him, following it no matter.

Pidgin and Larry emerged into the postcoital lull. They sat on the curb by the Cutlass, by the tethered snail. Pidgin balled up paper trash and threw it on the slow-spiraled shell, asked Larry if toilet water and south america meant anything to him. Larry said it meant either this snail had migrated halfway across the world in the space of a single lifetime or else the continental plates of the americas worked like a lazy susan. He said it meant nothing. No wool had been pulled over his eyes; he was no sheepfaced Indian. He removed his jacket with ceremony and draped it over a sheared-off lightpole so they were three people on the curb. He brushed the jacket with a lint mitt and told Pidgin another story he didn't want to hear. A tribal story this time. He said it would function as the coda to his death song.

It was about the old days, about a man in his lodge one day knapping when the sky goes pitch black. The man closes his eyes and opens them again, and it's still dark. There are many things that could be between him and the sun. He lives in a time when things are still happening, when protean gods are traipsing over the landscape disguised as their handiwork. A world was being forged with laughter. The Knapping Man hears it in the new darkness, coming from above—a hollow, pervasive sound that lasts and lasts. The coals from the morning's fire glow under the ash. He doesn't stir them to warm his hands but walks out into the daytime night, and—because he's a hero in a story and because his bow is trailing at his side, leaving a thin line in the ground which he can backtrack if necessary—he bends it skywards, the bow, lets fly an arrow tipped not with one of his precious knapped points but with metal-heavy hoop-steel. It flies high and arcless into the blackened sky, comes down with a crane, the first of its kind, leaves a hole of light in the sky which will soon be all that matters. The Knapping Man eats the bitter bird over four meals, and then lives at the outside edge of camp for years, because his body has turned the warmbacked crane to flesh, and it's part of him now, swaying his judgment, making him a liability to his band: every nightfall he walks out into the dark, bends his bow at the heavens, and lets fly a solitary arrow, trying to end that darkness as well. His prayers run deep; he had been a hero in another lifetime, in a different world. He had brought light. Now people are dying around him. The night persists, refuses to be pierced.

'Just like that,' Pidgin said, a half-mock.

Larry shrugged, said the night was massing against him now, he could feel it. His senses were expanding, the mortal coil was unwinding like a da Vinci whirlybird let fall from the maestro's hand. Pidgin said no, he had lived through it—Larry—he *was* living through it. Pidgin traded him a story to keep him there, corporeal. It was a memory, not a thing he could make up. He called it The Rabid Earmole. He'd heard it from an old RV Indian standing at Four Corners. Pidgin had been two days out of Clovis then. The postdoc anthropologist he'd thumbed a ride with had pulled over for some authentic dancing. The dancer was a twelve year old Kiowa-Comanche girl with budding hips. She moved like water, talked with her hands. She was accosted by the postdoc for pictures, life stories, tribal memorabilia. She said she was only twelve—ten fingers, then two in the afterspace. Pidgin stood back, leaned on the RV where her grandfather was leaning. Painterlike, they talked of the qualities and the depth of shade, because that was all that mattered. The old man nodded to the girl being led to concessions by the postdoc and said she could take care of herself, that one. Pidgin said her hair was pretty. The old man paused then changed directions, asked Pidgin where he was from instead of what tribe he was. Pidgin lied Hobbs anyway. It came natural. The old man leaned deeper into the shade and asked Pidgin what he thought about this whole colonization thing? Pidgin at fifteen didn't believe in aliens. The old man said colonization in the more local sense: the European tide, the diluvial americas. Cline Stob had told Pidgin the answer to this already, prepared him. It was rote. Pidgin recited: 'It would have happened one way or another. Had to. If not them then someone else.'

The old man coughed, kept his mouth covered, then burrowed his pinky into his left ear as if chasing an invasive and contagious thought, and said there was a time he'd had faith in his granddaughter's generation, collecting in knots at roadsides.

Pidgin looked to Larry. 'But there are people like me in those knots,' he said.

'Just because Cline said it. Whatever else he was, he wasn't Indian, Pidge. It's not something he could catch from your mother, y'know.'

Larry breathed fog onto the rhinestones of his star jacket, polished them, straightened the cuffs, asked did Pidgin's epilogue here involve the postdoc, the postdoc's tiny dancer, and the flock-blue interior of his car? Pidgin asked back did it matter that the Knapping Man wounded his own band not with flint points, but ones made of hoop steel? That that's why they were dying around him? Larry smiled, said that that old man asked the same BS colonization question of everyone. He'd never left the four-corners area. He had no grandchildren, was a cultural landmark. He was the tawny automaton at the gate of the amusement park and the amusement park was called Terra Nullius. Larry had encountered the old man in his youth as well. They all did. Pidgin stung, said at least he used recognizable characters: he had never seen, heard, or smelled the Knapping Man before. Larry said look harder: it was all happening, with or without their consent. He could no longer be held here, not even by stories he already knew. He was part of a more immediate one. His voice was calm, measured, fatalistic. Pidgin opened his mouth to argue, to get Larry to raise his voice in anger at the generic, sling some more Latin into the mix, but Larry shushed him, asked did he hear that? Pidgin hadn't. Larry said it was in the ground, laid his ear to it like a movie Indian, fingertips too. He told Pidgin it probably wasn't so safe on the curb anymore for pedestrians.

They watched each other's backs, Larry towards Portales, Pidgin Utah, and it was from Utah direction that it finally came, a motion at first low on the indistinct horizon, out of perspective, unreduced to a common point. It approached zigging and zagging, tacking into the wind, muscles bunched beneath the piebald hair. A single coyote. Pidgin tracked its progress towards them. It moved with animal intent, with hunger, its coat mucused down. Pidgin swallowed the lump his gum had become: by how much of the visual field the coyote displaced, it should already be mid-air, at arm's length. But it wasn't. It was still hundreds of yards off, its rolling shoulders cresting over an out of place double-decker bus, its feet light on the ground, its black lips curled in a smile. Pidgin felt it in the asphalt then, the approach of the poetic death Larry insisted upon. Matter was being conserved. Pidgin eased forward, away from him. The coyote reached the jobsite and skirted the pit, wary of it, intrigued in its way. But undelayed. It still hadn't made a sound, hadn't betrayed itself, wouldn't: it was in stalking mode. Larry was a mouse under the grass. The only mouse. He turned up at the last instant, breathed in the prewarmed air of a ridged black mouth, and then with a dip of canine neck was snatched from above, replaced by a foreleg that was gone too in an instant, held pad-up to the chest as the coyote leaped easy over the nearest row of buildings, never breaking stride. It was gone, had never been. Larry. Pidgin sat in the Cutlass, the mites in his eyebrows moving invisible over his skin. He rubbed them still.

In the rearview mirror Larry's star jacket reared lifeless and hulking. Pidgin slung it into the pit too, held close to his thigh the banktube he'd plundered against his will. In the Cutlass he inspected it as morbid duty dictated: it was Cline Stob's resistance piece in duplicate—the original on brittle engineering paper with unidle pictograms, the copy on vellum in Larry's grand hand, both undeciphered. And there was another thing too, under them, a photograph from the first generation of cameras, when shutter speed could be sundialed in. A barefoot Indian with a wide scarf tied around his head. The exotic. He was mounted on a white horse and the saddle was English, polished to brown glass, mane and tail combed with care. The Indian's camera-side bare foot was hooked lightly in the stirrups, his knee bent at the proper angle, his back held military straight. He had been posed. The photo was worn at the edges where Larry had held it, looking into it for something. There were no words on the back. It existed out of time. Pidgin left it in the tube with the letter because maybe it was nonlinear medicine against the algorithm, an antidote of some kind.

Pidgin didn't want the tube, the cylindrical parcel. He knew what it was worth.

He sat in the Cutlass again, burdened, surrounded by Clovis. When Charlie Ward appeared by the driverside door, gas can in one hand, cases of looted spirit gum in the other, Pidgin said he wasn't going to let this bullshit consume him. He slung his hand around the headliner to show. Charlie Ward grunted that he understood. He said he was going west for a windshield, grandson. Pidgin said he could do that, he could do that. It was settled. Charlie Ward gassed the car back up and they were in motion again, gutting the asphalt with the rock snail, the car sitting lowrider-deep in the road, dragging sparks. It wasn't a fast getaway. They screeched slow and halting around corners, the Cutlass stalling over and over, vacuum-locked, the chain too hot to touch anymore. Finally at the edge of town some weak link snapped and the snail cartwheeled into a field, moving faster in death than it ever had in life, and Pidgin and Charlie Ward slingshot ahead, freed, blowing spirit bubbles that stuck in their hair, coated their chins, tangled their fingers in stringy grey matter. The new religion. Pidgin watched the upturned bowl of the sky for missing pieces spanned like crane wings. He asked where Charlie Ward had been, and Charlie Ward shrugged, said back and forth. His security guard outfit was fresh pressed, had crisp ridges down the arms and legs. The tin badge shone.

'You going to arrest me, yeah?' Pidgin asked.

Charlie Ward replied with his foot, buried it deeper yet in the Cutlass. It didn't respond. Their speed was legal, and there were keys in the ignition. They were two longhairs going from place to place now, crossing no state lines even. Looking for a windshield. Charlie Ward told all the same stories in all the same order: cars cars cars, the occasional Mexican Wasp. The bandit-black Trans-Am and Hopiland was third from the end in the coup succession, and Pidgin was a nameless passenger in it, a white-knuckled accomplice, both feet on the dash. It was an attitude of reluctance. He watched his depersonalized self in Charlie Ward's tale, asked him to tell it again, felt himself already becoming the uneasy rider in the windshield story they were currently making. Each movement became heavy, labored with eventual description. The effort needed to sustain even the vagaries of a breathing pattern put him to sleep, where he dreamed he was in the Cutlass heading west, looking for the windshield that would solve it all. Charlie Ward was talking and driving and driving and talking.

When Pidgin woke it was an incomplete action, and he had to claw up through layers and layers of false wakenings. On the bench seat again, the nap real between his real fingers, he tried to claw up even further, out of New Mexico, but he was plateaued. The Cutlass was motionless. Charlie Ward called it Chaves County, but that didn't matter; there was a sign out Pidgin's window. It read A-1 AUTO SALVAGE, had a UFO stenciled in in the background, the two A-1 mechanics dismantling it for parts, tinkering those parts into Edsels and Studebakers and Saabs, in that order. The UFO was a familiar disc of light in the sky to Pidgin. He clamped onto the dash, not breathing, not doing anything until Charlie Ward reached across the seat, touched Pidgin's line of underlip hair. Charlie Ward was wearing a polished bone thimble on the reaching thumb when he did it, touched Pidgin. It was unaccountable; it was an old man trick: the thimble on hairstub made a jawdeep scratching sound that pried Pidgin's fingers from the dash vinyl and pushed him out of the car by the marrow. It wasn't light yet, but close. Charlie Ward said she was always open, that was a thing about her.

'She?'

'Her.'

They got no further without proper names. They walked through the gate, were met by no junkyard dogs.

There was a kerosene lamp hung on the open trunk of a makeless car. It guttered yellow with their entrance gust and Pidgin understood what Larry had meant about the senses expanding. He could no longer reel them back in. Two manshapes stepped as one from behind two wrecked panel vans. 'I think they're calling to you,' Charlie Ward said, and then eased down a carwide aisle of parts, unqueried. The two men were the mechanics from the sign. Both flat-eyed and dark-skinned. The one who approached from the north wore a Thoth-Amon shirt and stage boots; the one from the south had a motocross breastplate and was poking a screen into the top of a Dr Pepper can. They sat in the lee of a third panel van and smoked, passed the can around twice before there were any words, any introductions. The Thoth-Amon mechanic began it. He asked Pidgin if he knew of the two of them? Pidgin shook his head no. Thoth-Amon shrugged it off, said in days past they had been the Skag Brothers, the Phillips Head Brothers, and the dual subject of an image-driven documentary called *Glory Dog*. Now they were Killbourne and Cornbleu, of Aughtman Wrecking Services. Pidgin said he was Pidgin. Cornbleu rustled against his bumper-stickered breastplate and said they weren't without the occasional briefing: they knew of Pidgin.

'From Clovis, yeah?' he said.

Pidgin nodded.

Cornbleu held up the can for inspection, said the pot too, it was from Clovis. 'We even bought it from a fucking *pirate*,' he said, 'here in the big NM, understand?' He laughed, lost his smoke, covered one eye then the other, left conversational room for appreciation or awe or acknowledgment. Pidgin had none of the three to give anymore. Killbourne filled the empty space with tightlipped staring. Cornbleu turned his head away, leading with the tripartite brow of his right eye. It was a ducking motion. Killbourne continued his glare and explained that there were still a few procedural wrinkles to iron out: they'd only won the A-1 contract six months ago, only met her a few weeks back. Their duties here were vague.

Pidgin backpedaled. 'Her?' he asked for the second time.

Cornbleu said it, still looking away: 'Jackie. Jackie Feather, man. Jacqueline. The sweetheart of yesterday's rodeo. The Salvage Queen, y'know, shit. Used to do seances and shit over in Texas? That's how she financed this place, the yard. Bought it for less than two grand twenty years ago, then made it into this. *That* her.'

Pidgin nodded that he had seen her once, yes—indelible, shuffling. 'I didn't come here for a seance, though,' he said, 'that would be about the last thing I need.'

Cornbleu used his whole forearm to wipe his nose. 'She'll *tell* you what you need, compadre. Count on that.'

Killbourne rubbed his nose, stepped between them, said it was a good contract they had with her, as far as contracts went. But too, it was kind of long term temporary, would only last until they got together enough stake money to produce their TV pilot, in which they would be reincarnated yet again and sold wholesale to the public thirty minutes at a time. He made Pidgin guess the title and Pidgin guessed The Tonto Talk Show, with Cato on gongs. It got the necessary laughs. Killbourne passed the Dr Pepper can back to Pidgin, said to cash it if it needed cashing.

Pidgin negotiated the can to his face, rolled the lighter wheel four times slow, making sixteen sparks. Cornbleu laughed, said the sacred herb was getting to their honored guest already. Killbourne corrected: the THC was just doing the rete mirabile shuffle with Pidgin's psyche. It was a necessary dance. Without it none of this would make sense. Tonic clonic was a single word the way he said it, ran together in the middle. Cornbleu acted it out with his hand, from a sitting position.

Pidgin watched from an internal distance, trying to deal with the time lag involved, and said it was too late; he was already convulsed on the insides, spasmed out. He offered the spirit gum around. Killbourne and Cornbleu lined their hatbands with it with Hendrixian precision, said they were loyal. Dawn was miles away, an inchoate glow. Charlie Ward a metal noise rooting in the distance, an old man picking over trucks with his windshield measurements scrawled over the leathery back of his hand.

Cornbleu pulled Pidgin back into their three-pointed circle, pulled him back with a name.

'Glory Dog the Series,' he said, underlining *series*, spitting it like a bad taste, getting the jump on Killbourne. Killbourne swelled. He said it was better than Red Noise or Indian Time, no? Or, what, Young Pagans in Love? They were at it in silence, dagger-eyed and ham-fisted, maybe real brothers even. Pidgin looked past their rivalry and saw the insistent hem of a densely-beaded dress, the flash of a slim ankle, but then it was gone behind a car husk. Killbourne said to ignore it for now. They had a little more ground to cover first: Cornbleu produced the pilot episode of their long teleplay from inside his plastic breastplate. There were mimeographs, enough for all. Glory Dog the Series. It left them blue-fingered like jail. The working title of the first episode was multiple choice—either *The* Glitch, *Our* Glitch, or, in a different hand, Glitchman Rex.

'Only three?' Pidgin asked as Killbourne backed away, framing with thumbs and index fingers, but got no response. The shot was him and Cornbleu. Cornbleu narrated the introductions in rapidfire sentences, detailed the fast-cut glam shots that would orient the viewer to their Indian locale, the Native time slot. First there was a lone vole keeping nervous time, acting like he was on medicine. Next was a Ouida bird caught in a tailspin, which panned down to a shot which foregrounded the beauty and the economy of the dog travois. Last, of course, was the animated Pocahontas dancing and singing off-center, double D at least, piped like a primadonna, seen first on a handheld television set in a Roman Catholic stadium and then suddenly on all the sets the crowd was locked to. There were one-way dotted lines drawn from the tiny screen to the eye, and as the screen became the monitor of a video game, the eye became Iron Eyes Cody himself, roadside, thinking in Italian. The first season in a visual capsule. Cornbleu called it a spring-loaded suppository.

Pidgin didn't laugh; he was to play himself for most of it. He had scripted lines to follow, written in longhand, in a cursive peyote allowed. But still. He dropped the teleplay. Behind him Killbourne was warming up a decrepit theramin, and right beside him Cornbleu was wrestling from his breastplate a jawharp strung with catgut. He got it out, and after a few false starts they fell into a Zydeco-influenced getaway beat that would accompany Pidgin, scrambling across time. Cornbleu told Pidgin he was the good guy here, remember, but Pidgin kicked the teleplay away, blew at it, refused to touch it with bare skin, and his antics cued a laughtrack. When his back was turned to the canned laughter and to the idea of a camera Killbourne stood for, Cornbleu stage-whispered that Pidgin was doing fine, perfect, he was a natural Nature's Child.

Pidgin shook his head no, no, was rewarded with another laugh track, with one man laughing long and Spanish in the mezzanine. Pidgin cast about for the Mexican Paiute, for the *Y* on his father's chest that didn't need a question mark. Killbourne said to look at the camera, look at the camera. Pidgin found the teleplay in his hands again, leading him by the lips. He pantomimed the back and forth with Cornbleu, read his lines about how *The* Glitch had occurred circa 1610 or so, and those three core figures involved never died but transmigrated over the centuries, athanasiaed, cursed by instant karma to walk the earth, atone, make germ-line repairs, kill the damned butterfly, get back on that good red road and burn some serious rubber. He explained it to Cornbleu the Fawning Initiate first by way of failing sestinas and villanelles, and when that didn't work he retreated to the *Wargames* computer: the historical characters were jumping from actor to actor, running through all the options over and over, faster and faster, trying to escape the cycle, unbalance it somehow, spin it off track. But each time. The cast multiplied around them yet the triangle held, wouldn't go away, informed them all. It was different but the same: Pocahontas and her captain and the old chief, the first domino.

Cornbleu nodded, agreeing, pretend-seeing what had been within reach the whole time, imitating Pidgin it seemed, improvising with him, and when Pidgin studied the teleplay to find his place, the next line Sally had written for him, he saw that the cursif he had been reading was just the lowercase letter *A* over and over with a light touch, a weak pen, a hurried hand. There were no words there, only the shape of a mouth, of his mouth in the moment before he had said it all from nothing, nowhere. He exited stage left before the mechanical applause could start, removed himself from the shot, hid in one of the panel vans that still smelled of prohibition-era beerbread. When Killbourne approached to console or to prompt, Pidgin stopped him, said enough already, enough.

Killbourne held his hands up, palm out.

From his recess Pidgin said he supposed Golias was slotted for a guest appearance in episode two, after hours in the make-up trailer? Killbourne shook his head no with a smile, said Golias was old hat, European, African of late. Episode two was to be more about the Dog Days of summer, when the snakes were blind with their own milky skin, striking at anything, at heat. It was to be a nature digression for the sake of ratings—that's what the audience would expect from the Native timeslot—and would segue directly into the previews for the third episode, which would shufflestep from nature to the historical players by revealing their Platonic plight—how they were denied total recall, anamnesis, how they started each time wiped clean, yet still had at least the *potential* for rememory locked in their collective unconsciouses. It influenced their unthinking actions, so that they knocked the domino over again and again.

'And the fourth?' Pidgin asked, weary of his own voice.

'The fourth,' Killbourne said, 'the fourth episode is really like the next step from the second episode, like there it branched into two threes, get it?' Pidgin nodded; Sally had hardwired him to understand things being the same in number yet distinct. Killbourne rolled on, explained that the so-called fourth episode would be about a conscious renouncement of harquebuses and Spanish horses, it would be a format for the return to the old meaning of Dog Days, when Indians didn't need anything European, when horses were dogs. People would listen.

'Slow-ass going on foot, though,' Pidgin said, the desperate hole-puncher.

Killbourne shook his head no, it wasn't. 'They got around,' he said, 'the old old Indians,' holding both hands over imaginary ski poles that weren't ski poles, but the top part of stilts. 'You know what I'm talking about here.'

Pidgin turned in the direction of the Cutlass, in the direction of the volatile banktube forced under the bench seat like a pipe bomb. It was dramatic head movement and for once he hadn't meant it to be.

'How much are they paying you,' Pidgin asked, Rhine's hungry hands on him again, 'the truckers?'

'Cash on delivery,' Cornbleu said from the background.

'I don't want to be on your TV program,' Pidgin told Killbourne, 'on any damn program.'

Killbourne said he already was. He shook the script like a rattle, made a meek face, tendered an apology with cheek muscles. Pidgin didn't accept. That would be the first step. He said he wasn't looking at the Cutlass for any particular reason; he was just looking for Charlie Ward, and Charlie Ward was looking for a windshield, and that was all.

Killbourne nodded at the beaded dress hem undeniable four cars away, lifting and falling in the breeze occasioned by the predawn temperature dip. 'Now,' he said, 'she's waiting. I guess you can either go to her, or...' He indicated the Cutlass, the banktube that needed guarding.

Pidgin crawled from the panel van, kept his back to it, looked back once to Killbourne who had him framed with his hands, the frame tilted diagonal, his feet meanwhile easing Cutlass-ward. If Pidgin ever needed to be two people. He flipped coins in his head and drew mental straws and finally just leaned uphill, away from Killbourne, away from both of them, then covered the last two car widths in a bound, a two-legged pounce. The dress he had picked over the banktube was in motion too, though, ahead of him already. It was a young girl, the Kiowa-Comanche girl from Four Corners, the postdoc's tiny dancer, the automaton's grand-daughter. She hadn't aged. Pidgin wove in behind her and understood he had both feet fully in the amusement park now, was feeling his way down funhouse walls hammered out of junked cars. His distorted reflection in the chrome bumpers assaulted him, gave him a new kinesthetic, made him move like he looked. He rolled after the girl like a ragdoll, and it was because she let him, because she re-presented herself each time he lost her. He chased her and chased her, and she ran through the fluid dance steps she'd lured the postdoc in with, and then she ran on, to California, where she concealed herself in a pay-sweat and waited with the long, eightfold sight of a spider.

Pidgin could draw no closer than ten car lengths. It was enough. The postdoc wandered in, kneeling to catalogue the occasional hubcap-as-cultural artifact, counting his money against the pay-sweat sign, pulling the flap closed behind him. The white back of his index finger was the last thing of his in the world, and then it too slipped away and he left no brilliant, unfading afterimage. Moments later the sleeping-bag-covered frame shook itself awake. The postdoc screamed from within, a muffled plaint, and Pidgin felt his eyebrows grin at the situation, grin with the tiny dancer, for her, but it was false complicity. She emerged, undizzy with her deed, and began aging fast. Pidgin wheeled on swivelhips and fell into motion, his natural state. She was chasing him now, only her legs were getting longer and longer. Pidgin clambered over cartops and under shelves of bumpers and alternator innards. He rolled tires behind him and stood hoods in the teen dancer's way. She vaulted over most of the tires though, used the hoods as springboards to dive through the rest, and finally cornered Pidgin at the complicated door of a schoolbus sitting on its frame. PISD, Portales Independent School District, an extra *S* and *E* done with spraypaint long ago, forced into the narrow space between the last two letters.

The sky wasn't yet light except in the distance. Pidgin felt his way in, huddled against the emergency exit in the rear that wouldn't kick open. The girl-become-a-woman entered the bus through the folding door, closed it behind her, then began tearing the covers off the seats and wrapping herself in them, deep. She was still aging. Inside of ten steps she was the Salvage Queen, bent with years, her silverblack hair queued into a hard topknot, her weight focused over a single aluminum cane, bowing that cane. She didn't advance. She matched Pidgin stillness for stillness, directed her lined face out the unbroken window. Pidgin followed. There was Charlie Ward, singing the sun up, a crackless windshield tucked under his arm, duct-taped at likely stress points. Horse-thief in the AM.

'The night's almost over,' the Salvage Queen said, then looked back to Pidgin, leaning hard and nonchalant on the exit lever, legs crossed at the ankle. 'You wear his cowboy clothes well,' she added.

'That's because he's dead,' Pidgin said. 'Cultural hand-me-downs and all. That anthropologist guy you killed would have loved it.'

'Squiggly Leni,' the Salvage Queen said, fondly. 'The Slav.'

Pidgin tried to contain a smile he didn't think he had in him anymore.

'What?' the Salvage Queen asked, looking around.

'I thought you were talking about my uncle, at first,' Pidgin said, 'the *Slob*.'

The Salvage Queen leaned on her cane with both hands, let it guide her down to the edge of one of the seats. Pidgin sat too. She affected bemusement with him. 'He came to me once, too, you know,' she said, 'your uncle. Looking for her.'

Pidgin quit smiling.

'Your mother, I mean,' the Salvage Queen finished, turning to the front of the bus again, where there was a woman wrapped in a kimono, sitting alone. Staring stubbornly forward, shoulders stiff.

Pidgin closed his eyes, shook his head no, the Salvage Queen had it all wrong: he was looking for his *fa*ther. Big lanky white guy. Nearly ten years dead.

'You do miss her, though,' the Salvage Queen said, 'like she misses you,' and Pidgin's non-answer counted against him. She had used the present tense, *was* using the present tense. They sat like that for Pidgin didn't know how long, Pidgin afraid to speak, not trusting his voice, the Salvage Queen not interrupting him, Marina Trigo staring straight ahead.

'You don't understand,' Pidgin finally said. 'I just want out of all this.' He rattled the emergency exit lever to show.

The Salvage Queen said she would give Pidgin a song to take with him, then, if that's what he wanted so bad. Instead of everything else. She removed from her shawls a pen and paper, scrawled and talked, said Pidgin's *Glory Dog* monologue reminded her of the old days, before she passed the mantle on to the next set, when she was still in temporary love with the Captain Smith of her time. Pidgin said the herb and peyote had made that monologue up, it was only bullshit. He apologized for saying bullshit. The Salvage Queen wrote slow. She licked her pentip as if it were a pencil she was writing with. She shook her head no, said she'd seen *The Scræling*, after all, they all had. That was what it was all about, all right, where it started: circa 1610. John Smith and his Indian princess. Pidgin covered his face with both hands. His fingers were twitching. The protective sac around his awareness was being pierced at many points, and *The Scræling*'s BIA office was rushing in, the end of the story Pocahontas started. 'No,' he said, letting it rise in his voice, against the Salvage Queen, '*no*. It wasn't like it was. The video lied. I got away, see. I got adamnway.'

The Salvage Queen regarded him, said *yes*.

Her eyes glistened with it.

Pidgin held his hand out for the song because he knew it was the ticket home, out, because maybe he'd paid for it by saying *no* for her, but at the last moment her hand closed on the paper scrap, and the interknuckle regions of her fingers sprouted golden hair like wheat. Pidgin told her he didn't deserve this. He'd done nothing; he'd chanced on a grave robbery, seen a ghoul when he wasn't looking for one. He followed her shawled arm up from the back of her fingers and her features were rearranging themselves yet again. She could get no older though. There was only one place left to go. Pidgin backed to the exit door as her hard topknot submerged, was replaced by nascent-yellow sidehair. It was an unsubtle gender swap. Pidgin shook his head no and watched through a spyhole burrowed in the aevum, and she came at him in pieces, and the pieces ordered themselves into Redfield's Custer, a hard hand on his curved military sabre.

He sniffed the early morning air, considered it, then looked at this crumpled song in his fingers, held it at bifocal range. 'Toe the line or don't,' he read with the last of the Salvage Queen's voice, dropping the ticket underfoot with a grin, 'and that was all she wrote.'

'I got away from you,' Pidgin said.

'You sure about that?' Custer said.

Pidgin pulled on the exit lever until it broke off. Custer's harsh laughter rolled down the aisle, and Custer was approaching behind it, a direct military maneuver, all nineteenth-century brinkmanship swept out the complicated door. He drew his seventh-cavalry sabre. It gleamed. Pidgin closed his eyes and opened them, did it again, again, but still Custer persisted, approached. 'No,' Pidgin said, keeping his back to the wall, 'no.' Custer shook his head yes, though, yes. His legs were long, striding, a sound. He was in his prime, in his element. Pidgin said it one last time—that he got away—and then stepped forward, with the exit lever held low heavy and half-reluctant at thighlevel, half impatient. The line was toed. Like the Salvage Queen had said in her song. Pidgin tested the lever for weight, balance. It was there like it had to be. When Custer was two armlengths out, already a smell, Pidgin said aloud that he could run no more, he was out of time to traipse over, and was goddamn tired of traipsing anyways. It was a warning. His voice was as even as he could make it. Custer slowed, chewed the insides of his cheeks, appraised Pidgin, shook his head no but was unsure, his neck begrudging movement.

Pidgin drew closer, within reach, should he need it. Custer smiled one side of his face and extended the sabre between them, keeping things civilized, leaving time and space for his joke about this Indian kid with the deadwhite father, had Pidgin heard it?

Pidgin stepped back without meaning to.

Custer nodded, said this kid then, one day his dad's talking long-distance on the phone, to the late Marty Robbins, so the kid has to go outside.

'To wax the shelters.'

'To wax the shelters, yeah. Stop me if you know this one.'

'It doesn't sound like a joke,' Pidgin said.

Custer told him to just wait, it's a riot. So this kid's out there, waxing whichever shelter, when a lady walks up out of nowhere. A census-taker of all people. She knocks on the door, and, because the phone reaches that far, this kid's father puts Marty Robbins on hold, chocks the screen open with his foot, and immediately gets into a yelling match with this federal employee about who she's really working for and why. Typical stuff with him. But then the census-taker backs up from the fight before it can get out of hand, says she just want to collect the facts here, please, then points across the shelters at the kid, so dark in the sun, so Indian.

And standing there in the unlit door of the trailer the father's so white he glows.

'Him,' the lady says, 'he's not yours, anyway, is he?' her pencil cocked to record his answer, and the father looks along her finger to the kid, standing there waiting to be claimed. Expecting to be claimed. But then the father stares for longer than it should take, as if seeing the kid for the first time all over. Finally he just shrugs and shakes his head no. Probably no.

'He was just trying to mess up her data,' Pidgin said to Custer, when it was over.

'Tell yourself what you like,' Custer said back. 'But just because you never had a mother, don't go thinking the world owes you a father or anything.'

Pidgin was breathing hard now. 'How do you know,' he said to Custer, a schoolyard comeback, and Custer said this was the funny part, the punchline, get ready. Keeping the sabre between them the whole time, he loosened the chin-strap from his gaudy hat, pushed it off the back of his head, leaned his paunch out, then calmly removed his sideburns.

Until he was Cline.

He winked at Pidgin, and Pidgin shook his head no.

'Daddy's home,' Custer said in a low voice, applying pressure to Pidgin's sternum with the sharp point of his sabre, and Pidgin reflexively batted the sabre away with his lever. The lever's weight carried it through to bare seatback. It buried itself there. Pidgin placed a foot on the seatback to extract it from the springs and the stiff foam, never looking away from Custer, standing there like Cline.

'You're not him,' Pidgin said, insisted, terrified by what it would mean if he was, ready to give up if he was, accept all the benign inevitability of colonization BS he'd been spoonfed, forget the ending originally written for *The Scræling*, where the aliens come to colonize *america* with their advanced weaponry, and america tries to conscript Indians to fight, and the Indians just laugh while the credits role. Under his father's insistent stare, Pidgin already was already forgetting it, even, how it sounded, all of it, but then for an instant he saw through the disguise—the disguises—how Custer was just Birdfinger here, pretending to be Cline. Like always. Even down to the sidehair, the gut.

Pidgin laughed to himself, and when Birdfinger-as-Redfield-as-Custer-as-Cline cast a meaningful eye to the front of the bus, where the cardboard cut-out of Marina Trigo had been and still was, Pidgin shook his head no one final time.

'You don't know her,' he said.

Birdfinger-as-Redfield-as-Custer-as-Cline grinned the part of his face Pidgin could see, disagreed with a suggestive waggles of his eyebrows.

'I do know who you are, though,' Pidgin said. '*Uncle*.'

The blond figure turned to him then, nostrils dilating evenly, the blood draining from his lips, the dash from his posture. Everything else Pidgin took away with the rising backswing of the lever. It caught Birdfinger-as-Redfield-as-Custer-as-Cline in the fatty part of the throat, glancing across the larynx, felling him over a seatback. First he was on his knees though, his head nodding once to Pidgin in something like acknowledgment, thanks almost.

And *then* he fell. Like orchestra. Pidgin breathed in catches when it was done. His fingers were still twitching. The blond figure held his throat hard, trying for breath, for air, voice, words. There were none, though. His right leg pedaled a missing bicycle. Pidgin checked outside, for Charlie Ward in the new light, and when he redirected to the figure, saw the Salvage Queen there now, her side rising and falling in strained rasps, shawls spread around her like opera blood.

The world drew to a standstill, balanced on a sharp point.

What had he done, what had she done? Pidgin rearranged the names in his mind, to *Custer*-as-Redfield-as-Birdfinger-as-Cline, using him to get to her. But why? And there were so many other options too. All of which left her dying facedown at his feet. By his hand. Her aluminum cane bent, not a sabre, never a sabre. Pidgin let the lever slip away, and it rebounded off the rubber flooring, settled against the wall.

What had he done here.

What had he done just because his father lied to a census-taker once, because his uncle drew a picture of Marina Trigo once. Because the dead wouldn't rest for him.

He watched the Salvage Queen struggle for a few moments, then swallowed, unnarrowed his vision, and felt from seat to seat in the dim interior, making his way to the front of the bus—proud, unproud. Numb. The cardboard cut-out of his mother corrugated on the frontside, blank. Waiting to be filled in with memories Pidgin didn't have. He stepped down from it all without looking back, exited by the proper door and into the morning. He sang under his breath as he went, and his song was like this:

toe the line or don't
and that was all she wrote.

His new stage name would be Lido, not Golias. Lido who had struck an old woman down when she approached with a ticket in her hand. Low light didn't justify it, vague historical melodrama didn't justify it. But then again. God. New Mexico was too much with him; he was daisy-chained across twelve days. His breath was corrosive.

Meaning his cartilage-white trachea was intact, functioning to some degree. Pidgin touched it gingerly, and as he did, laughter carried across the husks of many cars. It was hollow, procreative. Pidgin rocked back and forth, sang his song of power until Charlie Ward approached.

'Did she find you?' Charlie Ward asked, the banktube there in his rear pocket, safe all along.

Pidgin held it all behind his eyes, nodded, looked away.

He had done it.

It was real.

The ride back to Clovis was the last time. Pidgin sat the passenger seat and Charlie Ward didn't speak. Pidgin became larger and smaller with each breath. They balanced the windshield across their laps. Mars rusting in the early morning light. Charlie Ward slid his thin leather belt from his jeans and held it out the window, whipped the Cutlass faster, faster, his dyed-black hair unbraiding in the fifty-five mile per hour wind, and they never had to stop for gas. Pidgin's breath caught once, reliving it, but he didn't confess to Charlie Ward, and Boz Scaggs didn't come over the radio, and nothing rose from the asphalt to halt their progress, their regress.

Pidgin said his mother's name aloud and Charlie Ward didn't ask him about it, apologized instead for Pidgin having missed the interment. Pidgin said no apologies: it started when he left Utah, or maybe it started at WWI, or 1610, or the thirteenth century.

'At least you filled in that hole,' Charlie Ward offered, and Pidgin nodded, unnodded; Cline Stob was still out there, after almost ten years of clinical death. Pidgin had failed even at that, and was still failing. He held the idea of a shovel steady over the dash because a shovel could repair the glitch in his recent past. He was thinking in glitch-terms now. He told Charlie Ward to ask him what he did for fun. 'So what do you do for fun?' Charlie Ward asked, but then Pidgin couldn't bring himself to answer because one answer was that he clubbed junk-yard proprietresses into the afterlife. It had almost been a confession. His hand remained over the dash, holding nothing, and he watched his actions become antics and half-feared a laugh track. Someone's grandmother was dying in the faded yellow bus of his mind. His throat constricted; the color and the texture of the road surface changed.

In Clovis, Charlie Ward coasted to the bus stop, shifted the windshield to the seat, groaned out of the Cutlass. Pidgin followed by way of the driverside door, child-style, framing himself for a moment with both hands on either side of the doorframe so he could pull himself the rest of the way out. Reentry. It was like he was arriving all over, hadn't been here for seven-odd years. He stepped down, let the heat loosen his joints, tighten the skin around his eyes. Here he was. The Unemerald City, the Land of Disenchantment, The Greatest Medicine Show on Earth. Unmade in Clovis New Mexico. Charlie Ward opened the trunk, and in the trunk was the paisley suitcase, and the paisley suitcase was the only thing that could have been there. He set it by Pidgin's leg.

He nodded goodbye grandson to Pidgin.

Pidgin nodded back yes.

Here he was.

Utah was catty-corner to him. He shouldered the suitcase, pocketed the volatile banktube, and walked back towards it, out of town, across the pastures and fields and fences and blacktops. Distance was nothing to him. His feet fell in the right place every step, ankle-deep in oversized pawprints, and the miles lined themselves up behind him. He told himself he had unfinished business to attend to: Cline Stob was still out there, improperly buried, unburied. Getting him in the ground was the last best and only shot. Pidgin told it to himself like that, insisted that there still was a shot, that he wasn't caught in the syndicated loop of a *Glory Dog* sitcom, cast as a Red Everyman, a neverkilled Crazy Horse. He stayed in motion to avoid it all gathering around him like an argument, prodding him through the many holes of his belt. He'd gotten past Sally's story. Now there was this one he'd made up when he was an adlibbing television character, giddy in the camera eye, swimming through organic hallucinogens. It should be easy: with his father he would bury everything all at once and it would be done. With a shovel. Like that.

Soon his destination was within shouting distance: the one-man monastery, the Goliardic hide-out. He didn't shout, though. He had traced the Mexican Paiute across New Mexico and Texas and now back to here, where he would have to be, where he was, in the flattened grass area where Larry had parked his truck for nine days off and on, in the clearing where there once had been a swordfight, duelists reaching tenderly for each other across generations. He was duded up for community service, too, the Mexican Paiute: sombrero, peasant leggings, hipbag and litter stick. In the trampled grass around him, where the deep pawprints scattered in a cascade, became piecemeal, coyote-sized again, there were dried mounds of baked and baking shit. The Mexican Paiute was spearing them and placing them in the hipbag, scooping what wouldn't spear. Larry. In a state of ordure. The Mexican Paiute allowed Pidgin to watch. He lifted his chin and smiled a coeval grin, and in a wash Pidgin realized the grin had been coeval all along. He sat in the heat and studied the Mexican Paiute as he collected the remains of the second to the last Goliard, not counting himself.

When it was done it was only noon, and they had no shadows. The Mexican Paiute squatted scant feet away from Pidgin, became a smell, held half of a sunwarmed burrito out. Pidgin forced his arm to accept, then his mouth. The beans tasted of adrenalin. The Mexican Paiute folded the foil of the burrito carefully, into perfect quarters, inserted it in his muslin shirt.

'Cline Stob,' Pidgin said, looking hard, as far away as he could, then right back at the Mexican Paiute. 'My father.'

The Mexican Paiute nodded yes. His eyes were flesh-colored, unwhite. He stood without the help of his spear, tested the air with his pushed-flat nose, and began the trek Cloviswards, inhaling regularly. Pidgin walked behind him as he walked, breathed as he breathed, became the missing shadow, the only difference that he was carrying a suitcase, not a litterbag. But that was a small thing. When they entered Clovis they walked against the absent traffic and no dogs fell in line with them, and Pidgin was unsurprised to be crossing the street to the twin quonset-style warehouses there on the south side of the road like half-buried beer cans. Or a banktube open to the ground. They had always been there, a tin facade patched on the facing side with galvanized sheets taken from a distant and mythical Saint George Street Brewery, the letters unfaded, disapposed, the partial dragon shape rearing over the pieces of the name still left. Pidgin recomposed it in his mind without missing a step. The Mexican Paiute led him to the quonset on the right, shifted the litterbag, dreamed a key into his hand from somewhere on his squat person and pushed the stubborn door open, entered. Pidgin kept one hand on the doorjamb as he crossed over, and suddenly the facade had an unimagined but inevitable interior: fiberglass light angling down in shafts from odd places in the roof, a wall-mounted collection of sharpshooter shovels looted from some impossible lost load of lawn and garden supplies, a cairn of broken concrete in the corner that used to be the floor here. Now it was back to ground again, though, not brown like skin but blinding white, crystalline—a lifetime of styrofoam crumbled into the semblance of snow, a mummified arm reaching up here, there, a headshape Pidgin had to look away from. The air was cool, foetid. It coated Pidgin's lungs, took his breath so he couldn't call the Mexican Paiute back from walking to the office part of things.

Pidgin was alone with the dead.

The gravesend motel.

It was Sally's picture all over again. This was the morning after she'd been talking about, 1890 all over. This was the pact the Goliards had made, the genetic script Sally had written. What he was supposed to complete for them. Pidgin laughed a little bit so he wouldn't cry anymore. Cline Stob was here somewhere, under this snow that would last forever, never biodegrade, his skin leathery—*hide* now—the rest of him dead, posed into an attitude of regret, a visual reminder. In the back of Pidgin's mind the Salvage Queen apologized below voice-level for the feature-length vision, and Pidgin closed his eyes once, accepting, and that was the first step; and the next was to repicture Birdfinger, not as Custer anymore, but as he was at Juanita's, immediately after the funeral, when, because Pidgin had unaccountably peed his pants, Birdfinger looked around and did too, just to draw some of the attention away. They had stood together when the meal was over, uncle and nephew, wetlapped, and it was still soon enough that Juanita called Birdfinger Cline on the way out. In his mind, Pidgin didn't correct her anymore, just slid down the warehouse wall to a sitting position, hummed Boz Scaggs for power, looked up at the huge american flag painted backwards on the rusted ceiling, with Goliardic happy faces in the place of stars, in some crude representation of the afterlife, all their feathers pointing the same direction away.

All that was left to do now was to lay the paisley suitcase on its side, release the twin alloy latches, let the fiberglass light warm the body of Flea the Dog, neither dead nor alive for tense minutes, but then waking nose first, cataloging over the ribbed-aluminum lip of the suitcase, extending one foreleg then another, eventually flitting from place to place across the damp earth, racing off stiffness, his mouth open, black lips pulled back in a canine grin, tongue carelessly placed. In the dogracing moments before the Mexican Paiute faded out a trap door, not looking back at his life's cache even, a long canvas roll over his shoulder that could have been anything—a hang glider, an inherited lodge, stilts—Pidgin asked him who he was, or had been, reasked in broken down Spanish: 'Quien es usted?'

In answer the Mexican Paiute looked past the massacre, over it, followed Flea the Dog's erratic course through the snow, led Pidgin to do the same, to appreciate the Airedale lope, discern the distinct sound of backwards causality locking the door of the warehouse, dial in the whisper of decomposition, the insistent plaint of a diagetic release. The blood in his own neck going systole, diastole, systole, diastole.

'A pides de boca,' the Mexican Paiute finally said, only once, across forty feet and twenty-two years: *As you want it. As it needs to be.*

A Vision of Delight

Gallup would always make Birdfinger feel a little fey around the edges; he'd spent two weeks there one night with gonorrhea of the throat and a carton of untaxed cigarettes. The way he told it to Stiya 6 was that he'd been a shade or two under the venereal weather, that it and the tar had changed his voice for a few days. Even Cline hadn't recognized him at first, over the phone. Stiya 6 asked again now *when* did Cline die? then cracked her window, ashed, forefinger tapping in advance. Birdfinger watched the red rockland lump by, didn't answer; all her belongings were grocery-bagged in the backseat, and because of them the Cutlass air was filthy with unasked questions, thoughts half-formed then abandoned, left better unfinished.

She said her father was in Gallup.

She said he'd been dying for months now, bad plumbing.

She said she had some friends who would smoke anything for free, and then maybe pay for more if they thought it was the deal of a lifetime.

Birdfinger said good, good, pretended the radio wouldn't dial in, tried to counter her lack of interest in her own past with undeniable trivia, minutiae she would recognize at a preconscious level: he told her that before the Goliards were the Goliards they had been a hairsbreadth away from being named after Jack Wilson; that their getaway truck ran rich and clean on paid-for airplane fuel; that Sally wasn't legally on the Cherokee roll call, would be unmustered for the Native hereafter, denied that graceland; that the madstones the Goliards carried on the off-chance of death were neither flashbombs nor Easter-style deer droppings but sunbaked balls of inedible cornmeal, which was the first and bluest ingredient for inedible chips. That she—Marina Felina Janey Stiya 6—had an ascending mole which passed from generation to generation, a lateral movement. That that mole was a marker. That now all his cards were on the table. Stiya 6 didn't speak for miles, and then when she did it was to say how her kidnapping grandmother had demoled her with wet string when she was five, over the course of two weeks on the run. It had been an act of charity, a cleansing, fourteen days tied in knots, living on sarvis berries and horse water; the scars she had were all from chicken-pox, which came later, pecking skin-deep holes.

Birdfinger said it didn't matter: he would take her to her father, and her father would remember where the mole had been.

'But he's almost dead,' Stiya 6 said in warning, getting defensive, stepping in front.

'Then he'll be able to see good,' Birdfinger said back just as quick.

They passed the city limits sign and didn't comment upon it. They were on schedule, off plan. Stiya 6 directed Birdfinger with a finger on the dash, left right right, and the Cutlass was sluggish with misplaced contempt, intractable. Birdfinger reeled curbward, blamed it on Gallup, on the fact that he had become stolen property, reeled back. The madstones on the seat by his leg were supposed to have been an illustration, physical evidence. Now they rolled back and forth from him to Stiya 6 like chemical messengers, a reminder of how far their conversation had decomposed and was decomposing. They pulled alongside an ape-hangered man, and the ape-hangered man paced them on Stiya 6's side, grinning a baleen grin. Stiya 6 tossed a stray eyebrow pencil in the general direction of his front spokes, a near miss. The man took the next right available to him, a less disastrous avenue. Stiya 6 extended a hand over Birdfinger's, where he had the madstones contained, pressed into the seat. 'Welcome,' she said, trilling an *R* in there where there was none. It was a nice effect. It unreveried Birdfinger.

'We used to talk some about making those blue chips,' he said without eye contact. 'Nachos and stuff. Whole goddamn meals, first and last suppers.'

Stiya 6 rolled her neck with the road, and it was like a nod.

Birdfinger told her ten years, his brother her husband had died nearly ten years ago.

'How did I take it, then?' she asked, firing up another cigarette.

'You didn't.'

'Oh. Yeah.'

She inhaled, staring at the windshield it seemed, and in the harsh white noise of radial tires the memory of her *then* at the end of *How did I take it* sounded like a test of sorts, a one-line interrogation, verification, a timid first step towards trust. Birdfinger lost himself in the rich acoustical world of replayed inflections, tongues against palates. Stiya 6's tongue and palate. She exhaled, and that cherished breath of smoke from her mouth lingered, nuancing into patterns and designs, waiting to be stolen, and Birdfinger did, filtered it deep and slow in his chest, eyes darting, right hand under hers again, absolutely motionless, left casual over the wheel, the warm secondhand intimacy in his lungs unbalancing him for long moments on end in which he could only follow Stiya 6's verbal lefts and rights. It was airborne nicotine; it was requited love. When he steadied himself in the fitted cup of his seat again, the Cutlass was straddling a handicapped parking space. There was no other kind.

The building in front of them was a restaurant called The Cowlich; in the rearview mirror was a stripjoint, The Wetnurse. The banner strung between the two said they were now under the same ownership, and the lettering used was neither celebratory nor threatening, just bland statement of fact, an announcement of progress, of the eventual coming together of daytime and nighttime pleasures. At most it suggested a covered walk soon enough, then a shared roof, then no dusk no dawn no dividing lines. The stretched banner whipped once with the wind, a lengthwise undulation devoid of emotional vagaries, fundamentally uninvolved, not conjuring a snake in water even, a tapeworm in caliche, and Birdfinger said to himself that this didn't feel like home, little black dog; Clovis had no need of such self-awareness, such invasive, mocking tones. It was what it was. And this wasn't. This was hers. In a voice he didn't recognize he asked about parking, but Stiya 6 was stretching the outside corners of her eyes in the mirror, forcing epicanthic folds that stayed, her skin dehydrated stiff. Madame Butterfly incognito. She said the parking spaces were for the maritime VFW crowd, Cowlich's main diners, who at sunfall would take part in an exodus across the street which would take hours; her new eyes were to play up to their military fetishes.

'They might know where my dad is, see,' she said.

'He's not here you mean?' Birdfinger asked.

'Of course not.'

Birdfinger followed anyway. He counted his steps in—*one penicillin, two penicillin*—went unshushed. Gallup. Cops in cars, topless bars. The coroner cruising slow at the outer edge of the parking lot, hertz-black and long of neck, biding, counting customers. He pointed his finger across space through tinted glass and New Mexico heat deadcenter at the bone certainty of Birdfinger's sternum. Birdfinger shook his head no, ducked out of harm's way, didn't extend his namesake in return around the rounded brick corner. He sucked his backside to the wall and told Stiya 6 his old man might have been Navy too, at least part of some armada or another, but didn't repeat himself when she didn't hear.

'Nevermind,' he said, lips tight, nodding onward. 'Food, beer.'

He held the door for her and she just fit past him. Inside, in a fit of nictitation, pupils creaking open, sawdust invading pantscuffs, Birdfinger let his hand fall lightly to the small of Stiya 6's back, and became her consort for the coming barbeque. Her first stop was the payphone, where she called the people she knew and alluded to a deal of a lifetime, not like the debauch of last year, no. She told them to cogitate on it, then, but they were here, with the three lawn bags of unmentionables, and not for long. She led Birdfinger to a table, arranged herself in view of the VFW men grouped around a one-man billiard show, sat with her back board-straight, an attentive posture, both restrained and suggesting carnal acts at the same time. Birdfinger pretended it was for him.

Aside from an Indian man in mirror glasses they were the only diners in the midafternoon. The back of the Indian's shirt read A REGULAR COWLICHER, and he was hunched over a kingsize table that held no fresh barbeque but two rows of unmatched side mirrors—one row angling towards him, the other away, already modified. Held close to his shirtfront was a Bud can and some left-handed tin snips. He performed for them, Stiya 6 and consort, unrolling the can with calloused nimble fingers, soldering it to the back of a car mirror with sartorial precision, so that the red outline hugged like an offset frame in a camera viewer. It was a drinking man's tactic. Birdfinger knew it well: the canskin decoration on the outside of the mirror, whipping by at what would appear to be hand level, would trick the police into so many double-takes and wasted sirens and retracted radio calls that eventually the driver of the car and the car itself would cease to exist as far as the law was concerned, would operate below its conscious level, in an underworld where school zones were bermed for speed, where residential was a slalom run, where headlights were a last-second resort for the weakhearted. When the Indian artiste had relocked his tin snips and settled his soldering iron in the ashtray, he turned his wide body around and said he was Indian Joe King, if they had to know, the font and drain of all things shady and otherwise in Gallup New Mexico. Stiya 6 asked what was he doing here, then?

Indian Joe King laughed a gap-toothed laugh, said his wares had saved the clientele more than once; the owners catered to him, gave him custom-fitted house shirts, a daily bespoke suit. He was a Gallup original.

'Bullshit,' Stiya 6 said. 'You're like the rest. I remember you when you where just plain old Indian Joe, when you used to yell at people walking by on the bridge.'

'My Johnny Cash years,' Indian Joe King said, caught, proud. 'Those people just kept on moving, moving, shit don't I know.' He walked his thick fingers on a haphazard slant through the air to show, and Birdfinger saw for a moment that that was the exact angle of the bridge to him, reeling drunk. He saw too that there had been better places to sit, tables less prone to idle talk. But none more in view of the VFW men, who were playing Yahtzee for money now on the green felt expanse, sentries placed over every farside pocket, keeping tabs on Stiya 6's strained third button.

Birdfinger tilted the beer in his glass, watching Indian Joe King's adam's apple dip into black-polyester range and hearing words other than his—Stiya 6's recentmost *then*, like a conversational tic, not a test. He shook his head no, though, drank down the beer, resettled the glass on the oversized rubber coaster that had pronounced holes, was shaped triangular to fit over the drain of urinals. UNIVERSAL brand. It held the glass in place well, let the condensation pass to the treated wood table below, which passed it on to Birdfinger's knee. The jukebox was a Dan Seals tribute, golden-plated at the edges, glitter in between, and the songs were paid for in advance and played all in order. They were easy lyrics. Indian Joe King reminded Birdfinger that they were Dan Seals'.

Birdfinger started, asked for the facilities, followed a backthrown thumb past the spare eyes of the VFW men, already two tables closer to Stiya 6 and still advancing.

There were no rubber drain-covers in the urinals, and no Larry-carved words in the stalls or walls. One of the few. Birdfinger left a forgery for him anyway, a response to the highbrow graffiti alone in a corner. *There will always have been a reason*, it read. Birdfinger added in Larry's fevered hand that that was no great consolation in the thick of things, hoss, then scratched the Indian happy face into place. It was a gesture of peace, a tag for the old days. He added the porcelain rim of the toilet seat to his mental files when he was through, backed away slow for a full view, came back to Stiya 6 who now had a silverbacked VFW ambassador sitting at their table, tossing out Cambodian pick-up lines for her, Vietnamese flyting words for any overcasual eavesdroppers. The one-man show, the Bill Yard of the place, Kinnewick by name. He said he was a cunning linguist, and said it fast, offered to Orient Stiya 6. It was an invitation. Stiya 6 smiled for the group of watchful VFW men, crossed her legs, rolled her eyes, and said simply no.

'Indian,' she said, 'not what you think. Molly Janro. Seth's daughter.'

Kinnewick spat into the sawdust then rolled tobacco out of his lip down after it, stalling, leaving space for Indian Joe King to watch them in eight different mirrors at once, for the VFW men to glare as one and talk behind paper-thin hands, for Birdfinger to flinch on his side of the table, at Stiya 6's name coming at him out of the clear sky at two hundred miles per hour, a jaeger bird, screaming: he had never bothered to ask, had followed her nametag; she hadn't corrected him either, until now. And still it was indirect. She flashed a quick smile across the tabletop, ordered barbeque all around with her hands, as if she was whipping it up herself, casting a spell for beef ribs. They came just as fast, sizzling in their cast iron pans-as-plates.

'Molly,' Birdfinger said, trying it out. 'Molly.'

He ate and reassembled her in his mind. The disappointed VFW ambassador drank his beer, polished his knife. He said there were extenuating colón-related circumstances that forbade thusly cooked meat, not to mention some gristly subterranean memories, surely the daughter of *Seth* would understand?

Their words drained across the room, into Indian Joe King's eidetic inner ear. Birdfinger watched them, added his own: 'Molly.'

Molly.

He paid little attention to the rest of the meal, to Kinnewick recalling with unnecessary precision where exactly in line Seth had been when they'd filed into this world through a hole thirty-four years ago, escaping an older, more violent one—the Bone Meal, the buried TommyHawk—where man ate man ate man, according to rank, their divergent edacities prefiguring the schism that would result aboveground, the repentant and the un- parting ways in grim silence, one slouching west like the end of a movie, to regroup, repress, the other suckling america on what it had already acquired an unholy taste for: milk that was only two percent removed from blood, yet white as the absence of sin. All that mattered was that in the end he proffered a last-known address that Stiya 6/Molly Janro/Janey Porivo/Marina Trigo/Felina folded as if valuable, secreted away in the fifth pocket of her jeans. Kinnewick accepted a niecely cheek kiss in payment, then sloughed away, not neglecting to drag a casual middle finger in Indian Joe King's direction, who responded in lackadaisical kind. It was acknowledgment, greeting. Birdfinger said to Molly that maybe this was his place in the world, his intended station in life; he could get a job as head greeter, revolutionize the industry.

Molly said her friends would either be here inside of ten minutes or not show up at all.

'Your name,' Birdfinger said, squinting, 'I guess I'm sorry.'

Molly shrugged, smoked, pushed her plate away.

Somewhere behind the bar a phone rang one and a half times, indicating some undisclosed schedule, and the VFW men wrapped up their Yahtzee game with IOU notes, began their hours-long exodus to the Wetnurse, lining themselves up by a hierarchy acquired at their beginning of time, with ritual empty spaces for those already crossed over, maybe a space there for Seth, maybe even a whole twin row absent, walking beside and among them, interwoven in sequence but all the same estranged, deferred to, their teeth filed to a sharp smile as they whip past on the interstate. In the grimed ceiling mirror, the missing and the currently-present would form a double helix, but as it was they were just a strand of shuffling profiles. Kinnewick raised his whole hand in farewell, mouthed good luck, passed. Indian Joe King saluted them away.

'They know him,' Stiya 6 said when they were gone, 'my father. Or, knew him. He's one of them. They don't know for sure anymore where he is, though. Or if.'

Birdfinger ordered blue chips to bring them together across the table.

Molly said she was from Idaho. Her father too.

'Seth,' Birdfinger offered with a chip, filling in.

'His hand, too,' she said, 'yes, okay? Everyone has them.' She pointed at the twenty-seven bones between the hand and the forearm, said there, the mole Birdfinger had been talking about, he had it, Seth, just past the business end of his watch tree. Meaning she must have too, before her grandmother kidnapped her those two weeks.

In the wake of her admission Birdfinger felt himself sag into a better place. He ate one blue chip and then another and then the whole basket, and they were good, and he was full: she'd said it, about the mole, under no duress, no immediate prompting. It was another timid move his direction, a pointed question, common ground she was allowing—needing. She was from Idaho. The gulf between them was already becoming less wide. Across it, Birdfinger could see her as she was. And she was beautiful. She hid it when the door opened the next time though, unfolded her eyelids, mussed her shorn hair even more, slouched. Birdfinger was already there, lived there. He smiled to have unexpected company. Her friends approached singly, interrupting the romance, feeling things out, patting Birdfinger down for wires then turning on each other for safety's sake, feeling armpits and camel-toes. There were eleven of them, mashed race and mixed gender, some in between, vibrating with tension, blurry.

'Wasn't sure,' Molly said offhand, about their shifting presence.

'Us neither,' they said back, 'not after last year.'

'Fluke.'

'More like the whole whale, dear Mags, beached in our damn garage.'

Molly's cigarette offer emptied her pack. A single match passed from hand to hand, landed hissing in beer dregs. Molly's friends lounged around the place drinking weasel pop and kola, formed themselves to chairbacks and cash registers and halfwalls. One of them with an aristocratic sneer per Falco suggested hooking a lightweight T-bar onto that banner outside, for senior citizen use, then got hit from opposite sides of the room with elevation problems and return-trip logistics and failing armstrength, drew his head in like a turtle under friendly fire.

'Goddamn,' Birdfinger said.

They nodded yes, exactly.

The worn business card they handed Birdfinger announced them as the Rundobogenstils, a Dram Vendor Society. Birdfinger suggested they reach for the acronym, buy a vowel or two, become DiVaS or primadonnas or something. They took the card back in a collective huff, and then as if Molly wasn't there explained her history with them via last year's debacle, how she'd pandered an out-of-state porn rag to them for distribution, an NRA-auspiced post-*Deep Throat* effort christened *Muzzleloader*. Molly Janro of course had a stunning cameo; she didn't look away when they said it, acted it, collapsed inwards in juvenile laughter. A woman emerged from the pile as the combined voice of the Rundobogenstils. She introduced herself as Patience Patience. She said *Muzzleloader* had been an affront, a greasy-palmed censor's miscarriage of decency; they had bought it solely to keep it out of circulation.

'I guess you can explain all your mistakes away like that,' Molly said, 'if you're that noble, I mean.'

'Then you admit it was a mistake.'

'I admit that it pandered itself, yes, that the multiple fold-outs were just smoke for the lobbyist personals-mocked-up-as-crosswords—'

'It's not about art, Mags.'

'Exactly,' Molly said, ripping her leg away from Birdfinger's consoling handpat. 'It wasn't. It had little value on the rack. Porn junkies saw through it in a glance or less. That's how the rods in their eyes are made.'

'Yet you sold it to us in good faith.'

'You were buying pornography in bulk, out of the back of a truck, Patience.'

The Rundobogenstils tsk tsked from their many vantage points, said Molly's overweight coxcomb of a friend should be honored they even came to this faithless meeting at all. Birdfinger stood out of duty, upsetting beer mugs, but they waved him down in concert, even Indian Joe King lending a spare arm.

It had been a compliment.

But still.

The Rundobogenstils asked Birdfinger how old he was anyway, how many decades did it take to eat that stomach full?

Birdfinger said he would be dead in dog years.

They watched him, close. Under all those eyes Birdfinger had no real choice in the matter: he barked twice, fast and mean, and the Rundobogenstils jumped as one, fell off half-walls, tumbled over chairbacks, and rose grinning, respect crossing their faces ear to ear, then being wiped away just as fast. They asked Birdfinger what he had for them, then? Birdfinger said patience patience, smiling and looking no one particular in the eye, and then extracted from his wallet the oversize, resin-doctored sample Molly had prepared en route, when she was still Stiya 6. The double front doors locked on cue, and everyone went through the obligatory wire pat again, part of the dealings.

Patience Patience brought to bear a turquoise-inlaid ceremonial lighter and said Birdfinger wasn't so funny.

'Breathe in,' Birdfinger said, indicating the lung path, 'I'm a goddamn barrelful.'

She did, then passed it on. The hashline. One by one they succumbed, coughing. Patience Patience asked what it was. Birdfinger said it was a beanstalk, he had traded a cow for it.

'What are cows going for these days?' Patience Patience asked.

Birdfinger shrugged, reluctant to offer the deal of a lifetime before the sample had made at least one more round. 'Grass, still,' he said, rubbing his scruff in thought, 'far as I know?'

Patience Patience almost smiled.

Each of Indian Joe King's mirrors reflected teeth, and his massive form shook.

Birdfinger asked the Rundobogenstils what their mission statement was, their creed, said at one time he'd had a mission too. They said he was never like them; Birdfinger said contraire, he was their clunky prototype, their coelacanth, Molly too: retrofigure back to ideals, essences, originals, they'd find him, and her. They all looked to her. She said they were in the fairy tale now, breathe deep of it. The Rundobogenstils shared an underbrow look, inhaled individually, watched Birdfinger close when his turn came. He held the harsh smoke in at liver-level, scratching his nose idly with the back of his hand, and when he could talk he did, lied that he was immune to the stuff nowadays, that was the only reason he was selling it.

Patience Patience said they, in turn, were immune to his solicitations.

Birdfinger said they had it all wrong: he wasn't here to make money, he just wanted to get the same cow out that he'd put in. He said livestock was going for cents on the pound these days, since they had inquired, and his trunk was weighed down with three fifty-gallon bags, uncounted and uncountable drams, a not insignificant amount, even for Gallup. He held the last of the sample between his thumb and forefinger, rotating for inspection, making them follow his lead.

'So what's it worth to you?' Molly asked.

Patience Patience locked eyes with her, didn't introduce herself all over again, like Birdfinger so wanted. Instead she answered Birdfinger's creed request, said they had none, they were past all that. 'In the afterlife,' she said, 'the *occupied* afterlife, missions are by definition pointless, falsely teleological, dependent upon a contrived linearity. And what you or a group of you believe is equally pointless. There you are, y'know.'

'In the afterlife?' Birdfinger asked.

'Sine loco. Fourteen ninety-two plus, and counting. Mags calls it a fairy tale. Europe calls it a social experiment. My grandfather calls it an accidental dream. We call it the spirit world. Not that traffic is below us, now....'

'Traffic in livestock,' Molly filled in for Birdfinger, but he was still fumbling with the afterlife concept, not ready to deal. In the commotion Indian Joe King peddled the idea of six sets of customized mirrors, traded for watches and baubles and doodads. Birdfinger gathered his thoughts, asked the Rundobogenstils why they needed chemical soothing then, if they were shades and all?

'Isn't that a pre-soothed state in the first place?' he asked.

'I said it was the afterlife, not Judeo-Christian heaven,' Patience Patience explained. 'And besides, when a shadow smokes a shadow, there's still something of an effect, if you hold it in long enough.'

Birdfinger started laughing then, raising the Rundobogenstils' eyebrows, and said that when he was a prototype, his group's mission had been nothing less than to halt the end of the world. He looked to Molly and corrected his *my* to *our*, apologized. She was tapping her foot in some code his unimmune senses couldn't latch onto. It was funny, he said, turning back to Patience Patience: his group had wanted the world not to end, and now here was this new group, his and Molly's inheritors—descendants—living *after* the end of the world.

The Rundobogenstils said his insight would likely go unrewarded this fine summer day.

Birdfinger said the reward was in seeing it, in speaking it aloud, giving it form. But there was business to attend to: he made talk about how he had friends in Tucson, already getting money together for the load in his trunk. 'But,' he said, clamping his forehead between fingers, 'the drive, y'know. Shit, it's a lumbar adventure for an old timer like myself.' He followed with a proposition of mutual gain, the banner deal of the afterlife: he offered to sell them the three mulched bags for any Seth-lead they might have and whatever modest cash they could scrounge inside of five minutes. He knocked on the table twice and said he was an easy man to deal with, when you got down to it. The Rundobogenstils reached deep in their pockets, came out with happenstance handfuls of cash which they piled on the table, all twenties, all willingly, and then delounged themselves from the many surfaces of The Cowlich, made movements towards the door. Patience Patience wrote an obligatory address on a napkin, teased Molly with it for a second—holding it out, shaking her other finger *not yet*—and then left it fluttering with the cash, joined the doorward funnel.

The barrel of the lock rolled once on graphite-slick brass and they were gone, and Birdfinger was just then realizing that their reflections had never shown up in Indian Joe King's mirrors, though they had occupied every conceivable angle. He realized too that they weren't Indian Joe King's mirrors anymore. He scooped one off the table and slammed the twin front doors open, lungs full to call out, but the parking lot was empty, the only sign of life the maritime VFWers easing across the road, holding their shoulders as if their lips were pursed. The endmost one cast a look back and Birdfinger saw that he was the acting rearguard; the whole line stopped with him, and that they weren't already stopped from the Rundobogenstils' prior exit made zero sense. Birdfinger had expected a van of sorts to be being boarded, a running board to be bowed with body weight, but there was only the Cutlass trunk, open and still, keys adangle. He collected them, walked the mirror back inside, to Indian Joe King, asked where was the van that should have been there? Indian Joe King waved the question away, said he had no truck with the dead himself, outside the occasional bauble, for novelty's sake. During the course of the Rundobogenstils' visit, he had made no more mirrors either, Birdfinger saw, and it was like no time had elapsed. But there was the money on the table, undeniable. Molly said not to ask, it was better not to know with them. Her words flushed clockwise, swirling over the broad table of Indian Joe King, who became the voice-over for the affair, said he was feeling something like pity for the two of them.

'Indebtedness, maybe,' Molly said, nodding down to the baubles he'd collected.

Indian Joe King shrugged, caught again, and to even matters up, scribbled a third Seth-address for them. Birdfinger said the Cutlass didn't quite get the mileage she did in days of yore. Molly stuffed a twenty in his mouth. Her fingers tasted of many things. Birdfinger catalogued them for miles, to the first trailer, where Dæstrom the bespectacled squatter stood risen from sleep on the other side of a lockable screen door. The idea of Seth bothered him like a horsefly. He swatted it away, began telling a personal anecdote about the Gallup pole that Molly claimed was more than generic; it was indigenous. They left him locked behind his screen, about to expose himself, become the neverspoken punchline. In the Cutlass moving in the direction of the Patience Patience-scrawled address, Molly counted the money aloud: three thousand dollars on the nose. She placed it between them, ignored it, then sneaked a look down. Birdfinger said object permanence was a rule of thumb in his car. He had *some* standards. Molly said it wasn't right; Birdfinger said it was more than he ever expected for weak tea.

'That's just it,' Molly said.

The second trailer was a charred rectangle on the ground. Molly walked from room to room to the exploded butane tank, said no, not like this. In the car again she counted through the three thousand dollars, held the bills up to the domelight, looked for telltale strings and fowl, erased the green color like a detective show, burned the corners of two of them. The flame was blue and yellow and smokeless. Birdfinger inhaled and proclaimed it was real government ink, he knew the difference. Molly shook her head no, no, it was too exact an amount for them to just *happen* to have in their pockets, and all twenties? The last trailer, in Indian Joe King's hand, was a gas stop away, and while Birdfinger pumped, Molly arranged the bills over the seat, her hands a bankteller blur, finally rising to her face slow, with hard edges now, in acceptance of defeat. She placed her feet on the dash as if to push it all away. She held three bills out to Birdfinger, the sequential serial numbers highlit with lipstick. Sixty dollars. A series. She began laughing in her chest, in her nose, behind her eyes, everywhere but her mouth. She told Birdfinger drive, drive, and coasting away without looking back at the waving clerk was already second nature to him.

Blocks away they pulled over, scanned at random, and all the numbers were of the same lot. It was unspendable, illegal tender. Molly acknowledged that the Rundobogenstils had matured in the last year, had grown up enough to get even with her, with them, for their garageful of *Muzzleloader*. 'I'm sorry,' she said, but Birdfinger was already saying not to worry, the only investment he wasn't recouping here was the lemonade and cookie money from last night. And that had been a date. Any money he owed around Clovis or Utah could wait too, had been standing long enough already that a few more months wouldn't matter much.

'Utah?' she asked.

Birdfinger drove and told her about the money he owed the kid—her kid, her money. It was a bold, abbreviated monologue. In the wake of it Molly was speechless, holding each of her elbows, shoulders drawn up, feet on the dash. Scared. Birdfinger said it was him that should be apologizing to her. She narrowed her eyes in response, maybe thinking, considering, reminiscing. Birdfinger left her to it, hoped he was in a good light. The third trailer was silent, right where Indian Joe King had said: baking in the sun, no cars, no lawn to speak of, though there had once been a sprinkler. Molly swallowed, stepped out of the car. Birdfinger followed her through the front door. The television was still on, smoking hot, talking episodic nonsense. Birdfinger inspected room by room as Molly sat the couch, hugging herself. He called back from each end of the trailer that it was empty, safe. There was just the smell. Molly began laughing at *safe*, couldn't stop. There were tears involved. She said her father Seth used to tell her stories he claimed were from Idaho but were likely lifted from ports and harbors around the Mediterranean; in them, she was an easily misled princess, he the aging-yet-able chief of some band of old-time stilt-Indians, always trying to reel her back in from misadventure; there were kidnappings and ransoms and emblematic raiding parties and regretted elopements and bedsheets shinnied down and wooden boats in the harbor with mysterious strangers and in the end there were always apologetic reconciliations celebrated by give-aways and recounted in song, until he was breathless, Seth, and the next story always began with the slow-acting poison from the last one, and how the chief had managed to gamble his daughter back again against all odds, tuck her in, leave the door open just a crack.

Birdfinger nodded that that was all good, he guessed. He said it like a question though, only partially asked. Molly shook her head no, extended a hand, held his fingertips, and told him he could go, please, she was here now. And thank you. For bringing her and all. Birdfinger stood with his feet on the carpet two feet above the real earth and retasted every last thing in his stomach. It burned his throat. He breathed out once, and it caught.

'You're sure?' he asked.

Molly nodded yes, didn't look back up.

Birdfinger made it apparent that he was honoring her request, being prevailed upon. He backed away slow, looking at her on the couch, where she always was, where she always had been, and then made himself get into the Cutlass, drive, drive. He came back once to tell her to lock the door behind him, but she didn't answer, was maybe still on the couch, staring. He left again, and it was harder this time. He talked to Net as he drove, said *see, see,* hovered his hands over the wheel as proof of his leaving, of his knowing when to leave. But then he returned a second time, asked if Seth was back yet, he had to know about the mole, just that one thing, for closure. He bagged the cash money in an old T-shirt and left it pendant on the doorknob, swinging, counting time. He made another gas run, shook a fleetfooted clerk from his fingerhold on the Cutlass bumper. He looked for The Cowlich for the first beer of many, but it was nowhere. He swallowed hard, was unsure where he was anymore in relation to Seth's trailer, if that's what it even was, God. It could be anybody's. He tore through the daytime backroads, found the trailer by providence, sat a hundred yards down the road, rehearsing things to say to her. 'Goodbye,' he tried, one of many that he couldn't get right. He was afraid to leave again, afraid of losing the address after all these years of waiting.

The five o'clock traffic eased by and the trailer park hooded its lids, watched the Cutlass. Birdfinger shook off the weight of their suspicions, stared at the trailer, trying to make a curtain part, a door open. It wasn't happening. He upped the ante in response, retaliation, tried to draw her out on the porch, but she didn't do that either, was maybe still on the couch, alone, scared of where Seth might or might not be. Birdfinger explained it to Net that he couldn't just leave her there like that, got no answer, had to assume an approving nod. It's not like he was meaning her harm. He coasted into the driveway, engine off, so he wouldn't disappoint her, sound accidentally fatherlike: but Seth wouldn't knock on his own door. He would have a key. The bag of illegal tender remained. Birdfinger knocked soft, didn't say Molly's name but *hello in there*.

Molly said to come in.

Birdfinger pushed the door, the weight of a hundred and fifty illsorted bills carrying it farther than he had wanted it to go, spilling in too much daylight when he wanted it to be just him. Somewhere in the five o'clock traffic a siren wailed after someone screeching around corners, making a fast getaway.

'They're playing our song,' Birdfinger said, tilting an ear.

Molly looked up at him, shook her head no. 'You were only a criminal in your mind, Bird.'

Birdfinger looked at his stolen self and said he was going to take that personally, when he got the chance.

But she'd said his name. She'd said his name.

She said too that Seth wasn't coming back.

She said that she had to be at work by midnight, if possible.

Birdfinger helped her stand, led her past the door where she collected the surfeit of illegal tender, opened and closed the Cutlass door around her, held his hands over the weatherstripped area where her window met the roof and made a groove, closed his eyes in thanks. It had been close. He had almost lost her to Gallup. For the pre-Albuquerque part of the trip back to Clovis, they were behind a milk truck with a SEC 8 license plate. Birdfinger pushed the lighter in and out and said the driver had to be a military reject; Molly smoked and said he was probably a dyslexic bullrider. For the post-Albuquerque part of the trip, the bumpersticker of the car in front of them said all in caps for them to drink more milk; the bumpersticker unsettled Birdfinger for unspecific reasons, but the car sped up and slowed down with them, was unpassable, got great mileage. Birdfinger slurred on any america that would allow billboard technology to become so personal; Molly said it reminded her she was thirsty. They made it to Squanto's by midnight, and once there they didn't talk of Gallup, of Seth. The way Birdfinger already remembered it she had been on the couch, waiting for him, tying bedsheets in knots because her hair had been shorn in a failed assault.

He had rescued her.

He had insisted she take the illegal tender with her too, rubber-banded in her purse, as token repayment for past misspendings, and because he'd yet to find the kid and do it right. She had accepted, leaned her slight mass into the sensor of the grocery store door, left an afterimage which wouldn't let the door close behind her. Birdfinger understood. He said her name after she was gone: Molly Janro. Her belongings were still in the backseat. He unloaded them into the trailer, moving her back in. He made it into three trips because three trips was significant effort, which meant significant reward.

Two days later the money was still unspent, unspendable. Over a breakfast that was a dinner for Birdfinger he said it was a bad take, the livestock money the mulched stalknub had turned into, and Molly said you have to be criminal to use words like that, like that: *take*. Birdfinger said he was, he had been. Molly laughed over her french toast, added more syrup, said she knew *she* was, or had been, at least, in her time, though she wasn't necessarily proud.

'What're you getting at?' Birdfinger asked.

'Nothing.'

'Then tell me nothing.'

She prefaced her response with a bite of french toast, chewed long, shrugged. 'It's just that...' she said, using her fork to extend punctuation, 'we have all that money. It seems a shame.'

'Your money,' Birdfinger said.

'Token money.'

Birdfinger realized then that in not so many words she was asking for payment, that in accepting the debt she was accepting who she was. That there was that debt still between them, linking them across the years, the gulf. He smiled. He said if only they could take that money to the bank, launder it in style, like in the movies. He said it in jest. Molly followed with the timed observation that Friday was payday at Squanto's. Maybe they could.

'We?' Birdfinger said.

She fed him a french fry as reward, reminded him she was still on cash-drawer probation.

'We,' she said, reenforcing the notion, making it unidle. 'Partners in old-time crime. Bonnie and Clyde.' She picked spice cans off the halfwall with her finger gun, one by one, plink plink plink. Birdfinger waited for them to fall. They didn't. He made his way to the porch.

'We have to live here, though,' he said, 'I mean, after payday or laundry day or whatever.'

Molly leaned straight-armed on the railing. 'Why?' she asked.

Birdfinger had no answer: because his brother built this porch; because the kid might show up here one day; because without him the renters wouldn't have anybody to make them feel legitimate, anybody to ease their squatterguilt; because this was where his history was; because he could no longer fit his life in the Cutlass all at once. He said it was paid for, the trailer, a first generation family heirloom with seventy-one thousand miles on it, no longer mobile. Molly said Clovis wasn't all it was cracked up to be in the tourist brochures.

'We have tourists?' Birdfinger asked, and then she was close to him, the back of her forearms against his chest in a convincing fashion, saying Birdfinger would wear a mask of course, and it's not like he would really be *stealing*: he would just be holding up register 6, failing at it for the cameras, leaving the illegal tender in unquestioned trade.

Birdfinger said there were too many variables in a plan like that.

They ran through it over and over, trying to figure it out better, all afternoon, and it finally came down to the hard fact that the only catalyst that would make this hypothetical grocery store stick-up artist abandon his *take* would be having the fear of God appear in his general area, which meant some sort of authority figure, which tended to mean sidearms, or at least blunt pocket objects. And Birdfinger said the Goliards were against real guns, more or less, even the blunt threat of a gun. Larry had had a sword, even.

'It's in the creed like that?' Molly asked.

'It's a flexible creed,' Birdfinger said.

'Perhaps situational,' Molly amended.

But still, there was no other way to force authenticity into the proposed laundry trip. Birdfinger offered to just get a job, maybe play an out of town gig or two, tag along with the rodeo or something, they knew him now. Molly shrugged like what did it matter anymore, like Clovis was strangling her. She paced back and forth like a pool hustler, like a caged panther. She said she was still grieving for Seth, she guessed. She began to say *if only* too, but Birdfinger interrupted, said this was the only place she could have come, okay?

She nodded okay, and her disappointed head motion spread to Birdfinger, who was watching her close, who fell into the obligation of give and take, caved, said if he could he would locate a third party, a catalyst to complete the masquerade. He looked away when he said it, told himself it was about requiting love, about conscious efforts to do so, about lengths. But it was about her. It was all about her. He took her to work and dropped her off at the door again, retired to Clandenstein's, repaired back to the trailer, meditated on the solaces of lawful delights he was missing out on around the clock: Molly slept on his bed, at his request, and he didn't know whether she'd say *come in* again in answer to a soft knock on the door. It could have been just a one-time trick. Perhaps it was enough that she was in the trailer. He had told it to one of the whiskeybent Clandenstein regulars like that, and the regular had looked into the near distance and said he was no expert, but this being exiled to the couch bit sounded a tad self-imposed, no? Birdfinger had talked to an alternate regular after that, about the same thing, about how his feelings for his brother's wife were never carnal, polluted. This next regular had revived the six-foot, redheaded idea of Net, asked what had she been then, some kind of Fanny Hill or another? and Birdfinger left with his tab four beers heavier, nodded once to Truck in defeat, once to Net in submission.

The next morning over dinner when he still hadn't found a third party or even began looking, Molly said she didn't so much like this being a creditor, it didn't fit right. Birdfinger said no, it was a good thing—for both of them: he owed her. She was a tablewidth away, croissant in hand, hand rising, teeth parted to accept. When she was gone again with the Cutlass this time, he told himself to follow through, follow through: he plundered the closet of unmentionables for his criminal outfit, stayed there all day reliving. It wasn't there though. He made do with a ski mask modeled in the bathroom mirror, didn't recognize himself, counted that as another good thing. But then again maybe he could ask her for pantyhose, for her smell on his face for courage, second wind. He buried the ski mask. Everyone at Squanto's would recognize his build anyway. Everyone in Clovis. Which meant he had to find his crime outfit, his warshirt. Midafternoon he did: it was duct-taped in plastic, had become the nest for a bowling ball monogrammed with AAA, a display model. The warshirts had been Cline's idea, but he had had Marina to make his—hot-glue the fringe in the right place, tie-die it the old way, play the right songs over it, breathe the right smoke in the right directions. Birdfinger had had to make do. He had in style. His shirt was retaliation against having to have a shirt: it was sleeveless, v-necked, and large over the stomach had the ironed-on image of Rodan the pteroble lizard, swooping down over an arm-shielded populace, the sweeping motion of the leathery wings inferred in the missing next frame, the bodycount too grisly for display, higher for being unseen. But it was there. The shirt was about more than the imminent threat of bodycounts, though, too; it was a shirt of invisibility: since Rodan had never existed, neither could a Rodan shirt, and—Birdfinger had extended it in explanation to Larry—if the shirt wasn't there, neither was the wearer. Poof. Larry hummed the magic dragon tune, smiled one side of his face, and said he was maybe going to get him a Mothra shirt, so he could remember what it was like to have been a giant South Pacific caterpillar, and after that they didn't talk anymore about it.

But the shirt worked.

Birdfinger only got caught when he refused to run.

And then it had been for her.

He left the shirt in the bag under the bowling ball, refolded, never washed in an automatic washer, held in place by the sixteen pounds necessary to keep it in place, corporeal, part of this reality. He was remembering it all now. Everything was falling into place. He placed himself on the porch, beer in hand, in the headlights of providence: let the third party come to him. That was the only way.

The afternoon trudged past, first in the form of an emergent renter who claimed in american to speak no american, next in the form of a prank, a Clovis Wildcat standing into the roof of a shelter then crawling out headsore, half-sure he had been abducted from his post-game stupor by a carload of extraterrestrials and then deposited in their temporary holding facilities, in await of the mothership. Birdfinger quieted his probe-complaints with a beer on the house, pointed in the direction of Clovis with his namesake, made up an alien tongue to click directions in. Two down, no luck. But then the real heat was just beginning; the afternoon was embryonic, yawning in the womb. It became a field day. The cats crept bellydown into the shelters in timeless fashion. A boot heel fell heavy and unquestioned out of the sky, thudded under the trailer, and in the still possibility it left the sun leaned over, white hot, pressing all life down, farther and farther, until something stood against it: a gopher emerged from the ground, pulling itself out of the distance, out of the flatness of the horizon, gesturing four directions in sequence and then becoming an old Indian in grey braids, describing a slow parabola at the outer limit of Birdfinger's vision. Birdfinger felt himself become an axis, and it was a new sensation—central, flatfooted. He stepped away from it, got the gopher man's attention by beating on a shelter top, waved him in.

The gopher man approached with caution, testing the air the ground the slant of the sun. 'The longhouse man,' he said from a studied carlength off the porch, his words clipped.

Birdfinger looked back at the trailer with different eyes, turned back to the gopher man, nodded yes, it was his place. The gopher man was wearing what had once been a security guard outfit, too. The first thing Birdfinger said to him of consequence was that sometimes providence was a beautiful whore with long lashes and delicate fingers, and sometimes he had the right change for her. He emptied the spittoon among the shelters, in trade. The gopher man didn't collect the spent money but nodded, introduced himself as Charlie Ward, removed his shoes in answer to a porch invitation, fell into a steady cadence of car-stealing stories. He smelled of kerosene, so Birdfinger tried to replace the burning scent with beer, tried to incline his torso to where he would appear duly regaled by grand theft auto. He didn't want to mess the situation up, scare this Charlie Ward into town. There was no eye contact, only words welling up, receding, capturing for moments at a time New Mexico tearing by at one fifty plus, leaving you, placing you beyond it: Birdfinger's torso inclination ceased to be an effort. His back became sore with attention. When Molly got home, still in her Stiya 6 nametag, eyes still tracking waist-level groceries from right to left, sizing up Charlie Ward an item at a time, holding a cigarette to her red lips, Birdfinger placed a hand over her lighter, shook his head no, flared his nostrils in a way that meant airborne kerosene. Molly repursed her lighter with a smile both understanding and disappointed, and with that small sacrifice it was begun, their criminal enterprise, with no porchside fireworks, only a meal of corn chips and beans and gameshows on the stacked TVs, movies into the night.

'An evening in with the extended family,' Birdfinger announced, seated with a drink within reach, *Solaris* winding down Cyrillically. The family was unresponsive, digesting, blinking during the commercials' assault, reposing themselves during the shows. He said it again to himself: an evening in with her, and the third party he had provided. He redefined himself as that, as a provider, remembered the broad strokes of the past—him and the kid—which made of him almost a father, allowed him to sit in the role of head of the household, husband. He put Charlie Ward to bed easy with some subtle penlight action, used it to change channels on the vistavision, the one with sound, so the words no longer matched the perched tube's picture. It was an old trick; the kid had been the unwilling test case. But still, Birdfinger had to do a sustained forearm pinch to stay conscious himself. And Molly fell victim of course, after a nine-hour shift, on the other end of the couch from Charlie Ward. In the mismatched dialogue flooding the room, Birdfinger climbed her inchmeal with his eyes, Molly, Felina, and felt a stirring, an overload, because when he had climbed her before she had been an even breathing on the other side of a hollow-cored door, and there had been little chance of her catching him excuseless, since her breathing pattern would change nanoseconds before that, leaving Birdfinger time to reach four feet over and flush the toilet, the lack of evidence in the bowl swirling away, becoming evidence if it came to that, to lying. But it never did. She slept. He watched her on the couch with the gopher man risen from the earth to play his part in their crime, and two hours passed, and his forearm was bleeding from the waking effort, and for a few moments the ten o'clock news dialogue synchronized with an exchange in a thirsty brown and white western, and it was enough to stir Molly.

She asked so Clovis was in a range war, now? and Birdfinger shushed her, indicated Charlie Ward. He led her to the kitchen. He play-acted normalcy and asked how was work, and Molly play-acted back, told him about all the different kinds of squash and the irregular stock numbers assigned them on a daily rotating basis by Espe Wilson, her paranoid assistant manager. Her fingers danced over a ten-key pad with each different squash type, and she said it was stimulus-response, her hand was developing birdsmooth ears, claiming autonomy.

'Askutasquash,' she said, in example, and her fingers raced through a number.

Birdfinger said he knew some post office personnel with the same quirk. After time it would develop into trigger finger, lock into place, ba bam bam bam.

They had nothing to talk about.

Birdfinger reached: 'Charlie Ward,' he said, 'mister third party. He was sent.'

'By who?'

'I don't ask questions anymore.'

'Because the answers.'

It wasn't a question. Birdfinger made himself a tuna fish and lithium sandwich. He liked them better in the afternoon. Over the third and final bite he accidentally called Molly Marina and she accidentally answered, rolled her eyes, laughed in spite of herself over the immaterial foam of a root beer. There were so many things that could happen. The moment branched; Birdfinger followed:

He told Molly that he got Charlie Ward on the bargain rack. 'Ninety-seven centavos,' he said, showing off, 'exact change.'

'He's too old, though,' Molly said.

'Experience,' Birdfinger argued. 'He's already a criminal.'

'You argue proper mindset.'

'I claim ability, Mags.'

'Don't call me that, please.'

'It's your Gallup name?'

'This is Clovis. I'm reminded daily.'

'Home.'

'A station in the rails. Riley switch. A layover.'

'He's not too old.'

'He falls asleep with popcorn in his mouth then wakes chewing. He told me about the Salian Dynasty when I didn't ask.'

'It wasn't from memory.'

'I'm saying his mind wanders.'

'But you wanted him for the job.'

'*Job* isn't your word here.'

'You wanted him, though, yes?'

'I wanted someone *like* him.'

'He's nobody to you. Another drunk Indian.'

'Maybe it's about trust then, or reliability.'

Birdfinger rubbed his eyes, ground his teeth, made like realization was washing over him in the middle of a lukewarm domestic dispute: 'You're protecting him, aren't you,' he said, 'that's it?'

'I'm rejecting him, Bird.'

The name, again. From her. Birdfinger continued, posited connective tissue: 'You kept getting him beer after beer, so he wouldn't have to get up.'

'You're misinterpreting.'

'You took his side in the movie debate.'

'I like westerns.'

'But that one's been on for three nights now?'

Molly shrugged. She said she liked the Indians in the movie, liked to watch them try to run with their quivers and their Robin Hood bows and their wigs, said she liked the Rod Serling narration, the one Indian at the end standing on that last piece of reality that's yet to crumble away.

'It's not a comedy,' Birdfinger said.

'Just because he's laughing doesn't mean you're supposed to,' Molly said back, then smoked a cigarette under safety of the range hood, vent humming. Her eyes through the dense smoke were reinspecting Charlie Ward asleep on the couch, pants unbuttoned, chin down and back.

'It's just that my father used to tell me about him,' she said, blowing smoke towards the living room.

'Him?' Birdfinger asked, motioning to Charlie Ward.

'He was the one they left behind,' she said. 'After that submarine accident. He was the one of all of them who couldn't mentally handle what they'd done to each other.'

'Do I want to know?' Birdfinger asked, and Molly shook her head no, he didn't. 'Whatever he had to do, though,' Birdfinger led off, 'that must mean he's capable of…helping us here…?'

'Okay already then,' Molly said finally, 'it's him or nobody, I guess.'

Birdfinger smoked her cigarette with her, coughed sticky menthol, went back to it again and again. He told her she didn't have to sell out Charlie Ward if she didn't want to, they could find somebody else probably, maybe, but she ignored the consolation prize, the false concession, scratched food matter from the vent grille. It fell on the thin metal of the range, pinged and pinged again. Birdfinger breathed in, swallowed, steeled himself, practiced the words in his head and then timed them while the back of Molly's index finger nail was elevated, prescratch, her left leg counterbalancing.

She was everything.

'I—' he began, didn't finish.

'Yes?'

'...'

'...'

'You were born in June. You were all born in June. That's one thing.'

Molly smiled, withdrew her finger, kissed Birdfinger once on the cheek before he had even been aware she was so close.

Close enough to feel the heat of her breath.

Give me my sin again, God. Birdfinger said nothing to unstall the moment.

Molly appraised it, the milked stillness, shook her head. 'It's just pity, I suppose,' she said, explaining the peck, waving it away with the twin backs of her cigarette fingers.

Pity. Birdfinger smiled, found his voice, said he would earn more, then, would get hit by a bus while trying to catch leprosy from an armadillo, if that's what it took. It was his third good line to her.

Molly looked away. In the story of them Birdfinger was narrating inside in monosyllabic prose she *tore* herself from his chest. He helped her scrape food matter from the vent hood and she repeated minutes and minutes of information about Frankish kings gone pious—Clovis the First, four syllables for three words—and on; Birdfinger absorbed the history as her mouth gave it shape. Now here they were fifteen-hundred years after the fact. And again they were run out of things to say to each other. Charlie Ward felt his way off the couch and into the distinct lack of banter, said he had to go somewhere, tonight. He answered Roswell direction to Molly. Birdfinger proffered the keys she'd returned him, flipped them end over end over the tabletop.

'My treat,' he said, 'just bring her back in one piece.'

Charlie Ward hesitated; Birdfinger conceded: 'Like she is now, then, more or less?'

Charlie Ward touched his finger to his forehead in salute, in gratitude, and Birdfinger said tomorrow they would peel that uniform for him and wash it. He looked to Molly and she nodded yes already, yes.

'Now though,' she said, not to be doubted, 'tonight.'

She did it in the sink, Charlie Ward covering himself with Cline's slickbacked duster, and the steam enveloped the three of them, clung their hair to their foreheads, collected in their ear whorls and drained inward with the head tilt of speech. Conversation ceased. Charlie Ward offered the first drink of his fourteenth beer into the pattern of the linoleum which the kitchen was forever too small to quite reveal; Birdfinger did likewise, winced. Molly kept her back to them, washing, drying, ironing with purloined starch, holding the electric cord of the iron together in her teeth where it had frayed apart. She was a force; she said she used to work in the crisp-linen bowels of a high-dollar motel. Birdfinger and Charlie Ward nodded appreciation. When she was done Charlie Ward was a new man with keys in hand—a security guard minus gun or nightstick.

'Tomorrow that hair,' Molly said to him in goodbye, and then he was escaped at last, heading Roswell direction for old-man reasons, and Birdfinger was listening to Molly sleep through the door again, and the next afternoon he was red-eyed, stiff of neck, moseying around behind Squanto's and feigning directionlessness, wearing civilian dress, whistling strong with his clean lungs. The first preliminary step of the *job* had been the third party,

Charlie Ward; the second step now was in the commercial-sized dumpster, in a clear plastic bag from register 6, a bag supposed to be marked with bright yellow tape and supposed to contain brown-paper money bands that the camera would *expect* Molly to be tucking in front of her knees, in the trash.

Birdfinger smiled from the criminal foresight of it all, congratulated himself on the details, then rounded the corner with confidence and got hit deadcenter with what turned out to be a chest pass, not a bullet. A red white and blue striped basketball. The ABA all over. Bonito Bonita snapped his fingers for change. He was between Birdfinger and the dumpster, at the free-throw line of a Nesmithian hoop. Birdfinger breathed shallow and fast, bounced the ball back. Bonito Bonita snagged it before it got to him and shot it blind towards the basket, rimming it off the front, already telling Birdfinger he hadn't seen that.

'I haven't seen anything,' Birdfinger said.

'So what you got for me this time, ese?'

Birdfinger turned his pockets out, smiled, said he just came to forage the dumpster a bit, in peace. He defined peace as the lack of hassle. Bonito Bonita winked his unpatched eye and fanned out the crisp money bands, repalmed them. 'You mean this old trash?' he asked, uninnocent.

Birdfinger became grim, nodded.

Inside of five minutes it was one-on-one, to eleven, for possession of the brown-paper bands. Birdfinger pointed out that there were some thirty-odd years between them; Bonito Bonita eased the patch across his face to cover what he called his shooting eye and spotted Birdfinger ten points, making it a one-shot game. Birdfinger tied his shoes with care, checked the ball for Bonito Bonita, then placed a hand on the pseudo-bagboy's skinny chest, to keep track of him, counteract his eel-slick motion. His namesake curled around fabric. Bonito Bonita smiled, leaned back on one leg, jersey taught, and rainbowed one high over Birdfinger that made no noise going through. Point. The next three were liquid-smooth drives, two to the left, one to the right, which Birdfinger called back on account of traveling.

'There's no traveling here,' Bonito Bonita said.

Birdfinger said he was just preparing a proper appeal.

Bonito Bonita conceded, drove to the right again, flaunting the exact same move, dribbling high this time and off Birdfinger's knee even. Point. Birdfinger said everybody was a showboater when they had the ball. It became his chorus, his taunt. After three more drives and one hail-mary from the other side of the dumpster, in two-point land, Bonito Bonita accepted the dare, rolled the ball to Birdfinger, forfeiting possession. Birdfinger dribbled indirectly to the top of the key, stalling to see if he was right- or left-handed. He decided he had to be right, because surely he would remember if he wasn't. But he couldn't tell from his dribbling. He bounced the ball to Bonito Bonita to check. Bonito Bonita withdrew a needle and air-pressure gauge, made a game of pretending to look under the hood for hints of the oblique.

'I make this one,' Birdfinger said, leading with his eyebrows.

'Yeah, okay. What the hell. Just don't let anybody ever tell you I'm not a sport.'

Bonito Bonita rolled the ball back to Birdfinger, making him wait for it, lean over at the end. When he stood he bounced the ball away from him with backspin, so it returned. Bonito Bonita said he would let the double dribble slide, considering that it might be a recent addition to the game and all. Birdfinger laughed. He said for every year he had on Bonito Bonita he had maybe ten pounds as well. He turned his back, protecting his tenuous dribble, watching it close, waiting for the defensive contact Bonito Bonita was lax to supply. Birdfinger forced him into it, began backing goalward so that Bonito Bonita had no choice but to apply forearm pressure. It was enough to lock onto. Birdfinger did. He focused all his weight and with one dropstep butted Bonito Bonita deep under the basket. Bonito Bonita rubbed something like anger from his lip and returned, became all reaching hands and anticipation, forcing Birdfinger farther and farther out, until he was on the backside of the dumpster as well, standing over the gumwad Bonito Bonita had used to mark his once in a lifetime shot. The ants were already organized into two-lane traffic.

'I'd call backcourt,' Bonito Bonita said, 'except now you've picked the ball up. Not in my interest anymore.'

Birdfinger said there wasn't any backcourt here, remember? He was standing over the gumwad, his dribble once and for all lost. He told Bonito Bonita he'd given it up on purpose, he didn't need it anymore. Bonito Bonita asked Birdfinger if he could still make out the goal. Birdfinger laughed, spit, said a wordless prayer, and then shot two-handed, back swayed, flinging from the chest, following through so that both thumbs kissed then parted ways, pointing finally at the basket, palms down, wrists limp. The ball had zero spin, and that was something. The lines were individual. They made the shot easy to track. Bonito Bonita looked twice at his watchless wrist, tapped his toe, began finishing the whistle Birdfinger had started. And then. The red white and blue ball came down with the full weight of every last bit of Birdfinger's desire on the dull front of the rim. It was enough to dislodge it from the lightpole it was attached to. It hung one-armed, wounded. A sheared bolt rattled on the concrete. The ball rolled back past Bonito Bonita and then past Birdfinger. No two-pointer.

Bonito Bonita said to Birdfinger that he was a luckless man among luckless men.

Birdfinger said that's why he hated Chinese food.

Bonito Bonita didn't get it, was the one behind for once.

'Because all the fortune cookies know my damn number,' Birdfinger explained. 'Trust me, it sucks.'

Bonito Bonita laughed, held his head about the wounded hoop, flipped back his patch to see it in its entirety, and gave the brown-paper bands to Birdfinger, said please, leave before you rip a whole in the ether or someshit. 'Too, man,' he said, 'I never did this, sabe? They'll say I'm going soft.'

Birdfinger said he wasn't proud either, but it was only a half-truth. They parted ways for the second time.

'So we're even,' Bonito Bonita said after Birdfinger.

'We're eses,' Birdfinger said back, emphasizing the Spanish, not looking over his shoulder, rerounding the corner to tuck the bands neat in his wallet, displace the two illegal twenties he was carrying just in case. Molly picked him up by the USPS drop boxes qua urinals, caught him unzipped, shaking off. He said old habits die hard. He fanned the brown-paper bands, smiled behind the success they stood for, surrendered them.

'Was it like I said?' Molly asked.

'Instamatic,' Birdfinger said, the shot of his life midair again, floating, ineffable.

'Good,' Molly said. 'Maybe you're a criminal after all.'

'Maybe my ass,' Birdfinger said, smiling.

Molly smiled with him a bit, but then looked over with premoistened sad eyes, said she'd entertained the notion but in the final analysis she just wasn't a Gemini, much less a Cancer, like he wanted her to be. She didn't even know how to pretend to have been born in June. She apologized. Birdfinger said it wasn't really something you could just decide to or not to accept; you were born into it. And she had to have been. He asked to see her driver's license, but she claimed it had been collateral for a busfare gone bad. Birdfinger made plans for an afterhours excursion. Molly called him on them: 'It's doctored anyways,' she said, 'a Rundobogenstilian special. They have a machine.' Birdfinger played at confusion, laughed with his shoulders, asked *what* leftalone purse silhouetted against the many-paned kitchen window? Molly laughed at the same time, and they laughed too long, didn't stop until they needed to curl their lips inward with concentration, bite them lightly as their hands attempted to desequence the illegal tender into a non-eye catching order.

Over the kitchen table they made three stacks of fifty bills each, found the progressive numbers difficult to escape once seen, dreamed up an involved three-card montyish shuffling system to counteract their knowledge.

Molly crossed and recrossed her hands and said she'd always heard that three-card monty dealers would be a shoe in for the gold if air-hockey was ever added to the Olympic agenda. Birdfinger met her halfway: he said he'd always wanted to write the lyrics of a song about a man wanting to fall from the sky like marble, the force of the impact shattering away all the extra from the true him, the statue within, his potential.

'DB Cooper song?' Molly asked.

Birdfinger said no, maybe, whatever it took to keep this give and take going. But then he looked at all the surely-stolen money in his hands, arranging itself in three systematic piles, which, though not quite sequential, were similarly random, which wasn't random at all. They looked for a way out and finally had to turn to Charlie Ward, stumbling in, dew beaded on his starched-slick security shirt. Charlie Ward obliged them, resequenced the one hundred and fifty bills into numeric order, their initial state. Here they were again. Bristol fashion. Charlie Ward retold a coup story about mismatched plug wires on a pinto, about the oddball firing order that resulted, that pushed the car fast fast, and told it in such a way that he got the message across that nature was fickle, meaning any sequence or lack of sequence was random, any order—the more outlandish, the more loyal to probability, to the eventuality that such a thing had to happen sooner or later. And now was later.

'Look around,' he said. Birdfinger didn't; he saw the horse thief snag a beer in the distraction, looked away polite at the last moment. Molly said to Birdfinger that it had to happen or be happening in some possible world, she guessed. And maybe it would work in their favor, play on her assistant manager's well-documented paranoia. She was taking Charlie Ward's side again, protecting him. Maybe because they were both Indian. Birdfinger relented, agreed about the possible world, said he just wished his hometown Squanto's wasn't going to be that world: the remote likelihood of a coincidence of that order being unearthed at any hour by any clerk could shut his faculties down one by one over the postcrime weeks, sap his wherewithal; he made plans for another nighttime excursion, this one to rearrange bills in the dark, where the numbers couldn't force themselves on him. Molly didn't call him on it this time. Driving her to work for another shift, he traded her an unquestioned, prolonging crawl over backroads for agreeing that yes, neither of them would roll on Charlie Ward if it came to that. She in turn allowed *roll* to go unquestioned, painted Charlie Ward as a bystander, an interloper, an old man who had agreed to play his part before they'd even fleshed that part out completely. He remained simply a necessary catalyst for Birdfinger: he had paid ninety-seven cents for him, owed the world nothing more.

That night at the kitchen table with the unopened purse, Birdfinger looked through the dark at what would be the thermal-enhanced image of his hands, and they were green from ink, and he began washing them. He was the only one at the trailer; Charlie Ward was establishing presence by the newspaper racks of Squanto's. Foresight again. It was going to be an involved three and a half minutes. Birdfinger tasted dread, retasted it as debt, a restorative function. Slept.

The next day was Friday, payday.

Birdfinger eased his warshirt over his head with all attendant songs and required smoke levels. It took forty-five minutes. When he was dressed and ready he drove through Clovis, both hands on the wheel, noticing all the things he had never noticed before—the brick and metal buildings that had no insides for him; the uneven but sharp line where they stopped reaching and the sky took over, unperturbed. He would describe it to Molly like that. He was supposed to meet her in the breakroom for the final go-ahead. He parked by the drop boxes for luck, locked the Cutlass, and made a show of not knowing the all-too present spectacle of the Indian security guard chewing ashtone gum just to the left of the automatic door. It swished and he entered the air-conditioned cold, beelined the breakroom.

Molly was there waiting, playing it cool for fifteen minutes. Stiya 6. Rita Hayworth's vinyl heartbeat remained. Birdfinger said he could go for some Marty Robbins right about now. Molly turned on him.

'Who?'

'El Paso man,' Birdfinger said. 'Cowboy balladeer.'

'I know who he is.'

She rose, brows furrowed, digging at something. She made her way to the vending machine wall some joker had labeled HAL, and as she was punching in the root-beer code Birdfinger made mention of his Rodan warshirt, plucked it from his chest to show. Molly came back pouring, inspecting the shirt.

'Like the sculptor?' she asked. 'So you're a thinking man now?'

Birdfinger shook his head no. Her styrofoam cup overflowed, airy brown foam roiling down onto her hand. She breathed it in without coughing, did her eyebrows once at the shirt as Birdfinger explained its many-tiered history. She asked if he needed hitdice to get a shirt like that going? and then held her hand over her mouth, cutting herself short, containing the laugh.

Birdfinger studied his motionless hands in response to the unexpected hitdice gibe and then followed the table to Molly sitting expectant across from him, saw her through the immaterial foam of her root beer and caught up with himself, recognized the moment replaying, the moment when he had just called her Marina in the kitchen, three syllables like three words he had meant to be meaning, three syllables she hadn't meant to acknowledge, reciprocate. He said it again—'Marina'—and she looked up, over, began an apologetic smile, and the moment soundlessly unbranched, met itself again, parallaxed back together around the lump of fear Birdfinger hadn't been able to get directly around as one person. It was gravitational lensing, it was the war-era dingy-green motorcycle separating from its sidecar around an obstacle and then rejoining, drawn back together by the brute memory of that obstacle. He realized then that it was the only way he could have gotten from the trailer's safe kitchen to this breakroom, this point in crime; the lump of fear had been fear of no longer being able to storm a place and a situation with nothing but bravado and a sense of mission. Birdfinger took Molly's accidental hitdice gibe and the self-doubt it kindled as evidence of the second branch resynchronizing with the one he had followed, evidence of that sudden jar of a moving sidecar reattaching, doubling the inertia, pushing him on. But the second branch had been different; he remembered it in a rush:

It began the same, but earlier in the week, with him becoming a keyring-giver, Charlie Ward stalling the automatic Cutlass three times before clearing the driveway, then vapor locking towards town, foot too far into the accelerator, Birdfinger following the next day to collect the brown-paper bands, rounding the rear corner of Squanto's and not walking into a basketball scenario but instead approaching the dumpster from upwind, digging through it with the mop handle already there, dislodging the yellow-taped bag, accidentally lofting the money bands up and out, giving them to the wind to play with. He gave chase, of course, tried not to create disruptive eddies as he reached for the bands, but it was hard not to do, and they cartwheeled out and out, and by the time he had them there was something in the distance still, and it was red white and blue, an ABA basketball, and when he got to the basketball and it was just a basketball, there was something still farther off, and it was a mound of dirt, easily sifted away to reveal a small-caliber handgun wrapped in plastic, still in cosmoline. On his knees with the money bands tucked into the relative shelter of his wallet, Birdfinger had contemplated the gun, the elements, and finally pocketed it, tacked into the wind, to the square block of Squanto's, to the trailer where Charlie Ward resequenced the illegal tender with autistic precision and confidence, rationalizing the order with a pinto of indiscriminate color and velocity, the lagtime after his explanation giving Birdfinger time to mentally note that yes, maybe it did have to happen in some possible world—maybe even this one—but if it did, then one thing it would no doubt succeed in doing among others would be to generate interest in what would have to be the colorful past of this three thousand dollars, and the three of them were an intricate part of that necessary past.

Molly had looked at him across his lengthy objection and asked like she meant it did he have a better idea then? Looking at her he hadn't, and she had said don't expect too much from the ace management team at Squanto's, and now here he was in the ineluctable Apache breakroom, at the sink washing his hands of the sticky root beer foam the table was coated with, listening to footsteps approach uneven down the hall and seeing for a moment the distinct shadow of the Gout Blues salesman before it ducked headfirst into the wall, another restroom. Birdfinger didn't follow; he was in the belly of things now. His actions and reactions were already acting and reacting without him. He nodded yes when Molly called him by name, whispered did he have the money on him?

'But not Bird,' he said, as much as he liked it, 'remember?'

'Then what?'

Birdfinger sat down, didn't let on that he was reconciling disparate memories of singular events. He focused on the question at hand: his chosen name in the Goliard days had been Bat Masterson, always said at least once within hearing of some federal employee, then covered up as if it had been a slip, not intended for the teletype. This time he stole Cline's old name, unused for years: 'Juan Ortiz,' he said, 'call me Juan if you have to. Never J.O. or Jo.'

'That's a girl's name.'

'Felina.'

'Juan.'

Birdfinger said for their purposes Charlie Ward would be Laughing Boy, and when Molly agreed and he had reconciled his memory to the point where he could look at things head on, he asked Molly how it would look, the both of them on break together and then her register getting hit by him minutes later? It was an accident of timing, appearance, *now*, but later it would be coincidence, evidence. Molly had no answer, so Birdfinger followed through for her, realized that in some possible world his presence here could serve as insurance for if the robbery actually worked—Molly would be suspected, would *have* to run, leave town, and his Cutlass was the only way, and he could no more turn her over after all this time than he could let her go alone, again.

He said please not to make fun of his shirt.

Molly looked down.

They ate dunking sticks for cover, to look unscheming. A bagboy passed on some stockroom errand and told Molly careful there, donut face, and Birdfinger stared him down until Molly stepped between, said no commotions, no attention, not now, not this late in the game. Birdfinger idled his voice down and asked her where was the gun, and she looked around and said to stop already—it was with Charlie Ward, to complete his security guard outfit, give Birdfinger a reason to spill the cash over the barcode scanner, right?

'And I gave it to him,' Birdfinger said, 'just like that? Of sound mind et cetera.'

'You said it had no bullets.'

Birdfinger didn't burden her with the waking memory that he hadn't been able to get the cylinder out or even rotate it, to see proper. He had had to resort to weighing the gun discreetly in Vegetables, then comparing that weight to what the manufacturer claimed over the phone unloaded weight was. He told Molly he could no longer do this, that there would come a better and more likely day, that this would have to be a dry run. Molly paced, rubbed her eyes, breathed in catches, started to argue but didn't. Finished her dunking stick. Asked Birdfinger if this was what he really wanted. Said his name as Juan Ortiz. Made it feel like Squanto's was just another post office from the less and less distant past, another *hit*.

Birdfinger nodded once okay, for her. But still, even. The old days had been easy yes but there had always been Cline too, running point, like an image of Birdfinger already taking all these chances. It had been the source of his bravado, Birdfinger's, the visual sense that each step was already taken, precursed, the knowledge that it wasn't the last. But now. Now he just had Cline's name to draw on: Juan Ortiz. It would have to be enough. He trailed his hand out of Molly's and walked the aisles with it, the name, nurtured it, blocked Squanto's out and tried to replace it with history, with a place already cased and cased well.

He was a Goliard again.

His steps were long and intentional. He lumbered up the cereal aisle. In the recesses of the startling white Inuit dairy section with seventy-two distinct flavors of milk, he rolled Molly's unworn pantyhose over his giveaway blond hair, wore it like a linebacked toboggan, the leg trailing down his spine, moving Samurai-style behind his head in the stainless-steel butcher door set swinging by a cartful of ribs. Birdfinger qua Juan Ortiz watched his reflection go side to side across the door, then settle, become dead-eyed. He was ready. He told himself today was a good day to repay certain longstanding debts, and to be repaid—seek reparations for happenstance birthing order: to rewoo with action the one who should have been his to woo in the first place. The security camera buzzed by on its plastitrack without hesitation, because technology was too sophisticated to relay warshirts back to a central monitor. Birdfinger had become invisible. Rodan. Juan Ortiz.

He stood in the register 6 line with both names and a box of frozen peas. Traded the peas for a twenty-five cent Gemini scroll, a personal touch for what was supposed to come off as an impersonal robbery, a detail to linger over later, like the oddball image of Charlie Ward aka Laughing Boy trying to disentangle a grey bubble from the tip of one his grey braids. He was under glass, on the other side of the automatic door, ready to approach at the intentional hint of commotion. Studying him close, Birdfinger faltered, realized he might be the one under glass, Charlie Ward the spectator. His wherewithal collected near the drain, and he was digging in his pocket for an honest twenty-five cents for what would later be a letdown of a gift when a thick finger at kidney-level made him look up, see that Squanto's had become smaller in his disattention, had contracted to the size of a branch post office, was dated by twenty years now. He never found the quarter.

The one customer in front of him was buying a book of stamps; the man behind, with the finger, was the salesman, the Gout Bluesman, returned from his bathroom sojourn wearing a hat that smelled like sandwich meat and rattled like medicine. And Cline, Cline was in the wings nearby, nodding approval, waiting for Birdfinger to hand the pretty clerk his typed note demanding the impossible. The Rundobogenstils had said with their slouched demeanor that guerilla tactics like this were passé, but then they were children, had never ridden in the back of a truck faster than radio, screamed across Texas with a bedful of intercepted knowledge so hot they had to wrap it in lead. They had never been a part of it. They could never know. Birdfinger pitied them their ignorance, because he *was* in it, now, up to the waist and it was rising, coloring everything, foregrounding Laughing Boy rechewing the salvaged gum, trying to wipe it off his finger, settling on Molly in the numbing presence of squash, fingers dancing over keypad, eyes cast down in seeming nonrecognition. This was the first place he had seen her outside the salesman's cocktail napkin. Birdfinger rotated to him, this salesman, nodded at the next register, said he was going to be awhile, sir. The salesman sloughed off the *sir*, replaced it with the sound of *yibbidy yibbidy* said slow, and then nodded towards the pressing matter of register 6, where Molly was mouthing the shape of the word *next* and meaning *now, now*.

Birdfinger heard, heard it all, shied away from it, had to sing an internal El Paso for soundtrack power, for the criminal resolve necessary to palm and wield the dummied-up roadflare. The pantyhose fell over his face on cue, and the run petering both vertical ways from his left eye was an insect crawling, and he was masked, invulnerable, Juan Ortiz. The roadflare brandished in a held-high hand would intimate dynamite to those uneducated—to those not raised by a stripmining father. It was in his pocket, almost drawn; the act was almost begun. But first there was the matter of the Gemini scroll. He rolled it across the counter to Molly. She swallowed, looked from it to him, and then scanned it in defeat, because there was no real law against the wearing of masks in public places. Birdfinger could see it like that on her face. He smiled through nylon.

'A gift,' he said, flatlipped.

Molly let it roll to the end of the belt, spin there unreceived. She looked to the salesman, the next in line, with his handful of remedies, but Birdfinger wouldn't allow it, the soundtrack wouldn't allow it: he pulled the roadflare with the candlewick fuse waxed on. He said the words to this Stiya at register 6 who was already stabbing the panic button for the camera, her store training overriding her self-preservation instincts, as rehearsed: 'Everything,' Birdfinger said, loud enough for all the other Stiyas, '*I want it all.*'

The commotion was officially begun; in the periphery of things Charlie Ward attempted to navigate the door he didn't seem to be trusting. Birdfinger felt the hose leg down his back like a tail now, like a braid, remembered the flesh-colored hose on the skin of his face—Molly's flesh color: he would be an overweight Indian in the first-hand accounts. With white hands. He said it again, to Molly: 'Everything you've got, miss pretty.'

The *miss pretty* tag was a little Goliardic flourish.

The salesman presented him with the necessary lit cigarette. Juan Ortiz teased the candlewick with it, smiling, then unsmiled at the entrance of Laughing Boy, feigned a bodylength flinch, began to narrate aloud his fear, their history, how Laughing Boy here had spoiled his first *heist*, in Virginia of all places, and since then had chased him all over the US of a. He said it like that: *of all places*. Molly's forehead met her hand. Laughing Boy assumed the peace-keeping stance, leading with the drawn pistol, legs wide, feet squared, braids flung behind the shoulders, walking forward as if haunted by the memory of a childhood spent on mediaeval leg brace gear. His chin was grey with spirit gum. The cameras swarmed, became a nascent buzzing mass. The assistant manager approached on unbended knee, presenting himself to fate, to Juan Ortiz; he came bearing coupons, recounting the names of those who had doubted that it would end like this, with fireworks like the Fourth, the birth of a nation. Birdfinger said it didn't have to, goddammit.

There was now one too many people involved.

The assistant manager was unrehearsed, was introducing himself as if 'Espe Wilson' had been in the script when they'd been rehearsing back at the trailer, written in all along.

Birdfinger could improvise too, though: he took a hostage, Molly, all he really wanted here anyway.

'Old man,' he said to Laughing Boy, redrawing attention, 'I don't think so.' Charlie Ward looked in the direction of the assistant manager, coupons in hand, smug with the end he had accurately anticipated, and then back to Birdfinger, the gun going with his line of sight, an obvious strand of gum snaked around the trigger guard. Birdfinger tried to spy down the barrel for certainty, got none. He said aloud that every good criminal knows when to make his exit, but then a thing happened: he had Molly in one hand and the roadflare in the other, and he had to ash. It was a basic need. He brought the roadflare hand to the cigarette, and when the cigarette returned, ash dumped discreet behind the register, under everyone's eyes, the candlewick was smoldering into flame. The assistant manager started laughing, derobing himself for his own reasons, and Molly asked liplessly what did mister Juan Ortiz *want* here, before he *left*.

A teletype somewhere woke. 'The money,' Juan Ortiz said, 'all of it, now.'

The candlewick didn't burn like the Old West fuses, either: it gave light. Birdfinger used it to collect the bills Molly intentionally stiff-fingered down behind the register, ahead of schedule. He bent over her and her hand was in his pocket and he almost cried for the sudden and public nearness. The trade was made, had been made. He stood with a handful of illegal tender. The assistant manager was nude, dimpled, talking last words, taunting Laughing Boy, telling him he might as well just let it happen, it was bigger than all of them, had nearly four hundred years behind it already. Charlie Ward shook his head no, even said it, but then the assistant manager was talking shrapnel talk, was bemoaning the loss of the register 6 girl, his newest niece, his best little Indian of them all. Charlie Ward qua Laughing Boy shook his head again no, but now Birdfinger didn't know who to. The assistant manager massaged barcodes into a liturgy. Birdfinger resisted it with Marty Robbins: his only chance was to run. Laughing Boy motioned Birdfinger away with the gun though, away from Molly, Felina. She wasn't breathing. 'No,' she said, 'no.' But the candlewick was burning, the assistant manager dancing with himself, one hand held at his center of gravity, the other orchestrating the end, the rebeginning.

'Remember,' Birdfinger said to Charlie Ward, '*remember*.'

Laughing Boy did, or seemed to, but then motioned Birdfinger away from Molly, and Birdfinger played along, spun her out like a dance step, got a meager clap from the floorbound salesman. At the last instant of contact between their fingertips, too, Molly dislodged the illegal tender from Birdfinger's hand, tearing the brown paper bands they'd placed together. The money fell in improbable sequence. Birdfinger could see it by candlelight. It was beautiful. Alone now and moving slow he followed the cast light to the nub of wick just as the roadflare began hissing magnesium sparks, and he dropped it without thinking, and the assistant manager ovalled his mouth Munch-style, giddy with the fall, waiting for impact, and the grey gum wound around the trigger guard of the once-buried gun tightened in fear, and like that the hammer fell, and Juan Ortiz was in the post office again, flailing back against a magazine rack, into the *Star*s stacked three deep, and there was smoke, yes, only it wasn't from the gun, but the flare, the fireworks, the birth of a nation.

Birdfinger was unshot; the gun was unfired.

And it didn't matter: Laughing Boy advanced on swivel hips, even after the dynamite ruse had become transparent, even after the assistant manager was realizing aloud he had been duped by a comedy of errors into revealing himself, even after his old-man pupils ceased swimming and focused on Birdfinger with recognition, or on the pair of Birdfinger and Molly, Molly cradling Birdfinger's head in her lap, holding a stiff arm out at Charlie Ward, saying no, no already, it's over. It wasn't. Charlie Ward was breathing fast and hard and mad and telling Molly to get out of the way, girl, get out of the damn way. She didn't though, so the broken record played on, and the grey gum stretched again over the trigger guard, and through the smoke of the roadflare and the sobbing of the assistant manager and the internal soundtrack of El Paso and in spite of Molly placing herself between, there came a muzzle flash, a seventeen-inch finger of flame, and Birdfinger felt it in his sternum, in Molly's already starting wail over his already dying body, heard his heartbeat vinyl through the PA, and then the salesman was panting over him with a penlight, searching for life, but he was already too far away to see Birdfinger, walking at an uncouth pace over a shinnery field in Canyon Texas, looking back at the pale disc against the clouds that was the Ford's tilted headlight and feeling it real in his chest where he couldn't deny it that no, he had been moving the wrong direction, the thing to do was to turn, backtrack, walk back to her.

Red Noise: An Old Man Stumbles Out of the Plainsong and Into the Dumbshow

Litmus Jones was deep in the cinderblock shed, redefining pillbox: three days ago, his fedora had been lined with coldcuts and remedy bottles. The bottles were lined up on the dash now, by height, each sampled in turn and in turn found to hold no remedy: the Gout Blues were a state of mind, not to be handled off the shelf; Litmus' left wingtip had been carefully peeled away from his foot and placed on the dash, settled into the fingernail-deep dirt, nestled there because placement was an issue and there had been time to take issue. Three days. The dash belonged to a red-on-white late-sixties Ford. The shoe was bronze in the ambient floodlight feeling in through the two-brick wide window, the only break in the cinderblock monotony. It was enough. Litmus rolled the final coldcut into a tube and began finishing it. He was a salami man. He said it like that, like the salami in his hand and in his mouth wasn't enough, wasn't doing it.

'I'm a salami man,' he said, for the ritual. It was something.

He could no longer remember why New Mexico, why Clovis.

Three days ago he had been uninvolved in what the radio was calling a daring daylight grocery run that ended in tragedy. The night DJ had asked tragic for whom, man, for *whom*, and then neglected to spin the promised record for half an hour.

Litmus could no longer remember why this bench seat, this shed.

On the dash in deference to the bronzed shoe were cross-temporal reminders, an internal dialogue gone the way of souvenirs: a plasticlear bracelet that had been there on the dead man's wrist an hour before the coroner; a business card with the text of The Wish to Be a Red Indian handcopied on back, deGermaned; a sepiatone telephoto, dogeared and thumbworn—strange outlaws of the yellow and brown past staring out of it still; a coaster from a local bar, pierced through button style with #6 guitar string, because the blue ribbon or the gold medal had been lost in drink, become unrecoverable; and, near the vent window, half of a *Star* Litmus had squirreled away for mother-warned days like these. No demo case no vacuum cleaners no lightning rods no sewing machines. Litmus was leaving clean, going to. Like the Kafka-piece said, he was shedding possessions like nobody's business. He read it to himself again, just for the comfort of suspecting it was meant for him: *If one were only an Indian, instantly alert, and on a racing horse, leaning against the wind, kept on quivering jerkily over the quivering ground, until one shed one's spurs, for there needed no spurs, threw away the reins, for there needed no reins, and hardly saw that the land before one was smoothly shorn heath when horse's neck and head would already be gone.* He wasn't Indian, though, that was the thing that kept getting in the way. In the skewed rearview his face was pancake #12, even, the color of fear, of waking after two unrecoverable weeks. All he had to show of it was on the dash. And no matter how he arranged them, the souvenirs didn't make any sense—the telephoto was still a carnival special, with the same guy pasted in there twice; the flipside of the Kafka business card still read STUD SERVICES / HOURLY RATES; the guitar-string still didn't match with any calloused indentions on his fingertips.

Litmus closed his eyes in defeat, but then slammed them open. Everything was the same, but still, he recatologued, finally settled on the up-ended and top-heavy rectangle of ground afforded him by the small window. It was like television: first, as had to be, there was nothing, and then came an old man made up like a glassine turtle. It was a gibbous night, so the old man wasn't out of place, there with his belly scant millimeters off the ground, legs and arms splayed, fingertips and toes dancing, advancing, a windshield strapped lengthwise down his back. His grey hair was untied, still wrinkled from braiding, and the way it moved with the wind made him part of the grassland. Litmus had read it that way in a coffee-table book once.

He remembered that.

He concentrated for more, anything, but as he drew his face closer to see that coffee table from his past, his anxious breath wisped the recollection away, and he was again watching the soundless approach of the turtle man. Or still. The old man was all stealth and patience. Plodding, plotting. His line of movement would lead him to the cinderblock shed, to the driverside seat of the red on white Ford. It had taken him thirty-four years to cover less than a quarter mile. 'C'mon, old man,' Litmus said, and breathed for him, reached out for him with his mind, whatever he had leftover from his two weeks, and the old man tensed with the invasion, corded the muscles along one arm and shifted his weight to it, then turned his head slow, first to the right—to the open field to the east—and then back to the west, the trailer that from Litmus' perch was a sheared-off corner from which he had to reconstruct the rest. The old man had a name for a flash, but then it was gone, reclaimed into plurality, time, and only his physical shape remained, part of the grassland, moving only when it moved, as it moved. He held his brokencrawled stance for an impossible succession of minutes and Litmus was afraid for him, for his thirty-four year crawl, and it was selfish fear: he had been in the shed three days. His two bowel movements were in a drainpan in the corner, doused with kerosene. He apologized to whoever found the pan. He could no longer even remove his left foot from the floorboard, from the fortress he had constructed around it. He was chained to this truck, should probably just put the plasticlear bracelet back on, tag his inflamed toe, and have done with it.

Even the old man was leaving: slowly, like ash blowing away, he turtled out of windowview, and it would be hours and years and decades before he would reach the cinderblock shed. But he would; he had to. As Litmus turned away in defeat, back to the dash maybe, the stillness the old man had left behind collected, penetrated Litmus' peripheral vision for a moment, and in it he could make out hulking, amorphous forms, wresting power back and forth.

There were illegal full-nelsons and bone-shattering leglocks and crowd-pleasing grimaces, but no crowd, which meant they were struggling for real, the forms. It was a dull-eyed anger. The thermometer clipped onto the truck's visor twenty-odd years ago said it was at least 1492 degrees Fahrenheit, a local one-liner. Litmus wiped his forehead and tuned the radio into the Lonesome Loser dedication hour, where the wrestling match played on, where a drunk man claiming FFV stock was dedicating selected song lines to a pie-shaped wedge of the local population who knew who they were. The night DJ-as-instigator prompted him, and to the night DJ's delight the man actually broke into song, but Litmus spun the radio dial away from his voice before the lyrics could cross the FM. He didn't need that, on top of everything.

He swallowed the last of the salami, savored the aftertaste as long as he could, allowed that maybe the red-on-white Ford hadn't been such a good idea. It had felt right at the time, though. And nobody had found him, and now there was a horse thief approaching at a landspeed best measured by calender. That had to mean something. Litmus turned at last to the half of the *Star* not wadded in the drainpan. It occupied him.

The first story was bootlegged from *Indian Country*, was a study weighing the likelihood that the Ghost Dance phenomena of the late nineteenth century had actually been Saint Vitus-related, an Indoeuropean brain fever the *Ind*ians had never had the time to develop immunity to, that this is how religions are born. There were obligatorily grainy shots from movie recreations. Litmus recognized the actors. Next was a heavy-tailed salamander under glass, an oversized relic found dead in the Andes, suicided on the only stepping stone in its rainwater pool. The locals had had to make deals with the carrion birds for the carcass; the paleozoologists said they had to assume the damned thing was trying to evolve, *now*, when all that shit was supposed to be over and done with. Litmus had to supply the cursewords himself, as the *Star* asterisked out the vowels, provided a legend at the bottom for those with time to reconstruct: * = *a, i, o, e, or u*. Litmus had time, and vowels aplenty. He studied the mottled skin of the great and noble salamander on the redramatized stepping stone, commended it, turned the page on it, turned three on it, to Gallup, to the security-camera shots of a bank robbery where the robbers evidently used some bluescreen technology to move invisible behind the registers, picking and choosing three-thousand dollars one twenty at a time. Aliens ghosts telekinesis or a new audio-visual cult and/or plague come to visit New Mexico?

Litmus didn't fill in the multiple choice, skipped the single column claim that there was a predator on the loose with a taste for geriatric flesh, skimmed the retractions and corrections in an effort to reconstruct the prior issue. It was futile, though; there was only this *Star*. Last in it then, right before the managing editor's full-page tongue-cheeked prediction that this year's predictions would be on the next page, was the lead-in of a story by the hotshot staff photographer, an attempt to tie together the rumors that the Navy brass never ceased experimenting with the so-called Philadelphia technology, but used it to try and get rid of the overproud radio talkers from WWII. The article's claim was that there was physical evidence of the immaterial in the vicinity of Clovis, a scuttled accident of interdimensional proportions. The article was a call for help, for substantiated rumors, eyewitnesses, survivors, a reveille; the photographer admitted he was trading that month's salary for this verso-page write-up here. It was a plea. His home phone was in parentheses, all the prime numbers asterisked, and there was no legend, only a last minute footnote for the undecorated seamen not to feel guilty for living as they had had to; Litmus laughed, accidentally looked deep enough into the page that he saw underground, into the steel belly of things. He quit laughing. Tried to unfocus but the white meat and red remained, persisted, insisted.

It was his twelfth time through the articles, now. They were more and more familiar with every read, yet made less and less sense. He told himself it was just a d*mn tabloid, smiled with cleverness. But still. He pitied the Andean locals their ill-advised deal: carrion birds were single-minded, infinitely patient. They would wait over the village's left shoulder until the locals turned only to their right, and that's how religions are born: from fear, not infections. From dabbling in Saint John's wort, conjuring demons. Litmus flipped away from their page, the price they had paid for fame, and noticed that this issue of the *Star* was old enough that the staff photo of the boy wonder showed him with skin as mottled as the heavy-tailed salamander. It was like *it* was spreading. Litmus held the paper at arm's length, saw the wave of floodlight split by dual windowscreens into inchwide particles falling on his forearm, and then dropped the paper fast, wishing it were heavier, something with heft, throwable. As it was it fell too close, left the distinct chance for infection. Litmus opened the door, aware he was still chained by the toe to the cab of the truck, aware he had been alone with his thoughts and his fears for too long. It didn't matter. With a floormat he fanned the *Star* into the recesses of existence, even tried blowing it further away, and that's how he was when he realized he was no longer alone: standing in front of the hood was the old man, risen silent from the grassland, the glass shell on his back. Litmus ceased fanning, and the dustmotes collected overhead and fell on the heeled and the wheeled alike.

'Laughing Boy,' Litmus said, recognition rising in his throat.

The old man tightened his lips in response, and Litmus flinched, scanned for a gun, evidence of sidearms, found none. The old man shook his head no, offered no name to replace Laughing Boy, said it was too late already for names to matter anymore anyway, he'd had enough. Litmus understood: he himself was a salami man, nothing else. The old man stepped neat out of his glass shell and said he wasn't coming back this time. It was another warning. Litmus considered the last three days and the two blackout-weeks before and nodded okay, him neither. Not fucking ever. That they shared—not names, gifts, verbal coquetry. That and the work: the broken windshield popped out under Litmus's arm-focused weight like a Tucker commercial, and the replacement snugged into the seal so tight Litmus had to open the door, yawn for his ears. The old man laughed, drew closer, his hair tucked into his shirt collar, and tattooed the flank of the truck with his soot-black hand, dragged fingerwide pinstripes to the no-frills grille, circled one eye.

The night was afoot.

His pocket was inside out and it was a tanned scrotum.

The Thunderbird engine turned over under his forefinger and thumb, and coughed kerosene residue once, twice, then began to even out rich on airplane fuel, the gauges coming to life under the old man's insistent glass tapping, the cinderblock shed aswim with carbon monoxide. Litmus' eyes teared up, his lungs dry-heaved. 'Now,' he said, breathless, forcing the shin-high vent closed, 'goddammit now already,' and the old man dropped the truck into low and it whitesmoked across the slick concrete across the narrow confines of the shed and then it was leaning into the already collapsing door, and they were in the pasture, unscratched, the old man with his head out the window, his hair decollared, his foot heavy with speed. By the time the bias-ply tires and the tall gears registered blacktop, the old man was recounting his past deeds, enumerating them in open council, daring Litmus to shake his head no. Litmus didn't, couldn't. He held his hands palm-down against the dash and realized the combination of fuel and engine and gears driving them would never top out. By the time they cleared town, the old man had raced through his auto-theft stories, was glossing over his starring role in the daring daylight grocery run, where one S.P. Wilson had stripped naked, danced over a man dead for three-hundred years already. And the old man went on, was stepping into something altogether different now, narrating the minutes-ago past, catching up with himself, telling it in a way that Litmus could see it through his grassland eyes:

He had been angling over the pasture towards the cinderblock shed for eleven hours; the sun on his glass shell had made the grass smoke on either side of his shadow, giving the illusion he was burning across the land. But it was taking all day. Dark came like a chattel when he called for it. By then he was close too, already whispering to the Thunderbird Ford to calm it. And then a thing happened; it was like a finger reached into his mind, made him aware of the young woman on the longhouse porch, refusing to let herself cry over the blond mound of corpse. The woman who knew Seth; the corpse who had been the man who had become someone else in the moments before death, whose lips were now blue with cornmeal. That was to the right. To the left was a green-eyed ragdoll dancing closer and closer, following the sky down to the trailer time and again, the leadlined bulge low on his side not unbalancing him. His loping familiar was there too, the dead-eyed dog. They took the upwind approach to the porch—dog inspecting the scentless windshield—and by the time the ragdoll got there, the woman had stepped inside, and he had time only to lay one hand on the chest of the blond corpse and one on his own in private ritual before he had to shoulder it easy, softshoe off the porch, start stealing away.

The old man said he had known the green-eyed ragdoll when the green-eyed ragdoll was still a man. But now. Now he was loping off with his familiar, with his debiered prize, off into the Clovis night. The screen door opened and closed behind him once, though, with a hollow aluminum sound, a childhood sound, and it slowed him, the ragdoll, turned him around at the edge of the floodlight.

There stood the young woman, taller than life, hipshot into the wind, her black hair half across her face, one hand on the redwood porch railing. Across the old man's glass back she was seeing the ragdoll with the slung blond corpse, and the ragdoll looking back became in her presence all green eyes and hesitation. After an indefinite period of waiting he chanced a word below his helmet—*mother*—like a question, an over-the-shoulder recognition, and the young woman narrowed her eyes in response to the weight of the almost-familiar, the half-recalled, and as the old man disentangled himself from the spiderwebs connecting the two of them at unlikely points, Litmus looked back once through Charlie Ward's letdown greyblack hair and said it in a voice he hardly owned—that she never died—and then New Mexico in his peripheral vision began to slip away with the gathering speed of the Thunderbird Ford, with the singular determination of the old man, and Litmus patted the dash for more, leaned into the wind with it, and the asphalt on the other side of one-sixty became glass placid and their painted horse was running running hard, the pistons firing 15426378 15426378, the sound of their pipes falling behind them, so that for moments at a time they didn't need the truck at all.